Last Call

"Laura Pedersen's wry, bittersweet story charts the unlikely romance between a dying yet still vibrant man and a nun whose faith has abandoned her. While much is lost in this gentle tale, much is gained too, and by the novel's end, the characters are granted the kind of wisdom and acceptance for which we all continue to long."

—Yona McDonough, author of *The Four Temperaments*

Beginner's Luck

"Laura Pedersen delivers . . . If this book hasn't been made into a screenplay already, it should be soon. Throughout, you can't help but think how hilarious some of the scenes would play on the big screen."

—*The Hartford Courant*

"Funny, sweet-natured, and well-crafted . . . Pedersen has created a wonderful assemblage of . . . whimsical characters and charm."

—*Kirkus Reviews*

"This novel is funny and just quirky enough to become a word-of-mouth favorite. . . . Pedersen has a knack for capturing tart teenage observations in witty asides, and Hallie's naïveté, combined with her gambling and numbers savvy, make her a winning protagonist."

—*Publishers Weekly*

"A breezy coming-of-age novel with an appealing cast of characters."

—*Booklist*

"A fresh and funny look at not fitting in."

—*Seventeen* magazine

LAST CALL

laura pedersen

BALLANTINE BOOKS

NEW YORK

A Ballantine Book
Published by The Random House Publishing Group

www.ballantinebooks.com/BRC

ISBN 0-345-46191-6

Manufactured in the United States of America

First Edition: January 2004

2   4   6   8   10   9   7   5   3   1

Inscribed

to

Judith Ehrlich

"If you love someone anything is possible, even miracles."

— MR. LUNDIE, BRIGADOON

ACKNOWLEDGMENTS

Special thanks to Carolyn Fireside for her passion and creativity, Maureen O'Neal at Ballantine Books for her steadfast support, and to my literary agent Judith Ehrlich for her imagination, dedication, and encouragement. Ongoing appreciation for everyone back at the kibbutz—Willie, Julie, Aimee, Michael, Elliott, Cecilia, Lucy, and all the critters.

LAST CALL

J oe-y! Come down here and eat some breakfast," his mother calls into the hollow tunnel of the antiquated dumbwaiter.

"What are the choices?" shouts back a high-pitched youthful voice.

"*Yes* or *no*! Get down here and eat some oatmeal before you leave."

When Joey enters the kitchen Diana bends to kiss him while at the same time maneuvering her hand across his forehead to check for fever. "You feel warm to me." She studies his face for unnatural coloring and a runny nose. "It could be the start of a summer cold."

Her son is a boyish-looking eleven-year-old with wide-set expressive brown eyes and a moon-shaped face that has high ridges hidden just beneath the surface, suggesting that he'll inherit his mother's striking cheekbones, straight nose, and generous mouth.

"Eat some oatmeal before you leave," Diana insists with an urgency that implies oatmeal has been officially designated a miracle cure for the common cold.

"I don't want any yucky oatmeal." Joey pushes her hand away. "Grandpa's taking me to a baseball game. We'll get hot dogs."

"Based on how late he arrived home last night and the racket he made getting upstairs, we'll be lucky if Grandpa takes out the garbage. I'm surprised he didn't wake you up. Or worse, give you nightmares."

Diana leans over the old-fashioned steel sink to adjust the calico curtains, diverting the glare of the formidable late June sun. The shiny copper-bottomed pots lining the far wall cast flickering circles around the room like a disco ball. From outside in the backyard drift the gentle melodies of summer—the plaintive chirping of young sparrows fidgeting in their nests, shrilling crickets, and the silky ripple of tall grass in the breeze.

The tranquillity of the morning is abruptly broken by an exuberant burst of song. A chorus of "Will Ye Go, Lassie, Go" reverberates throughout the stairwell of the three-story town house in an accent containing a velvety Scots burr, and accompanied by the sound of steps being taken two at a time. On the final "go," a dynamo of a man with an unruly mop of salt-and-pepper hair slides across the threshold to the kitchen as if tagging home base. Without missing a beat before the start of the next verse he rescues his grown daughter from slaving over the stove and skillfully waltzes her around the room, gaily accompanying them in his lilting baritone:

"I will build my love a tower, near yon pure crystal fountain, And on it I will pile, all the flowers of the mountain."

He moves with the confident agility of an acrobat. His daughter Diana, however, wearing a stiff vinyl cooking apron and brandishing a wooden spoon above her like Lady Liberty's torch, is a reluctant dance partner. After a turn around the island she glances at the stovetop to signal that the pot may boil over if her attention is diverted for another second, and attempts to pull away. He finally releases her with an abrupt chortle followed by a kiss on the forehead. His flashing green eyes and solid reassuring jaw are softened by a fan of laugh lines, indicating that he's accustomed to achieving his objectives, even if only temporarily, like this morning's dance.

"Not bad for a man supposed to be pushing up the heather!" proclaims Hayden MacBride, a square-shouldered man of medium height, medium build, and medium age, all of which are in sharp contrast to his outsized personality. He seizes two spatulas and concludes his grand entrance with a drum roll on the countertop.

Not to be left out, Joey grabs the salt and pepper shakers off the kitchen table and places the matching pewter grinders up to his face as if they're binoculars and he's a fan at his grandfather's impromptu concert. This elicits a merry smile of approval from Hayden and a scowl from Diana.

"Just think how much better you'd be feeling if you hadn't skipped your doctor's appointment," she reprimands her father, thereby informing him that he'd been found out when the medical office called looking for him. "Not to mention take your pills, stop drinking, and come home before midnight."

"You're absolutely right," replies Hayden. "Let's not mention it!" Having spent a lifetime embracing joy he's not about to let impending death get in his way.

"Well, I'm making another appointment," says Diana. "The doctor said you're a candidate for this experimental treatment that's just been approved for testing."

"Oh please, Diana," replies Hayden. "There's no cure for this thing and you bloody well know it. They're just wantin' to use a bunch of desperate fools as free guinea pigs."

Father and daughter have had this conversation a hundred times in the past two weeks and both players know their lines by heart. And they're both well aware that neither will prevail, no matter how many times the scene is performed.

However, with Diana's attention momentarily diverted by Hayden, Joey sneaks around the corner into the dining room and returns with a brown paper bag that he passes to his grandfather behind his mother's back. Then Joey moves to distract her by lifting the lid off the pot and licking the spoon so his grandfather can whisk the parcel into the front hall without being observed.

"Joseph!" his mother scolds on cue. "That's disgusting!"

Joey scrunches his face at the lumpy beige goo. "Gross."

Hayden returns minus the brown bag and wearing a tan straw hat tilted rakishly over one eye. He peers into the pot. "Double, double toil and trouble; fire burn and cauldron bubble." Also making a face he asks, "Porridge in summer?"

"It's called oatmeal here, Dad. And it's good for you."

"Well it's called porridge in Mother Scotland and 'tis favored by the very young, the very old, and the very *poor*."

"Stop filling Joey's head with stories about witches and murders." You can hear the capital letters as she speaks. "He's going to have NIGHTMARES."

"It's bloody Shakespeare's *Macbeth*."

"I don't care if it's Dr. Spock. And don't curse. And don't fill up on junk food at the game." Diana examines the green-and-white-checked dish towel she's been using to determine if it should go into the wash. She throws it down the chute to the basement just to be on the safe side.

"Hey Mom, how do you get a Highlander up onto the roof?" asks Joey.

"I don't know," Diana says distractedly.

"You tell him that the drinks are on the house!" Joey laughs like crazy and a suppressed smile causes the corners of Hayden's vivid green eyes to crinkle.

Diana's eyelids flap up like window shades upon hearing the punch line and she peers critically at both father and son with such foreboding that it could earn her a part in *Tomb Raider*. "Stop letting Joey sit in with your Scottish cronies and their bawdy jokes! And don't let him race up and down the bleachers in the hot sun." Diana stresses "hot sun" as if the sun is the enemy rather than the patron of all life. "And make sure you take his inhaler."

"Do I look like my head buttons up the back, woman?" demands Hayden.

"Did you sign my Little League permission slip?" Joey asks his mother.

"We'll discuss it when your father picks you up on Sunday. *If* your father picks you up on Sunday." Her expression is one not just filled with doubt but impending doom.

Joey can't stand the way his mother and Hayden are always saying bad things about his father. In fact, this shared hatred seems to be the only thing about which the two of them ever agree. "Mom, there's nothing to *discuss*. Dad said it's *fine*."

"Joey, you have *asthma!*" Diana states the condition as if it's already claimed two hundred lives while they've been speaking. "Dad doesn't talk to your doctors. I think you should play golf again this summer."

"I don't want to play golf," whines Joey. "I want to play *baseball*." Why can't his mother see that by treating him like a boy in a plastic bubble she's not only depriving him of a normal childhood, but preventing him from making any friends in the new neighborhood. In fact, if it weren't for his grandfather, he'd be spending all his free time playing video games and solitaire. Joey moans and tilts backward against the refrigerator as if he's just been stabbed in the heart by Macbeth's dagger. "Golf is *stupid*. It's a bunch of old farts talking about the stock market. I want to play *baseball*."

"Hey, watch who yer calling an old fart now. I've only just turned fifty-five. And mind what you say about golf. It was the Scots who invented it and I daresay I managed to close more than a few deals on the fairway." Hayden removes a large plastic pasta fork from the rack on the counter and playfully clunks Joey over the head with it. "C'mon now, we're off like a new bride's nightie."

"*Dad!*" Diana protests what she considers to be risqué speech for the ears of an eleven-year-old boy, and also the mishandling of her cooking utensils. Why not just drop an eyeball in the garbage can rather than go to the trouble of poking it out?

"See you later Di-Di. There's a copy of my life insurance policy on your dresser. *Please* look at it and then file it someplace where you'll be able to find it. After all, you *are* the principal beneficiary. And there's some Con Edison stock for you and Joey. Your sister Linda inherits whatever's left in my bank account, which, believe me, is a lot less."

"Dad, *puh-leeze*." She waves her right hand in the air as if fending off an airborne plague. "I've told you that I don't want to discuss it."

The older man's lighthearted manner evaporates like an eclipsed sun, and as his voice rises in frustration the Scottish brogue becomes more pronounced. "Well, if we do'an' discuss *it* then who's goin' to make sure I do'an' have Jell-O with teensy marshmallows served up at the funeral and that all me clients who never paid their premiums on time aren't sit-tin' in the front row handin' out their business cards? And who's goin' to make sure I get cremated in me pajamas so that a good suit do'an' go to waste?"

"*Dad!*"

"Do'an' *Dad* me! There's enough money in that policy for Joey to go to college. Which is about four years' tuition more than your ex-husband the sculptor, or rather the sculpture, will ha' put away when the time comes."

Joey stuffs chocolate chip cookies into his pockets while his mother is preoccupied arguing with his grandfather. Since Diana and Joey moved from Westchester back to the family home in Brooklyn, grandfather and grandson have become adept at distracting the common enemy so as to provide each other with windows of opportunity to accomplish all the things of which she disapproves. In other words, most everything. They wriggle and scamper about like a herd of ferrets so that she can only con-centrate on one at a time.

After just three short weeks of living under the same roof, it's reached the stage where Diana insists that their combined antics are responsible for her first gray hairs and almost chronic neck tension. This is not at all what she had planned. By moving in with her father it had been Diana's inten-tion to nurse Hayden back to health, not bring sleep loss and stress-related illnesses upon herself, in addition to raising her son around whiskey, revelry, and bad language.

Hayden turns back to Joey. "Ready to go, slugger?"

"Aren't you going to take your mitt, honey?" Diana, whose womb dou-bles as a tracking device, reminds her only child.

"Oh, yeah." Joey stands on his toes and pecks her on the cheek. "It's in the car." He feels faintly guilty about lying to his mother, but on the other hand, if she knew what they were really up to she'd never again let him set foot outside the house with his grandfather.

"It seems as if the two of you have attended a baseball game every day so far this summer." Diana punctuates her speech by scraping the glutinous oatmeal into the disposal. Then she begins scouring the sink with Comet, the way she does all surfaces, as if the regular application of cleanser can cure her father and son of their respective ailments.

"That's the wonderful thing about havin' a bloody awful team. It's easy to get tickets." Hayden is not a bad liar so much as his daughter is a good detector of lies, and thus he says this hurriedly and then beats a hasty retreat out to the driveway. In the bright summer sunlight his green-and-red-plaid I BRAKE FOR HIGHLANDERS bumper sticker stands out against the rusty chrome.

Hayden takes care as he maneuvers the station wagon through the tree-canopied side streets, past rows of stately old brownstones with stoops framed by wrought-iron railings, and out onto the main drag. "All I need is to have a fender bender. She won't be able to snatch away my driver's license fast enough." He heads down a wide avenue flanked by brick row houses that have green-and-white-striped metal awnings and green shutters with copper eagles nailed to the front. Plastic furniture is scattered to the side of driveways like buckshot and a few large American flags hang at doorways in anticipation of the Fourth of July.

Hayden drives past St. Benedict's Church and then turns onto the expressway and toward the wealthier neighborhood of Brooklyn Heights, with its nineteenth-century town houses and streets lined with ginkgo trees. Flatbed trucks rumble past as they haul their loads of scrap metal to the East River junkyards. He makes his way around bright orange cones, big black barrels of gravel, and construction workers waving checkered flags in order to slow drivers down. "Brooklyn will be a great city if they ever finish it," jokes Hayden.

"It's amazing that Mom actually believes we go to a baseball game every day," says Joey. He makes no secret of the joy he gets from putting one over on his perpetually vigilant mother.

"She do'an' follow sports. Diana will never understand payin' good money to watch people purposely injure themselves."

"How many funerals are we gonna hit today?" asks Joey. Most of the time he enjoys them, but after three in a row it can become depressing, all those people crying and blowing their noses and the women with their makeup all messed up, looking as if they're preparing to head out trick-or-treating.

"I found three that look promising. The newspaper is right in the backseat. Check the death notices. I reckon there's a fine chance of procurin' some roast beef and shrimp scampi for lunch today."

chapter two

Every morning since he was diagnosed with terminal liver cancer, Hayden has ritually pored over the obituaries as if they're the real estate ads and he's in the market for an apartment that must meet very specific guidelines. Since death itself is nonnegotiable, he has decided to take charge of the factors he can control, and find the best way to carry out the deed on his own terms. Without a doubt it's been difficult for Hayden to wrap his mind around the entire enterprise of dying, especially being a person who has always found so much pleasure in life and so desperately desires to watch his grandson grow up. But in his opinion, the alternatives to taking matters into his own hands for a swift send-off are even more frightening. Some of these people lay in a coma for weeks with tubes and machines running their entire bodies! Everything except their minds, that is. He can't imagine such indignity.

And the *last* thing he wants is some nursing home keeping him alive as an asset to their bottom line. Having spent thirty years in the insurance business, he's well aware of how that can work. Nor does he have any intention of lying unconscious while a hospital chaplain anoints him with holy water, his least favorite brand of spirit.

Thus Hayden has determined that the best way to explore his options is by attending funerals and interviewing the relatives of those who've just cashed in a cancer patient. Given the occasion, it seems natural to inquire about the final hours and whether the death took place at home or in an oncology ward, and about hospice care, the Hemlock Society, barbiturates, and self-regulated morphine drips. He reasons that by taking Joey along, the boy will gradually become more comfortable with death, and it won't be as traumatic when Hayden's own time comes.

"This first fellow, Richardson, is having his memorial service at Central Presbyterian, and so they'll surely drop some money on a reception back at the house," says Hayden. "He was a member of the New York Public Library and the Brooklyn Museum of Art."

"So what did he croak of?" asks Joey.

"Acute asthma," Hayden answers with grave seriousness, though his green eyes glimmer with mischief.

Joey's momentarily alarmed before realizing his grandfather is only teasing. "C'mon. Does anyone really die from asthma, Grandpa?"

"Do'an' be ridiculous." Hayden leans over and rumples his grandson's butterscotch hair. "Richardson died o' The Cancer, of course! Do you think I'm cruising these things for the petit fours and to hear 'Greensleeves' choked out on the oboe? This is a serious medical inquiry into the pros and cons of euthanasia."

"Then if I'm not going to die, why won't Mom let me do anything?"

"She's a worrier. Always has been. Diana had more sick dolls than any little girl I ever knew. And not just a flu—oh no, Diana's dolls contracted the rubella and smallpox and leprosy and leukemia—all requiring toothpick tongue depressors and wee IV drip bottles fashioned out o' pipe cleaners. Her Barbies would have automobile crashes and boating accidents and get bitten by poisonous snakes and require antivenin to be flown in from remote jungles. Sometimes I think she should spell the name Di with an *e* added onto the end."

Imagining his mother as a neurotic young girl rescuing her dolls from the jaws of death brings a smile to Joey's face.

"Your mother grinds vitamins into my tapioca pudding," Hayden states with a chuckle. "She thinks I do'an' notice."

"But if you know, why do you let her do it?"

"It makes her feel better. Like when you let her check your forehead for fever even though you feel fine. Relations are a willful lot."

"Are we going to attend funerals all summer long?"

"Why not? For an old barracks bag, I still ha' a lot of wind left in me!" Hayden takes one hand off the steering wheel and pounds his chest. "Besides, these forty-year-old oncology doctors don't know a blessed thing about death. Wouldn't know it if the grim reaper crept up and bit 'em in the arse."

"I wish you weren't going to die," says Joey. He doesn't entirely understand how a person so alive can be expected to die. How do the doctors know for sure that Hayden is going to die soon and why can't they give him something to stop it? Down deep Joey is convinced the doctors must be wrong and that whatever is showing up on their X-rays will eventually go away on its own, same as a cold or a headache, or like when he had the chicken pox last summer.

"We've already discussed this Joe-Joe. Everyone has to die. Some boys never even get to meet their grandfathers."

"Yeah, but then they can't miss them when they're gone."

"Good point. But I just told you, I have a bit o' time left." Hayden's tone turns more serious, like that of a pilot soothing his passengers during some unexpected turbulence. "We'll see all the Mets games and maybe even get front-row seats to a Rangers game this winter. An insurance buddy of mine is a friend of the manager. And we'll pick out a dog for you. A boy's dog—a golden retriever or a German shepherd. And you'll have friends in the neighborhood by then."

Hayden is in the process of trying to teach Joey everything he knows in just a few short months, from the practical—how to read the weather by the shape of the clouds and to tell time by the angle of his shadow—to the philosophical—why women are inclined to say yes when they mean no and vice versa.

"I'll *never* have friends if Mom doesn't let me *play* something. All the guys are practicing baseball and soccer and playing water volleyball at the community pool. And she says dogs have dander that will make my lungs collapse."

"The doctor says you'll grow out of the asthma, and you will. You haven't had an attack in months and you haven't been in the oxygen tent for o'er two years now."

"But you just said that the doctors don't know anything."

"Just for the record, I preferred it when you were five and didn't question me when I told you that purple-eyed monsters lived under the stairs. Joey, doctors know all about the asthma. It's in the first week of medical school. Furthermore, you need to be strong and healthy so you can climb to the top of the toboggan run during the winter carnival and scatter my ashes on the way down. You'll be twelve by then."

"*Grandpa!* I hate it when you make jokes like that."

"Who's joking? And do'an' be like your muther. She won't allow me to discuss my own death, and it just so happens that it's what I want to talk about sometimes."

"It's not my fault that I don't want you to die." Joey can't imagine a world without his grandfather. Even when Joey and his mother lived in Westchester, hardly a week went by when grandfather and grandson didn't see each other. Hayden would take the train up after work and announce his arrival by starting to play his bagpipes at the end of the block and then walk toward the house. His pockets would be brimming with treasures such as plastic bugs, disappearing ink, firecrackers, and all sorts of novelties that would cause Diana to throw fits.

"Always remember that you're Scottish, Joey." Hayden's brogue lilts upward in pride. "We do'an' get exercised about death. Unless of course a child dies. Now *that's* a tragedy. But for a fifty-five-year-old Highland geezer such as myself death is just as natural as a harvested field of wheat left to go fallow at the end of the season—its job is done."

If the truth be told, the actuarial tables at Hayden's insurance office had promised him another 21.6 years, and privately he is more than a bit miffed about getting shorted. But Hayden knows that to a boy Joey's age he must appear ancient. Fifty, sixty, seventy—there isn't much difference to an eleven-year-old. And by talking positively about the situation Hayden forces himself to remain upbeat and free of apprehension. He keeps remembering that his own father didn't make it to the age of forty and never had the good fortune to see his children grow up, and thus he should be thankful for the life he's already enjoyed.

"Okay," Joey agrees. "Only, if you're allowed to talk about dying then I'm allowed to talk about *not* wanting you to die."

"Hmm. I suppose that's fair enough." The kid has a natural instinct for a deal. He'd do okay in life. Hayden swings the car into a Sam's Club a few blocks from the funeral home so they can use the men's room to change into the dress clothes stashed in the paper bag.

"It's too bad I can't tell Mom how much use I'm getting out of my navy blue blazer," Joey says as they walk through the parking lot. "She thinks I only wore it once for that stupid school concert."

Grandfather and grandson examine themselves in the restroom mirror like nervous grooms, checking for any signs that might broadcast their status as interlopers. Hayden takes a handful of water and pats down his disorderly hair, a dark brown thatch recently streaked with gray, as if an early smattering of frost had wafted down upon it.

"Do you really think they'll have good food at this one?" Joey asks as they exit the enormous store, toting casual clothes and sneakers in paper bags. "I liked the one where they had hamburgers and ice cream sundaes for the kids."

"Those Irish Catholic welders certainly know how to throw a party—open bar, closed casket. However, this fellow was a doctor, a thoracic surgeon at Mount Sinai Hospital. They'll probably have carved ham and smoked salmon. Those old money Presbyterians do everything understated—you could be eating off a hundred-dollar chunk o' china and not even know it."

"I bet they have brand-name scotch," Joey adds knowingly.

"And what does a wee lad like you know about brand-name scotch?"

"I learned it from you. It means good hooch like Dewar's and Johnny Walker Black and maybe Chivas Regal. Not rot gut."

"Well, as long as we're on the subject of hooch, do your old grandpa a favor, will you? If you're going to be hooverin' up the alcoholic beverages then either drink vodka or let's buy some mints on the way home. Last week I had to tell your mother that some bloke spilled beer all over you at the ball game. Fortunately, she do'an' know the difference between the smell of brewer's yeast and Drambuie."

"I just wanted to see what it tasted like." A sheepish Joey slides down into the passenger seat.

"Right, and I drink martinis for the nutritional value of the olives. Do you think I was never eleven years old, that your old grandpa sprung up with the heather after yesterday's rain?"

chapter three

The parking area at the funeral home is full and the MacBrides are directed to the overflow lot on the grass next to the blacktop. Always a good sign—with an excess of mourners it's easier to blend in and mingle. As they walk toward the main entrance Hayden leans over and whispers to Joey, "I'll bet a lot of his patients saw the big write-up in the newspaper."

Once inside, they follow the DR. RICHARDSON signs, respectfully keeping their heads bowed while passing vacant-eyed mourners in search of coffee and restrooms, enormous vases overflowing with fragrant white azaleas, and strategically placed boxes of tissues. Over the past three weeks Joey has noticed the one thing all funeral homes have in common is that they keep the air-conditioning at full blast. He assumes they're worried about the smell from all those rotting bodies coming up from the basement.

Hayden makes a beeline for the casket since that's where the family always congregates. His modus operandi is to chat up the relations in order to get invited back to the house for further research. If the guest of honor died at home he can usually even wangle a tour of the sickroom. Did the deceased prefer the shades up or down? Did he mostly read, watch TV, or listen to the radio? Did they rent the hospital bed or buy it? Who's the best supplier? Were private-duty nurses hired?

First prize is of course an open-casket liver cancer corpse. In these instances Hayden feels as if they'd attended school together, only that the cadaver graduated slightly ahead of the mourner. The newspaper said that Dr. Richardson died of lung cancer, but you can't always go by this. If a patient outlives the initial diagnosis then most malignancies spread, and the only reason they still call it such and such a cancer is due to a system of nomenclature that permanently identifies you by whatever you were struck with first.

This time it's a closed casket, causing Hayden to comment, "So much for doctor heal thyself. He must o' looked a wreck at the end."

Although Joey can't bring himself to tell Hayden, there are a few things about the funerals that he doesn't really like—the boring talk by the minister or rabbi, and the people moaning and crying. At the same time, he has to admit that there are some things he really enjoys. If it's an open casket then seeing an actual dead body is really freaky. Joey likes to challenge himself to see how close he can get to the corpse and then imagine it jumping to life and running up the aisle. He also has a good time counting how many Mass cards the person received and peering inside the shiny limousines. Sometimes during the eulogy the funeral director even lets him put the flags on the hoods of the cars out in the parking lot. But most of all, he enjoys meeting the other kids.

Hayden is pleased that Joey doesn't cling to him after they view the body. A natural born socializer that kid is. Or a "people person" as they said in Hayden's days as an insurance salesman. Joey can always land a job in sales if he doesn't make it as a catcher for the Mets, his dream job.

And circumstances being what they are at funerals—distant cousins arriving from far-off places and throngs of wriggling children, many who've never met before—Joey is immediately accepted. There isn't any of that competitive schoolyard stuff. The boy simply informs them that his grandfather is a friend of the family and he's in like Flynn.

Sometimes Hayden observes Joey playing cards or video games with the other kids and knows that his grandson is going to be just fine after the mess of the divorce settles down, Diana stops fussing over him, and he makes some friends at his new school. After one funeral there was even a game of kickball out in the street. Joey was so excited to be pitching the ball and running bases—something Diana never would have allowed.

However, if Joey *had* suffered an asthma attack and Diana found out that Hayden had let him play kickball, it's certain she would have euthanized him faster than you put down a decrepit cat that pees all over expensive new carpets. Hayden keeps the inhaler in his pocket, just in case, though he doesn't tell Joey this. In truth, Hayden finds it amazing that with all of Diana's precautions and ministrations Joey hasn't already voluntarily checked himself into an iron lung for safekeeping.

As Hayden takes up a position near the casket, pondering the fine line between life and death, a strong arm claps him on the shoulder followed by a voice that would be considered loud for a wake. "Crazy Hady MacBride!"

Hayden turns to find the last person he expects to see, T. J. Cory, a young colleague from the financial services division of his old Brooklyn office. Effectively concealing his surprise at being discovered, Hayden gives T. J. a hearty greeting and a big smile, successfully disguising the fact that his mind is racing to figure out how Cory is connected to the deceased.

T. J.'s eyes well up with tears as he tells Hayden, "Your coming to the funeral will mean so much to Mom! You have no idea!"

Mom? Dr. Richardson can't be T. J. Cory's father. Hayden hadn't seen T. J.'s name in the paper. On the other hand, T. J.'s first four names were something that sounded more like a Civil War battleground than an insurance salesman. But Hayden manages to stay one step ahead of being found out.

"Actually, I'm sorry to say I wasn't aware he was your dad, T. J.," says Hayden, his brogue swelling and making this confession sound all the more heartfelt.

"Stepfather," interjects T. J.

"Yes, oh, now I see," says Hayden. He scours his memory in an attempt to recall something pertinent about Richardson from the obituary, but all that comes to mind is the fact that he was a navy veteran. "T. J., I'm here to pay my respects to a fellow member of our armed forces."

T. J.'s eyes practically leap out in front of his nose and he puts a beefy arm around Hayden and starts steering him over to a fifty-ish woman in a black dress and black lace gloves just a few feet away. "Mom, Hady here was in the navy with Dad!"

The small woman looks up at Hayden as if he's a ghost. "You survived the rescue in the South China sea with Marvin? I'd heard that everyone else was gone." She hugs Hayden and presses her face into his chest.

"Well, ma'am." Hayden stiffens slightly as he imagines himself in the navy and tries to place the South China Sea, but a group of people have surrounded them and all talk at once. Apparently T. J. has informed the relatives that another survivor is in attendance.

"You simply must say a few words," insists Dr. Richardson's brother Drew, an ophthalmologist.

"Oh yes," concurs T. J. "Especially how you were in the water for two days with the sharks."

Joey arrives at Hayden's side, intrigued by the word *sharks*, and not surprised to see that Hayden has so quickly ingratiated himself with the entire family. Hayden introduces his grandson and they all solemnly shake Joey's hand as if he's the offspring of a great war hero.

"No, I couldn't speak," Hayden demurs.

"Oh, you must say a few words!" the widow urges Hayden as if he'd be shirking his duty not to say a few words.

Joey looks up at his grandfather for a signal that they should make a run for it.

Drew comes huffing back over after a brief word with the minister. "It's all set. You'll speak first, Officer MacBride."

Joey's mouth drops open at the word *officer*. The closest Hayden has ever been to the armed forces was when they went to buy Joey a sailor hat at Reliable & Franks military surplus store outside the gates of the Brooklyn Navy Yard.

Before another word can be said the minister walks to the podium and the mourners take their seats. The family pulls Hayden along with them to the front row. Meanwhile Hayden quickly puzzles together what he knows—he and Richardson are the same age so it must have been Vietnam. They must have landed in the water due to a ship or a submarine sinking. And there were sharks. That was settled. He'd go with the sharks. To bolster his confidence, Hayden reminds himself that supposedly there aren't any other survivors who can contradict his story.

When called to the podium Hayden clears his throat and the fear of being found out translates into an appearance of mournful solemnity. He starts by saying how wonderful it was that Marvin devoted his life to medicine, to helping people, and yet it was no surprise. His brogue swells as he recounts how Marvin was always concerned with the well-being of others, even that tragic day when they were in the frigid shark-infested waters of the South China Sea, praying to be rescued. Hayden takes a pause as if he hesitates to revisit those terrible two days in his mind, no less talk about them. But then he steadies himself and tells the story about the explosion and the waves as high as a house, and finally, the sharks.

"You'd swim over to your buddy through the freezin' cold water thinkin' he was still alive and tap him on the shoulder from behind. The torso would bob once and there wouldn't be anything below the waist."

The audience gives a collective gasp.

"The thing about a shark is he's got lifeless black eyes and when he comes at you he doesn't even seem to be alive until he bites you."

After a deep intake of breath from the assembled crowd, the room is dead silent except for the hum of the air-conditioning.

"And when he bites, those black eyes roll over white. Yes indeed, a lot of men went into the water but only a few came out."

There's an involuntary moan from somewhere in the back and Hayden decides he'd better not press his luck. So he closes by saying how it was Marvin's idea to all form a circle against the sharks and how he encouraged everyone not to panic because certainly they'd be rescued. And if it hadn't been for Martin's bravery and calm assurance there wouldn't have been any survivors and thus Hayden would always be eternally grateful to his old pal.

After the ceremony Hayden is mobbed and embraced by appreciative mourners. T. J. and Drew insist that he come back to the house. But after such a narrow escape Hayden insists he must get Joey to a made-up baseball practice and they quickly exit.

On the way to the parking lot Joey is lavish in his praise for Hayden's speech. "That was incredible, Grandpa, especially the part about the sharks. In fact, it sounded as if I heard it somewhere else."

"I stole a few bits and pieces from Robert Shaw in *Jaws*." If Diana knew that he and Joey rented scary movies on rainy afternoons when she was at work she would disconnect the VCR.

"Well, they bought the whole story!" Joey crows.

"It was really wrong o' me, Joey. I just didn't know what else to do. T. J. caught me by surprise and before you knew it—"

"But they *loved* it. It made them feel better."

Hayden knows that's true, but still worries about setting a bad example for his grandson. On the other hand, sometimes you have to bend a rule or two in life, and that isn't such a bad thing for a young person to learn.

"It did seem to lessen their sorrow a wee bit," he agrees philosophically. The way Hayden sees it, no matter what did or didn't happen in the South China Sea, the poor bastard probably performed some unsung good deeds along the way and so it all balances out in the end. And death is the end, no two ways about it.

chapter four

By the time the funeral duo exits the second reception across town in Canarsie, it's late afternoon, and time to change back into their game clothes and head for home. Hayden pulls up to Canarsie Beach Park, over-looking Jamaica Bay, where bronze plaques along the pier explain the varieties of birds indigenous to the area and a golden age club in matching T-shirts storms the waterfront with arms pumping and backs slightly hunched against the breeze.

Suddenly a well-formed young woman spilling out of a skimpy orange bikini top and cutoff denim shorts struts toward the boardwalk from the back of the parking lot in gold plastic high-heeled sandals. "Look, look," Hayden nudges Joey with his elbow. "She's taking the twins for a walk."

Joey turns and stares at her with appreciation in his wide blue eyes. He tries to let out a low whistle but doesn't have the technique down yet. The object of their admiration gives the MacBrides a smile as she passes them by to join a muscular man carrying a cooler.

Hayden and Joey change back into their casual clothes in the men's room behind the outdoor ice cream stand and then buy large pistachio cones with chocolate sprinkles for the ride home. "We'd like sugar cones, along with an eight-by-ten glossy of yourself," Hayden says to the woman serving them, causing her to giggle with delight.

They take a shortcut through Seaview Village, driving past block after block of ranch-style and split-level houses that feel more like a middle-class suburb than Brooklyn. Joey looks longingly at the children bicycling and playing kickball in the neighborhood's quiet streets. They serve as a painful reminder that as much as Joey adores Hayden, he wouldn't mind having a friend his own age so they could trade baseball cards and play video games.

They're two of his favorite things, and his grandfather knows absolutely nothing about either one.

Before entering the town house Hayden insists on a quick debriefing session to ensure that they have their story straight—who played, who won, what the score was, what they ate, and so forth. Rigorous rehearsal is mandatory. "Your mother," Hayden is fond of reminding his grandson, "possesses the cross-referencing skills of a lifetime employee at the Library of Congress."

It's during moments like this that Hayden feels a twinge of guilt—coaching an innocent boy to lie and thereby setting a bad example. If Joey grows up to be a mobster Hayden is convinced it will be entirely his fault. Though if his grandson becomes a funeral director or a caterer that will probably be his doing as well. However, he absolves himself in true Scots' fashion with the knowledge that all three occupations pay a good wage.

"Now Joe-Joe, do'an' forget," Hayden adds, "tomorrow we're going to a baseball game for *real*. So we do'an' need to sneak out any extra clothes."

"Good. I'm getting bored with all this death."

"I admit it's an acquired taste, like the bagpipes."

As far as Joey is concerned, the funerals are all starting to look the same, and his grandfather often becomes subdued on the way home, absorbed in his own thoughts. Joey prefers it when his grandfather is cursing out the opposing team after a Mets game or giving him pointers on how to flirt with the girl at the ice cream parlor. On those days Hayden is filled with an endless supply of good humor and gives Joey tips on driving, car maintenance, and the best places in Brooklyn to take a woman if you want to kiss her. His grandfather believes Brooklyn to be the most romantic place in the world, much more so than the tourist-infested Manhattan.

When they finally enter the house it's half past five in the evening, prime appliance time for Diana. As usual, she has the vacuum blaring, washer spinning, dryer tumbling, dishwasher churning, blender whining, and the microwave whirring while it defrosts a bird for dinner. Hayden has purchased three extension cords and reset the fuse box at least a dozen times in the weeks since she and Joey arrived. The good thing is that with all the racket covering the sound of the car engine as they turn into the driveway, it's usually easy to sneak into the house and stash their funeral clothes in a closet before she even realizes they're back.

Sprawled across the sofa and glued to the TV is Diana's no account ex-boyfriend Anthony, not to be confused with her no account ex-husband

Evan. *How does such a bright and attractive girl constantly attract such good-for-nothing men?* Hayden repeatedly asks himself (and Diana). Even her senior prom date did prison time right after graduation for acting as wheelman to a Brighton Beach Russian mafioso. Hayden remembers the incident all too well, since it took the boy away from his regular job at his uncle's chop shop and Hayden got stuck with the corsage bill.

"What's *he* doing here?" Hayden hisses at Diana, who's in the kitchen making Anthony's favorite sun tea with freshly squeezed lemons and a tray of snacks. Hayden views Anthony as a giant primordial toad who basks on the sofa in the glow of the TV until food appears, at which time his head sinks into his shoulders and he proceeds to slobber and gorge himself.

"He's relaxing after a hard day of work," replies Diana.

"Any more relaxed and the sheep will be counting *him*," remarks Hayden. "I thought you two broke up after he *borrowed* your credit card."

"Now Dad, he's paying that money back, every cent." She anxiously twists the thin gold chain around her neck. The only thing Hayden does that truly bruises Diana's feelings is constantly criticize her choice in men. The rest of his comments and antics only serve to annoy her, or else drive her to the brink of despair with worry.

"You could bring a tear to a glass eye." Hayden looks at the tray of hors d'oeuvres with eyes that are like the windows on an old-fashioned cash register toting up the cost.

"He needed the money for supplies. Oil paints and properly stretched canvases are very expensive."

"Is that what he told you? I think the only stretched canvas your Michelangelo has ever seen is while lying facedown in a hammock."

"That's enough now. Besides, Joey likes him. This summer Tony is going to teach Joey how to fish," she says brightly. "A nice safe sport where he won't get hit in the chest with a ball."

Hayden switches on the coffeepot. "The only reason Joey likes him is because he hasn't made any friends in this neighborhood yet. Right now the lad would gladly play freeze tag with all the inmates on Riker's Island."

Diana switches off the coffeepot and foists a glass of prune juice on him instead. "Dad, you *know* you're not supposed to have coffee."

Hayden sips the juice and then makes a face. "I'm going to die a healthy man." He puts down the glass and stares at his daughter for a moment. She's stunning in a lavender silk T-shirt and a flowing peasant skirt splashed with indigo, fuchsia, and turquoise, practically dancing across the parquet floor with the light quick steps of a gazelle. Suddenly he is overcome with the urge to protect her and unmask this freeloading buffoon once and for all. Dying would be easier if he knew that he was leaving Diana and Joey in the hands of a trustworthy male.

"Just watch how cheap he is." Hayden proceeds to call into the living room, "Hey Anthony, we were thinkin' of goin' over to Vittorio's in Bensonhurst for some Italian food? Any interest?"

"Thanks Mr. MacBride, but I should really get back to the business." It further irritated Hayden the way Anthony regularly referred to his job as a floorwalker at Home Depot as "the business," as if he owns the entire chain.

"That's too bad. Well, what if the daughter makes us a bite to eat here, some pork chops or rack o' lamb?"

"Oh, that sounds great!" Anthony yells back from the living room. "I can never turn down Diana's cooking."

"*Sgiomlaireachd,*" sneers Hayden, knowing Diana will understand the Highland Scottish word for someone in the habit of dropping by at mealtimes.

"Dad, *please*. Now don't embarrass me."

"*Me* embarrass you? *He's* the one who said that Barcaloungers come from Barcelona." Hayden heads back toward the door. "I'm goin' over to the hospital supply center."

"Dad, will you please stop haunting hospital supply stores. You've been there almost every day this week. Besides, it's almost six o'clock. They're closed."

"Then I'll go hospital supply *window shopping*. Maybe they've invented a new sofa with an ejector button. I know you'd rather I peruse garden supplies, but unfortunately I do'an' have that kind of timeline."

"Suit yourself," says Diana. She hates her father's jokes about dying. It makes what's going to happen unbearably real. "But I don't want Joey going. He'll become a mortician if he keeps hanging around with you."

"The pay is good," Hayden replies cheerfully. "Besides, you think it's better that he sits in his room playing solitaire on the computer the whole day long?"

"Better than watching you haggling over coffins? *Yes.*" Why couldn't Hayden just teach Joey to play chess and take him to the movies like other grandfathers?

"That was the Neptune Society I signed up for, Diana. They take your ashes out to sea. I've told you a thousand times that I do'an' want to be buried. The earth is for the living, not the dusty remains of the dead. Would you *please* read my funeral instructions, it's quite clear—"

Joey enters the kitchen. "*Mom,* why'd you take down all my baseball posters? I can't have an asthma attack from just *looking* at sports."

"No, but you'll take the paint off the walls with all that tape." Diana had allowed Joey to put tape on the walls of his old room. But she doesn't want to act as if Hayden's home is her own, even though that's what he keeps insisting they should do.

"So we'll cover it with more posters," Hayden comes to the rescue. "Tape away!" He gives Joey a hug of camaraderie.

"Yeah!" Joey hugs him back. "Thanks, Grandpa."

"Okay," Diana grudgingly agrees. "But don't make a mess by changing them around all the time." She's determined to maintain some authority by having the last word on the matter. "Once you decide on a place then that's *it.*"

"I'm hungry." Joey glances toward the stove and the oven for signs of cooking. "When's dinner?"

"Ask Ant'ny," says Hayden in a fake Brooklyn accent. "He's the charter member of the Clean Plate Club."

chapter Five

As Hayden and Joey head for Shea Stadium the following morning, the Brooklyn-Queens Expressway thunders and quakes with end-of-rush-hour traffic. In the distance the skyscrapers of Manhattan rise and melt into a pale gray sky. Hayden squints into the glaring sun, attempting to realign his vision after a few medicinal whiskeys the night before.

"We just need to pay a quick call at the hospital." He delivers this news to Joey only after turning off the expressway.

"But Grandpa, you *promised* no death today," complains Joey. Why won't it just go away, this stupid Cancer Monster attacking his favorite person in the world, this double-crossing disease that doesn't hurt while it kills.

"Now do'an' get your skivvies all in a twist. We're going to a baseball game for real. The Bone Factory is just a pit stop. Cyrus is passing off some special pills to me. And he may not be around much longer, if you know what I mean."

"Pills? I thought you decided to sit in the car with the garage door closed," says Joey. Every time he opens the garage door Joey holds his breath, terrified that he'll find his grandfather's lifeless body slumped over the steering wheel.

"When did you start law school? Besides, that was last week. Cyrus says pills are better—that I may not have the strength to crawl out to the garage. And if *someone* should find me tryin', she'd tie me down." Joey and Hayden both understand exactly who that "someone" would be.

"Cyrus knows what he's doing. He was a pharmacist."

"You talk about Cyrus as if he's already dead."

"He very well could be by the time we arrive." Hayden scowls at the slow-moving traffic. There must be an accident up ahead. "Cyrus is going to take the same pills himself. Only the stubborn old goat is determined to stick around long enough to attend his grandson's bar mitzvah."

Joey appreciates that Hayden and Cyrus have a lot more in common than just cancer. Not only do the two men both possess sharp business sense, but they share a great enthusiasm for their adopted country. Cyrus had fled a dictator-ruled Romania with his family when he was seven, old enough to remember the poverty and lack of opportunity in his country. After attending the Bronx High School of Science and Fordham University, he'd gone on to earn a pharmacy degree at the University of Buffalo, mostly paid for by scholarships and financial aid. Eventually he'd opened a chain of pharmacies in Brooklyn and Queens and made a small fortune. And who would know better than Hayden, since he'd similarly built a career in America and sold Cyrus plenty of insurance over the years.

The oncology ward is bustling as patients are wheeled past with IVs dangling from metal racks overhead, and clipboard-carrying doctors and nurses efficiently scuttle up and down long corridors and into white rooms with beige rubber molding near the floor. Walking past the open doors the visitors are hit by a series of different smells—the aroma of flowers, sharp disinfectant, and the odd sour smell distinctive to places where people are waiting to die.

Hayden doesn't ask Joey if he'd like to wait in the lounge. Nor does the boy try to avoid being part of the pilgrimage. If it's true what his grandfather says, that he is really going to die soon, then Joey wants to be with him every possible minute. So he faithfully traipses after Hayden to the bedside of sixty-two-year-old Cyrus, haggard and wasted, dying of pancreatic cancer. Cyrus's wife, Hannah, kisses the new arrivals on the cheek and tells them she's going to use their visit as a chance to get some breakfast. Before leaving she tenderly caresses her dying husband's forehead.

Despite the hopelessness of his situation Cyrus is delighted to see his old friend. "Did you have any trouble finding the place?" he jokes in a thin raspy voice.

"No, I slipped an orderly a fifty and he took me right to you," Hayden kids him right back.

Suddenly their banter is interrupted by a ferocious shrieking coming from the next room, followed by the thud of cheap institutional furnishings smashing into the shared wall. Hayden and Joey both flinch and Cyrus covers his ears, as if this is the sound of death itself. When the uproar finally subsides, Cyrus lifts his hands from his ears and shakes his head as if his resolve to ignore the cacophony is wearing thin.

"Nothing to worry about." Cyrus motions for them to take a seat. "Goes on all day long. Have you ever heard a dying person make so much noise? Talk about a death rattle." Then he adjusts the cardboard sign hanging around his neck.

"What's that, Uncle Cyrus?" Joey inquires and points to the big hand-lettered placard spelling out DNR in shaky red block letters.

"*Do Not Resuscitate.* That means they'd better not try to jump-start me once I'm on the train heading downtown. Or I can sue their stethoscopes off."

"The hospital gave you this?" Hayden skeptically examines the poor penmanship and unevenly torn cardboard.

"No, of course not. I made it myself. The nurse only puts a discreet notation in my chart and a little card on the door. But I don't want anyone making a mistake in the dark." He shows them the penlight hanging around his neck that he switches on to illuminate the sign while he sleeps. "Joey, open the night table drawer there and hand your grandpa the orange pill bottle."

"Are you sure you have enough for yourself?" Hayden examines the half-full bottle. "I wouldn't want to leave you short, not at a time like this, anyway."

"Believe me, I have everything I need. And with these, we're not talking about all that many." His voice turns serious and drops to a whisper. "I made those pills myself. They're illegal and they're death bullets. Once dissolved they can fell a rhino in five minutes." He glances toward the open door to make sure no one is hovering in the hallway. "You don't pop them and then change your mind and call nine-one-one, okay? Because you won't be around to dial the ones. Take all six."

Hayden nods in understanding and shoves the pill bottle deep into his pocket. As he does so, the prospect of death suddenly seems very real, as if up until now he has only been playing the part of a dying man in a movie. For the first time a sense of dread briefly penetrates the consciousness of Hayden MacBride.

As he studies Cyrus's ravaged face, Hayden asks, "So, uh, not to be meddlesome, but when are you going to, you know . . ." They're interrupted by more shouting and what sounds like the crashing of bedpans and metal instruments against the common wall.

"Ugh, who can die with all this commotion," grouses Cyrus. "Day and night she carries on, screaming about the Lord, priests running out with their hands covering their heads, red Jell-O splattered on their backs like blood. In fact, go over there and put one of these on her door." Cyrus taps his finger against the DNR sign on his chest.

"Get out!" A shrill female voice can be heard above the commotion. "He has forsaken me! Get out!"

"Sounds like one of those folks being deprogrammed out of a cult," says Hayden. He'd occasionally received requests from clients who'd been brainwashed into cashing in their life insurance policies and signing them over to the grand wizard. The family would inevitably hire lawyers to try and prevent the financial forkover.

"Go and see if she wants some downers, just enough to give her a good night's sleep," says Cyrus, the friendly humor evaporating from his voice. "Send them over with a bottle of champagne and tell her they're compliments of room four-nineteen. We can't get in any trouble for dealing drugs, at least not where we're going we can't." He takes an unmarked plastic bottle from his nylon pouch and shakes out a half dozen triangular blue pills.

Hayden wraps them in a tissue, places them in his shirt pocket, and gingerly pats the spot as if caring for a large wad of bills. "I'll peek in on the way out." He hesitates, not wanting to confront the finality of their parting. "I guess we're off to the ball game."

"If the Mets lose I'm going to kill myself," jokes Cyrus.

"Aye, me, too," says Hayden.

"Cut it out, you guys," says Joey. Why did they always sit around and make jokes instead of searching for a cure? "I hate it when you two talk like that."

"It's just like being married," Hayden says to Cyrus while nodding toward his grandson. "Okay Joe-Joe, let's get you out o' this morgue and go find the alkahest."

"The alkahest?" comments an amused Cyrus. "That's a word I haven't heard since college."

"It turns things into gold," Joey knowingly informs him. "And holds the secret to eternal life." Whenever Hayden takes Joey somewhere he doesn't want Diana to hear about, such as the ice cream parlor before dinner, he announces that they're off in search of the alkahest. Only Joey secretly harbors the hope that he'll really find it and save his grandfather's life. Thus he's always on the lookout for new books about sorcery and magic.

Hayden shakes hands with his old friend and then leans over and kisses him good-bye. They both look serious for a second but won't allow themselves to be overcome by emotion.

"The bar mitzvah is tomorrow?" asks Hayden.

"Ten o'clock," replies Cyrus.

"You're going to the temple?"

"If it kills me."

"Then . . . I . . . I guess I'll see you in a few months," says Hayden.

"Don't try and tell me you believe in heaven and hell and all that malarkey."

"No, of course not. I just thought that maybe you did." Lately Hayden wishes he could buy into the whole afterlife business so that "good-bye" wasn't so damned final. It seemed as if it was easier to let go for those who believed they were indeed on their way to a better place.

Just then another crash is heard from next door followed by more angry screams.

"On your way out," Cyrus tells Hayden, "would you *please* inform her that I'm busy dying over here. And another thing, you're a slick talker, try and stop Hannah from having me buried. She won't listen to anything I say, as if being sick automatically makes you senile. And you know what I really want for my send-off."

When Hayden acknowledges Cyrus's request with a knowing smile, Joey looks quizzically at his grandfather, who makes a motion with his head to indicate that he'll tell him later.

As they enter the hallway, three nuns come rushing out of the room next door as if they're being chased by the devil himself. Cascading after them are a telephone, water pitcher, black leather-bound Bible, and other bedside paraphernalia. A nurse walking down the corridor calmly dodges the barrage as if it's an hourly occurrence that everyone has become accustomed to working around.

"Mind if I have a look-see?" Hayden says to a nun cowering in the hallway outside the door. But she appears to panic and rushes off down the corridor without replying.

"Wait here a minute, Joe-Joe." Like an advance scout checking for signs of enemy artillery fire, Hayden warily enters the room.

I told you to get out!" a woman hollers and a ceramic vase full of flowers comes flying toward Hayden. He ducks and it crashes and splatters directly above his head.

"Jayzus, Mary, and Joseph!" says Hayden. "With an arm like that you should be pitching for the Mets."

"Who are you?" The woman in the bed shouts and picks up a blue plastic lunch tray, apparently ready to hurl it at him. "A priest? Another specialist?"

"I'm Hayden MacBride. Nice to make your acquaintance. And no, I'm just a visitor. My friend Cyrus is tryin' to die in the next room and you're keepin' him from it." His brogue bubbles to the top in indignation and he rolls his *r*'s more severely.

Hayden edges closer. Her pale blond hair is shorn, not very stylishly, making him wonder if perhaps she's just come out of brain surgery. That could also explain the fits. Otherwise, without any makeup she appears no older than forty, though a distraught forty. Her face is flushed with anger, bright blue eyes resembling a pair of shattered prisms about to spill over with tears. But he finds them enchanting, like those on an old-fashioned china doll.

"You don't look very ill to me," says Hayden.

"Well I *am*. Inoperable lung cancer." The anguished patient slowly lowers the tray but stares at him with enough loathing to indicate that she might yet fling it. "And it's . . . it's just not fair. I've prayed my entire life and now *this*."

"Terminal liver cancer," says Hayden matter-of-factly, pointing to his midsection. He then lifts the chart that is chained to the end of the bed. "It's never fair."

"You sound vaguely familiar," says the woman. "I mean, your voice. That's a Scottish accent, isn't it?"

"Well done." He flashes a good-natured grin that could illuminate dark places and the rows of permanent furrows that cross his square forehead deepen when he smiles, which is most of the time. "Most Americans think it's Irish or English. Though I have a feelin' it only sounds familiar because yer thinking of a famous Scottish actor, who shall remain nameless, and is known for copyin' my accent in films."

"Sean Connery!"

"I didn't say it." Hayden self-consciously smoothes his perpetually disorganized hair.

The patient calms slightly. "I haven't seen a movie in ages." She loosens her grip on the lunch tray and offers Hayden a small hand. "I'm . . ." she pauses as if she's become so addled that she can't remember her own name. "My name is Rosamond. Rosamond Rogers."

"The accent was always a good opener when I used to sell casualty insurance. And speaking o' casualties, what's with all the hollerin' and hurlin' of furnishings over here?"

"I'm sorry for disturbing your friend." As she apologizes a solitary tear drifts down her cheek. "I haven't been taking the diagnosis very well. It all happened so suddenly. And now they want to do all these treatments and tests when I'll probably just die anyway."

"So then why stay here?"

"Because it's a *hospital*, that's why!" Her anger quickly returns.

"I *know* that. What I mean is, why sit around and let them poke and prod you if they're just torturin' you? Besides, doctors do'an' know what they're doin' most of the time anyway. More or less killed my poor wife. And then they said I was supposed to kick the bucket three months ago. But look!" Hayden throws up his arms in Olympic medalist fashion. "Here I am!"

Rosamond Rogers scrunches her brow and finally loosens her fingers on the plastic tray. While she's framed against the white hospital sheets, he can't help but notice she's the antithesis of his wife, slender and fair, whereas Mary was raven-haired and shapely, exactly like their daughter Diana.

Rosamond's countenance slowly shifts from trapped to pensive, as if it hadn't occurred to her to just get up and leave.

"Aggressive inoperable malignant tumor," Hayden says and drops her chart. "Looks pretty hopeless to me."

"Are you a doctor?" she asks.

"No, but death by The Cancer just happens to be my favorite hobby these days. Aside from baseball, o' course. Speaking of sports, my grandson and I are on our way to a baseball game. Why don't you come along?" That would get her out of Cyrus's hair for good. By the time she checked back in again he'd most likely be gone, and if not, it was doubtful the same room would be available. Besides, some baseball would get her mind off her troubles. Baseball cheered everyone up.

"We're Mets fans." Hayden throws on the charm as if he's selling a million-dollar insurance policy. "They're playin' the Cardinals. Are you a Mets fan?"

"I've never been to a baseball game." She ponders the invitation, as if this is a forbidden outing, or something even more outrageous, like Hayden has suggested firebombing the United Nations. Pushing aside the movable table holding the lunch tray, up until then a prospective weapon in her hands, she finally says, "That sounds splendid. Would you mind waiting in the hall while I change?"

Hayden exits and vaguely wonders if he's just started a new career as a social worker or, alternatively, asked a woman out on a date for the first time in thirty years. Before he became ill his sweet twenty-six-year-old neighbor Bobbie Anne had been bothering him to ask a woman out. Well, now he'd done it. And a feisty one, at that.

Hayden locates Joey counting tiles on the floor of the patients' lounge at the end of the corridor. The boy was forever counting things. Hayden is beginning to think he'll grow up to be a math teacher. Or else a bookie. Wouldn't that give his mother a fit!

Joey is relieved to see his grandfather return. He believes that if The Cancer Monster has a secret hideaway, it's probably here in the hospital, maybe in the basement or up on the roof.

"So? Did you give that lady your Suicide for Dummies lecture?"

"I prefer the term *self-euthanasia* if you do'an' mind. And yes, I have convinced her to check out," he announces, ever the proud salesman.

"She already took the pills!" Joey exclaims, not even trying to hide his astonishment for the benefit of the other patients in the room. "Wow, Grandpa, you could sell ice to Eskimos." He parrots ones of Hayden's favorite sayings.

"No, no. I mean check out of the hospital in the traditional sense of the word. I've invited her to the game with us. And here she—"

Hayden is struck dumb as Rosamond appears in full nun regalia, like a vision out of a stained-glass window—long black habit, white wimple, black cloth veil, large cross on a long silver chain dangling above her waist. Her face is smooth and pleasant now, dairy-fresh skin and a small upturned nose. "I'm ready!" she announces.

Unable to hide their shock, Hayden and Joey simply stare at Rosamond and then at each other, mouths agape.

"You didn't tell me she was a nun," Joey whispers to his grandfather.

"I had no idea," replies Hayden. "It wasn't on her chart."

chapter seven

It's an exuberant summer afternoon that fills the landscape with motion—flocks of birds crisscrossing the sky, trees swaying and trembling in the breeze—and the confused noisy jumble of wildlife and traffic that combine to make a sort of disjunctive parade.

Outside Shea Stadium Hayden listens carefully to the coded shouts of scalpers in an effort to determine which way the ticket market is going. Almost as much as the game itself Hayden loves the haggling—lowballing, arguing, and then pretending to walk away.

Sometimes by waiting around he can get a bargain as the sellers worry they might end up stuck with their wares. Alternatively, holding out until the last minute on a day like today can result in overpaying for seats in the stratosphere. Bad weather or a potentially boring game can send prices tumbling. But today is gorgeous, the teams are closely matched, and Hayden is possessed by a sudden urge to abandon his usual thriftiness. He pays a little more than he normally would for three tickets behind third base, where Joey can study the catcher.

Once inside the cavernous arena Hayden sends Rosamond and Joey on ahead while he waits in line at the snack bar. Rosamond is overwhelmed by the noise, vibrant color, activity everywhere one looks, and the overall energy of a fast-filling stadium. The hospital had seemed loud and crowded compared to the solitude of the convent, but this is like nothing she's ever seen—music blaring from large overhead speakers, people in animal costumes dancing on the field, shouts for refreshments from a man with a large box strapped over his shoulders, fans yelling to friends, waving mitts in the air and shouting "charge" on cue to a loud horn overhead.

It's easy for Hayden to locate Joey and Rosamond in the stands without checking his seat number. Lots of people are wearing black and peering out from underneath baseball hats, but she's definitely the only one with a wimple and veil. More than a few spectators nod and point at the nun in the stands, but their attention is fleeting. This is New York, after all.

Rosamond sits between Hayden and Joey, who take turns attempting to explain the lineup to her. But when Rosamond asks about scoring a "run-home" they simultaneously stifle laughter and realize they're going to have to start with the basics of the game. She doesn't know a bunt from a base.

Whether or not she ever figures out exactly what's happening on the field, one thing is certain, Sister Rosamond loves doing The Wave. It appeals to her ingrained fondness for group ritual, like standing in chapel and outstretching your arms to connect with the Holy Spirit. Whenever they rise she moves with the soft delicacy of a reed in the breeze, as if possessed by a natural sensuality, which doesn't go unnoticed by Hayden.

Rosamond also enjoys the Crackerjacks, hot dogs, and pretzels, all of which she enthusiastically chomps away at, making Hayden think that her medical condition certainly hasn't affected her appetite. Or else hospital food is a lot worse than it looks.

When passing the box of Crackerjacks during a particularly exciting play, she accidentally spills some on the man in front of her. Only when he turns around with his Brooklyn sneer that says, "Hey, you throwin' the Crackerjacks, you wanna fight?" and finds himself face to face with a beaming fan in a long black habit and three-inch cross topped with a crucified Jesus, he just laughs and gives a shrug that says, *Now I seen everything.*

Whenever Rosamond starts to cough, which is often, Hayden passes her his large soda and politely holds her Crackerjacks and places his hand on her back while she waits to catch her breath and take a sip. And it doesn't escape his notice that she doesn't flinch or pull away from the contact. On the other hand, Rosamond's so caught up in the action down on the field he's not sure she even notices.

It's an exciting game and in the bottom of the ninth inning when the score is tied the Mets' weakest batter strides toward the plate. After he takes two strikes looking, Hayden whispers to Joey, "Five dollars says he knocks out a homer."

"Grandpa, he's the worst hitter in the entire league! And the Cardinals' pitcher is on fire."

The batter kicks the dirt off his cleats, taps the plate, and warily eyeballs the pitcher. "Then is it a bet?" asks Hayden.

"Of course!" says Joey and they shake on it.

With two strikes and three balls the batter for the Mets hits one solidly over the fence behind second base, and Joey is momentarily torn between happiness for his team and disappointment at losing the bet. But he's rewarded shortly afterward when the board flashes GAME OVER, with a final score of six to five, Mets on top. The fans exit the stadium cheering and shouting, slapping backs and playfully punching one another. Maybe this season will be different after all.

After the game Rosamond asks to be dropped in the Brownsville section of Brooklyn, in front of a cloistered convent tucked away behind a dark gray stone wall. It's the only one of its kind left in the borough, she tells them. From a distance the old building appears abandoned and foreboding, standing alone on a small hill, severely Gothic with its massive arches and soot-blackened stone exterior. With the roof sagging in places it looks more like a dilapidated fortress than a house of worship. And no matter how many fire escapes are attached it could never be enough. The enormous weeping willow trees on the front lawn and rows of dark green hedges alongside the building are thick with solitude.

"Listen," says Hayden, quickly wondering what might make the best case for seeing her again, "I've been doing some research into all this death and dying folderol, and I'd be happy to share my files if you're interested."

A dark shadow crosses Rosamond's face, as if she's forgotten how she became acquainted with Hayden in the first place.

"I mean," Hayden continues, "if you want to give me your number—"

"There's no telephone here."

"Oh, well, then I'll give you my address—"

But Sister Rosamond is already shaking her head from side to side indicating that this is also forbidden. She carefully rearranges her habit before exiting the car. Beyond the tall iron gates the warm summer sun can be seen dipping behind a tomb of dark gray clouds.

"Then I guess it was nice meetin' you," Hayden calls through the window on the driver's side. He's surprised to feel so disappointed at being turned down, the sting of the no-sale compounded by the personal rebuff. But really, what's the point? He's dying, she's dying. And to top it off she's a nun. They're as different as chalk and cheese.

"Thank you so much," she says through the open window. "For a few hours I forgot about all my woes and felt like a schoolgirl during recess." The simple daily routine of the convent is supposed to free one's mind to concentrate on God. Yet Rosamond can't remember feeling so exultant as when the batter hit a surprise home run during the final inning and hundreds of spectators collectively gasped before bursting into wild applause. And Hayden reached around and squeezed her shoulder as if they'd known each other forever.

However, this unexpected surge of emotion only increases Rosamond's sense of being a complete failure as a nun. On the twentieth anniversary of taking her vows she's not coming at all close to fulfilling her calling, to achieving a state of exhilaration in her love for Him and progressing toward grace through the power of contemplative prayer and devotion. Instead, she feels spiritually bereft, with a heart like a dried-up riverbed. And now this terrible disease, certainly meant as a test, is muddling her faith worse than ever rather than providing the focus and clarity she so desperately craves.

"So long," he and Joey both shout as Hayden slowly turns the car around in the narrow gravel driveway lined with tall dark elms. The onset of dusk makes the chinks of remaining light that filter through the trees appear as if gold dust is falling to earth.

As they pull away Joey glances out the back window. "Hey, Grandpa, stop the car. The nun is chasing us!"

And sure enough, in the rearview mirror it appears as if a diminutive Darth Vader complete with flowing black cloak is awkwardly dashing after them through the deceptive shadows of twilight.

"It's Attila the Nun!" Hayden rolls down his window.

"Perhaps you can pick me up on Friday at ten?" she asks breathlessly. "I'll say it's a doctor's appointment."

Hayden nods in agreement, but before they can make further plans she turns and runs off again. Rosamond hurries through the hedge and back toward her world without television, newspapers, radio, movies, fashion, or men, except for Father Edwin, who comes to administer the sacraments and hear confession. Back to a place where the passing of time is marked by the changing colors of the altar clothes, and the vitality of someone such as Hayden MacBride is noticeably absent. Rosamond briefly stops in front of the permanently open but empty grave located at the entrance to the chapel, an ever-present reminder of the rich reward that will be hers after death.

A nun's time on earth is negligible to what awaits her in heaven, and thus she's not supposed to fear her demise. Only now that Sister Rosamond is actually faced with the prospect of death, she cannot bring herself to acquiesce so easily. In fact, she finds the very idea of her life ending so early to be nothing short of terrifying.

The station wagon merges onto the expressway and they ride toward the setting sun. Hayden is quiet, which is unlike him after an exciting game, since he usually enjoys recapping all the high points and errors. But this evening his mind is far away, pondering all the strange turns that his life has taken since Mary's death—the encounter with his neighbor Bobbie Anne, being diagnosed with The Cancer, and now meeting a nun who likes baseball.

In the tranquil atmosphere Joey decides it's the perfect moment to ask about something that's been on his mind lately. "Grandpa, what do you do if a girl tries to kiss you?"

Hayden laughs and checks his rearview mirror before changing lanes. "Well, if she's a sweet lass you close your eyes and you let her. Why? Was the Sister trying some funny business while I was in the loo?"

"*Grandpa!*" says Joey, making sure Hayden knows that this time he's well aware that he's being teased. "It's just that yesterday this girl at the funeral snuck up and kissed me."

Hayden goes directly into his repertory of Scottish folk songs, thumping the steering wheel while crooning "*Sing the praises o' my dearie*" from "The Peerless Maiden."

"Cut it out. She is *not* my dearie!"

"And why not? A girl doesn't peck a boy on the cheek if she doesn't fancy him."

"I ran away."

Hayden slaps his right hand on the top of the headrest and then pats down his ungovernable mane with his palm. "Good heavens! So she wasn't exactly the kipper's knickers then?"

"She was awright, I guess." Joey looks out the window. "At my old school the guys used to say that Mom is sexy."

Hayden chuckles as he does a mental review of the supporting evidence—the eyelash extension on the dresser that he swatted mistaking it for a giant fly, the early pregnancy test sitting on the bathroom ledge that he thought was a science project belonging to Joey. Diana's appeal to the opposite sex is more than a bit disconcerting even to him. When she was an outgoing and eye-catching young girl with red ribbons tying back luxuriant hair that was like crushed black velvet he was thrilled that his daughter was destined for beauty, radiance, and intelligence. And of course it's a blessing to have a sexy wife. But a full-grown sexy daughter?

"I'm sure what they meant was that your mum is very attractive, which she is—gets that from your grandma. There's no need coming to blows about it if another lad feels the need to pay a compliment."

"Sometimes I wish she was like all the other moms."

"And let me guess, all the other boys say they wish that they had a sexy mum like yours."

"Yeah, that's exactly what they say. How'd you know?"

chapter nine

The house is quiet the next morning. Too quiet, decides Diana, as she prepares to leave for the start of her second week as a receptionist at a nearby medical center. Her father was usually the first one up, unless of course he'd snuck out of the house the night before and drunk with his friends until all hours.

She fixes a tray in the kitchen and then tiptoes into Hayden's bedroom and gently closes the door behind her so as not to disturb Joey, who's still asleep in the next room.

Hayden's eyelids pop open at the sound of the old wooden door meeting the slightly warped frame. "Jayzus, you gave me a fright! Was dreamin' about the day I married yer mother and then I see her comin' through the door."

"Sorry, Dad. It's just that you're normally up by now and I wanted to make sure you were okay." Diana hands him a glass of freshly squeezed carrot juice and puts a dish of sliced grapefruit on his bedside table. Her hands possessed a curious authority, but not calmness. They were constantly in motion, nervous fingers searching for tasks to perform and objects to dust or straighten.

Hayden tries to recall if maybe he forgot to close the front door or made a lot of racket when he crept in at four A.M. But his brain is foggy, and to be perfectly honest, he doesn't even remember climbing up the stairs or getting into bed.

"Was the hospital supply store showing a late-night double feature on broken hips?"

It was no use trying to hide the fact that he'd been out late. Somehow she knew. Instead Hayden moves to Plan B, and gaily attempts to gloss over the matter with humor. "I went over to Alisdair's to help him alphabetize his liquor cabinet. He has trouble with his *B*'s and *P*'s. And then, before you know it, he's making mint juleps with peppermint schnapps instead of bourbon." Hayden squints critically at the juice glass that's been planted in his hand and at the bowl holding the grapefruit. "What's all this?"

"Breakfast!"

"Breakfast for a jackrabbit! And I'm not bedridden yet, if you don't mind. I'll go to the diner for some griddle cakes." But obviously hungover, he doesn't make any attempt to rise from the bed.

Diana dismisses the subject of his breakfast plans with a roll of her eyes. "Dad, I need to talk to you about something."

"If it's about that nasty herbal tea you've been trying to get me to quaff, it would frighten the French."

"No, no. It's about the neighbors." She sits down on the edge of his bed.

"Did Paddy go off on another bender?" asks Hayden. "Ha! I warned him not to retire from the transit authority. The sobriety tests kept up his consciousness—in that he was conscious a lot more." Hayden laughs at his own joke and then trails off coughing. He takes a sip of the violently orange carrot juice but this only serves to make him gag and gasp even more. "Oh, me bagpipes for a Bloody Mary. Can't you leave me to my own vices?"

Diana ignores his dramatics and sly wordplay. "No. And I'm not talking about the neighbors behind us. I mean next door on the left. That Ellis woman."

Hayden immediately stops coughing, wipes his mouth with his pajama sleeve, and visibly stiffens. He knows what she's about to say and preempts her. "Her name is Bobbie Anne and she's a good lass tryin' to raise two wee ones by herself." His brogue always becomes conspicuously thicker when he goes on the defensive, which doesn't escape Diana's notice.

"So then I take it you know that she's a . . . that she turns tricks while her children are at day camp." Diana whispers this as if someone might be trying to listen in from the hallway.

Hayden pulls himself up to a full sitting position. "Do'an' say it like that! The husband died during a peacekeeping mission off in some godforsaken place where Jayzus lost his sandals and the government do'an' give her enough to get by on."

"So then why doesn't she get a job like the *rest of us single mothers?*"

"Because her daddy didn't pay for her to go to six years o' college, for one thing."

Diana feels her face flushing with anger but refuses to let him lay on the guilt about her constantly shifting college major, which added two years to a four-year liberal arts degree. She looks him straight in the eye as if to say "That's no excuse and you know it." However, Hayden had signed the lime-stone town house over to Diana just the week before and thus she knows what's next in his arsenal—daughters being handed paid-for homes with no monthly rent or mortgage payments.

Diana rises and glowers at him before turning to leave. She may have in-herited entirely too much of her mother's artistic disposition, at least in Hayden's opinion, but she also picked up a good deal of her father's quiet but fierce stubbornness, a gene passed down from generations of rugged Highland farmers and fighters.

Hayden is quick to note that he needs one final thrust to confirm his vic-tory. In a more conversational tone he adds, "She had a job selling wedding gowns at some fancy boutique on Madison Avenue—left at six every morn-ing and arrived home at night after her kids were in bed and her entire check went to baby-sitters and commuting costs. She couldn't even pay her taxes."

"Maybe she could work from home, start a day care—"

"Diana!" he says sharply. "Mind yer own business, will you please?"

"It *is* my business, Dad. I don't want my son growing up next to a whore—"

"*Do'an'* say that Diana. I'm warning you!" He swings his arm out to point and practically knocks over the juice glass. Tall patches of Scottish accent erupt once again. "Bobbie Anne is nothin' of the sort. She just offers neigh-borhood men a bit of comfort. For all we know it stops them from worryin' an unwillin' wife or gettin' drunk and hittin' their young'uns."

"I can't believe this. You're defending a *prostitute*."

"Now I told you not to use such language. It's her home and her body and it's a free country. And by God, where else is she going to make two hun-dred dollars a day tax-free and be able to stay at home and raise her little girls?" Hayden realizes that he's made a serious error by quoting an exact fig-ure, which is not likely to slip past Diana. Her eyebrows are already heading north toward the ceiling fan.

"Or whatever she earns," he hastily adds. To further the distraction Hay-den attempts to rise but takes a deep breath, coughs, and collapses back onto the bed. It's impossible to tell if it's the hangover, his liver, or whether he's simply feigning some sort of a spell in an effort to divert her attention.

"Oh, Dad!" Diana's caretaker instincts overwhelm her argumentativeness. She reaches to help him but he pushes her away. Diana is wracked with guilt by Hayden's illness, his willful self-destructiveness, and most of all, her inability to get him in for treatment. She understands that what the doctor has suggested is experimental and there are no guarantees, but he won't even try.

Hayden insists that such quackery is simply a scam either to drain his bank account or else to test a new generation of drugs that could eventually be patented and sold for millions. And so in his opinion they were looking for victims, not volunteers. Hayden knows from the way he feels inside that his cancer is much too far advanced to be stopped, even by an organ transplant.

If only her mother were still alive, thinks Diana. She's certain he would have tried the treatment for Mary's sake. "Then will you at least *please* stop drinking?"

"I'm fine." Hayden produces another convincing cough, just to be on the safe side. "And if I really thought the liquor would kill me I'd have a lot more o' it, believe you me."

Without a doubt Diana brings out the best and worst in Hayden. She reminds him so much of Mary and he loves her so completely that he never wants her to be hurt by life. Likewise, it drives Hayden mad (and often to drink) that he can't prevent her from making what he considers to be bad choices, especially when it comes to men and managing money.

"Then get dressed and come downstairs and I'll make you some apple cinnamon pancakes before I go to work." When would she ever learn? It was no use arguing with an insurance salesman. Her mother was the only one who could ever best Hayden in a verbal duel. Or else properly lay on the guilt to bring him around.

Hayden's cough quickly subsides and his sea-change green eyes light up. "Pancakes?" His brogue recedes. "The way your mother used to make them?"

"Of course." She smiles back at him and heads downstairs to the kitchen.

Before rising Hayden takes a deep breath and savors the lingering aroma of Diana's fragrant perfume, which has recently replaced the chronic household odor of burnt toast and stale tomato soup. Yes, it was a brand-new day. And he actually has a date lined up for later in the week! Okay, she's a nun.

Then again, it made sense to befriend someone who believes in an afterlife, seeing as they don't have much time left in the current one.

He walks over to the window and looks out at Bobbie Anne's postage stamp of a backyard. She's hanging wash on the line, as she does every morning about this time when it's not raining. Hayden breathes a sigh of relief that Diana didn't pursue the subject of his intimate knowledge of Bobbie Anne's rates. Besides, he can't ever tell her the truth anyway.

chapter ten

Five months earlier, the week before he'd been diagnosed with The Cancer, Hayden had paid a professional call on Bobbie Anne. It was the one-year anniversary of Mary's death and Hayden felt so wretched that he was preparing to get extremely drunk and start the car with the garage door closed in order to join Mary, wherever she was. Or at the very least, escape an anguished existence without her. She had been his compass in life. And though he'd been tempted several times throughout the years by attractive female coworkers and clients in distant cities, where he could have easily had a fling, he was never unfaithful.

While swigging scotch and fashioning the garden hose into a suicide apparatus he'd seen the fresh-faced and curvaceous Bobbie Anne in the adjacent backyard shaking out some rugs, her gorgeous hair that appeared reddish-gold in the sunlight hanging loose about her shoulders, and making for a striking contrast against her creamy complexion. In the neighborhood it was rather common knowledge that she saw men between ten and two. And so with his mind clouded by grief and whiskey he'd put down the hose, crossed the yard, and requested an appointment.

Bobbie Anne smiled pleasantly, as if Hayden was asking to borrow a cup of sugar. And in her friendly southern drawl she instructed him to arrive at eleven the following morning and confirmed that her fee was indeed two hundred dollars in cash.

Hayden immediately abandoned the hooch and hose and worked himself into a complete panic over the upcoming "date." He picked up the phone to call and cancel a dozen times but was too nervous to even dial her number. And standing in front of the bank teller was the first time in his life that he wished he had accepted one of those plastic cards that enables a customer to enjoy the anonymity of an ATM. Hayden was convinced that the woman behind the bulletproof Plexiglas partition knew exactly what he wanted the money for, because in all his twenty years at that branch he'd never withdrawn more than a hundred dollars in cash during a single visit to the bank.

Having lived as a bachelor for a year Hayden was also afraid that his appearance had deteriorated, much like the backyard, which since the day of the funeral had been slowly overtaken by weeds and undergrowth. At work his secretary regularly arrived with Tupperware containers filled with food for Hayden to take home and instructed him to get more rest. She was suspicious that outside of work hours he'd abandoned himself to alcohol and disarray. And a visit to the town house would have proved her instincts to be correct.

To be on the safe side Hayden went to Gus the barber for a haircut.

"Big business deal?" joked Gus.

"No, it's a personal, I mean a social—"

"Oh." Gus nodded and gave him a big wink in the mirror. "Then you'll want my Ladies' Man Special. That's thirty dollars and cheap at the price."

"Thirty dollars!" His regular haircut was only ten. "What can I possibly get for thirty dollars—a little off the top and ten years off my age I would expect."

"Trust me," said Gus. After cutting Hayden's hair he gave him a shave and trimmed his ears, neck, nose, and eyebrows. Yes, it was worth it. Except for the slightly unhealthy pallor of his skin, Hayden looked as if he'd been dry-cleaned.

He arrived at Bobbie Anne's a full twenty minutes early, like a senior citizen attending a retirement party. Everything he wore was brand-new except for his khaki pants, and those had been professionally washed and pressed, just to be on the safe side.

"Hey there, Hayden," Bobbie Anne said in her welcoming drawl. She was from Athens, Georgia, which was where she'd met her Brooklyn-born husband, Derek, while he was stationed at an army base there. According to Bobbie Anne, her father was the owner of a prosperous furniture store and a deacon at their church, and her mother was a long-standing member of the exclusive local garden club. Bobbie Anne and her sisters were all sent to an expensive girls school, spoke perfect English complete with proper usage of who and whom, and yet possessed no practical skills aside from those required to be good wives to wealthy men—interior decorating, flower arranging, table setting, and menu planning.

When Bobbie Anne became pregnant by a Yankee enlisted man, the son of a Polish-born electrician and his immigrant wife, and one of eight children, her parents were devastated. Her mother sobbed while her father banged his Bible on her dresser repeating, "Why'd you get on the train if you didn't want to go to Atlanta?" Eventually her aunt Winifred arrived from Savannah to mediate, if one could call it that. The choice was being disowned or else a stay at the home for wayward girls and unwed mothers, following which the baby would be put up for adoption. Bobbie Anne didn't score any points by asking why she'd never heard of homes for wayward boys.

And so now, at twenty-six, Bobbie Anne was a widow, still lovely, but with lines creasing the corners of her soft violet eyes, and a gentle slope to her breasts from having nursed twin girls who were now eight.

She led Hayden into the small square living room. It was furnished inexpensively; most decorative objects, such as calico wreaths and decoupage boxes, appeared to have been handmade by Bobbie Anne, or else were art projects created by her daughters. She acted as calmly and naturally as if she'd invited Hayden to brunch, or they were standing and talking while taking a break from cleaning up their yards, as they often did when Mary was still alive and he actually cared about keeping up the house and lawn.

Hayden placed the money on the coffee table, eager to get it out of his possession. Before leaving he'd counted and recounted it ten times. Exactly two hundred dollars in crisp new twenties. Though he wasn't sure what to do about a gratuity. In business one didn't normally tip the owner of an establishment. And when you did offer a gratuity for service it was usually afterward, not before.

"It's so nice of you to drop by, Hayden." She wore jeans that fit snugly and a short-sleeved hyacinth-colored cotton sweater that looked pretty against her long flowing copper hair.

"It's kind of you to have me over." He was careful not to say invite because she hadn't exactly invited him.

Bobbie Anne offered him tea or coffee. He declined. She came over and lightly touched his elbow and her far-seeing violet eyes stared into his luminescent green ones. "How've you been, Hayden?" Her voice was smooth and comforting like warm honey. "You look slightly peaked."

"Oh, I guess I've been a wee bit lonely, bangin' around that big old town house all by myself." The truth was that he'd been feeling tired, anxious, and without appetite for weeks. However, Hayden wasn't about to go to any doctor just to hear that he was "suffering from depression." At his insurance company practically everyone was taking pills or going to therapy as a way to try and get happy, from the president all the way down to the temp workers.

But Hayden was descended from a long line of hearty farmers who picked up their axes and guns when necessary and made do the rest of the time, not pill-poppers and crybabies. His was a vigorous soul that had always possessed joy, not sorrow. Anyway, Hayden despised doctors. They certainly hadn't done much to help his poor Mary with her heart condition, telling her to get on a treadmill, following which she had a stroke right there in the doctor's office. Yet they always managed to send out their bills, whether they saved a body or killed it.

"Of course you're lonesome, darling." Her eyes widened with understanding and continued to gaze into his, as if waiting for him to blink as some sort of a signal. "It'll get easier as time goes by. Just keep telling yourself that, even though I know that right now it's impossible to believe."

He'd heard such sentiments before, but her gentle manner and languorous drawl made the words sound natural and comforting, and not as if she pitied him. For a moment Hayden considered using the argument that had become his favorite for the well-meaning but nonetheless annoying advice-mongers, which was that *no one* could comprehend the magnitude of his loss. But then he remembered that Bobbie Anne had also lost her spouse, and that she must have loved her husband very much to have broken with her family in order to marry him. Perhaps she did understand.

"After Derek died I used to pretend I was acting in a play to get through the long days and even longer nights," she continued. "And then one morning life just suddenly became real again."

What happened next was not at all what Hayden had intended. He started to sob. All the grief he'd kept inside since the day of Mary's death suddenly exploded to the surface. Hayden wiped his eyes with his shirtsleeves but it was no use, his chest was shaking and he was sputtering. The storm was just beginning to brew. He wept all the tears that had been locked away in his heart since the previous spring.

Bobbie Anne took a step closer and put her arms around him and Hayden put his around her and was relieved that she couldn't see his face, only feel him heave up against her. They stood like that for a long time while he wept. Then they sat on the couch and he explained how he still expected Mary to show up, to appear out of the shower with a white towel wrapped around her soft sheet of black hair. And how both his daughters had invited him to come and live with them. Only he didn't want to leave the neighborhood and his friends of the past twenty years since they were all that he had left of Mary. They still included her in the old familiar stories that they recounted and the memories they held dear. One might say, "Ah, now this is a good pudding but Mary's was a better one." In that way the private language of old companions served to keep her spirit alive, and thus was a comfort to him.

Then as swiftly as the emotional tempest had arrived it moved on, a prairie swept by a tornado. Hayden took a deep breath and actually smiled at the thought of coming over to make love to a woman less than half his age and ending up crying and having her counsel him. Normally it was Hayden the insurance agent who was called upon to act as minister to distraught policyholders right after tragedy struck, or else to comfort one of his own daughters after Mary's tenderness could perform no further healing.

However, Bobbie Anne spoke in a way that didn't leave him feeling embarrassed. "You'd be surprised how many of my friends," which was how she graciously referred to her customers, "get the intimacy over quickly and spend most of the time discussing their wives and jobs," she'd assured him. "In fact, one psychiatrist talks the *entire* visit, and only stays for fifty minutes instead of the full hour. I don't even have to tell him when it's time to leave. He just automatically looks down at his watch at the exact right moment and says, 'I think our time is almost up. Why don't you make an appointment for next week with my secretary?' "

Hayden supposed that Bobbie Anne would have to mark him down with the talkers and rose to leave. He'd been there for slightly over an hour.

But she playfully tugged at his sleeve and he sat back down on the couch. Then Bobbie Anne pulled her sweater over her head and placed his right hand on her left breast. And she kept her hand there, upon his, for a moment, while she leaned in to kiss him on the lips.

Now, when Hayden fantasizes about the event, it is this part he always finds the most exciting, her hand on top of his, his hand on her breast. And then the kiss.

They made love until they tasted of each other. The great fire in Hayden's nature magnified him as a lover, and when she climaxed he wanted to believe that it was real. Yet he had to face the fact that a woman in Bobbie Anne's business either faked orgasm or didn't bother at all. And so he didn't ask.

"You're awfully sensuous under that wry Scottish exterior," she remarked while they were getting dressed. Bobbie Anne's life had been hard and she was wise in many ways, an emotional clairvoyant of sorts who knew what was on his mind without being told.

"I . . . I like a woman." He realized that this sounded rather silly. But it was true. He'd been with a fair number of women before falling in love with Mary. "I mean . . . I like their softness, their voices, their thoughts, the way they see the world so differently."

The next morning when Diana appeared from Westchester for her weekly inspection, she took one look at Hayden's gaunt face and sallow skin and trundled him off to the doctor. He was too tired to protest, which only served to alarm her even more. Tests followed. Hayden was not dismayed by the hepatitis diagnosis since it could be treated. The liver cancer could not, unless he wanted to be a guinea pig in some unproven drug trial with a mile-long list of side effects. Hayden's first thought was not about himself but about Diana and Joey. Who would watch out for her when he was gone? And who would ensure that Joey would learn all the things about life that a mother cannot teach her son? This last issue particularly troubled him. With his life suddenly being wrenched from Hayden without his permission, suicide was out of the question for the time being and life had all of a sudden become very precious.

When Hayden's insurance agency announced they were closing the Brooklyn office Diana insisted that he accept the early retirement package with full health benefits rather than try and commute into Manhattan every day. And much as he would have liked to continue working to the very end, he did not want his coworkers to witness his inevitable decline. Hayden was known throughout the entire company as the perpetually energetic and good-natured colleague who was quick with a joke and a smile, and that's how he wanted to be remembered. Not as some washed-up salesman who everyone was humoring because of illness, who brought everyone down by serving as a constant reminder of their own mortality, that life could indeed turn on a dime, and there was no insurance policy on earth to stop it from doing exactly that.

Hayden never returned to Bobbie Anne for professional reasons, but they'd remained friends and often chatted in their adjoining backyards. Sometimes he baby-sits her apple-cheeked little girls on weekends while she shops and runs errands. And when she arrives home he'll burst into a rousing chorus of "My Bonny Lies Over the Ocean," much to the delight of her daughters, since he changes Bonny to Bobbie, and the twins gleefully chime in *"Bring back, bring back, oh bring back my Bobbie to me."*

chapter eleven

Hayden is aware that time should fly now that he's officially dying, but the hours between leaving Rosamond and picking her up again three days later crawl by as if he's a four-year-old anticipating Christmas.

When Friday morning finally arrives Hayden briefly worries that she's forgotten about their hastily arranged date, or worse, she's changed her mind. But ever the optimist, he takes the newspaper and spends almost two hours planning their afternoon.

They'd start with a couple of funerals, and then, since it promised to be a nice sunny day, they'd drive out to the crematorium near Bethpage on Long Island. Afterward he'd take Rosamond to his lawyer friend in Garden City to draw up a health-care proxy so they couldn't keep her alive on machines for months after she should have been dead.

After Diana finally departs for work, Hayden and Joey quickly change out of their pajamas and get under way. A recent thunderstorm has swept the pale sky clean of everything but a single cloud. Roadside construction workers remove their yellow slickers while standing on asphalt that is shiny and iridescent with streaks of oil.

Hayden stops at the Sunoco station and shows Joey the proper way to pump gas into the car and check the oil. When Diana's not around he's been teaching the boy basic husband skills—how to mow the lawn, reignite the pilot light, and even take apart the pipes under the kitchen sink to retrieve lost rings. "You come from resourceful stock—the Scots invented the telephone, the TV, the steam engine, and even the electric light."

"You forgot the bicycle," adds Joey, who's heard this list recited many times before, especially after his grandfather has had a few drinks.

"Ah, indeed I did. If you're so smart then . . ." Hayden pauses with a twinkle in his eye, "what's the only thing you should ever add to whiskey?"

"More whiskey!" Joey shouts as Hayden finishes the *y*.

"We'll make a Highlander out of you yet, despite all these subways and skyscrapers." He clamps his hand on Joey's shoulder as the boy struggles to open the hood. It's at moments like this, while watching Joey's young hands fumble to find the hidden latch or use a heavy tool properly, yet slowly gaining skill and confidence, that Hayden profoundly regrets he will not see his grandson grow into a man.

On the drive over to the convent Hayden is relieved that Joey is preoccupied with a new video game. Otherwise the lad might notice his grandfather's nervousness, his continual efforts to smooth down his damp hair with a pocket comb, and his repeatedly checking the rearview mirror for anything off-putting, such as a coffee ground stuck between his front teeth.

When Hayden rings the old-fashioned bell of the convent a small door of rotted wood creaks opens and inside it he finds a notepad and pencil, which suggests a primitive version of a bank's drive-through window. He writes "Sister Rosamond" on the pad and pushes it back into the cavity. The message disappears into gloomy darkness and is met with ominous silence.

Hayden goes from heart-racing excitement to heart-pounding dread in a matter of five minutes. He finally returns to the car and is about to leave when an iron gate off to the side of the massive building cries out in protest and Rosamond appears from around the corner of a tall hedge.

She floats toward him, as if years of gliding through the silent corridors of the cloister have left her weightless. Her step is so light that not even the sparrows and cedar waxwings feeding along the path are disturbed by her passing. Upon seeing him leaning against the freshly washed station wagon, a smile plays across her lips that shapes her face into a shifting collage of hope and fear.

Once they're all settled in the car Hayden brims with enthusiasm. "I found a woman about your age who died of esophagus cancer. I thought we'd start with her funeral in Park Slope and then hit an ovarian cancer memorial service just for the hell of it. I mean, you never know where cancer is going to spread to next. It's like trying to track a jaguar through the jungle."

Rosamond appears shocked by this pronouncement, or else his use of slang, or most likely both. "Did you know either of these women?"

"Of course not," says Hayden. "I was trying to match up your disease, so you can start gatherin' information, you know: when she was diagnosed, what kind of treatments they tried. I don't want to influence you one way or another, but in my opinion those homeopathic patients go the fastest—the people who start ordering celery-eucalyptus pills and the like from Guadalajara. What a racket! In my next life I want to be a vitamin salesman."

Rosamond doesn't appear amused by this stab at humor. Or by Hayden's plans for the day. With her time so limited she'd prefer doing and seeing all the things she's missed, to live as fully as she can in whatever time is left. It was Hayden's sheer exuberance that she'd been fascinated by in the first place. "It all sounds rather depressing," she replies sadly.

"Oh, it's *not*," Hayden says passionately. "Tell her, Joey."

"We have a good time at funerals," Joey concurs, but not very convincingly. Though he doesn't say it out loud, the fun is wearing off, despite Hayden's constant reminder that the first three letters in the word *funeral* spell f-u-n. "And at the Jewish ones you get to wear a hat and then throw dirt onto the casket at the graveyard."

"No funerals, please," says Rosamond.

"Well then," says Hayden, attempting to salvage the situation, "there's not *only* funerals. I have a friend who works in a nursing home for the terminally ill and he can get us in there. Or there's the Death and Dying section of the Barnes and Noble superstore." He holds up a cassette. "And I have an audiotape version of *Final Exit*—it's very detailed, about gettin' your papers organized and then committing suicide."

Rosamond blanches at the word *suicide*. Then she becomes a bit teary-eyed. "I don't want to hear about that either."

"Maybe the cemetery . . ." Hayden's voice trails off, perplexed and disheartened that he can't seem to make a sale.

"No cemeteries. No funerals. No death!" she announces. "I had such fun at the ball game. It made me realize that there are so many things I've never done. . . . I entered the convent when I was nineteen, after going to an all-girl Catholic school and working for a year as a kindergarten assistant." She wipes the tears from her eyes. "I haven't had fun in twenty years. Except for the hospital, I haven't been anywhere in two decades!"

"Oh, you want to go to another *ball game*!" Hayden suddenly cheers up again. Okay, so she's in denial and unwilling to face reality just yet. "Darn. The Mets are away this weekend."

"It doesn't have to be a ball game. I mean, I haven't been *anywhere*."

"Then . . . well, uh . . . Joey . . ."

But Joey understands right away. It's as if Rosamond has been in school her entire adult life and this is the first day of summer vacation. She wants to feel the sunshine on her face and have a good time without worrying about scowling grown-ups, surprise quizzes, and homework assignments. And quite frankly, he wouldn't exactly mind a break from his grandfather's recent fascination with death either.

Let's go to the Long Island Game Farm!" says Joey. "I saw an ad on television. It's exit sixty-nine on the expressway."

Hayden glances at Rosamond. She finally looks pleased.

"Long Island Game Farm or bust!" he announces and turns the station wagon around. In rotating the steering wheel Hayden has the odd sensation that what's left of his life may be taking a turn as well.

"That sounds lovely, Mr. MacBride."

"*Mr. MacBride?* Sounds as if I'm bein' measured for a coffin! Please, call me Hayden."

"All right, Hayden." She glances shyly down at the floor mat. "Then please call me Rosamond."

"I do'an' know if I have that much breath in me lungs, you know, if we get to be regular mates. How about Rosie, like a Rosie by any other name couldn't be as sweet." Hayden laughs at his mangled reference to Shakespeare.

Rosamond blushes and says, "Oh, nobody's called me that since . . . I guess nobody ever has! You're the first, Mr. MacBr— I mean, Hayden."

They speed eastward on the Long Island Expressway, none of the electronic signs overhead blinking with news of accidents, construction, or slowdowns. Hayden is amazed by the level of comfort the signs offer a driver—explaining why you're being delayed and how long it's likely to last. Whereas twenty years ago, before the signs, drivers sat and stewed, some anxious travelers climbing atop their cars to peer ahead or else leaning on their horns in frustration. But with the advent of the information age they've all calmed down and now yammer away on cell phones, repeating to anyone who will listen what exit they're near, why there's a backup, and how this will alter their estimated time of arrival.

In the absence of heavy traffic and delays they turn into the Game Farm parking lot in slightly over an hour. From the sideways glances of the other visitors, an observer would think that none of the patrons had ever set eyes on a nun before. Hayden and Joey nudge each other with amusement as children tug at their mother's sleeves and point to the three of them. And when Rosamond sits in the petting zoo feeding a baby lamb from a bottle, after doing double takes practically the entire clientele turn their cameras and camcorders toward the sight. It amuses and charms Hayden that only Rosamond is oblivious to the fact that wearing a long black habit and surrounded by an array of barnyard animals she brings to mind a Christmas pageant.

The trio enjoys watching the lions laze in the buttery sunshine and the quietly contemplative zebras with their stocky striped bodies that stand out against the green and brown hues of the simulated jungle. In the primate section an ape beats his chest and then swings to the ground on a large black rubber tire attached to the end of a thick chain.

"Hey Grandpa, where does a gorilla play baseball?" asks Joey.

"I don't know, Joey. Where *does* a gorilla play baseball?"

"In the *bush* leagues!" Joey laughs so hard he bends over and Hayden smiles approvingly at his grandson's enjoyment of jokes.

"What do gorilla attorneys study?" Hayden shoots back.

"What do gorilla attorneys study?" Rosamond and Joey say in unison.

"The Law of the Jungle," replies Hayden.

Joey jumps up and down with excitement and Rosamond covers her mouth with her hand but laughs a warmhearted laugh, the kind left over from a girlhood filled with close friendships.

"If you're laughing at that joke then we're in real trouble," jokes Hayden.

But Rosamond points and Hayden turns around to see the gorilla imitating Joey by jumping up and down. When the big ape finally stops and sits down, a female drops from a tree branch above and begins to groom him, picking through his brown fur and eating anything that catches her fancy. While the male gorilla patiently waits, his glassy eyes look directly at Hayden, so full of expression that he seems almost human.

"It's pretty easy to see where we come from, eh?" Hayden says to no one in particular.

"You can't possibly mean that," responds Rosamond.

"What? You think some Guy in the Sky with a white beard made us and he's up there watching like Santy Claus to see if we're bad or good?" Hayden laughs out loud at the very proposition. "Fact o' the matter is that a week-old human baby is less developed than a week-old gorilla."

"But the laws of evolution are made by God," Rosamond says firmly.

For someone with such a gentle tone of voice, Hayden observes, she can be awfully bullheaded. First she doesn't want to go to any of the places he's picked out and now, barely an hour later, she's trying to convert him. And to think that Diana is constantly accusing Hayden of being stubborn! Obviously his daughter doesn't have any nun friends.

"Wait just a minute." Hayden turns to her. "I thought you fired God after he gave you the death sentence."

"I believe in God," chimes in Joey as he beats his chest and watches with delight as one of the apes mimics him.

"Then why did God give you The Asthma and a mother who won't let you play baseball or have a dog? And a father who do'an' pay child support?"

"Maybe he's testing me," Joey replies.

"I should have never let you go to Mass in Westchester with Diana and that Catholic furniture-maker boyfriend of hers." Hayden pronounces "furniture-maker" with distinct disdain.

"Hayden, you don't *go* to Mass," Rosamond corrects him in a stiff but amiable voice. "You *assist* at Mass. It's one of the seven sacraments, not a spectator sport."

"Oh, so now the two of you religious fanatics are ganging up on me? Just like Diana and the furniture-maker. Is this how it's goin' to be?" Hayden's brogue strengthens to accentuate his mock outrage.

"And what's wrong with crafting furniture?" Rosamond asks. "Jesus was a carpenter."

"Well your Jesus probably didn't owe so much in back taxes that his furniture was sold at public auction along with the car he owned jointly with his gullible girlfriend who never bothered to put her name on the title."

"Let's get cotton candy," says Joey. He doesn't feel like talking about God or his mother's disastrous love life.

Eyeing the large cones of pastel pink, blue, and yellow hanging from the pushcart stand, Rosamond has to admit that they look magically enticing, especially after so many years of brown and white fare, such as rice and over-cooked pot roast or meat loaf and mashed potatoes. She orders strawberry and Joey chooses lemon and they delightedly pull tufts off each other's cones and hold them up to the light before letting the sparkling pink and yellow spun sugar dissolve on their tongues.

As they climb into the car to return home Joey invites Rosamond to sit in the backseat with him so he can show her his baseball cards and teach her how to use his Gameboy. When the station wagon pulls up to the convent it's almost dinnertime even though the summer sun is still an hour away from the horizon. The evening is like velvet, soft and warm. A few faded apple blossoms drift onto the windshield through the sweet, perfumed air. Whereas the game farm was loud and vibrating with life, the convent is tomblike in its silence and makes one feel as if it's possible to hear the seconds ticking in the air. The dark stone arches yawn gloomily in front of them. Rosamond is smiling and Hayden is feeling satisfied that he managed to please her after such a rocky start.

"Grandpa, can we take Rosamond to the circus?" Joey senses that he's found his ticket out of constantly going to funeral homes. And he's decided that Sister Rosamond is fun to be with, even if she is a nun. "This morning they showed the horses on TV."

"The *circus*? Haven't you just seen enough nature for one week?"

"I haven't been to the circus since I was a little girl," Rosamond says wistfully.

"Wait just a second!" Hayden's schedule is full up with planning his imminent demise, and there isn't time for nonsense like clowns and horses. "I thought the whole purpose of our meetin' was to get you informed about dyin'. So you can decide if you want to stash away some plastic bags and make a will and that sort of thing."

"But I don't own anything," Rosamond reminds him. "I'm a nun."

"There are still lots of bits and pieces you need to think about tendin' to. You can't just leave all the arrangements to others—well, you can, but you'd be crazy to do it."

"I don't want to make arrangements to die. I want to spend the little time I have left enjoying life!" All those eager shouts at the baseball game and the happy children at the game farm. For a short while it had made her forget what was looming over them. "I want to go to the circus!"

Joey gives her a covert low five in approval.

Hayden looks suspiciously at Joey as if he's now certain that the two of them are in cahoots and have been secretly plotting against him.

"The circus, eh?" Hayden turns to get Rosamond's reaction. But what he notices is not her eager smile so much as the transformation in her appearance. The summer sunlight has turned her skin the color of apricots while the grayness in her eyes that morning has faded away, revealing china blue irises that seem to reflect the intensity of the sky overhead.

"C'mon, Grandpa. Let's take Sister Rosamond to the circus. Kids under twelve are only ten dollars. And maybe there's a discount for nuns, too!"

"A discount for nuns?" Hayden is amused. "At least you come by your sales ability naturally. I suppose I should be proud."

"Hooray!" shouts Joey. "We're going to the circus."

"Well do'an' tell your mother until after we've been or she'll throw fits about your asthma and the possibility of bein' mauled by a lion."

As Rosamond steps out of the car to go and do battle with her soul after having violated so many rules, Joey is also faced with an internal struggle. He stares at his cherished Mike Piazza baseball card, the one Rosamond had been most interested in since he'd played so well at the game they'd gone to see. It was worth almost twenty dollars.

They all say good-bye and she turns toward the gate. Hayden starts the engine. Joey yells "Wait!" He leaps out of the car, runs after Rosamond, and shoves the baseball card into her hand, the cardboard still warm and sweaty from being clutched so tightly, making it painfully apparent that enormous deliberation went into giving up such a prized possession.

Rosamond can't really accept any sort of material gift, which is technically considered to be a worldly possession. But the look of sheer joy on the boy's face after battling his conscience reminds her of the teachings of Paul, and the glory in being a cheerful giver. She's deeply touched at being on the receiving end of such an obvious sacrifice. In taking the card Rosamond places her hands over his. "Thank you," she says. "I know how much you value this and I'll always treasure it."

Joey feels his face become warm. He turns without a word and scampers back to the car.

"You gave her a *baseball card*," says Hayden. He makes up his mind to spend less time teaching his grandson about car maintenance and more time on communicating with women. "Let's talk a moment about flowers." Hayden points to the brilliant goldenrod and Queen Anne's lace dancing in the gentle evening breeze along the roadside. "Wildflowers are everywhere, women love them, and best of all, they're free!"

chapter thirteen

As Hayden and Joey pull into their neighborhood a light rain begins to fall. The sidewalks are wet and sparkle as if diamonds have been mixed into the cement. Alongside the front stoops the lilac bushes sift raindrops through their dusty heart-shaped petals and the potted geraniums nod to one another. The residents will be relieved that they won't have to water their boxes of sweet william and hanging planters of pansies, violets, and petunias. Then there are the plastic roses and plastic daisies that people in Brooklyn still favor. They'll get a nice rinsing from the rain, as will the white plastic chairs and red children's wagons that have been left out in the narrow front yards.

Joey is only upstairs for a moment when he shouts, "Mom, where's my computer?"

"Anthony took it to be repaired, hon," Diana calls from the kitchen.

"But there ain't anything wrong with it," Joey yells back.

"Don't say 'ain't'!" Diana reprimands him. "I don't know much about computers, but he's going to add memory or something like that to make it run faster."

"Has the cheese slid off yer cracker once and fer all?" asks Hayden, settling into the living room to mark up the obituaries with red and black Magic Markers.

"Oh hush!" Diana says angrily. "You always assume the worst about my boyfriends."

"That's because they always *are* the worst. And not exactly what you'd call heavy thinkers!" He points a finger to his head for emphasis. "I just do'an' understand it, Diana. You're pretty, you're intelligent. You have a fine education. I mean, it's the liberal arts and so it's not good for much of anything, but what is it with you and these ne'er-do-well blokes?"

"They're not *ne'er-do-wells*. They're *artists*. You know, not everyone is only concerned about the bottom line the way you are, Dad. Vincent van Gogh never had any money during his lifetime and now his artwork sells for millions!"

"And I might take this opportunity to add that he went crazy and killed himself. It's not about being coldhearted." Hayden raises his voice. "It's about taking responsibility and being—"

"And being like *Linda*! Why don't you just say it! Married to a congressman with a big retirement account filled with mutual funds!"

"It has nothin' to do with your sister."

Diana is upset and wipes tears from the corners of her eyes. "I don't want to fight about this anymore! Why don't you just move in with Ted and Linda? Your constantly campaigning son-in-law would love nothing more than for all the people at their church and the PTA to know they're caring for his ailing father-in-law."

"Why must you always bring up Linda? What's she got to do with it?"

But Diana only stalks out of the room.

Hayden would never admit it to anyone, least of all Diana, but he quickly becomes bored at Linda's perfect Tudor-style vinyl-sided home in New Jersey—the cookie-cutter houses, the neighborhood men comparing their lawns and cars, his daughter's politician husband, Ted, droning on about the missile defense shields and the Kyoto treaty and stopping to pump everyone's hand and make babies scream with his Halloween grin. All Hayden can ever concentrate on are those two barn door–sized front teeth, which act as a large umbrella above the lower lip. On the positive side, Linda never nags Hayden about his drinking. But this only serves to take half the fun out of it. She simply gives him a tight smile and says, "It's your life, do what you want."

Joey observes this argument from the top of the stairs while contemplating the absence of his favorite three distractions—computer games, the cartoon network on AOL, and pornographic Web sites.

Hayden looks up at him. "So Joe-Joe, how about a math problem? What do you think the odds of getting your computer back are? Fifty-fifty, one in ten?"

"I like Tony. He's going to take me fishing." Joey wishes that his grandfather didn't always have to say bad things about his mother's boyfriends. And also about his father. It only ended up getting everyone all upset. His mother then yelled at him to clean up his room and Hayden usually went out and got drunk.

"Too bad there's such a big gap between liking a person and trusting a person—about two thousand dollars in this case," says an irritated Hayden. "See, Joey, you can like the guy at the deli. But don't trust him to put the ketchup in your bag. Always check for it yourself."

"My dad says you're too clinical."

"I do believe he means *cynical*. And though I have a couple of adjectives for your dear old dad I'll save them for a judge. Meantime tell yer insolvent, actually there's a word for him, tell your insolvent father that bein' cynical pays the bills," Hayden harrumphs, "if you ever see him again, that is. A wolf may lose his teeth but ne'er his nature. Remember that."

Diana returns composed and wearing fresh lipstick. "Joey, after dinner I want you to go straight upstairs and clean that room! A mess like that is a perfect place for mice to start nesting. And they carry all sorts of infectious diseases. Now wash your hands and come to the table. I made a nice roasted chicken with fresh broccoli. You two have probably been gorging yourselves on junk food all day."

"I don't like broccoli," says Joey. "Why can't we have porn?"

"*What?*" Diana's entire body straightens up as Hayden looks on with amusement.

"You know, peas and corn," says Joey.

"Because tonight we're having broccoli. There's an article in *Time* magazine listing all the vegetables that help fight cancer."

"Diana, darling"—Hayden kisses her to make up for his recalcitrance—"I think you mean *prevent* cancer, not turn back the tide for someone who's already been *struck down* with it." They take their places around the dining room table.

"This is one time when you're wrong, Dad," Diana persists. "There's a list of foods that are good for people who've already been diagnosed. Cruciferous vegetables possess many cancer-curing properties. I'll bet you didn't know that."

"What's 'cruciferous'?" Joey pipes up.

"Anything that has a cross at its base." Diana makes a cross with her two forefingers to demonstrate. "For instance cauliflower, cabbage, radishes, broccoli—"

"Is Rosamond cruciferous?" asks Joey.

"Who?" Diana asks.

"Saved by the broccoli," Hayden says to himself as he dramatically drops a single stalk onto his plate and passes the bowl to Diana. "So, how's the new job at the bone bendin' factory?"

"It's an HMO, Dad. The doctors are all very nice. And two are pediatricians so there are plenty of children around, which I enjoy."

"I do'an' understand why you didn't just become a doctor. Scotland has produced some of the best doctors in the world—James Lind discovered the cure for scurvy, the Scots were the first to teach anatomy, and practically invented public health programs. And they train darn good nurses, too. It sounds to me as if you do all the same things that a nurse does at this new job and get paid a quarter as much."

"We've had this discussion a hundred times. I didn't know what I wanted to do in college and so I majored in psychology. And unfortunately it's useless without a graduate degree. Besides, I thought that I might like to be a painter and college was just supposed to be a backup."

"That was your mother's fault, always takin' you girls off to museums and exhibitions and givin' you drawing lessons. I'll say you should have been a painter—a *house painter*. Yesterday I received two quotes. These criminals want four thousand dollars to paint this place—inside and out."

"You should talk to Tony. He has some friends—"

"Thanks, but the last thing I need on my payroll is a bunch of knuckle draggers in three-piece suits with bright red bows hanging from the mirrors of their shiny new Camaros. Honestly daughter, do you think I came up the Clyde on a bike?"

"Oh, Dad. Tony could get a discount on all the paint and supplies at his business."

"It's not his *business* fer Chrissakes! It's a *chain store*. He's an *employee at a chain store, not a majority stockholder*! Besides, I'd rather do it myself. What do you say, Joe-Joe? Should we paint the house together?"

"Yeah, that'd be fun!" says Joey.

"Dad, stop kidding around. Joey can't paint with his asthma. And you can't with your, your, you know . . ."

"With my *liver cancer*. It's not going to go away if we try not to say it, Diana."

"I know, I know." She scoops a large helping of broccoli onto her father's plate.

chapter Fourteen

Before leaving for work the next morning Diana makes Joey and Hayden plate-sized western omelets with cheddar cheese and big chunks of ham. And she doesn't argue when Hayden turns on the coffeepot or refuses the glass of vegetable juice she attempts to put in his hand.

"To what do I owe this high-cholesterol treat?" asks Hayden. "If it were your dear departed mother doing the cookin' then I'd know there was an expensive new frock in the closet." Hayden chuckles at this reminiscence, elbows Joey, and loudly whispers, "A man supplies, a woman buys!"

"No new cars or clothes. But you're going to be mad at me," Diana says as she scrapes the bottom of the frying pan. "I saw Bobbie Anne in the backyard early this morning and I . . . I had a word with her about . . ." she looks at Joey, "about, you know, considering a different career."

Hayden glances up from his plate and scowls at her. "And what did she say about that, Hardhearted Diana?"

"She told me to mind my own business, in no uncertain terms."

Hayden laughs loudly and thumps his fist on the table. "Good for her!"

"Honestly, Dad, whose side are you on?"

"Why hers, o' course!"

Diana practically throws the toast onto his plate, storms out of the kitchen, and leaves the house only after a sufficient banging of doors, tsking, and loudly clacking her high heels across the hardwood floors. Though once in the driveway her paranoia overtakes her anger and she goes back up the front steps and calls through the screen door, "Don't drink out of the tap today. It smells like sulphur. There's filtered water in the refrigerator."

Hayden rolls his eyes upward and makes a circle next to his head with his index finger to indicate that Diana is crazy with all her worries and this elicits a host of giggles from Joey. Since moving in with his grandfather Joey no longer takes to heart his mother's endless warnings about rabid squirrels, carbon monoxide poisoning from sleeping without a window cracked open (but not enough to catch flu from a draft), blindness from playing computer games in the dark, and a long list of other maladies and dangers supposedly lurking around every corner. There was a time when he was afraid to open the front door because she had him so terrified that bronchitis was just waiting to swoop down like a giant pterodactyl and kill him with one breath.

There would be no dampening Hayden's high spirits on this Friday morning, not even the brief thundershower that rolled overhead while they washed the dishes. Something had definitely changed. After finally letting his heart grieve for his lost wife and adjust to the short time he had left, Hayden was beginning to be able to take stock of, and fully appreciate, what remained. And perhaps Rosie is right in that he should focus more on living than on dying.

"You realize," he tweaks Joey, "that by taking you and your nun friend to the circus this afternoon, I'm not only missing a terrific autopsy on the telly—pulmonary tuberculosis—but also a lecture on alcoholic hepatitis at John Jay College."

Joey giggles. "She's your friend, too." There's something about the way Rosamond and his normally outgoing grandfather hesitate around each other that causes Joey to sense they might like each other. Whenever he wanders off to look at something or buy popcorn Hayden and Rosamond appear almost nervous when he returns, as if they're afraid of being seen together without him. Joey likes Rosamond, but he knows that it's in a different way. Or if it's not in a different way, he realizes that he's too young to ask her to marry him.

When they pick up Rosamond, Joey pleads with her to sit in the backseat with him so that he can show her more baseball cards. Hayden shrugs and says, "So now I'm to look like the chauffeur, is that how it's going to be?" But he courteously opens the slightly rusted door to the back so she can climb in.

Hayden heads down the gravel driveway and the entrance to the convent slowly disappears from view. Once he's turned onto the boulevard Hayden announces, "We're stopping at a funeral."

"Oh, Grandpa!" moans Joey and buries his head in the space between the backseat and the car door. With Rosamond on his side of the battle Joey's been more open about objecting to Hayden's never-ending quest for information on dying. "It's the same stuff over and over again—rest in peace, blah, blah, blah."

"It's Cyrus," Hayden says softly. "I know he told us not to bother, but I have to show respect to the family."

"Oh," says Joey. "Sorry."

"Is that okay?" Hayden says to Rosamond. "Cyrus was your neighbor in the hospital—the man responsible for introducin' us."

"Of course," says Rosamond.

The synagogue is set back behind a crowd of billboards in a neighborhood that was once predominantly Jewish and is now largely made up of Islanders from Jamaica, Barbados, and Trinidad. Hayden places a yarmulke on his head and passes one to Joey but decides against handing Rosamond the black headscarf. For one thing, it won't show up against the black veil atop her wimple, and furthermore, it seems a rather overt clash of faiths.

Hayden settles Rosamond and Joey in the second to last pew and then makes his way to the front and speaks with Cyrus's widow, Hannah, and her daughter, while the rabbi and a few relatives huddle at the nearby dais. But all that Hayden can think of is how dismal Cyrus would have found the proceedings. His friend had wanted to be cremated and for there to be a big party, culminating with his ashes being launched in a rocket of red, white, and blue fireworks on the Fourth of July. Only Hannah wouldn't hear of such a "cockamamy scheme."

Rosamond has never attended a funeral outside of the convent, where they are long solemn affairs in Latin performed by the attending priest. Thus she's astounded by how social the event is, despite the sad circumstances. People mill around talking, hugging, crying, calling to one another to come over, and even smiling upon exchanging heartfelt condolences or news of babies, engagements, and graduations. The mourners seem to find as much solace in their busy exchanges as the nuns found in their silent contemplation.

Finally a serious-looking man in a dark suit goes around asking people to take their seats and then taps the microphone, apparently more in an effort to get the service under way than to make sure it's working. What follows are a few philosophical musings about death by the rabbi and a long-winded speech about "how short life is and that God is in the small things" by a cousin whom Cyrus despised. This is certainly not what Cyrus would have wanted, thinks Hayden. He considers stealing the corpse after the funeral and bringing it to his friend who works at the crematorium. It would easily fit into the station wagon. But he no longer possesses the strength for such endeavors. And besides, Diana would definitely have him institutionalized if she caught him grave robbing.

Instead Hayden privately resolves that the next night he and Joey will sneak into the cemetery and light a couple of rockets atop Cyrus's plot. At least it's something . . .

"Are they poor?" whispers Rosamond as they wait for people to exit by row. "They certainly didn't spend much on a casket."

"No, no. Cyrus left the family in fine shape. It's a pine box, sort of a FedEx coffin. The Jews have a special next-day delivery deal with God."

"Oh." Rosamond is aware that as the mourners slowly leave they all stop in mid-step for a few seconds when they notice her nun's habit. And for those who are in danger of missing the spectacle, a few well-placed whispers, nudges, and nods bring it to their attention. "I feel like a penguin escaped from the zoo," she whispers to Hayden.

"Don't worry," he tells her. "Think of it as a little quid pro quo. The Orthodox Jews always try to get into convents when nuns take their vows."

Rosamond looks at him, obviously puzzled.

"You know, to represent the groom's side." Hayden laughs out loud at his latest joke and so does Joey. "God, Cyrus will love that one when I tell him."

"*Grandpa!*" says Joey.

"What, you don't think Cyrus and I agreed on a secret way to communicate so he could give me all the details after he died?"

"Now stop it," Rosamond chides him. Hayden has taken to regularly teasing her or engaging in some outrageous behavior intended to cause her to laugh, or else scold him, not unlike a schoolboy pulling the pigtails of the girl on whom he has a crush. Only Rosamond feels embarrassed by his attention, and even guilty about condoning some of his more racy remarks by giggling at them. However, as soon as Hayden's interest is diverted, Rosamond finds herself subconsciously hoping it will soon find its way back to her.

chapter Fifteen

As they emerge from the Brooklyn Battery Tunnel in Manhattan, Rosamond opens the window and leans her head out in an effort to touch and taste New York City, and thereby internalize the pulsating atmosphere where dreams can come true and the truth can be elusive. Most of the structures—office buildings, town houses, corner stores, and restaurants—are the same as those she's seen in Brooklyn. But like most people born in quiet places where the appearance of propriety at any cost is favored, Rosamond has always imagined that New York is a magical city. For almost twenty years she'd gazed at this commanding skyline from within the closed walls of the convent, and now here it is, right at the tips of her fingers. She reaches her arm out the window so that the palm of her hand can absorb the consecrated air as they turn up Broadway.

Rosamond attempts to register every sensation at once—the man hawking newspapers to passing cars, a police cruiser with its red bubble swirling and siren blaring on the left, a school bus on the right with a red stop sign that swings out into the next lane of traffic. A school bus—could there really be children in a place like this? The news and movies of her childhood portrayed New York as the home of sailors, chorus girls, and mafia. It was the place where sultry heiresses posed in fancy nightclubs with long black cigarette holders, tossing off clever quips and come-hither looks to down-on-their-luck private detectives.

Through a series of sharp turns Hayden maneuvers the car into an underground parking garage manned by fleet-footed attendants who dart about shouting and waving flags. As they dive into the headlong rush across the busy streets and crowded sidewalks Hayden automatically takes Joey's elbow. Rosamond quickly grabs Hayden's other arm, terrified that she's going to be swallowed by the masses or fall into one of the gaping, steaming holes in the ground, barely cordoned off by a thin strip of flimsy orange tape.

Hayden feels the small feminine hand around his biceps and a satisfied smile appears on his face, that of a strong, capable man protecting women and children in a dangerous world. For a moment he is reminded of taking his daughters trick-or-treating and how they'd come racing to the corner out of breath and terrified after having encountered a ghost or a witch, and find such relief in his mere presence, sometimes even leaping into his arms. It's a heady experience to know that another living being is so dependent on you for safety and reassurance. It also makes a person strive to live up to those formidable expectations for as long as possible. Who doesn't want to be viewed as having such heroic powers?

Rosamond is astounded by Hayden's self-assuredness in this madhouse of humanity. He effortlessly navigates their route and Joey stays close at his side, more curious and intrigued by his surroundings than fearful or anxious. If it were up to Joey they'd pause to take the flyers from every hawker, gaze into overdecorated store windows, and stop at every umbrella stand to watch the lightning-quick vendor deal hot dogs, ice creams, and sodas as if they're playing cards. And every time he clanks open the aluminum hotbox the delicious aroma of hot pretzels saturates the air. But the second they turn the corner the wonderful smell is overwhelmed by the foul odor of a dozen cigarettes as a group of smokers stand huddled together outside an office building puffing away while nervously glancing at their watches.

No one so much as looks at her nun's habit. And it's no wonder. Within five minutes Rosamond sees two men with shaved heads wearing saffron robes, several women in skimpy halter tops and short-shorts, and a seven-foot yellow and orange chicken passing out menus in front of a take-out restaurant called The Cluck Hut.

Joey almost trips several times from peering up to the tops of tall buildings in search of his idols—Superman, Batman, and Spider-Man. Or else one of the bad guys, such as Cyborg II or Brainiac. New York was not only the model city for almost every important superhero's home, it was also the place that monsters such as Godzilla always wanted to destroy. Joey was constantly pleading with Hayden to take him to the Empire State Building in order to imagine what those last moments were like for poor old King Kong.

After a few more blocks Rosamond begins to adjust to the hustle and bustle of street life, settling into the pedestrian rhythms with the beats tapped out by "walk" and "don't walk," and loosens her grip on Hayden's arm. Still, the city is so much more real with sights and scents and sounds than she had ever imagined. Her jewel box Manhattan always had a lovely soundtrack, usually by George Gershwin or Richard Rodgers, and smelled like the briny seacoast air of the small town in Maine where she was raised. And when the television was turned off the house was still except for the wind nudging a shutter or the cat scratching at the door to go out. Rosamond is simultaneously intrigued and unsettled by the chaos of the city in comparison to the well-ordered universe of the convent. As far as she can tell, there is no way to feel near God in such a hectic and untamed place as this, to find peace of the soul and the cleanliness and order that enables one to master the mind and all of its powers.

The circus is held under a bulky blue tent behind Lincoln Center on the west side of Manhattan. The high-pitched voices of eager children can be heard rising from every bleacher like rows of trilling and chirping birds anticipating a windfall of seed or bread crumbs. Rosamond and Joey, also caught up in the excitement, share a green slush drink the color of a chemical spill and an overflowing tub of caramel-coated popcorn as the band strikes up, indicating that the show is about to start. Hayden relaxes amid the chaos and treats himself to the cold beer he smuggled in under his jacket. Looking around at all the poles and wires holding up the temporary structure he guesses as to how much insurance is involved in such a venture, especially after one factors in the coming and goings of several enormous elephants.

The lights in the audience dim and the ringmaster suddenly appears from out of a cloud of pink smoke. He introduces red-nosed clowns in hobo suits and oversize floppy shoes, amazing acrobats on stilts, breathtaking jugglers of fire, tightrope walkers, and stunt riders atop low athletic-looking horses with long braided manes. A magician makes his swimsuit-clad assistant disappear into a wardrobe only to turn and find her standing behind him dressed in an elaborate ball gown.

Rosamond is exhilarated by the sheer lavishness of the spectacle—the showy costumes, dazzling colors, and eight-person band above the center ring playing high-spirited music. It reminds her of when she was a girl and a traveling carnival would set up shop on the edge of her otherwise quiet coastal fishing village at the end of every August. And for the next five days everyone went around in an altered state—normally quiet and staid fishermen sneaking off to the beer tent, while otherwise kind and neighborly women became fiercely competitive in contests of pie baking and handicrafts. Meanwhile teenage boys were preoccupied with proving their manhood at games involving shooting and strength, and by entering boxing matches. The little children ran around pell-mell, alternately terrified and thrilled by the freak show and the flying swings, safe in the knowledge it was the only time they could get their clothes dirty without reprimand and for dinner eat caramel apples, fried dough, and saltwater taffy.

Then one morning the field was empty, with only large patches of dead grass as evidence that such a grand and decadent moment had ever occurred. The carnival disappeared as quickly as it had arrived, and the villagers returned to their shopkeeping, lobster traps, churches, and hearths as if it had all been a dream. And it was a dream, at least in the sense there existed a collective conspiracy to overlook anything untoward that may have transpired during the five days of bedlam.

Joey is mesmerized by the death-defying performances that include exploding cannons, angry lions, and audacious motorcycle jumps. And then there is the famous Shondra Family flying trapeze act—two muscular brothers hanging upside-down, soaring high above the audience as they swoop from one end of the tent to the other, sending their daring wives and sisters spinning between them. There's even a boy no older than Joey who manages a double somersault while being tossed through the air like a giant watermelon. Why couldn't Joey have been born into a circus family, with his mother smiling and applauding on the tiny platform from which they pushed off on their heroic missions, just like the happy Shondra mother, her trim figure outlined in an orange-and-gold-spangled costume, matching headband, and heavily made-up face.

Hayden is secretly pleased that his two guests are so thoroughly amused, but finds that his own joy is to be had in continuing to play the pessimist. "People payin' good money to watch other idiots tryin' to kill themselves," he grouses as they prepare to leave. "Who are the real fools now? Ask yourselves that."

"Oh, Grandpa," says Joey.

"Oh, Hayden," says Rosamond.

When they exit onto Columbus Avenue it's raining again and the wet hissing sound of trucks and taxis roaring through puddles fills the city air with noisy dampness. There's no sky now, just a ceiling of umbrellas overhead. Between the scaffolding, restaurant canopies, and umbrellas of others, they hardly get wet.

Hayden leads Rosamond and Joey down to Fifty-ninth Street, past the enormous black glass skyscrapers that are headquarters for brokerage firms, media empires, and under the awnings of world-class hotels such as The Plaza across from Central Park. The eighteen-story cast-iron building with the green copper roof resembles a French chateau, only with flags flying out front as if it served as an international border crossing. Joey imagines that it's a place where spies meet to exchange top-secret information and brief-cases filled with millions of dollars.

Passing the Pulitzer fountain in front of the grand old hotel they head toward the General Motors Building across the avenue and into the famous F.A.O. Schwarz toy store, where sensory overload strikes the second they pass through the revolving doors, as if they've entered a parallel universe. The massive space is crammed from floor to ceiling with luxury toy cars, enormous stuffed animals that talk and wave, and every movie tie-in known to Hollywood. From all directions come the sound of train whistles, rockets popping, dolls crying, light sabers dueling, and a lion roaring from some-where within an artificial jungle suspended overhead.

When they arrive at the top of the escalator a smiling employee with an old-fashioned leather aviator hat and goggles approaches Joey and shows him how to fly a balsa wood airplane so that it loops back to him like a boomerang.

Meanwhile Hayden and Rosamond are fascinated by the living room–size Lego space station. Toys had certainly advanced from the marbles and blocks of their youth.

The worker in charge of Legoland admires Rosamond's nun's habit and says, "Fabulous look!" Meanwhile he's outfitted in a red-checked shirt, denim coveralls, and an engineer's cap, obviously compliments of his em-ployer. "Are you demonstrating the *Sister Act 3* action figures?" he asks Rosamond.

"Sing-Along Sound o' Music," interjects Hayden.

"You should have been here when we had the *Braveheart* display," the young man replies to Hayden, obviously picking up on his Scottish accent.

Hayden smiles broadly and with a strong brogue states, "Indeed, I should o', lad. I could ha' played 'Sons o' Scotland' on me pipes."

"Wow," says Lego Man. "Has anyone ever told you that you sound just like Sean Connery?"

"Never heard o' him," says Hayden as he takes Rosamond by the arm and leads her away.

By the time they leave the store the rain has stopped and so the three tourists walk across the street to Central Park. Sitting on a bench they eat ice cream cones from a street vendor while enjoying the endless parade of children, dogs, tourists, cops, skateboarders, and Rollerbladers.

As they drive across the Williamsburg Bridge the Manhattan skyline once again glows in the distance, awash in silver, like a holy city in an ancient legend, proudly presenting a noble facade to the outside world, and yet careful to keep all its secrets just slightly out of reach. The city is like a human being, thinks Rosamond, with a familiar exterior and a complicated and perhaps truly unknowable interior.

Despite having had a wonderful time at the circus and the toy store, Rosamond seems distressed when they finally arrive back at the convent.

"What's wrong?" Hayden asks. "Did you forget your keys?"

"Hayden . . ." Rosamond begins haltingly. "I can't stay here anymore." Her voice contains the fretfulness of a front-row student suddenly assigned to detention.

Placing his hands on her shoulders, which are shaking like muscles that have been held under strain for too long, he asks, "Are they giving you the heave-ho? Why, those rotten bastards!" Hayden has no idea how convents work but imagines it's like the strict boarding school he'd attended in Aberdeen for a year, and that Rosamond is being expelled for breaking the rules.

"Oh no, they've been wonderful about my illness. But I can no longer pledge myself to God," she says, her voice as delicate as a sigh and her sorrow spilling out far beyond the borders of consolation. "But this is the only home I've known for the past twenty years. I have no other place to go. It's so awful—I can't stay, and yet I can't leave."

Rosamond and Hayden stand in the driveway silently staring at each other in the gathering gloom, their shadows growing taller on the stone wall.

Joey has never before seen his grandfather speechless. Nor has he ever before seen grown-ups acting so dumb. He pulls on Hayden's sleeve so that his grandfather leans down and then Joey whispers, "Ask her to sleep over."

When Hayden straightens up he appears to have awakened from his trance. "Then you should sleep, I mean, you should consider yourself a guest of the MacBrides for as long as you like. Go and pack your things and we'll wait for you right here."

"I don't really have anything—just a nightgown and a few books."
She looks up at the towering dark gray building. "And I'd rather not go
back . . ."

"Right. Then hop in the car," he says cavalierly, as if they're off on a
great adventure. He pulls out of the driveway spraying dust and gravel in his
wake, as if they're being chased.

chapter sixteen

When Diana pushes open the front screen door with two overflowing bags of groceries the first thing she sees is a boy about Joey's age patiently explaining how to work the channel clicker to a nun. Could she be in the wrong house?

"Hi, Mom," says the boy.

"Joey? Oh, my!" Diana turns toward the archway into the kitchen where Hayden is standing holding a cup of tea in one hand and a cocktail glass half-filled with bronze liquid in the other.

"Rosamond, it is with great pride that I introduce you to Diana, The Duchess o' the Sidelong Glance."

Only Diana is too startled to do anything but look from Hayden to Rosamond in disbelief. Sometimes hysteria overshadowed the social graces inherited from her mother.

Rosamond rises and extends her hand, attempting to hide her surprise at Diana's appearance. She has imagined Hayden's daughter as a shy young woman in a gingham jumper carrying a basket of flowers on her arm. And yet standing before her is the raven-haired version of Marilyn Monroe, wearing a tailored midnight blue pantsuit with matching high heels. And there is certainly nothing bashful about her—from her long strides and full red lips to her unrestrained figure and sharp glances.

However, there is also none of her father's sparkling conviviality. To Rosamond's great surprise, her swift movements and darting eyes don't communicate self-assuredness so much as doubt; doubt that anything good can last, doubt that anything that lasts can possibly be good, and doubt even that the sun will come up in the morning.

Unaware that she's being appraised, Diana sets down her bags on top of Hayden's new large-screen TV and takes Rosamond's hand, though not without giving her father a censorious look. "It's nice to meet you, Sister." Diana can only assume he's started to interview private-duty nurses. But a *nun*?

"Actually, I suppose I'm not really a sister anymore," the nun tells her. "I guess you should just call me Rosamond."

"Joey's going to be a lion tamer!" Hayden announces in a concerted effort to add annoyance to aggravation.

"Don't be ridiculous, Dad." After all these years Diana still can't always tell when Hayden is trying to get a reaction out of her solely for his own amusement.

"To the first asthmatic lion tamer," Hayden says and raises his glass in toast fashion. He hands the cup of tea to Rosamond. "Maybe they'll even find some asthmatic lions for him to train."

"I want to be shot out of a cannon!" exclaims Joey. What could be more exciting than flying through the air with a thousand fans breathlessly waiting to see if you were going to live or die? Though that doesn't mean he's given up on becoming an astronaut. Because he'll still do that part-time, when the circus is on vacation. But that's only if he can't be a baseball player.

"You took him to the circus, didn't you? You do things like this on purpose just to upset me—what about all the *animal hair* and his *asthma*?"

Hayden ignores her. "Where's Ant'ny-the-Sofa-Tester?"

"He had to work."

"Hope it isn't too much of a shock to his system. Though I imagine the couch can use the rest. Speaking of rest, I'm moving into the death chamber," says Hayden and points toward the room at the back of the house on the first floor.

"Oh, Dad!" Diana scolds him and nods toward Joey as if he shouldn't say such things around a child.

Rosamond, on the other hand, appears shocked at hearing such an unusual announcement. She hadn't been into somebody's home in over twenty years. Did people sleep in vaults now, with extra oxygen pumped in to help them rest?

"Okay then, the *sunroom*. I'm giving my room to Rosamond. Tonight I'll sleep on the couch in Linda's old bedroom."

Diana is considerably more surprised to hear that the nurse is moving in with them that very night than about Hayden's latest round of planning his demise. She peers at Hayden to see if there's been a turn for the worse in his health and concludes that he looks much as he had the past few weeks, a bit pale and weary around the edges, but for the most part upbeat and energetic. And knowing how careful Hayden is with his money, she finds it astounding that he wouldn't have waited until the last possible moment to hire outside help and pay rental on a bed.

"Uh, Dad, isn't full-time nursing a little bit premature?" She turns to Rosamond. "I mean, I'm sure you're very competent and all but—"

Hayden starts laughing and slaps his knee. "Rosie's not a *nurse*!"

Joey starts to explain, "We met her at the h—"

"Shea Stadium," Hayden quickly jumps on top of him and Joey bites his lower lip while Hayden finishes. "She's a baseball fan who needs a place to stay for a while."

"It's *your* house," Diana replies tersely. She glares at him as if he's lying through his teeth or else gone senile from The Cancer. But she knows better than to grill Hayden, especially in front of an audience. If instead she quietly observed him and watched for clues, the truth eventually emerged. With Hayden anything is possible. Perhaps the nun has a gambling problem or is an alcoholic.

She takes another look at the fully habited Rosamond, now seated on the couch with her back perfectly straight and hands folded neatly in her lap. Diana guesses the nun is older than she by only five or six years, making her about forty-one or forty-two. Rosamond's skin is smooth and free from wrinkles, apparently untouched by the damaging rays of the sun and worrying about baby-sitters. In fact, the only sign of internal tumult in her placid countenance lies in her eyes, which are cat blue and bright but wary—and there is something odd about the way she hardly takes them off Hayden.

Diana very much doubts the baseball story. But why would he lie? And where else would Hayden have encountered a nun? Has he suddenly started attending church? Did he make up the stadium story because he's embarrassed by the fact that he's turned to religion in his hour of need? She decides to interrogate Joey later. It's obvious he knows more than his grandfather is letting him tell. He always bites his lower lip like that when something is afoot that he doesn't want her to know about. But as it turns out, waiting won't be necessary.

"Rosamond is dying, too," Hayden cheerfully continues. "And she's enlisted me to help her to work out the details."

"Inoperable lung cancer," adds Rosamond. She surprises even herself with this public declamation. It sounds ominous to hear the words spoken aloud. For while they were at the circus she was able to put aside thoughts of the death sentence hanging over her head like a storm cloud, threatening to cast down its lightning at any moment.

"Oh no!" Diana's hand shoots up to her fluttering heart. Every day she imagines contracting a deadly disease and now here is a woman just a half dozen years older who's done exactly that. Which only goes to serve as additional proof for Diana that one can never truly worry enough.

After Diana recovers from the initial shock of hearing that such a healthy-looking woman is deathly ill she nods toward her father and says soothingly, "Well, you couldn't be in more capable hands. Dad has made quite a study of the process."

Rosamond begins to nervously finger her habit and Hayden turns the conversation in a less prickly direction.

"Di-Di, is there a chance you could lend Rosamond something to wear until she can go shopping?"

"Yes, of course." Diana attempts to get a sense of Rosamond's measurements despite all the dark billowy covering. "In fact, I think we're about the same size."

"Good, because she's getting out o' the nun business."

Diana refuses to fall into another of Hayden's traps by asking why, since it's hardly likely he'll tell the truth, especially now that he's obviously had a few drinks. For the time being Diana can only speculate. Has he converted Rosamond to his breezy atheism? Or is the reason more sinister, does she need a disguise because she's in hiding as the result of a scandal, something Hayden might know about or even be involved in, such as an insurance scam? She knows he's always lived honestly, but lately he keeps referring to the fact that he'd planned on leaving a more sizable inheritance, and had counted on working at least another ten years.

"It will feel strange to go shopping after two decades of wearing the same thing every day," muses Rosamond. "Actually, I don't even know where to begin." And it's true, she has only the vaguest notion of what people wear these days. From what she'd seen in the hospital, people dressed much more casually than they used to, even for work.

Rosamond recalls that as a young girl she'd adored pretty clothes, sewing outfits for her dolls and making suits from construction paper for pictures of people that she would cut out of magazines. Only the latest fashions had been the last thing on her father's mind, especially after her mother passed away. He was a fisherman through and through, more concerned with practicality—keeping dry and washing the sea salt off your boots so that the soles didn't rot. So until she entered the convent, most of her days had been spent in a plaid school jumper, blue church dress, or else coveralls and oilskins for helping out on the boat.

Upon hearing that a gullible consumer is headed directly into the commission books of potentially insincere salesclerks, Diana's maternal instincts go into high gear. "I have tomorrow morning off. I'll take you shopping."

"And in the afternoon I'll show her around the hospital supply store," adds Hayden. "I already called to have my bed delivered."

"Oh Dad, we're not really going to have a hospital bed in the sunroom."

"Diana, you *said* I could die here with you. Now are you sure you wouldn't rather I go to your sister Linda's house in Nouveau Jersey?"

"No, of course not. It's just that . . ."

Hayden and Rosamond and Joey all stare at Diana as if she might suggest a magic potion that has the power to ward off death.

"It's just that . . . why do you have to sound so *excited* about it?" Diana finally manages to articulate her difference in philosophy. It's not normal to view dying as an adventure. "And why must you always discuss these things in front of Joey?"

"What? Would you rather tell Joey that I've moved to Brigadoon until one day he stumbles across my ashes in an urn under the kitchen sink?"

"Oh, *Dad*," moans Diana.

chapter seventeen

At ten minutes after nine the next morning two burly deliverymen arrive with the hospital bed and Hayden directs them to the sunroom in the back of the house. It's a modest but cheerful space with a bay window looking out onto the small square of lawn that passes for a backyard.

"Joe-Joe, isn't it a grave-nudger's dream?" Hayden bounces up and down on the mattress. "Why don't you man the controls and take it on its maiden voyage?"

Joey sullenly shakes his head "no" and stalks out of the room.

Undaunted, Hayden begins to experiment with final poses—lying on top of the bed, hands crossed above his chest and head propped up slightly by a pillow. When Rosamond enters the room wearing one of Diana's pale yellow summer dresses he leaps up as if he's both astonished at the transformation and delighted by what he sees.

Rosamond pretends not to notice his pleasure, although she has to admit she's been hoping he'll make some comment, even if it's just one of his jokes or sarcastic remarks.

"Well, well," says Hayden.

"Well what?" asks Diana, following Rosamond into the room. "Dad, isn't that dress attractive on Rosamond?"

"I've seen more meat on a butcher's pencil." Hayden hadn't realized what a slender figure Rosamond was hiding beneath her flowing habit.

Rosamond looks away, crestfallen, despite her initial feeling that even a sarcastic acknowledgment would do.

"*Dad!*" scolds Diana.

"I didn't say anything bad!" Hayden protests, a bit abashed. "It's a lovely frock—nice as ninepence. You have a terrific sense of style, Diana. I've always said that about you."

"You've never once said that about me," she corrects him.

"I haven't? Well, I've always thought it. Except for that short black leather skirt you wore in college."

Rosamond breaks into a deep bronchial cough, and everyone is swiftly reminded that all they're doing is temporizing, savoring what should be an ordinary moment as a way of staving off the grim reality of their situation.

As soon as Rosamond has caught her breath Diana announces, "We're going shopping in the city—Lord and Taylor, Macy's, then Eighth Street in the Village for shoes."

"Have fun." Hayden fumbles in his pocket and hands Diana his credit card. "It's on me. And make sure to get something for yourself."

"Why, aren't you coming?" Rosamond appears surprised and feels a stab of disappointment.

"Dad, shopping?" Diana scoffs. "He never even went into the department stores he insured."

Hayden is momentarily uncertain of what to do. "No, I mean, well I, Joey, that is . . . I've got to . . ."

Just then Joey appears in the hallway and gives Hayden an angry look. How many times did he have to tell his grandfather to stop acting happy about dying?

"I'm going with them," says Joey without looking at his grandfather. "Mom is letting me pick out my birthday present."

But Hayden mistakes the fury in Joey's youthful countenance for determination and hops off his new bed. "Then that settles it. I'd better go and get me loafers."

Diana's jaw drops in amazement while Rosamond smiles self-consciously. When Hayden goes upstairs to change his slippers for shoes, he's shocked to find that Linda's old bedroom, now a sewing room, is experiencing a snowstorm of white feathers, constantly renewing itself from the air swells created by the ceiling fan overhead, which someone has turned on high. On the floor he finds the slashed carcasses of three pillows. It's only now that Joey's strange mood sinks into Hayden's consciousness. Apparently the hospital bed has not been perceived as an all-around success. The lad wasn't known for throwing tantrums and destroying bedding. In fact, the worst thing Hayden can recall him doing was getting Silly Putty on the couch cushions, and that was an accident.

Hayden switches off the fan and the delicate feathers drift downward until they come to rest on the floor, bedspread, and bureau. Now why would Joey go and do something like this? Then Hayden remembers the morning of his father's death, when he'd stalked out to the barn and broken up the hay bales, pitched the lose straw down onto the floor, and then buried himself underneath the huge pile.

"Dad, are you okay?" From downstairs comes the ever-vigilant voice of the woman able to channel Florence Nightingale.

"Yes, yes. Just polishin' my shoes." He closes the sewing room door so that his daughter doesn't find the mess before he can sneak back in later and clean up while Diana's preparing dinner. And there were extra pillows in one of the closets. Mary used to stock up whenever linens went on sale.

When Hayden appears on the landing Joey is fearful that his grandfather is going to yell at him. Or worse, tell on him, which means he'll be grounded and the birthday present will be postponed, if not canceled. And knowing his mother, she'll probably call the Wildlife Refuge and find that goose feathers carry deadly diseases, and they'll all have to check into the hospital for painful tests and blood transfusions. But Joey decides that he doesn't care if he gets punished. He's not sorry he did it. His grandfather shouldn't have ordered that stupid deathbed.

Except that Hayden only pulls Joey close and, as if nothing had happened, says, "So we're going shopping! It's just like Christmas in July. Almost makes you wish it was snowing, doesn't it Joe-Joe?"

Diana is too concerned about making it to the stores before the lunchtime crowd to pay attention to Hayden's exchange with her son. And thus the pair are able to leave without tripping her radar, except for the white feathers that Diana plucks from the back of Hayden's bushy mane as they climb into the car.

Once inside the large air-conditioned department store Hayden and Joey peer from behind a rack of bathrobes and eye the heavily made-up models offering perfume samples and makeovers to the passing parade of shoppers. Then Hayden pulls Joey over to the lingerie department where a mannequin dressed in only a skimpy black negligee holds their attention for a long period of time. Fortunately Joey seems to have reverted back to his normal, amiable self.

They wander through the racks of pastel-colored bras with matching panties and leopard-print teddies. The heart-shaped sachets tied with pink ribbons emit a powerful blast of hydrangea, and when combined with the silk nightgowns brushing up against their arms, leaves them slightly dizzy.

"May I help you?" asks a gorgeous young woman with aquamarine eyes and long strawberry-blond hair who is poured into a clingy and low-cut purple sheath dress.

"No!" Hayden practically shouts. "I mean, yes, we're lost." Hayden looks at Joey and places his hands on his grandson's shoulders. "We've lost this poor child's mother. Perhaps you could direct us to ladies' sportswear."

The woman smiles knowingly and says, "Right on the other side of those escalators." She points a burgundy-tipped finger toward the opposite end of the store.

Hayden and Joey pause at the brightly lit jewelry counter, glass cases glittering with stones and gold chains in all shapes and sizes resting in dark green velvet-covered trays. "Joe-Joe, let me give you a little lesson about women. See all this stuff here?" He points to the bracelets, earrings, and necklaces. "It all has a secret code with women. Men don't have a copy o' the code. But we've figured out most of it," Hayden whispers conspiratorially. "Do'an' ever buy jewelry at the start of a relationship, because then you don't have room to grow. After six months or a year you get her a nice pair o' earrings." Hayden taps on the case to indicate the gold hoops. "Then on the second Christmas you buy the bracelet. If she's expectin' an engagement ring but you're not quite ready you can stall with a necklace containing her birthstone."

Finally Hayden points accusingly at the diamond rings. "These you don't go near under any circumstance, unless you're very very sure you want to marry the lass. There's no such thing as a friendship diamond, no matter what her sister tells you, do you understand me?"

"But what about *after* you're married?"

"Oh, that's easy. She just charges whatever she likes and brings it home, holds up what you bought for her, and you pretend to have a heart attack when the bill arrives."

Hayden hears Rosamond's cough coming from the women's clothing department followed by her voice. "That's too expensive. I mean, I think I only have six months or something . . ."

"Don't be ridiculous," insists Diana. "You sound just like Dad. He won't even renew his magazine subscriptions. I could just as easily say the same thing about a New Year's Eve dress—that I'm only going to wear it once so I shouldn't pay very much. But that's no way to live."

"At least it isn't if you have credit cards," Hayden says to Joey as they approach the women, but Diana overhears him.

"Very funny, Dad. Now come back here to the changing room and keep an eye on our things."

Hayden and Joey sit down on an overstuffed pink velvet couch in a lounge area along with a number of men who are dismally waiting, covered in shopping bags and women's purses. Some are sleeping with their heads tilted back and mouths open as if they've been there for days. Three are huddled around a portable TV watching a ball game. Joey and Hayden play paper, scissors, stone while Diana reviews the nearby metal racks to see what other shoppers have rejected.

Two of the men have started laying side bets on Joey and Hayden's game in order to help pass the time. "Joe-Joe, now don't just throw out anything— you need to have a strategy," Hayden counsels his grandson. "You have to try and determine what I'm thinking and then head me off. To be successful in life one must always anticipate."

Rosamond eventually emerges from behind the curtain wearing a tangerine-colored summer skirt and a white blouse with flowered lace trim. Diana rushes over to adjust the collar and turns up the cuffs on the sleeves. "What do you think?" Rosamond twirls around, unaware of her spontaneous and profound femininity, but anxious for Hayden's reaction.

Several of the men wake with a start and like trained lab rats automatically drone: "Terrific," "I love it," "Is it time to go?" But upon realizing it's not they who've been summoned, after an appreciative look at the attractive stranger, most either turn to the ball game or doze off again.

Hayden gazes at Rosamond approvingly. To him it appears as if she's ready to dance on a moonbeam. "It's . . . it's more lovely than the fair city o' Perth." And it is, at least on her. He's seen figures more shapely and faces more strikingly beautiful, but never such perfect grace. Her sweetness fills the room like a gentle perfume and even a few of the men continue to gaze upon her with pleasure.

"Thank you. Diana picked out a few things. She thought the white cotton blouse gives me continuity with Catholicism and that the flowers are nice and cheerful for summer."

Thrilled by Hayden's reaction, Rosamond turns once again to examine herself in the long mirrors. She's not so much captivated by the dainty look of her new clothes as by the weightlessness of the fabric. Without the heavy cross and layers of thick cotton for ballast, Rosamond feels as if she might float up toward the ceiling like an escaped helium balloon. For the first time since before checking into the hospital almost two months ago, she's not experiencing that ever-present shortness of breath.

"I'm always tellin' Diana that she inherited a wonderful sense of style from her dear departed mother," Hayden says as he continues to admire his new houseguest.

She, in turn, feels the pink flooding her cheeks, and unaccustomed to being the center of attention, darts back into the changing room.

chapter eighteen

On the afternoon of the Fourth of July, Hayden takes Joey out front and shows him how to change the gas tank on the grill and then fire it up for a cookout. Joey reminds his grandfather that he wants his hot dogs charbroiled until they're black and crunchy.

"I can already taste the cheeseburgers with pickles and catsup, a big bowl of barbecue potato chips, and onion dip," says Hayden as he loudly smacks his lips. "And then washing it all down with some cold beers and a shot of whiskey."

Getting into the spirit Joey says, "I'm going to roast a whole bag of marshmallows and melt chocolate bars onto graham crackers and show Rosamond how to make s'mores!"

As they continue to plan their dream menu, Diana strides out front with a platter that appears to contain mushy flat tennis balls, not freshly made hamburgers and foot-long hot dogs. "This looks like pond scum," says Hayden.

"Or mold," suggests Joey and pokes at one of the spongy green "hamburgers" with his finger.

"Better than burgers!" announces Diana.

"Garden boogers," yells Joey, quickly picking up on their uncanny resemblance to snot.

"Joey, stop that at once!" his mother insists. "For your information, they're sage patties, free from nitrates. We'll eat them on whole wheat buns and instead of potato chips loaded with carcinogens I've made a delicious tropical fruit chutney that we can have with frozen yogurt. I read that sage possesses regenerative properties for the liver. And that the tannic acid found in mango has a healing influence on the blood vessels while guava relieves asthmatic respiratory distress."

"Chutney?" Joey proceeds to stick out his tongue, gag, and pretend to vomit onto the grass.

"Oh, bloody hell," says Hayden and grimaces. "Diana, darlin', you are about to spoil my favorite holiday."

Hayden is forced to wonder if Diana is truly his biological daughter—garden burgers on July 4th? Ah well, he'd just have to mooch off the neighbors. There was an overwhelming sense of collegiality among the residents of the block, and with Hayden's reputation for being a promoter of joy and enthusiasm, he was a sought-after guest. The neighborhood children were especially big fans of Hayden's, since he always purchased a large quantity of whatever they were selling for school or Little League. Despite his characteristic thriftiness, Hayden's heart always went out to a young salesperson.

"Come on now," pleads Diana. "Rosamond is very excited about the almond milkshakes that I'm making. According to my book on Chinese herbs, they're supposed to help with lung problems."

After Diana heads back into the house, Hayden attempts to cheer Joey. "Don't worry. She's not going to pee on our parade. Winners never quit and quitters never win, always remember that."

By late afternoon the rest of the neighbors have gathered in front of their town houses, barbecuing and partying, and waiting for the fireworks to begin. The Haitians and Dominicans have organized a steel-drum band at the end of the street and play languid upbeat rhythms. A jumble of white, black, brown, and Asian children begin jumping around together and shouting for a sprinkler to be turned on.

Hayden is especially fond of Brooklyn's immigrants—Russians, Mexicans, Nigerians, Koreans, Orthodox Jews, and families from the Caribbean. Some live together in communities and maintain their separate cultural identities. But most join the hubbub of integrated neighborhoods and preserve the best of their native lands—recipes, music, crafts, and dress, such as the many colorful cotton skirts and headscarves worn by the Jamaicans and Trinidadians on the MacBrides' street. The neighborhood is filled with the singsong speech of the West Indies, where people stress the ends of their words and vibrant conversation is a form of entertainment.

Hayden often thinks that if only the rest of the world could see the results of this grand experiment—people exactly like them, worried about paying their rent and raising their kids right, but without paying much mind to the color or religion of their neighbors. Whether Asian, African, or American, people want a decent place to live, decent food to eat, to be around long enough to watch their children grow and prosper, and not be pushed around by lunatics with guns. If they'd just realize there was only one life, this one, and there was only one race, the human race. Then perhaps all the killing could finally come to an end.

Hayden and Joey pretend to eat their sage patties by biting into the rolls. But as soon as Diana runs into the house for a phone call they quickly toss them into the trash.

"I do'an' even think the raccoons will make a run at those," says Hayden.

"What's wrong?" asks Rosamond. "I think they're good."

"Call me when your old convent publishes their recipe book, *Someone's in the Kitchen with Jesus—101 Things to Do with Campbell's Mushroom Soup,*" quips Hayden. "Then we'll let *you* be the taste-tester."

Fortunately, when it's time for the tropical fruit chutney, Tony arrives to take Diana to the giglio festival in the Italian and Polish neighborhoods where the North Side of Williamsburg meets Greenpoint. His brothers are running a booth of carnival games and his sisters and aunts will keep them busy at the church bingo game until long past midnight. Diana assumes that Joey is excited about attending the festival and riding the Ferris wheel, an activity his mother has deemed asthma-safe.

So Diana and Anthony are surprised when Joey begs off, saying that he wants to watch the fireworks in the park across the street. What his mother doesn't know is that her son has other, top-secret plans.

As soon as Tony's shiny black Monte Carlo has turned the corner Hayden and Joey both grab one of Rosamond's hands and make a dash for the Palowskis. Just three doors down, Ed and Sophie are barbecuing for their nine children, six brothers and sisters, and umpteen grandchildren, nieces, and nephews, as they do every year.

There's always plenty of extra food since most of the family work at local packing plants, warehouses, trucking companies, and the Costco in Long Island City. The leftovers, slightly irregulars, and those boxes that just never made it onto the forklift are known throughout Brooklyn neighborhoods as "swag." And people constructed elaborate barter systems, such as beans for toilet paper and pet food for baby food, depending on where the neighbors and various members of the household were employed.

The three party crashers are ushered to the overflowing picnic table and finally dig into greasy cheeseburgers, vats of potato salad, and charbroiled hot dogs. And Hayden is given his very own family-size bag of potato chips. Rosamond bites into a hamburger just off the grill and the juice trickles down her chin. Without a free hand to wipe it off she turns away embarrassed. But Hayden mops it with a napkin and laughs wholeheartedly, then bellows with amusement, "Now that's a burger! And it doesn't leave grass stuck between your teeth."

"Yes," agrees Rosamond. "It *is* rather tasty."

Joey enters into a marshmallow-toasting contest to see who can make theirs the brownest without letting it catch fire. Then there's freshly sliced watermelon that dribbles down arms and necks and sets off a seed-spitting war. For the adults there's another watermelon filled with cantaloupe and honeydew balls that have been soaking in vodka. Hayden doesn't mention the secret ingredient that makes it taste so refreshing. "Now *that's* a fruit salad," he says to Rosamond as they finish drinking the leftover juice in the bottom of their bowls and go back for more.

Rosamond can't understand why, but she begins to feel flushed and lightheaded. "I have the strangest urge to do jumping jacks," she whispers to Hayden and then releases a girlish giggle at the very thought of such a spectacle.

"And who in the heck is Jumping Jack?" rails Hayden, who has by now had several beers and fears that Rosamond has taken a shine to one of the fellows at the party.

"Jumping jacks, silly," Rosamond says and demonstrates by moving her arms up and down. "At the convent I used to lead calisthenics every Tuesday and Thursday."

"Well why didn't you say so. C'mon, everyone!" Hayden announces to the thirty or so partygoers lounging around talking and laughing with drinks in hand. "Rosie's going to lead us in some exercise, and lord knows a few of you could use it." Hayden nods toward some of the more pronounced potbellies in the crowd.

"Hayden, I didn't mean for *real*," protests Rosamond.

But he's already haphazardly assembled the group, and started the jumping jacks by shouting "hut two! hut two!" and there's nothing for her to do but join in. Fortunately the participants appear to think that this is an excellent amusement and they all hop up and down chuckling and giving each other high fives until they tumble onto the grass laughing. Even the normally sedentary Ed Palowski sits up in his lounge chair and claps two empty beer cans above his head.

Once it grows dark enough for the children to light sparklers and draw their names in the evening air, Hayden tells Joey it's time to head home so they can proceed with their scheme. The only task left is to make up some excuse to give Rosamond.

As they walk up the driveway Hayden says to Rosamond, "Okay then, Joey and I are off to uh—to look at some hunting rifles. We'll be back in about an hour."

"Oh, I haven't been to a sporting goods store since I was a girl." Rosamond's giddiness is accompanied by a sudden taste for adventure. She makes a note to get the recipe from Mrs. Palowski for that delicious watermelon basket. It certainly was restorative.

Standing slightly behind Rosamond, Joey points down toward the spot on his arm where one normally wears a watch. It's almost ten o'clock.

Hayden makes a show of looking down at his watch. "Actually, they're probably closed. We're going to the twenty-four-hour outdoor garden center to look at some fertilizer for the backyard—very dirty stuff."

"I wouldn't mind going for a drive." Rosamond enjoys being in Hayden's company, even when he's just going to fill the car with gas. It seems as if something always happens in his presence. Occasionally they ran into an old business crony of his and the two exchanged quips, or else they might see a man wearing a shirt covered in a blinding print and Hayden would lean over and whisper, "South Africa called. They want their flag back."

It's Joey who ultimately decides that honesty is the best policy. "We're going to set off some rockets on Cyrus's grave," he confesses. "We could get arrested. But you're welcome to come if you want."

"Why not?" Rosamond is definitely up for the adventure, even if she doesn't fully appreciate the stakes. "I used to love fireworks when I was a girl. We would smuggle them into Maine from Canada on my father's boat—great big sizzling flares, screaming rockets, and red pinwheels."

"Okay, then," Hayden relents. He has to admit that her daring is impressive. "But wear the old penguin suit, just in case. It may come in handy."

chapter nineteen

The gates to the small Jewish cemetery are secured by a rusty but effective padlock. It's an old graveyard and the trees and shrubbery have long ago outgrown the original landscaping plan. This makes for dark dense patches that loom in the corners like giant rock formations. A sudden gust of wind rustles through the branches above them as if the breeze has a secret it's trying to tell. And for a moment the air swirls about them like water.

Joey runs ahead carrying a flashlight that illuminates thick canopies of cobwebs slung between the surrounding hedge like silver wires strung with tiny diamonds. Eventually he locates a place near the back where a couple of bicycles are leaning against the fence and there's a gap in the shrubbery. By climbing from pedal to seat it's easy to scale the fence.

"Probably some kids daring each other to spend the night in the graveyard," concludes Hayden. "Let's give them their money's worth." His voice is filled with bravado and mischief.

Joey is the first to hop over the fence, then Hayden chivalrously holds the bicycle steady for Rosamond as she climbs up, lifting her thick cumbersome skirts with one hand and using the other to lean on his shoulder for support. Just as she's at the top of the fence, Hayden shines his light on her head, the stark white wimple making her face ghostlike against the surrounding black. Some shouts can be heard a few yards away along with the trampling of dry brush and several "ouches" as heads collide and toes are stubbed against tombstones in the rush to hide. When Rosamond is safely over the fence, Hayden follows. He's glad it's dark so she and Joey can't see the effort that it takes him. The physical sureness and capability he'd always taken pride in had recently changed to a sense of limitation and uncertainty.

Once they locate the correct plot, Hayden and Joey line up ten empty Coke bottles and pat them down into the fresh earth of Cyrus's grave. After placing a rocket inside each one they stand solemnly in front of the plastic marker for a few moments, as if it's a shrine. But the silence is soon interrupted by the rustling and whispering of frightened boys trying to find their way back to the fence in the darkness.

It's a moonless night except for a pale pewter halo behind thick dark clouds, and even Hayden has to admit that this particular cemetery ranks high when it comes to spookiness. Every willow branch dangling along the path makes you feel as if a spirit is tapping you on the shoulder, or running a long bony finger down your cheek. And with their rounded tops, the tombstones and tall, thin monuments resemble shadowy and misshapen soldiers about to descend upon anyone who dares to disturb the dead.

"Shouldn't we say a few words?" Hayden asks as they stand atop Cyrus's final resting place.

"How about the Mass for the Dead?" suggests Rosamond.

"Too Catholic."

"Then how about something from the Old Testament?" says Rosamond. "Psalm Twenty-seven—The Lord is my light and my salvation; whom shall I fear? The Lord is the strength of my life; of whom shall I be afraid? When the wicked—"

"I think Cyrus got enough religiosity from Hannah."

"We learned the dreidel song in school," offers Joey.

"Wrong holiday," replies Hayden. But the word *holiday* sparks the solution. "I've got it! 'This Land Is Your Land'! Woody Guthrie was one of Cyrus's favorite customers and he was always playing Guthrie's albums in the back of the store." Hayden professes to be a Guthrie fan as well, though for an entirely different reason. The musician who so famously chronicled America was of Scottish descent.

Hayden leans over to set off the first rocket but his short match runs out before the fuse catches. "Bloody hell. I forgot to bring a lighter."

Circumstances being what they are Rosamond chooses to ignore his bad language. She pulls a votive candle out from the folds of her habit like a magician producing a dove. "Here. Use this." Her ingenuity produces nods of approval from her co-conspirators.

Once the fuses are lit Hayden and Joey and Rosamond stand a few feet back and begin softly singing *"This land is your land, this land is my land, from California . . ."*

As the rockets hiss and shoot up into the inky black sky they hear an enormous ruckus off to the side as the group of interlopers has apparently decided to run for their lives. Ghosts are one thing. But it would seem that Armageddon put to folk music is quite another. The sound of scrambling through hedges is followed by a moment of illumination from the explosives, during which a half dozen lithe young bodies hurl themselves up and over the fence as if their very existence depended upon it. The rusty metal fence squeaks and vibrates until they've all made it safely to the other side. The last rocket makes a low arc and explodes just a few yards above Cyrus's grave, showering it in sparkling blue lights.

"Now that's a Fourth of July those kids will remember," laughs Hayden. "And one that will make 'em take out lots of insurance when they're older."

"Believe me, I'll always remember it!" Rosamond is so caught up in the excitement she's forgotten that there's no reason to be storing up memories for old age.

Joey will never forget the night either. Though not so much due to all the action in the cemetery as for the close call when they get home.

Hayden has miscalculated Diana's return and instead of preceding her by a comfortable margin he finds her pacing the living room, anxiously awaiting their arrival and on the brink of calling the police.

"Dad, where on earth have you been? I called Alisdair and Paddy and Hugh and *nobody* has seen you, sober or otherwise." She pauses to take a breath and only then absorbs their appearance—Joey's torn T-shirt, black soot covering Hayden's hands, brambles stuck to Rosamond's habit, which she hadn't worn since the day she arrived. "*What* is going on?" Her voice rises a full octave and her eyebrows meet overhead to form a dark, angry V.

Unprepared for this surprise encounter, Hayden and Joey are briefly stumped as they both work furiously to concoct a story that Diana is likely to believe. However, all Hayden can think of is to say that they were out in the golf course searching for golf balls, and he instinctively knows that she'll never buy it, at least not at this time of night. His eyes dart from Diana to Joey like a runner about to steal second base.

"We were praying." Rosamond comes to the rescue.

"Yes," Hayden quickly and enthusiastically agrees. It passes through his mind that she could have had a tremendous career in sales. He hadn't realized how fast she is on her feet. "Rosie took us on a vigil."

"You're trying to make me believe that you were off *praying!*" Diana scowls at Hayden and straightens up to her full height of five-foot-nine so that she's almost staring him in the eye. She further expands her domination over the available space by placing her hands firmly on her hips.

But it's Joey who ultimately acquits them. "Praying." Clasping his hands together he gazes up toward the overhead light fixture as if it's the Blessed Virgin Mary herself. And with a beatific smile on his youthful face he begins to chant, "The Lord is my light and my salvation; whom shall I fear? The Lord is the strength of my life; of whom shall I be afraid?" His wide-set eyes and fresh pink skin give him an expression of angelic innocence.

Diana's caught off guard and her face goes momentarily blank. For the first time ever in dealing with her father she's been completely trumped rather than fobbed off or cleverly evaded. Not only that, she's aghast at having sounded so offensive in front of Rosamond, especially when her friend is wearing her ecclesiastical uniform, on duty for God.

"I'm *so* sorry," Diana apologizes. "It's just that I didn't know where you'd gone and of course got myself all worried and so I . . . I . . ."

Rosamond lightly touches Diana's shoulder as if to confirm that she's absolved of all sin and says good night, though her own conscience gives her a prick on the way out of the room. Well, they *had* been praying. She puts it down as a sin of omission and assigns herself twenty Hail Marys and a handful of Our Fathers before going to bed. Stopping for a moment in the kitchen she fills a glass of water to calm the coughing spells that often wake her during the night. Through the window over the sink it's possible to see the iridescent red and green flashes of neighborhood fireworks cascading back to earth like falling stars.

"Perhaps they have it right," muses Rosamond. "It's best to go out in a blaze of glory." And though she could not see it, her eyes reflected the flickering lights, and something awoke deep inside of her.

chapter twenty

Although she's only been an honorary member of the MacBride clan for two weeks, Rosamond's insistence that they focus on living, not dying, has taken effect, and the household settles into a new rhythm. To the delight of Diana and Joey, a peculiarly submissive Hayden is no longer constantly indulging his morbid obsessions, and he and Joey aren't sneaking off to funerals every morning.

Instead, the three friends pass the warm summer days attending baseball games and fishing for striped bass and mackerel in Jamaica Bay and the Atlantic. Or else roaming the Brooklyn Botanic Garden, admiring the voluptuous magnolias and sweet-smelling crabapple blossoms. It's inevitable that at some point while gazing around at all the beautiful blooms Rosamond will recall the power of the creation story, sigh and say, "Life began in a garden."

"Actually, life began in the sea," Hayden contradicts her.

"Flowers need water," says Joey, diplomatically suggesting that they might both be right. And this, combined with the glorious color and fragrance of the Cranford Rose Garden, is enough to make them leave the age-old debate for another time, giving Joey the opportunity to go and hunt for Godzilla, the monstrous ancient turtle.

When it rains they head for museums in any of the five boroughs, making the selection by blindfolding Joey and having him randomly drop his pencil point onto the list. The only rule is that they must visit everyplace once before starting to repeat.

At the Metropolitan Museum of Art in Manhattan, Rosamond and Hayden relax by the fountain with the bronze Pan figure in the center located at the end of the statue gallery. They admire the large Tiffany stained-glass panel and Hayden splashes Rosamond with a handful of water whenever she turns away. Of course, the one time Rosamond splashes Hayden back the guard comes running over and Rosamond, who has never been publicly reprimanded for anything in her entire life, practically faints with embarrassment.

"I told her to stop it," Hayden soberly informs the guard. "It's not as if we're in a playground."

Joey darts in and out of the reconstructed ancient Egyptian tomb with other mummy-obsessed young boys. Hayden notices how his grandson's arms and legs are beginning to seem too long and gangly for his still soft boyish body, and wonders if he'll grow to be tall and wiry like the men on Mary's side of the family. Her brothers had all distinguished themselves as long-distance runners and college track stars. Or perhaps he'd develop the strong back, shoulders, and hands of the MacBride farmers and become a wrestler or a football player.

When Joey finishes with the Temple of Dendur they walk past a display of Chinese pottery and musical instruments on the way to the European wing. Wandering among the nineteenth- and twentieth-century paintings Rosamond is soothed by the luminous impressionist landscapes and cathedrals of Renoir and Monet. She's fascinated by the way small brushstrokes are used to simulate reflected light and how the broken colors manage to achieve such brilliance. And when they arrive in the rooms holding paintings from the Renaissance she's captivated by the sumptuous *Madonna and Child with Two Angels* by Botticelli, and Filippo Lippi's dramatic *The Annunciation*.

Without thinking Rosamond reaches out her hand and touches Hayden's arm, but she's so startled by the sensual power of their contact that it causes her to draw away just as quickly. Hayden's equally stunned by the electricity of their connection, but because she jerks her hand away he assumes Rosamond must have touched him by accident, or without thinking. There's no way of asking, but he secretly hopes it was the latter.

Hayden is also captivated by the paintings, though he admires the works for their sensuousness, vigorous style, and delicate coloration. He stands for a long while in front of enchanting mythological scenes such as Ameto's *Discovery of the Nymphs* and Titian's *Venus and the Lute Player* that allude to the triumph of love and reason over brutish instinct.

Following close behind Hayden and Rosamond, Joey is mesmerized with the paintings for an entirely different reason. He's counting and mentally cataloging all of the naked women, and constantly reshuffling his Top Ten List of Breasts, which he'd started the week before when they attended the Salvador Dalí show at the Brooklyn Museum of Art.

On the way to see the weapons and armaments, Joey's favorite exhibit, they pass through the gallery of large thirteenth-century paintings and trip-tychs depicting gory battle scenes, the birth of Jesus, and Christ dying on the cross. Joey reads the description below one of the paintings and asks Rosamond, "Did Jesus Christ want kids to call him Mr. Christ, or just Jesus?"

"I believe everyone addressed him as Jesus," says Rosamond, trying not to smile. "Christ wasn't his last name. It means 'messiah.' So it didn't mean that Jesus was born to Joseph and Mary Christ, but Jesus the Messiah."

"Oh, like Robert the Bruce," says Joey.

"Who?" Rosamond appears confused.

Hayden nods to indicate that Joey should explain.

"Robert the first, the king of Scotland who won Scottish independence from England in the battle of Bannockburn in 1314."

Hayden interjects, "He may have been a messiah to the Scots but I doubt the English viewed him that way." He chuckles. "Anyway, Bruce is from the French *de brus*, and it was the name of the clan, the way I'm descended from the MacBride Clan."

"So it should really be Jesus the Christ," says Joey. "Like Winnie the Pooh."

Rosamond and Hayden both laugh at the comparison, especially in front of such dramatic works of self-sacrifice. But Joey doesn't understand what's so funny and feels sheepish whenever Rosamond shares in a joke at his expense.

chapter twenty-one

The one time that Hayden and Rosamond leave Joey to spend the afternoon with children his own age at the municipal pool they feel awkward in being alone together. It's as if their de facto guardian is missing, instead of vice versa.

For Rosamond the situation is particularly uncomfortable since cloistered nuns almost never do anything in pairs, due to a rule intended to discourage any special friendships from forming. The order warned that such friendships could diminish the community as a whole, and more important, interfere with their individual commitments to God. The sisters normally worked in threes instead of twos within the walls of the convent, and likewise three went if a nun had to be escorted to an appointment on the outside.

If she were to be honest with herself, Rosamond's major concern at the moment is that exactly what the mother superior had warned against is indeed happening, that she feels a special friendship between herself and Hayden, and that it's wrong for so many reasons. Yet he fascinates her. Never before had Rosamond encountered anyone whose enjoyment of life, even in the face of death, was so boundless and sure that he had the ability to call up a surge of gladness in the heart of almost everyone he met. She is awed by his faith, not his faith in any particular thing so much as in himself, and his view that life itself is a garden of pleasure to be enjoyed, not a trial to be endured. Whereas her sisters treated most earthly delights as a test of one's will, and therefore most urges and desires were obstacles to be suppressed or surmounted.

For his part, Hayden is excited about this chance to be together, just the two of them, and is determined to make the most of the opportunity by finding out if Rosamond might be attracted to him the way he is to her. His anxiety stems solely from the fear that he may not get the answer he's hoping for.

In order to set the mood Hayden puts on his favorite CD of Jean Redpath singing Robert Burns songs and places the speakers on the windowsill so the sweet Scottish melodies can be heard out in the backyard. Next he mixes Rosamond a glass of electric orange–colored Mango Madness Snapple with seltzer water and bubblegum ice cream, a concoction she discovered while experimenting with Joey. Its appeal, they've explained to him, is not so much in the taste but the way the combination fizzes and sputters in the glass like Alka-Seltzer and decorates the mouth and tongue with a hallucinogenic rainbow of colors.

Hayden pours a scotch for himself and together they sit side by side in lawn chairs out in the backyard and enjoy watching the neighbor, Mrs. Trummel, periodically hurl lemons out her window at the sleek little rabbits diligently turning her garden into a salad bar. Only between her bad eyesight and even worse aim, the rabbits don't bother to glance up from enjoying the rows of carrots, cabbage, and Bibb lettuce long enough to defiantly wriggle their noses at her.

When they're finally settled Hayden is unsure of exactly how to make his move. It's been so long since he approached a woman. Should he ask her out on a formal date? That seemed rather silly since they'd been spending every day together for the past two weeks. They sit in silence for a long while as a pleasant soprano version of "Amang the Trees" with a Scottish lilt floats out across the lawn.

"Would you care for some cookies?" Hayden asks, well aware that he sounds considerably more formal than he'd intended.

But before Rosamond can reply a hair-raising holler of *"damn critters"* is heard from next door and a hard round lemon hits Hayden squarely on the shin.

"Or perhaps a wedge of lemon," he ad-libs and picks the fruit up off the ground.

Rosamond laughs and looks over at the agitated Mrs. Trummel, leaning out the back door and threatening the intruders with poison. "No, thank you. But let me know if she starts throwing strawberries."

"I wish she'd play for the Yankees," says Hayden, and tosses the lemon up and down like a baseball.

Rosamond nods and smiles.

Hayden continues to search for a smooth transition to the topic of dating. "It sure is a pleasure to have some company," he begins haltingly. "Not that Joey isn't great company."

"No, of course not," Rosamond agrees almost too quickly. "He's a wonderful boy. I've enjoyed getting to know him. And it's been such a long time since I've been around a young person. It's very refreshing." As she takes another sip from her effervescing ice cream soda Hayden can see that her tongue has turned a dark shade of purple with a bright green patch at the back.

Realizing that to find the right words is a futile pursuit, he decides to move on to Plan B. He places Mrs. Trummel's lemon on the small white table and casually stretches his arms above his head and lowers one so that it rests on Rosamond's back with his hand atop her shoulder. Only she jumps up and lets out a surprised cry as if a wasp has stung her. The ice cream soda flies up in the air and lands squarely in Hayden's lap, the cold liquid causing him to also let out a holler and leap to his feet.

"Oh no!" says Rosamond and covers her face with her hands.

Hayden scoops a glob of ice cream off the front of his trousers and Rosamond tries to help by plucking at the small red, pink, and orange squares of sticky bubble gum that now cover his midsection. Mrs. Trummel, however, has chosen this exact moment to rush the rabbits in her garden with a broom.

Seeing Hayden standing there with Rosamond down on her knees profusely apologizing and preoccupied with his crotch, Mrs. Trummel looks as if she's witnessing an indiscretion that requires turning her broom on the two of them. And perhaps the only thing that stops her is that they're all interrupted by the arrival of Joey, sobbing and holding a blood-soaked towel up to his face.

Mrs. Trummel, having raised four boys and three girls, is considerably less shocked by the sight of a bleeding boy than she is by whatever Hayden and Rosamond appeared to be doing. "Fight," she proclaims while removing the blood-soaked towel and expertly tilts Joey's head back to get a good look at his injuries. "One fat lip and that'll be a black eye tomorrow," she says. "Put some ice on it. And protect your face next time, Joseph. Even my *girls* know that."

Sitting at the kitchen table Rosamond listens to Joey recount the story of the scuffle down at the pool while Hayden wraps ice in a washcloth and covers it with a plastic bag. Just as the boy is starting to calm down Diana arrives home from work. Dropping her packages onto the floor she sprints to embrace her son. "We have to get him to the emergency room right away!"

"Jayzus, it's just a shiner and a fat lip, Diana," says Hayden. "Do'an' make things any worse than they are. You should have let me take the lad to boxing lessons over at the Y like I told you in the first place."

"I just don't understand why boys have to be so mean. Who would do something like this to an innocent child? Are you sure you didn't say something to make them angry?" she demands while pressing the icepack to Joey's face.

"*I told you*, every time I put my towel down another one would come over and say it was *his* spot," Joey mumbles through her hand. "And then they wanted a five-dollar 'parking fee.' " His voice begins to quaver in a conditioned response to the tears welling up in the corners of his mother's eyes. Sometimes he hates her for overreacting to every cut and scrape, as if a black eye is equivalent to the plague. If only he'd grown up playing ball with other boys and going to camp in the summer. But now it's too late. The bullies sniff him out right away, like sharks heading for blood in the water.

"Okay, that's enough boo-hooing," announces Hayden and pulls Diana away from her excessive ministrations. "Wet sheep don't shrink. They shake off the water." He hustles his grandson past both women. "Let's go and get some ice cream."

But the mention of "ice cream" suddenly brings Hayden and Rosamond back to the terrible moment when all the chaos began. Hayden can't tell if he's angry or just plain disappointed by Rosamond's reaction to his overture. Bloody hell, she didn't have to screech and jump up like that. Was the thought of him as her boyfriend *that* terrifying? How about a polite removal of the offending arm and one of those ridiculous lines that women are so great at: "I really like you, but only as a friend." Or in their case she could have just as easily said, "With us both dying I don't think it's such a good idea."

For her part, Rosamond is still in a state of shock. She thinks constantly about that first day at the baseball game when Hayden casually placed his arm around her shoulders, and how it made her spine tingle with pleasure. It was so memorable and thrilling that the next time they went to a game she'd made sure to be right next to him when it looked as if the Mets might score a home run. So why did she have to scream like that and spill ice cream all over him? It was all so horribly embarrassing. She's too chagrined even to glance in his direction.

Hayden keeps his hands on Joey's shoulders to avoid meeting her gaze as he gruffly asks, "You coming, Rosie?"

"I . . . I'd better help Diana with dinner."

Diana senses that something disagreeable has transpired between Hayden and Rosamond. She takes a closer look at them and her eyes settle on the multihued goo covering the front of his khakis and Rosamond's hazard orange–stained lips. "Dad, *what* is that all over your pants?"

He irritably barks back at her, "After thirty years in the insurance business I've finally fallen victim to an Act of God."

chapter twenty-two

When Joey comes back alone from getting ice cream with Hayden, and Diana hears a car pulling out of the driveway, she immediately senses that something is amiss. "Where's your grandfather?"

"He said he's going out," replies Joey.

"What else did he say?" Diana insists.

"Not to wait up." Joey goes directly to the kitchen sink and washes his hands before dinner without being asked in an effort to improve her mood. It's not been lost on him that Diana always gets grouchy whenever Hayden goes out at night. And by checking the clock all evening she inevitably orders him off to bed much earlier than if she's happily watching one of her favorite movies.

Throwing up her arms as if they're goalposts for a place kicker, Diana turns to Rosamond. "I *hate it* when he goes and gets drunk with those crazy Scottish friends of his. They should all be in detox."

"Oh dear," says Rosamond, feeling responsible for Hayden's departure. This must be what is meant by the expression "driving someone to drink." Fortunately Diana doesn't appear to blame her. Nor has she asked about what transpired in the backyard. And Rosamond has been too embarrassed to volunteer any information.

Once they're all sitting at the dinner table, Diana turns her attention back to Joey's bruised face, though his pained expression is more the result of a bruised ego. Diana examines the patches of green and yellow appearing beneath his swollen left eye. She reaches out to touch the scab forming above his split lip but he pushes her away.

"Well, I think we've had enough excitement for one day," concludes Diana.

An hour after Joey is sent off to bed, Rosamond sits in her room trying to concentrate on a book while the voices coming from Diana's TV in the next bedroom murmur in the background. When she hears a car pull into the driveway Rosamond jumps up, tosses the book onto the bed, and pushes back the curtains. The station wagon is parked half on the lawn and half in the driveway, and a slightly stooped Hayden is careening toward the front porch. Rosamond checks her face in the mirror, straightens her hair, and rushes downstairs to meet him.

Only there's no sign of Hayden anywhere on the first floor. Opening the front door she finds him leaning against the house with one hand on his midsection and the other gripping the metal railing along the steps. Even in the dimness of the porch light she can make out beads of perspiration on his forehead and that his normally ruddy complexion has turned ashen.

"Hayden!" she cries, alarmed to see this normally effervescent figure so debilitated. "Are you trying to *kill* yourself?" Rosamond takes his arm in an effort to help him inside but he shrugs her off and manages to stumble over the threshold on his own steam.

"No, it's The Cancer that's killing me. I'm just the battleground." He turns so that his face is only a few inches from hers and she can smell the sweet but tangy aroma of whiskey on his breath. "What do you care?" he jabs an accusing finger into her shoulder.

"Why of course I care," she says so quietly that it's impossible to tell whether she's afraid of waking Joey or of the words she's saying.

"It wasn't as if I was goin' ta hurt you this afternoon!"

"I know that," she replies, trying hard to sound convincing.

"Then why'd you jump away from me?" His voice rises sharply on the word *jump*.

"I honestly don't know."

"Yes, I think you do." Once again he pokes at her shoulder where a summer-weight cotton sweater covers her blouse. "Bloody Brides of Christ. Two layers of clothing over twenty layers of thick skin."

"Dad!" Diana comes racing down the stairway. "*What* is going on here?" But she doesn't wait for an answer. It's obvious that Hayden has been "overserved," as he likes to put it. She places his arm over her shoulder and half drags him toward his new room at the back of the house.

Hayden goes along with Diana more because he welcomes the support than he's ready to call it a night. Though he manages to turn his head and yell back at Rosamond, "I wasn't goin' ta hurt you!"

When Diana returns to the living room Rosamond starts trying to explain recent events, but her words come out in a jumble and tears begin to fill the corners of her eyes.

Diana places an arm around her new friend. "It's okay, don't cry. Believe me, I can figure out what happened. I've been there a million times. But don't take it personally. Dad's drunk and he didn't mean what he said. Let's go watch *Algiers* with Hedy Lamarr and Charles Boyer. It starts at midnight."

Rosamond, feeling uncharacteristically fragile, searches her pockets for a tissue. "But, what he said, I mean . . . he did, I mean . . ."

"Listen Rosamond, a man thinks that a woman has rejected him and immediately there must be something wrong with *her*, right? It can't possibly have to do with *him*."

"But he's so angry with me."

"Oh, he's not mad, he's just embarrassed." Diana waves dismissively in the direction of Hayden's room. "You'll see, it will all be okay tomorrow. He probably won't even remember that he saw you tonight. Welcome to family life." She nods toward the stairs. "In the meantime, you'll find that TV boyfriends are much better companions. You don't need to wear makeup or high heels, and the minute they become annoying you just switch them off and go to sleep."

chapter twenty-three

The next morning Rosamond nervously waits for Hayden to emerge from his room, hoping that Diana is right and that he won't remember last night's altercation. She wishes, in fact, that there were some way to erase *all* of yesterday from his mind.

At nine o'clock Rosamond starts back toward Hayden's room for the third time, but upon reaching the closed door turns away, realizing that she can't bear another round like last night. Only what can he possibly be doing in there? On a normal day, he'd have already been to the gas station and the newsstand by now.

Just when Rosamond is about to send Joey into the room, Hayden comes marching through the front door singing "The Blue Bells of Scotland" with great gusto.

"Oh where, tell me where, is your Highland laddie gone? Oh where, tell me where, is your Highland laddie gone? He's gone wi' streaming banners, where noble deeds are don' And it's oh! in my heart I wish him safe at home."

Rosamond's anxiety disappears as she laughs at the picture of Hayden she's had in her head all morning, angry and ailing in his bed without anything to eat or drink. So sure was Rosamond that he was still in his room she hadn't even thought to check if the car was in the driveway.

Hayden waltzes gaily past her, stopping just long enough to drop a small box covered in gold wrapping paper into her lap, and then disappears into the kitchen with a bakery bag. She doesn't know what to make of the situation. *He* is giving *her* a present? When she's the one who acted like such a frigid fool? Although maybe it isn't a present at all. Perhaps it's another of his suicide potions.

Rosamond tentatively peels away the paper and opens the box to find a shiny new charm bracelet with six charms already dangling from a silver chain. She carefully studies each one—the Empire State Building, an apple, a museum, a banner for the Mets, an adorable miniature rendition of the Brooklyn Bridge, and on the end a little fish. She can't help but wonder if the fish is intended as a symbol of Christianity or a memento of their fishing trips.

Glancing toward the kitchen Rosamond hears the sounds of Hayden making coffee and pushing down the squeaky lever on the old-fashioned toaster. He must have stopped to buy bagels while he was out. Hayden loved the reaction he got from the counter people and other customers when he gleefully ordered his favorite bagel, "an everything with nothing."

Rosamond is thrilled by the gift, but even more so with the idea of a man buying her a present. It was just like a scene out of the movies Diana is always watching. In fact, the night before last they were in Diana's room watching *The Old Maid* when a nostalgic Bette Davis said something to the effect of: "A woman never stops thinking of the man she loves; she thinks of him in all sorts of unconscious ways—a sunset, an old song, a cameo . . . and a chain." And Rosamond and Diana found it so breathtakingly romantic that they'd both hugged their pillows and sighed.

Holding up the bracelet and seeing it sparkle and shine in the morning light causes her heart to rise in her chest. But it abruptly falls back to earth as Rosamond remembers that she's not allowed any jewelry other than her cross, rosary, and wedding ring. She drops the bracelet back into its box as she painfully recalls the day she sold her mother's pearls to make a dowry that would be presented to the Church upon taking her final vows.

Then she extracts it from the box again. I *must*, she orders herself, stop reacting like a nun to every situation! That's what caused all the trouble in the backyard yesterday—Hayden wanting to kiss her and her seeing the frowning face of her mother superior glaring down at them through the tree branches. In fact, if she'd had visions as strong as that back when she was in the convent, as some of her sisters did, it's doubtful her faith would have faltered in the first place.

It's when Rosamond lifts the shiny chain for the second time that she notices the little handwritten card at the bottom of the box:

Going My Way? Your friend, H.M.

Rosamond assumes that Hayden's referring to all the places in and around New York that they've decided to try and see before they die. The Empire State Building has been at the top of her list and at the very bottom of Hayden's. He declared it to be a "bloody tourist trap." As to *your friend,* well, it could be worse. At least he doesn't consider her an enemy. She links the bracelet around her wrist and hurries into the kitchen to thank him before she has time for any more ridiculous thoughts or flashbacks.

Joey is leaning over Hayden at the table and pointing to an ad in the local paper for the annual Coney Island Mermaid Parade. "Please can we go, Grandpa? Please, I'll do anything—I'll wash the car and even clean out the garage. I'll pay for the gas." Joey is convinced that this event will provide an opportunity for him to see half-naked women.

Rosamond attempts to get Hayden's attention by pointing to the bracelet dangling from her wrist but he only gives her a dismissive nod and turns back to Joey. The urge to throw the bracelet right back in his face momentarily overwhelms her and she's further surprised by this newly discovered capacity to anger so quickly, and over something so petty. But why did Hayden give her a gift in the first place if he didn't want them to make up? Once again, Rosamond is lost at sea in the relationship game.

Then she recalls Diana's words from the night before—*he's not angry, he's embarrassed.* And she understands that the peace offering isn't supposed to be formally acknowledged, since that would only remind them of yesterday, which is what they're both trying to forget.

"Doesn't this look like fun, Rosie?" Joey attempts to enlist Rosamond in his campaign to attend the Mermaid Parade. "It'd be so much cooler than the craft museum, don't you think?"

"Museums are educational," says Rosamond.

"Mermaids are educational," says Joey. "Hans Christian Andersen wrote about them and there's even a statue of one in Denmark. When I get my computer back I can show it to you on the Internet!"

Hayden and Rosamond are susceptible to his boyish enthusiasm and agree to most of Joey's more reasonable requests. After all, it was Joey who landed them at the game farm and the circus, outings that put them solidly on the path to friendship in the first place, so they consent to drive to Coney Island.

Once they're in the car Hayden suggests to Joey, "Maybe you can work for Disney and make millions on turning those fairy tales into cartoons."

"I've decided to become a priest," announces Joey.

"What?" Rosamond and Hayden utter simultaneously and Hayden accidentally jerks the station wagon to the right as he turns to look at Joey in the backseat.

"Just kidding," says Joey and giggles. "Hey, what did the Buddhist say to the hot-dog vendor?"

"I don't know." Rosamond takes the bait. "What did the Buddhist say to the hot-dog vendor?"

"Make me one with everything!"

Rosamond laughs merrily, and Joey is thrilled by the attention she lavishes on him.

"Maybe you should become a stand-up comic," suggests Hayden. "I've never known a kid who can remember so many terrible jokes."

That's all Joey needs to get started. "Knock knock!"

"Who's there?" asks Rosamond.

"Mayonnaise," says Joey.

"Mayonnaise who?" asks Rosamond.

"Mayonnaise have seen the glory of the coming of the Lord."

Rosamond laughs again, but Hayden just groans and shakes his head as if he's forced to work as a bus driver for elementary school children. He digs around in the glove compartment and sticks a tape into the cassette deck. "You two acolytes may as well enjoy a little of the Gospel according to John and Paul," says Hayden.

Because it's unlike Hayden to play religious music, Rosamond and Joey look at each other with curious expressions as they wait for the tape to begin. After the first few chords Rosamond recognizes the song from when she was a girl and they all three sing along with The Beatles:

"When I find myself in times of trouble, Mother Mary comes to me . . ."

When the song finishes Hayden turns down the volume and says, "That's my vote for next pope."

"Paul McCartney for pope?" Rosamond laughs at the idea of her mother superior making such a ridiculous announcement following vespers, the time when important news was communicated.

"No, silly. He's probably Anglican," says Hayden. "I think the next pope should take the name John Paul George Ringo."

Joey bursts into giggles and Rosamond swats him on the back of the head and says "Oh *Hayden*," but he can see the smile playing across her mouth.

While they wait for the drawbridge over the Gowanus Canal to close, Hayden explains how people once used it as a dump for garbage, old furniture, and broken-down shopping carts. Eventually community efforts to clean it up met with success and there was no longer an acrid smell at low tide. Marine life soon returned. And a family of swans had even made its home under the Carroll Street Bridge.

The Mermaid Parade turns out to be unlike anything they expected. Much to Joey's disappointment, Hayden's amusement, and Rosamond's shock, more men than women are dressed up as over-the-top "mermaids." They strut about wearing teased wigs of red and green seaweed, Cleopatra-style eye makeup, pointy gold cones as breastplates, and skintight Speedos that melt into blue scales painted onto shaved muscular legs.

Still, the three remain to enjoy the music of the Sea Monkey Orchestra, antique car show, and to watch King Neptune lead the parade. Afterward they have a hot dog at Nathan's and stroll through the amusement park where Hayden convinces Joey and Rosamond to ride the ancient Cyclone roller coaster. Before entering the line Hayden shows Joey how to cheat up on his toes in order to make himself appear tall enough for the ride.

"I can't believe I'm doing this," says Rosamond and crosses herself as the man on the platform secures the padded metal bar over their shoulders. She's frightened and excited at the same time, which strikes her as exactly the way she feels about Hayden.

"Just think how close we'll be to heaven," says Hayden. The rickety coaster starts up the hill and several riders are already bravely raising their arms above their heads, or, alternatively, screaming in terror over what's to come. From the summit people appear to be the size of squirrels, and beyond the beach is the glittering dark green sea dotted with boats. For a moment it feels as if they're on top of the world, as the gears go quiet and a nearby carousel can be heard pumping out "Under the Boardwalk." When they suddenly drop perpendicular Hayden hopes that Rosamond will grab on to him in her fright, but she stoically grips the metal bar and emits a series of ear-piercing screams as the car navigates steep drops and turn after jarring turn.

chapter twenty-four

When Hayden, Joey, and Rosamond arrive back from their travels early enough, as they do this evening, Rosamond goes into the kitchen and offers to help Diana prepare dinner.

Never having been assigned to do any cooking at the convent, Rosamond isn't able to contribute much to the effort aside from chopping, stirring, and washing pots. Before becoming a nun she'd always eaten in school canteens. And prior to that a housekeeper or her stepmother had ruled over the kitchen at home.

However, Rosamond is eager to learn and Diana enjoys hearing about what the three of them have been up to all day. It was an excellent way to keep tabs on her father and son, since Rosamond's natural honesty wasn't tuned to what information might best be withheld from Diana, such as the morning Joey fell out of the boat while trying to net a fish.

When Diana discovers that Rosamond has developed no food preferences, the former nun explains that living communally is supposed to be an exercise in humility. And that catering to individual likes and dislikes highlights self-importance, thereby diminishing your ability to distinguish desires from needs.

Rosamond soon realizes that her breviary was missing one proverb: the way to a man's heart is through his stomach. She's noted how Hayden's entire countenance lights up over the prospect of a good meal and how he speaks so reverentially of certain favorite dishes made by his late wife.

Diana is amused by the fact that her friend's culinary experience has been firmly molded by the heart-attack-on-a-plate seventies—fried eggs and bacon for breakfast, spaghetti with canned tomato sauce or chicken salad mixed in a vat of mayonnaise for lunch, and for dinner meat loaf with vegetables boiled until they dissolve, or liver and fried onions.

So Diana introduces Rosamond to modern delights such as cranberry scones, Israeli couscous, roasted chicken with herbs de Provence, and the art of the vegetable stir-fry. And most important, the miracles of the microwave oven, Cuisinart, and Ziploc freezer bags.

Having a companion in the kitchen is equally pleasant for Diana. In addition to the fun of unveiling two decades of progress to someone who may as well have been sealed up in a bomb shelter, Diana realizes that she misses the company of her mother the most when cooking old family favorites. It's nice to have a woman to talk with again. Whereas every time Diana invites Linda and her husband to dinner, she only ends up feeling humiliated by some remark her sister makes, always along the lines of how charming it is that she and Joey are "poor but happy" and how sweet and old-fashioned it is that Diana "makes everything from scratch." The subtext is of course that cooking is a way to economize, not something that Diana enjoys and has a talent for. No, because that would force Linda to admit that Diana and their mother had shared something special together. Though it was true. The two women had spent many wonderful hours poring over recipe books, shopping and experimenting, delighting in their successes and joking about their failures.

Hayden and Joey are relieved that Diana has a project to keep her occupied in the evenings, which gives her less time to worry about their respective ailments and attempt to force jelly bean–sized vitamin pills on them.

After Joey is in bed and Hayden has gone to meet his drinking buddies, a.k.a., the self-styled Greyfriars Gang, Diana continues to catch Rosamond up on her favorite old romantic movies—*Casablanca*, *A Foreign Affair*, and *All This and Heaven Too*. Diana is also particularly fond of stories that feature love spoiled by terminal illness, plague, or nuclear holocaust, such as *Terms of Endearment*, *Outbreak*, and *On the Beach*.

Sometimes they page through *Vogue* and *Elle*, critiquing the latest fashions and making imaginary shopping lists. And despite an initial hesitation on Rosamond's part, Diana slowly indoctrinates her new friend into the womanly secrets of styled hair, manicured nails, and a touch of makeup. Though Diana suspects that Rosamond permits the makeovers more for Diana's benefit than her own, or perhaps in order to look nice for Hayden. It's obvious to Diana that Rosamond is fascinated by her father. Whether it's as a heathen who needs converting, a friend, or a love interest, she can't be certain. Although she is sure that there is a charm bracelet on her friend's wrist where there was no bracelet before.

It's usually only during these intimate moments, when the two women are alone together, and yet not staring directly into each other's faces, that Rosamond makes her subtle inquiries about Hayden.

This evening, while Diana is preoccupied with trimming Rosamond's bangs, the former nun tries to sound offhand when approaching her favorite subject. "Your father doesn't say much about his childhood." But the keen interest in her bright blue eyes betrays the false nonchalance of her voice.

"That's because Dad didn't really have a childhood," replies Diana. She's proud of how her father employed his solid work ethic and good humor throughout his life in order to overcome a difficult beginning. "It was the end of World War II and his parents had struggled to keep the farm going without gas or electricity, you know, doing everything by hand, even making their own soap and tallow. Dad's older brother lied about his age and joined the Royal Air Force at sixteen and was killed while dropping bombs over Berlin."

"Oh!" Rosamond flinches and Diana just barely avoids glancing her forehead with the scissors.

"Careful!" says Diana. "I'm just glad that Dad was only a baby because I'm sure he would have run off to join some Highland maniacs and happily led the charge. Anyway, when Dad was ten his father died of cancer, and soon after that they lost the farm. There was a sister, Fiona, between the two boys, but they lost her to scarlet fever shortly after moving to a slum in Glasgow."

"How awful!" Rosamond's eyes grow wide with sadness.

Diana decides to take advantage of Rosamond's preoccupation with Hayden's childhood and trims the curls surrounding her cheeks so they frame her face.

"Dad of course wanted to go out and work but his mother made him attend school. She went from house to house in the better neighborhoods and gave music lessons. Eventually one of the men took a shine to her, they married, and Dad went off to Edinburgh to work his way through the university there, which is where he met Mom, and then came to the States."

Diana pulls Rosamond's hair back for a moment but decides it looks better loose around her face. "The day after they arrived here Dad saw an ad in the *New York Times* for an insurance salesman and essentially sold *himself* within five minutes. After two years he'd won every award in the business and was the youngest regional manager in the company's history."

"But your mother was American, right?" Rosamond asks. Then she turns her eyes down shyly. "Oh Diana, I hope you don't think I'm being too nosy."

"Don't be silly. In the sixties Mom was an exchange student in Edinburgh from a good Episcopalian family in Westchester. They fell madly in love and when Mom's year ended Dad was too broke to even afford his ticket to America—he had to charm the pants off his future father-in-law long distance, which, being Dad, he did with no trouble."

Although she's not aware of it, Rosamond begins to smile as she imagines a handsome young Hayden overcoming all obstacles for the woman he loves, and having a marvelous time for himself while doing so.

When Diana finishes styling Rosamond's hair with some mousse and a blow-dryer she applies a few strokes of peach blush to her cheeks and forehead. She simply cannot comprehend how someone with such bright eyes, unspoiled skin, and lustrous hair can be terminally ill.

Studying her new look in the mirror Rosamond is reminded that hairstyles and makeup are the chief adornments of women, and as far as convent rules go, she's committed sins against humility. She automatically assigns herself five Aves, five Paters, and five Glorias. Then she remembers her new vow, which is to stop torturing herself with her old vows.

To Diana she makes an effort to appear pleased. "That's much better," Rosamond says with forced cheer. "Those pieces on the side would never stay behind my veil and then I'd be tugging at it all day until it ended up cockeyed around my face."

"Is that what you'd call a Bad Veil Day?" teases Diana.

When they hear Hayden's boisterous entrance in the downstairs hallway both women look at the clock on Diana's dresser and are surprised to find that it's already a few minutes past midnight.

"It sounds as if he's in good spirits," says an expectant Rosamond.

"More like distilled spirits," says a doubtful Diana.

"What *is* he singing?" asks Rosamond.

Diana hesitates to tell her but Hayden is coming up the stairs and his rich Scottish voice is only growing stronger. "It's Gaelic."

"Oh," says Rosamond. "It's a pretty song. What is it?"

"Mairi Bhoidheach." Diana purposely gives the Gaelic name, rather than the English translation, "My Pretty Mary."

The door to Diana's room is open and Hayden stops his song mid-word, startled at seeing his friend looking so lovely with her clear, intensely blue eyes set deep in strong arches, and full florid cheeks that spread warmth and promise like the sun.

Hayden takes a few steps toward them but stops to balance himself with a hand on the dresser. "Rosie, you've . . . you've changed something."

She's unsure of whether he's pleased or not with Diana's alterations. "It's just a bit of makeup and Diana trimmed my hair." She reaches for a tissue to wipe off the lipstick the way the girls in the convent school used to do when returning from a trip into town.

"No, no." He stares at her for a moment, "You're so . . . so beautiful."

Rosamond's cheeks flush and she demurely casts down her eyes.

"Not that you needed improvin' upon, mind you." Hayden takes a step closer, as if she may be an apparition and he won't be convinced she's real until he touches her. Only as soon as he completely lets go of the dresser he stumbles and Diana rushes to his side, grabbing his arm and shoulder in order to steady him.

"Whoopsee!" shouts Hayden, a merry expression on his face, "I'm afraid the boys had me on the drink 'n' drown plan tonight."

Diana attempts to steer Hayden back toward the door. "Dad, stop blaming it on the boys. *You're* the one who drinks too much. Now let's get you to bed!"

"Whee!" shouts Hayden as he spins away from her grasp.

Diana takes his arm again, more firmly this time, and says, "Hush, before you wake the neighborhood."

"Shhh," slurs Hayden and puts a finger to his mouth. "You know why yer not supposed ta talk in church doncha—so you do'an' wake anyone." He laughs uproariously at his joke.

"Stop making God jokes," says Diana, out of respect for Rosamond.

"I do'an' make jokes, God talks to me," insists Hayden. "For instance, just this evening He said, 'Hayden, don't make me come down there again!' " Hayden erupts in another gale of laughter.

Diana realizes that as usual, chastising her father only encourages him, and the best thing to do is separate Hayden from his audience.

Meanwhile Rosamond briefly considers that it might be bad form to be amused by such jokes about God, but Hayden is so charming in his mischief that she can't help herself. As father and daughter exit the room Rosamond allows herself a hearty laugh, which fortunately doesn't lead to her doubling over with a cough, but just a few short hacks, after which she easily catches her breath.

"Say good night," Diana says to Hayden as she finally maneuvers him into the hallway.

"But how can I miss you if you won't go away?" asks Hayden and chortles some more.

"Say good night, Dad," Diana says more sternly.

"Good night Dad," Hayden repeats and begins a new song in Gaelic as Diana leads him back down the stairs and to his room.

When Rosamond kneels down to say her prayers, thoughts of Hayden's silliness keep intruding until she finally has to settle for a quick Twenty-third Psalm and give it up for the night. At times like this she finds it impossible to believe that a person with the tremendous vitality that Hayden possesses could ever be taken from the world. Surely a mistake has been made *somewhere*.

chapter twenty-five

Before breakfast the next morning Rosamond works with Joey in the backyard, patiently showing him how to cast an adult-sized fishing rod. She stands behind the boy while holding his wrist in her hand and together they swing the long aluminum rod over their shoulders and around to the side so that the nylon thread sails out across the far hedge.

Inside the house Hayden sits at the kitchen table grudgingly drinking a glass of fresh carrot juice, waiting for Diana to pack her lunch and leave for work so he can make a pot of coffee and nurse his hangover without having to listen to her sermonize on the evils of caffeine.

Hayden is also mentally preparing for her to give him heck about being drunk two nights in a row, but she continues to chatter away as if nothing happened. Only he doesn't trust the cheerful front for a minute. Surely she's going to try yet again to persuade him to trade in the rusty old station wagon by claiming that it isn't safe because it doesn't have airbags and antilock brakes. Or else ask him to splurge on an air-conditioner as his penance, the way Mary once bought an expensive carpet right after he'd gone on a particularly colorful bender.

Hayden is correct that his daughter has a hidden agenda, but he's not even close to guessing what it is. After last night's conversation with Rosamond, Diana has changed her strategy with regard to reforming her father. It's obvious he isn't going to try the experimental cancer drugs for her sake, or even Joey's. But perhaps he would if he were in love.

"Rosamond's pretty, don't you think?" she begins innocently.

"Sure enough, though I don't think you have to fear anyone around here competing with you in the looks department. Every morning Pete at the gas station asks me why you don't call him."

"That was a *big* mistake. I should never have gone out with him in the first place. He just wore me down. Anyway, have you noticed that Rosamond's cough seems much better?"

"That's why they call cancer the silent killer, my darling. You do'an' cough yourself into a coma or start having seizures on the subway train." Hayden, who is always so careful to hide his failing resources, yawns and adds, "You just feel tired all the time and wonder how you ever used to make it to lunch without a nap." He stretches his arms out to his sides and yawns once more as if to exemplify his point.

Diana is stunned that Hayden has let down his guard for a moment. Only she can't decide whether it's a good or bad sign that he's started talking reasonably about his disease. Up until now he only trafficked in extremes, either making jokes about it or else planning his death for a Friday evening so that she won't have to miss a day of work.

"Maybe I should take Joey to the office with me today so you and Rosamond can stay here and rest up a bit," she offers.

"Rest?" Hayden clears his throat and forces himself up from the table. "We've got places to mow and people to tree."

Diana heads toward the door with her lunch in a brown bag. "The way you glad-hand around town all day a person would think you're running for president." She kisses him on the cheek. "Tonight I'll make some Collops of Beef and Oaty Crumbles for you and your friends."

Hayden can't believe he's managed to escape without a temperance lecture. And not only that, but landed one of his all-time favorite meals. He goes to the back window and shouts to Rosamond and Joey in the yard, "Last one in the car has a face like a hen layin' razors!"

At the prospect of an outing they quickly put away the fishing pole and dash inside the house to get ready.

Hayden enjoys taking Joey and Rosamond on explorations of Brooklyn's history and cultural diversity. Today he drives them to Brighton Beach, the once predominantly Jewish neighborhood that's now a jumble of Russians, Puerto Ricans, Dominicans, Mexicans, and African Americans. Still, the boardwalk between Fourth and Sixth streets lives up to its name of "Little Odessa." Small family-operated cafes offer black and red caviar, giant herring, and borscht along with cappuccino, vodka, and kvas, a homemade drink similar to beer, which Hayden rarely passes up an opportunity to sample. And being that he's on good terms with the hostesses and wait staff, he's always given special treats and the best seats available. Hayden inevitably asks if Abraham Lincoln used to request a table or a "Booth" and they just nod and smile heartily, unable to comprehend. And Hayden reciprocates by patting the person on the back as if they're indeed in on the joke.

While they relax at one of the inviting restaurants with swirled Cyrillic letters on the menus, Hayden attempts a conversation with a Lithuanian family at the next table. When that fails he shows the children how he can balance a spoon on his nose, which is always a great success.

Next they stop at the crowded Mrs. Stahl's for baked pockets of bread dough mixed with potato and onion, known as knishes, slather them with mustard, and wrap them to eat on the boardwalk. Down by the water groups of elderly people gather to kvetch, play chess, and people-watch, just like an old-fashioned town square.

Afterward Hayden takes Rosamond and Joey to some of his favorite monuments, including General Grant on his horse, presiding over Bedford Avenue near Huntington. Then they head to the Hall Street Kosher Café across from the Brooklyn Navy Yard, where Hasidim with dark beards wearing long black coats and wide black-fur-rimmed hats crowd around cases of fish, blintzes, and matzo balls. On the streets of Williamsburg it's not unusual to see Satmar families with eight or ten children. Joey is fascinated by the ringlet curls that the males, even the small boys, have tucked behind their ears, which Hayden explains are called payis. And Joey carefully studies the young mothers to see if they are really wearing wigs, as Hayden claims, and that it's not just his grandfather getting up to his regular tricks.

Rosamond is always surprised to see that another group of individuals, much like her order of nuns, has chosen to live according to their own religious beliefs in this bustling and in every other way modern city.

chapter twenty-six

On this particular Thursday they must be home early because Hayden's Greyfriars Gang is coming over. After moving in with Hayden, Diana had initially banned the raucous gatherings, claiming they were a bad influence on Joey, though her real motivation was to force Hayden to cut back on his drinking. But the men simply changed the location of their lively meetings to Duncan's home. He was also a widower, and without eating any proper food throughout the evening Hayden arrived home more intoxicated than before.

Thus Diana decided she was better off having the men 'round to their place, serving them a good dinner, and breaking the party up when things got out of hand. In fact, she finds that she actually enjoys preparing some of their favorite dishes, the way her mother used to do.

Rosamond helps Diana in the kitchen as the men gather in the living room. As the Glenlivet begins to flow they toast the Scottish-born American John Paul Jones for his raids on the British and hotly debate the new Scottish parliament.

"Preparing a meal while listening to the men in the other room makes me think of Martha," says Rosamond to Diana, who is removing the heavy casserole dish from the oven.

"I don't think Martha Stewart ever had to contend with a rowdy gang like this," says Diana.

"I meant Martha in the Bible, preparing a meal for Jesus and his disciples after Lazarus was raised from the dead," explains Rosamond.

"Oh," says Diana. "Well, it's safe to say that the ruckus the Greyfriars Gang makes can also raise the dead. We may as well go out there and introduce you and get it over with. Brace yourself!"

Diana leads Rosamond into the living room where the men are gathered around the TV watching *Chariots of Fire* on the VCR for the umpteenth time.

"He wins because he's runnin' for God, doncha see?" insists the devoutly Protestant Alisdair.

"Oh, so God do'an' like the looks of the rest of th' atha-letes?" Hayden loves to spar with his cronies and emphasize his points by applying his thickest brogue. "Get out of here will ye! Eric Liddell *wins* because he knew how to run in the Scottish Highlands. It gives ye good strong lungs."

Diana hits the pause button and nods to her father indicating that he should introduce their guest. Then she hurries back into the kitchen to make sure the soup doesn't boil over.

Hayden clears his throat and stretches out his arms as if presenting royalty. "Let me present my fellow Idleonians!" He rattles off the names of his cronies, "Alisdair Blaine, Hugh Drummond, Duncan Osgood, and Patrick Fitzgerald." Then he points to her and proclaims, "Rosie here was a nun, but she recently kicked the habit." He laughs uproariously at his own pun.

But Rosamond doesn't hear what Hayden says. Not accustomed to hiding her expressions, she is still staring at Patrick Fitzgerald, who is a *black man*. Almost half the nuns she knew were from Irish families, but she'd never met a black nun of Irish descent. Nor a priest, for that matter.

Hayden takes her shock in stride, as if he's used to pulling this joke on newcomers. "I know you're surprised that Paddy's got an Irish name. Or I suppose he's what you might call Black Irish." Hayden chuckles some more. "His grandmother was from Dublin, which at one time was a popular destination for the Moors. Anyway, we allow him to stay as a way of thanking Ireland for safeguarding the Book of Kells during the war. Isn't that right, Paddy?"

"Do you know why Scottish pipers march when they play?" Paddy asks Rosamond.

She thinks about the question for a few seconds and then shakes her head.

"Because a moving target is harder to hit!" Paddy shouts and slaps his knee.

"If ye do'an' take that back right now I'll get me pipes and play 'I Laid a Herrin' in Salt,' " threatens Hayden.

"And if you do *that* I'll start singing 'Danny Boy,' " counters Paddy.

"Well, I do'an' know as to how I'll recognize it since every song your people ever wrote is in a *minor key* and features a *bloody fun'e'ral*." Hayden continues in his lively whiskey-heightened voice, "Three Scots were in church one Sunday morning when the minister made a strong appeal for the orphans and ast'd everyone to give twenty pounds. So the three become very nervous as the collection plate nears and then one of them faints and the other two carry him out!"

Hugh, Alisdair, and Duncan roar with patriotic laughter while Paddy prepares to top him with an Irish joke. "Have you heard about Irish Alzheimer's disease? You only remember the grudges!"

Hayden is both pleased and slightly vexed by the way the Greyfriars Gang shows off for Rosamond and gives her appreciative glances. He's happy they find her attractive since it serves to confirm his good taste. However, Hayden's innate sense of old-fashioned propriety makes him reprimand the boys when they start becoming overly friendly by placing their arms around her waist while cracking a joke.

It isn't long before he delivers her back into the kitchen under the safe watch of Diana, who only appears among the Greyfriars to serve, clear, and scold. She loves them well enough; however, she's also taken them aside individually to suggest that all this drinking is literally killing her father. But will they say anything to Hayden or try to stop him? Not a chance.

From the kitchen Rosamond continues listening to the men's revelry. They've apparently embarked on a toasting competition, which Diana insists only serves to give the men an excuse to keep refreshing their drinks.

Paddy begins with an Irish blessing. "May you have food and raiment, a soft pillow for your head, may you be forty years in heaven, before the devil knows you're dead." Laughter explodes from the room followed by the sound of the men clinking their glasses.

Hugh counters with a Scottish toast. "When we're goin' up the hill o' Fortune, may we ne'er meet a friend comin' down!"

Hayden can be heard chiming in. "Here's to the heath, the hill, and the heather; the bonnet, the plaid, the kilt, and the feather! Here's to the heroes that Scotland can boast, may their names never die—that's the Highlandman's toast!"

Paddy quickly retorts, "May you live to be a hundred years, with one extra year to repent."

Alisdair takes his turn. "Here's to the health of your enemies' enemies. Here, here."

"No fair!" Paddy complains. "That's an Irish toast!"

Duncan shouts, "The Irish aren't the only ones with enemies, you know." The men descend into another round of good-natured arguing.

Diana watches with amusement as Rosamond eavesdrops. "You should have been here for Beltane when Hugh served haggis while Dad and Alisdair climbed out onto the roof and played 'Scotland the Brave' on the fife and bagpipes."

"*Roof* I understand. But Beltane and haggis?"

"Beltane is the fertility festival on April thirtieth, though the boys have figured out a way to make it last for an entire week. And haggis is minced heart and liver mixed with suet, onions, and oatmeal. It's supposed to be boiled in the stomach of the slaughtered animal, but that's where I draw the line."

"Draw a line for me, too," concurs Rosamond.

chapter twenty-seven

As the days dissolve into weeks, Rosamond's thoughts often return to her old life, not the convent itself so much as the simplicity of her former existence. It's not that God wasn't a complicated partner in a relationship, He was. But she's beginning to suspect that relationships between men and women are somehow equally as intricate.

Prior to her diagnosis, Rosamond had settled into a peaceful routine, though one could argue that she'd become almost like a sleepwalker. And from time to time she *was* concerned about the numbness creeping into her soul, but according to her Sisters, this was supposed to be a growing ecstasy as a result of her love for Him. Thus she would often pray to be overwhelmed by grace and filled with an awareness of divine presence in order to counteract what she feared was simply an increasing lack of sensation.

Then she met Hayden. And her interior exploded into a riot of feelings as if an overture had suddenly started playing in her barren soul, encompassing every emotion from fearfulness and trepidation to amazement and unbridled joy. They were the antithesis of the virtues she'd been trained to cultivate—piety, conformity, purity, duty, reverence, solitude, and compliance.

In an effort to bridge the gap between old life and new, Rosamond decides to start attending Mass at the Catholic church at the end of the street. It certainly wasn't the same as going to chapel five times a day, but it helped her maintain a connection with the past.

And though Rosamond rarely mentions anything about what went before, it's obvious to Diana that she's wistful for something lost. She often comes upon her friend gazing at the Hummel figurines above the mantel, silently moving her lips and twisting her wedding ring, as if in prayer.

It soon becomes apparent to Diana that Rosamond has no other friends in the area, and though she would never be so bold as to inquire, it doesn't seem possible for the former nun to go back and visit her old life.

"Why don't you come along to my book group?" Diana asks her early one evening as Hayden and the Greyfriars Gang settle in to watch *Braveheart*. (He has recently increased their meetings from once a week to whenever possible.) "It's with some old school friends in Larchmont, where we used to live. And driving along the water is so pretty this time of year."

"If you don't think they'll mind," says Rosamond.

"It's really more to socialize," says Diana. "We don't know how to play bridge. Our grandmothers tried to teach us when we were growing up, but back then we thought it was totally *uncool*."

Diana navigates the station wagon along the Bronx River Parkway and through a maze of overpasses and viaducts. Rosamond is fascinated at how the boarded-up buildings, billboards for discount mattresses, and auto junk-yards suddenly metamorphose into tree-lined neighborhoods with soccer nets in the front yards. The sun is low in the sky as they drive down Chatsworth Avenue, giving a shiny cast to metal signs, store windows, and gutters along the edges of building roofs as they catch the sharp slanted rays of light. Diana turns right onto Boston Post Road and then makes a left onto Larchmont Avenue. After passing the firehouse and police station she points to a gorgeous stone church in Fountain Square. "That's Saint John's, where my grandparents went. And where my parents were married." She pulls the car over for a quick look. "It's Episcopalian."

There's been a wedding, and Rosamond stares at the dozen or so people in their Sunday best posing for pictures out front, especially the beautiful bride in her white silk dress with a train so long that a girlfriend needs to carry it across the threshold so that it doesn't drag on the ground.

Looking at the bride and groom a tear comes to Diana's eye. "They're so lucky. I hope it works out."

"You'll meet someone," Rosamond encourages her friend. "When I was a schoolgirl we had a very short prayer: Dear Saint Anne, please send a man."

"Oh, there are plenty of men. I'm just afraid I'll never meet the right one. And have what my parents had, or even what annoying Linda and boring old Ted have."

"Of course you will. You're intelligent and attractive—"

Diana nods her head at these words as if she's been hearing them all her life, and nowadays only serve to convince her that they're not true, that people say them just to make her feel better.

Rosamond is again struck by the fact that for some mysterious reason she has yet to comprehend, Diana truly lacks confidence in herself.

"So how come you stopped going to church?" asks Rosamond.

Diana assumes that by changing the subject her friend is acknowledging that it's true, that she doesn't have much chance of finding someone.

"Same reason everyone stops going, I guess. It was more my parents' thing. And Joey's father certainly didn't have any interest in going."

"Was there anything you liked about it?"

"Yes. It made my mother so happy. She would save up all her problems, bring them here, and leave feeling that it was a brand-new week and everything was going to be fine. I was always amazed by how such an intelligent woman could leave a crisis in the hands of God. . . . Oh, I'm sorry, I didn't mean—"

"No, no." Rosamond involuntarily smiles that secret smile, the way nuns always do at people "on the outside" who act as if the daily grind were more important than their spiritual lives. Onlookers rarely understood how nuns could have committed their entire lives, hearts, and spirits to something that can neither be seen nor touched.

"What's so amusing?" asks Diana.

"Well, we get hit with that quite often," says Rosamond. "I imagine it's become a sort of refrain like men always saying how attractive you are."

"Oh." But Diana doesn't really see the connection.

"Listen," says Rosamond. "I'm not suggesting that you should start going to church again." They both automatically glance out the window at the handsome old church and the happy wedding party. "But it may be worth considering where your mother got her confidence—her confidence that you and Linda wouldn't be run over on the way home from school, that her husband wouldn't stray, that the bills would eventually be paid. You have to believe in *something*, Diana, even if it's not God. Even if it's just yourself."

"You mean like Dad? I *know* he doesn't believe in God."

"But it doesn't mean that at one time or another he didn't look fear right in the face and decide how to deal with it."

Diana briefly considers Hayden's difficult early life in comparison to her own relatively easy one. Rosamond was right, he did indeed possess the confidence of an evangelist.

A tremendous cheer goes up as the bride and groom dash through the crowd hand in hand under a shower of birdseed.

"The gardens are so beautiful," says Rosamond.

"So are the cars," says Diana. She gazes at the line of brand-new Mercedes and shiny BMWs out front, comparing them to Hayden's ten-year-old Ford station wagon with the rust patches on the doors. Diana had been forced to sell her little Mazda Miata when the child support and alimony checks stopped coming, shortly before they moved to Brooklyn. Now she was dependent on the subway and borrowing her father's car, just like when she was a teenager.

chapter twenty-eight

They locate a parking spot on the side of the road two doors down from Selma Thackery's sprawling brick ranch house, since the circular driveway is already filled with Audis and SUVs. A group of twelve women in their early to mid-thirties has gathered at the home of Diana's closest childhood friend. Some wear linen business suits indicating that they've come directly from high-powered jobs in the city, and others are dressed as if they were recently finger painting with active toddlers.

The group has just finished reading the new Andrea Aniston novel called *All for Love*, which is being hailed by the critics as a "thinking woman's romance." Only it isn't until they actually sit down for a discussion that it occurs to Diana the subject of the book might not be appropriate for one who has just fled a nunnery. On the other hand, maybe it will advance Diana's hidden agenda of Hayden and Rosamond falling in love so that he'll finally consent to try the treatment for his cancer.

Selma passes trays of dainty canapés and nori rolls that obviously came from a gourmet shop while Lynn Kohnstamm begins with a summary of the plot, just in case anyone didn't finish the book. Then she declares the meeting open for comments and critique.

"I think it's unrealistic that a married woman with two children would cheat on her husband to get back at him for having an affair," insists Magda Waterston.

"Why not?" counters Geraldine Baxter. "If it were the opposite, if the man found out his wife was cheating, I'll bet you'd believe it if he went off and had an affair."

"I'm not so sure," says another woman, sexier than most of the others in a black halter top and denim skirt. "Did anyone see that movie where the wife has an affair with that incredibly sexy French actor?" All the women except for Rosamond nod their heads to indicate that they'd indeed seen the movie and more than one face appears dreamy at the memory of their favorite male star. "Well, the deceived husband didn't have his own affair, he went off and killed the lover."

"That man is *so* sexy," says one of the women.

"To die for," says another.

"Is he *really* French?" asks another.

"He is," a quiet woman in a frumpy oversized sweater interjects. "He's a French citizen, born in Paris, France, January 12, 1966," she reports like an obsessive fan.

"Well, he can put those used books that he deals in on my bedside table any time of the day or night," says the halter top.

"He's too short for you," oversized sweater states authoritatively. "Five-foot-seven."

Clearing her throat in the manner of a high school teacher whose class discussion has run away from her, Selma asks, "What's your impression, Rosamond?" Like a good hostess she makes an effort to include their visitor, who appears slightly lost, and about whose background she is unaware. "Do you think Miranda should have had the affair?"

"Oh, I'm sorry." Rosamond is startled to be called upon and is still wondering who this mysterious man is they're all talking of and seem to know so much about. "I didn't read the book. And it's hard for me to even imagine such a situation, being that I just came from two decades in a convent and was recently diagnosed with terminal lung cancer."

The women stare at her and then look to Diana, as if their guest's life is a hundred times more interesting than anything they've *ever* read in a novel or seen portrayed on the screen. Meanwhile, at the mention of lung cancer, Selma grabs for the closest ashtray and immediately stubs out her cigarette. Before the discussion can go any further the phone rings.

A moment later their hostess returns from the kitchen and addresses Diana. "It's your neighbor, Mrs. Trummel. The police are at your place again. It isn't a Greyfriars night by any chance, is it?" She gives the group a wry smile. Having known Diana since elementary school, most of the women are familiar with her father's tremendous enthusiasm for social occasions.

"These days any night can be a Greyfriars night." Diana rises and gathers her things. "Especially since Dad splurged on the large-screen TV so that life-sized Scots and English can do battle every night thanks to DVD copies of *Rob Roy* and *Braveheart*."

Diana turns to Rosamond. "We'd better go. The Scots spend most of their time fighting wars; only when there isn't a war, they fight one another. Last week it was over who invented the jig—the Scots or the Irish."

As they say good-bye to the group something about the previous discussion suddenly occurs to Rosamond. "You know, there's a similar situation in the Book of John."

"John Grisham?" asks Selma.

"No. The Bible. A woman cheated on her husband and they were about to stone her. But Jesus said that whoever is without sin should be the first to throw a stone at her. So she was saved. But he said she must leave her life of sin behind."

The women nod at her, as if this is indeed an interesting take on *All for Love*, and all the more valuable coming directly from a convent.

When Diana and Rosamond open the front door *Braveheart* is nearing its end and all the men, along with Joey and Hugh's teenage son Andrew, are shouting and raising their fists at the TV during the final battle scene. Diana's eyes land on the bagpipes and snare drum on the floor next to the couch. By standing directly in front of the set she blocks most of the picture while muting the volume. The rowdy men boo her and angrily raise their glasses.

"Dad, were the police here again? And why is Joey still up?"

Hayden waves her off like an annoying mosquito. "Oh, Alisdair was playing along on the pipes while we were butchering the Brits. Old Mrs. Trummel trounced on us for making a ruckus."

"Okay boys, that's enough Gaelic culture for one evening." Diana extends the channel clicker like a lightning rod and turns off the TV set. "You've seen this a million times." The men continue to hiss and denounce her. Diana removes the two bottles of Lagavulin whiskey from the end tables only to find they're empty. Next she turns to her son. "Joey, go to bed right now or else your growth will be permanently stunted from lack of sleep!"

Rosamond also finds herself highly unamused by Hayden gambling so recklessly with his health. After her initial fascination with the merry Greyfriars Gang, she's come to agree with Diana. As well-intentioned as they may be in wanting to help take Hayden's mind off his illness, they *are* a bad influence. And the mornings following their rambunctious gatherings he's usually in terrible shape, barely capable of moving and unable to eat anything.

Rosamond is about to demand to know why he's so intent on killing himself. But even in his inebriated state Hayden anticipates her and slinks off to his room, quickly closing the door behind him.

chapter twenty-nine

In the morning Hayden lies in his new bed pretending to be asleep while waiting for Diana to finish in the kitchen and leave for work. His daughter, however, knows that he always fakes sleep on his side so he can keep an eye on the door and really only sleeps on his back or stomach. She noisily enters the room carrying a large glass of purplish-brown prune juice and the cordless phone.

"You look terrible!" She waves the telephone handset over his body like a laser pointer. "I'm calling the doctor."

"Don't you dare!" He makes a halfhearted attempt at grabbing the phone away from her. "It's bad enough he already wants me as a free guinea pig." His voice sounds throaty and nasal. "Besides, it's just a cold."

Diana examines the bedside table and finds a tumbler with an amber-hued stain on its bottom along with a spilled container of aspirin and glares down at him like an Old Testament prophet. "I think it's more like a High-land Hangover." She replaces the cocktail glass with the one containing the juice. "Dad, all this aspirin is ripping apart your stomach, and you *know* what the doctor said about drinking . . ."

"It's possible that Paddy overserved me just slightly," Hayden admits with a twinkle in his eye. "He has a heavy hand with the—"

"Please, I could hear you reciting 'Lochinvar' while I was loading the dishwasher."

"Luvely poem."

"All eight stanzas!"

"Now, Sir Walter Scott is a good example of a man who was devoted to his art and yet held a regular job," says Hayden in an effort to turn her attention away from his liquor consumption. "He was a lawyer and the sheriff of

Selkirk for thirty years. If you insist on marrying an artist, why can't it be one with a salary?"

"Don't change the subject."

Joey enters the sunroom in his pajamas and Hayden begins reciting: *"So faithful in love, and so dauntless in war,"* and then points to Joey who raises his right arm as if brandishing a sword and finishes: *"There never was knight like the young Lochinvar!"*

Hayden claps his hands and Joey beams with pride while Diana scowls at them both. Then Hayden leans his head against the pillow as if he could go back to sleep for another eight hours.

"You don't look very good," says Joey. "Are you going to die today, Grandpa?" Joey glances around the room to see if The Cancer Monster is lurking in a corner or else has a big, hairy green foot sticking out from under the bed.

"I do'an' think so. But as long as I'm under the weather we should use the situation as a trial run. Now be a good lad and fetch the newspaper and then make your grandpa a bender-mender of black coffee and toast."

Rosamond enters the room wearing a white low-cut silk robe, obviously borrowed from Diana, and sits down in a chair next to Hayden's bed. Diana rolls her eyes before leaving as if to say, "I give up, he's all yours today."

"So, did you play the bagpipes last night?" Rosamond asks.

"No darlin', I've given up me pipes until I can go grouse hunting back home in the Sidlaw Hills outside o' Dundee. Takes too much lung power." He explains this in an exaggerated brogue and then adds a cough for emphasis. Though Hayden uses the opportunity of moving his head up and down to take a surreptitious look at Rosamond in the flowing robe with a pink negligee peeking out from underneath and decides she's quite fetching from head to foot.

Once Joey has dutifully delivered the paper and toast, but no coffee, and headed off to watch cartoons, Rosamond asks, "Hayden, I was wondering, would you do me a favor?"

"Oh whistle and I'll come to ye, my lass, O whistle, and I'll come to ye—" but he starts coughing for real. After taking a sip of prune juice Hayden manages to croak out, "Robbie Burns."

"I've invited a young man over this morning," begins Rosamond.

Upon hearing the words *young man* Hayden's brows float upward like two twigs in a storm, not unlike Diana's when she's preparing to deliver an impromptu sermon. Hayden is willing to admit that he's been attracted to

Rosamond from the first moment her heavy silver cross smacked him full in the face when she leapt up to do the wave. However, he's also aware that he's fourteen years her senior. Though what should age matter if they're both going to die soon anyway? But more important, it's obvious from the backyard disaster that she's not thinking along those same lines. Still, that doesn't mean he'll allow someone else to threaten her honor!

Sensing that Hayden might be coming to the wrong conclusion, and very much not wanting him to, Rosamond adds, "Hank's a priest. At least he's training to become a priest, just a few more months to go. I met him in the hospital when he was doing rounds and then ran into him again last Sunday when I wandered over to the church at the end of your street. And . . . and I'd like you to speak with him."

Hayden is relieved that Rosamond isn't suddenly producing a beau so shortly after turning him down. Yet at the same time he's annoyed by this attempt to pour religion down his throat. "Oh Rosie, I thought ye'd given up on all this God codswallop."

"No, no, it's nothing like that," she insists. "It's simply that I don't believe this young man has the calling, I mean, I'm afraid that he's making a mistake."

Hayden laughs with no small amount of relief. "Well, what am I supposed to do about it?"

"There's something about you, Hayden . . . how can I say this so it doesn't come out sounding all wrong? You have a way of making people feel either much better or much worse about their religion. And so I fibbed just a bit. I told him you have spiritual conflicts that need immediate attention. I hope you don't mind."

"Glad to know I'm still good for something." Perhaps the way to Rosamond's heart is through performing deeds of heroism and chivalry like a Scottish Don Quixote.

"Wonderful, because he's going to stop by in a few minutes, on the way to Mass." She moves toward the door. "Now I must go and put something on."

Hayden shakes his head in an attempt to shrug off his hangover. "Does it have to be this morning?"

As if in answer to his question the doorbell rings.

chapter thirty

Embarrassed at being caught in her nightclothes, Rosamond pulls the robe tight around her before going to the door and directing the young man to Hayden's bedside. Henry Flaherty is tall, broad, clean-shaven, and crowned with a lion's mane of golden brown hair that makes him look like a schoolboy when it flops into his eyes, which is every time he wags his big head.

"Father Flaherty, I presume," says Hayden. Americans rarely catch his reference to when the *New York Herald* correspondent Henry Stanley found the famous Scottish missionary Dr. David Livingstone in Africa.

But Hank shakes Hayden's hand and actually acknowledges the reference. "I'm afraid my missionary work was in Guatemala, Mr. Stanley. And please just call me Hank."

Rosamond leaves the two men alone while she goes upstairs to shower and change. As she passes the hall clock she can't help but think what the mother superior would have to say about shuffling around in a carnation pink negligee covered by a silk bathrobe at half past eight in the morning. The nuns were out of their scratchy cotton oatmeal-colored nightdresses and into their habits by four A.M. And barely thirty minutes later they were kneeling on the cold marble floor of the chapel for morning prayers. Lauds was said at daybreak, thanking God for the first light, as at the beginning of creation, and for the light of Christ's resurrection. Following that the nuns chanted the first interlude of the Divine Office.

Meanwhile, Hayden is not so easily won over by the young man at his bedside and gives him a cold stare that suggests he should state his business and get a move on.

But the priest-in-training only stands next to the bed and nervously fingers the Saint Christopher medal hanging from his key ring. And Hayden gives in to his natural instincts for breaking the ice and making potential clients comfortable.

"You've got the map of Ireland all over your name and face there," says Hayden.

"Actually my mother's people are Scottish—Moncreiffe."

Hayden's sparkling green eyes ignite with interest. But he quickly realizes that Rosamond must have tipped Hank off. After all, hadn't Hayden confided in her that he used to snare his biggest customers by opening his sales pitches with a little Scottish lore? But Hayden can't help himself. And he's not about to fall for any sales pitch from God anyhow.

"That's from the Gaelic *Monadh Craoibhe*, meanin' 'the hill of the sacred bough.' " Hayden begins talking clans and tartans and becomes very animated. "Joey," Hayden calls into the living room, where the distinct high-pitched voices of cartoon characters can be heard coming from the television set. "Be a good lad and fetch my book o' Scottish clans from the coffee table!"

But it's Diana who comes through the archway and hands him the book. She's stunning in a mint green suit with a purple scarf tied loosely around her neck, smoke-colored eyes and crushed cherry lips prettily accentuated with makeup. Her dream-dark hair streams down her back the way night spills across an open field. And in her wake rises the smooth but insistent scent of vanilla.

Rather than be curious as to why a stranger is talking to Hayden about Scottish history, Diana is more interested in who the very attractive stranger is. Hank is unquestionably handsome and looks professional in a black cotton shirt and neatly pressed pants that emphasize his athletic build. Hayden introduces the two as Diana proffers one of her more flirtatious hellos, where her wide-set eyes and broad smile serve to heighten the sharp arc of her cheekbones.

"Oh, I wasn't expecting company." Diana smoothes her hair and straightens her skirt as if she's been caught in an old housedress.

"He's studying to be a priest." Hayden quickly clarifies the situation.

Diana reexamines the visitor's outfit. *"Oh."* She withdraws her hand in a businesslike manner. "Yes, of course. Well, have a wonderful time discussing religion with Dad. I'm going to be late for work if I don't leave right this minute." She kisses Hayden good-bye on the cheek and sneaks another glance at Hank while she's bending over, only to catch him staring at her figure, as she thought he might be. He looks away, but it's too late, his face flushes and his expression is that of a man who accidentally walked into the ladies' bathroom and wants to get out in a hurry. With a delicate wave of her fingers at the two men Diana exits the room.

Hayden coughs and takes a sip of juice. But this only makes him grimace now that he realizes it's been spiked with one of her vitamin concoctions. "Oh God, I need Rosie to make me a cup o' coffee." It's obvious that Joey's attempt was thwarted by The Nutrition Department. He turns to Hank. "I'm sorry but I'm a bit under the weather from last night."

"Party?" asks Hank.

"Oh, good heavens no," Hayden replies with the utmost sincerity. "Lips that touch wine shall never touch mine. Late night prayer vigil."

"Of course." Hank nods his head in understanding, as if the exhausting rigors of the supremely devoted are all too familiar.

After the small talk seems to come to a natural close, the younger man clears his throat and begins his prepared remarks in a serious voice that occasionally croaks with postadolescent uncertainty. "Mr. MacBride, Sister Rosamond tells me that you've lost your faith in God."

"She did now, did she?" Hayden's business instincts tell him that Rosamond may be trying to trick him with this rubbish about "the poor father-to-be not having the call" and that she's actually sent this Sky Pilot to convert him, her final good work before departing this world. Well, he hadn't dealt with sheep rustlers as a teenager and then been on the casualty and property side of the insurance industry for twenty years just to be conned by some wet-behind-the-ears Holy Joe. Two can play at the conversion game.

"Since being declared a goner from The Cancer I can honestly say I no longer feel His blessing." The truth of the matter is that Hayden stopped feeling the blessing of anyone he couldn't see with his own two eyes after his brother, father, and sister died by the time he was sixteen, his mother praying up a storm all the while. Because it wasn't God who eventually lent assistance to their plight, but the fact that after losing the farm he and his mother both worked long hard hours in order to get back on their feet. Hayden's religion was simple: Get an education and find work. Or as he liked to tell the trainees when asked for the secret to his success: show up, buck up, suck it up, and don't fuck it up.

And when your number is up, don't moan about it, especially if you had a pretty good run—food on the table, healthy children and grandchildren, and of course the love of a good woman.

"Do you think it would help if we prayed together?" Hank asks in his earnest baritone.

"No, no. I have too many unanswered questions. Faith can be a sticky wicket. For instance, if I accidentally back over a pregnant woman with my station wagon do you think it's God's will? And if my grandson kills for his country will he go to hell?"

The priestling appears momentarily distressed. "Of course not!"

"Then let me ask you something else, do you think Adam and Eve had navels?"

"What?" Poor Padre Hank is still totally unaware he's being strung along.

"You know, belly buttons, because that would imply birth, not divine creation."

"No," Hank muses. "No, they couldn't possibly have."

"But tha' would mean they weren't perfect human bein's then!" Hayden declares triumphantly, his brogue swelling. "And what about war? How can we say God is on our side while the other side is sayin' the exact same thing?"

Before Hank can attempt to answer, Rosamond reenters wearing a peach-colored sundress with white sandals, hands a glass of iced tea to Hank, and places a steaming mug on Hayden's bedside. "It sounds as if you're feeling better."

Hayden looks at the hot liquid with suspicion and wrinkles his entire upper body as he inhales the lemony vapors.

"Diana said that you were to have this herbal tea instead of coffee because of your ulcer."

"You realize that you're forcing me to pour a shot o' whiskey into this concoction?"

Rosamond ignores Hayden's threat. "Are you two having a nice chat?"

"I don't think there's anything more to be said." Hank looks down at the wedge of parquet flooring between his size thirteen shoes.

"Oh dear, I was afraid of that. Well, then, I have a proposal. Why don't we all go to the Empire State Building today? We still haven't gone there."

"No New Yorker has *ever* been to the Empire State Building!" moans Hayden. "It's a bloody rip-off for out-of-towners."

"Come on. You promised to do all the things that we've never done before we . . . you know . . ."

"How about tomorrow?" Hayden bargains.

Rosamond holds up her charm bracelet with the silver Empire State Building dangling from it. For a woman who apparently didn't want to act like a woman when it came to kissing, she'd certainly figured out how to run the guilt game. Then again, she was Catholic.

"Oh, all right," a grumpy Hayden acquiesces.

Rosamond looks at the young priest. "Won't you join us?"

"I have to do some marriage counseling. It's part of my internship."

"Oh, that's rich," says Hayden. "A single celibate twenty-year-old is counseling people on marriage!"

"I'm *thirty-one*," the boyish-faced Hank remarks with visible irritation toward Hayden. Then he turns his pleasant smile on Rosamond. "But thank you for the invitation, Sister."

"It's just Rosamond now, Father," she corrects him. Rosamond is somewhat shocked to hear the words as they come from her mouth, as if she's considering taking them back.

"And it's not Father . . . yet," Hank tells her.

Hayden scowls at this overly polite ecclesiastical blather, turns to Hank and demands, "So when are you coming back? I hate to remind you but I do'an' have all the time in the world."

"But . . . but." Hank is convinced that he has failed miserably in his mission to make Hayden a believer. "You want me to come *back*?"

Hayden also feels that he hasn't succeeded in the challenge Rosie gave him of testing the young man's resolve. But more than that, he's taken a shine to the young man. "How do you expect to restore me faith if you do'an' come back? Or am I that hopeless?" Hayden asks playfully.

But Hank regards his remarks with gravity. "How about Monday?"

" 'Tis Monday then."

"Go in peace," Hank says as he walks toward the hallway.

"Not in pieces," Hayden calls after him.

"Hayden!" says Rosamond.

He ignores her scolding. "Now why can't Diana date a nice young man like that?"

"Because you're too strong and her mother was too perfect," Rosamond says as she hands him the tea and neatly arranges herself in the chair next to his bed. It is painfully obvious to Rosamond that Diana's low self-esteem comes from idolizing her parents and being terrified that she can never live up to their example or expectations.

"*What!* What did you just say?"

"Hayden, I never knew your wife, but from all accounts she was beyond reproach."

Hayden smiles, recalling Mary's attributes. "She was a good woman, though she had a temper, indeed she did. Threw me out in the street one freezin' winter night wearing only the clothes on my back, not even an overcoat." He shakes his head at the memory, though without volunteering what he may have done to incur such wrath in the first place.

Rosamond doesn't ask, but assumes it had something to do with whiskey and possibly the Greyfriars Gang. "I can tell that Diana greatly admired her mother. Believe it or not, many young women came to the convent in large part to escape their mothers."

Aha, thinks Hayden, she never meant to be a nun in the first place. Her mother was probably trying to marry her off to someone she despised and fleeing to the convent offered the only escape. "Is that why you went in?" he asks hopefully. Hayden would love nothing more than for Rosamond to say that taking vows had all been a terrible mistake.

"My mother passed away a few hours after I was born. There were complications. And my father was a lobster boat captain up in Maine. When it was time for me to get an education he sent me to a convent school in western Massachusetts where his sister was a teacher."

Hayden looks at Rosamond with a mixture of surprise and concern. "I'm sorry," he finally manages to say, as if someone had just been declared dead.

"No, no. That's just the point. It sounds much worse than it is. I'm sure it *was* difficult on my father, because he loved her ever so much. But he eventually remarried and I would spend vacations with him and my stepmother. And because I never knew my real mother, I can't really miss her, except of course the idea of her. However, my aunt Kathy, my mother's older sister, was perfectly lovely and I had a wonderful time at the school where she taught, even though it was strict."

"So what you're saying is that by trying to be everything to Diana we didn't leave her room to be herself."

Rosamond folds her hands in her lap and looks past him, out the window, where the sky is painted in Easter colors and birds poke in the grass for worms. "Not necessarily. I just think it might be a challenge to live up to the example that you and Mary set. And so it's easier to go in the opposite direction, to not even try and come close in her work and relationships."

"You know what you can do for me, Rosamond?" Hayden raises his voice and bangs the mug down on the bedside table so that the tea slops over the edge.

"What?" Rosamond is suddenly concerned that she's offended him by speaking so boldly, but she knows no other way. They conversed very little at the convent, and when they did it was straightforward, constructive, and essential, such as when they reviewed their faults.

"Tell Joey to get dressed," Hayden announces in his grouchiest voice, "so we can go to the blessed Empire State Building!"

chapter thirty-one

It's a perfect summer day on the Isle of Manhattan, where the sun is an enormous gold disk glittering above the resplendent steel-and-glass skyline. The city appears to be a fortress of shiny windows with water towers placed high up on the rooftops, as if to prevent access by the enemy.

Atop the Empire State Building Rosamond peers with delight through the large coin-operated telescopes in an effort to find all the landmarks with which they've recently become familiar—the nearby Chrysler Building, with its gleaming art deco spire, the block-sized Museum of Natural History, and the great green expanse of Central Park. Who would have imagined that so many sober-looking gray apartment buildings were crowned by roof gardens with flowers, trees, and even swimming pools. Off in the distance it's possible to see the domed Williamsburgh Savings Bank Tower with its enormous illuminated clock.

Joey runs from side to side trying to find the best place to take a picture. It also occurs to him that he should ask for a telescope for his birthday since he could then spy on Mrs. Trummel's daughter Donna, who often comes home on weekends. Hayden briefly considers jumping from the observation deck when his time comes, but apparently insurance companies had already thought of that and carefully constructed barriers, making it impossible to leap to one's death without employing a rope and grappling hook.

When they pull into the driveway back home Hayden is still reveling in playing the resident curmudgeon. "We get a better view o' Manhattan from the Williamsburgh Savings Bank Tower right here in Brooklyn. And it do'an' cost any ten dollars to stand on line for over an hour just to ride up in a crowded elevator."

The three tourists enter the house and find Diana leaning over the lacquered maple table with sheaves of papers and envelopes haphazardly spread out in front of her. Hayden's first thought is that after having left a copy of his will and insurance policy to review, for the twentieth time, she's finally set out to get organized. However, her eyes are red from weeping and smeared mascara streaks her cheeks.

"Oh Dad! Joey!" She rushes to the entranceway and grabs all three of them. "I didn't even hear the car pull into the driveway." Her lips tremble and then her mouth draws tight. "Dominick died this morning! The scaffolding outside his dorm room collapsed—a freak accident."

Dominick was her younger sister Linda's eighteen-year-old stepson, who'd been attending college in Washington, D.C. But because he'd moved to Honolulu with his mom and her new husband when he was still in elementary school, they only vaguely knew of him.

Diana clutches Joey and Hayden and Rosamond in a group hug as if they are the ones who just barely escaped a fluke construction accident. Eventually she snuffles loudly, lets her arms drop to her sides, and searches for a tissue to blow her nose.

Hayden examines the jumble of papers she's been sorting through—old car payment books, rent stubs, canceled checks, and death certificates.

"I'm trying to find a list of our funeral plots," explains Diana between blowing her nose and wiping away the teardrops that are still forming in pools against her bottom lashes. "Linda said that she thought Grandpa Arthur owned some gravesites at Lakewood Cemetery."

"But why would they want Dominick buried with *our* family?" asks Hayden. Not that he minds. It's his view that death is a personal matter and people should do whatever they want.

"It sounds as if Dominick wasn't very happy in Honolulu. His mother's marriage is on the rocks again and she's had another one of her breakdowns," says Diana. "So they don't really live anywhere right now."

"I always thought it was Ted who drove his first wife mental by makin' her put on those silly hats and gloves when he was campaigning," inserts Hayden. "The big Jackie O. sunglasses she always wore I understood, what with those teeth of his—"

"Dad, not now," Diana scolds through her tears. "Anyway, his grandparents, who still live here, are organizing the funeral. It seems that Ted and Dominick had some sort of falling out back when he was in high school. I guess that's why we never met him."

"Still, it's his son," says Hayden. "And Ted's mattress is so loaded with money I'm surprised he can sleep at night."

"Ted wants him to be cremated. Apparently there's a big flap in New Jersey politics about the land that will be needed for cemeteries if the burial rate doesn't go down. But the grandparents are Italian Catholic and they're going crazy. So Linda thought that if we gave them a plot that we don't need it would stop all the arguing."

"Well, she's right," says Hayden. "I mean, she's right that Mary's dad did own half a dozen plots at Lakewood up in Westchester. But he sold them off to foot the bills for your grandma Phoebe's nursing home. There's only one left—mine."

"Oh." And although Diana releases an involuntary shudder at the mention of Hayden's grave she also realizes that she can't blame him for bringing it up, at least not this time. "Oh," she repeats and begins gathering up the papers.

"Give it to them." Hayden hands her the cordless phone. "I do'an' want it."

"But it's next to Mom. And what if I want it or . . ." Diana hesitates before she can add "Joey," wanting to avoid bringing up the worst-case possible scenario, that her son should predecease her. Or else put a curse on him. "Dominick never even met Mom . . ."

"It's not like being buried is a networking opportunity, Diana." Hayden solemnly nods his head toward the phone to indicate that she should call her sister. "I loved your mother very much and she'll always be in my heart, but I just do'an' want to be buried, simple as that. Not at Lakewood, not anywhere. Your mum and I lived our lives together, 'til death did we part. And even though it's not going to be eternal, it was nonetheless very blessed."

Diana is conflicted but finally takes the phone and offers the gravesite to her sister's family. What follows is a lot of "No, no . . . we couldn't possibly . . ." by Linda and her husband, Ted, Dominick's father. Finally Hayden gets on the line to conclude the negotiations, which he does in less than a minute, by making Linda and Ted feel as if they'll be doing Hayden a favor by taking the plot off his hands. And despite the fact that the circumstances of the conversation are abysmal, in an odd way it cheers Hayden to know he hasn't lost his touch—since all that is left for him now is the big close, The Final Sale, the one that only pays a commission to your beneficiaries.

After some more to-ing and fro-ing about deed and plot number it's agreed that the Brooklynites will drive the paperwork over to Linda's house in Flemington, New Jersey.

The three MacBrides and Rosamond silently clamber into the station wagon. Without saying a word Diana hands Hayden her car keys, a sign that she must indeed be terribly distraught. She knows that he's still a capable driver, otherwise she would never let him squire around his grandson, but since the diagnosis he'd been relegated to passenger status anytime they ventured out together.

"You definitely don't want to be buried then?" Diana asks Hayden as they leave the neighborhood.

"Nope!" Hayden glances in the rearview mirror to see if Rosamond displays any reaction to this statement. But she appears not to have heard. She looks serene sitting there and silently gazing out the window, like a dove with its wings folded.

Indeed, Rosamond is contemplating all the unexpected turns that life can take, and how death can arrive suddenly, announcing itself loud and clear, or else sneak in like a bank robber under the cloak of night.

"Joey's going to scatter my ashes," Hayden continues. "He knows where."

"I can only imagine." Diana rolls her eyes up toward the sun visor and releases a sigh that threatens to fog the vanity mirror.

Hayden knows his daughter is envisioning the ballpark, and not the toboggan run where Diana and Linda used to love to be taken when they were little girls.

"I'd still like to have a memorial service for you." Diana doesn't turn to look at Hayden as she says this. Instead, she reflexively checks the intersection ahead for oncoming traffic. "I mean, if you don't mind."

"Fine. But no prayers. Just poetry or a personal memory." Hayden raises his voice slightly so that Joey can hear him from the backseat. "Joey, how'd you like to recite a poem at Grandpa's funeral?"

"Do I have to memorize it?" Joey asks.

God, to be eleven again, thinks Hayden.

"No. Just read it out of a book. Anything by Robbie Burns will do."

"Of course you'll memorize it!" Diana says curtly to the backseat. "Of course he'll memorize it," she assures Hayden in a more soothing tone.

"Then you'd better go with 'Scotch Drink,' bein' it's one of the shortest."

Diana's good humor begins to evaporate with the suggestion of odes to alcohol at Hayden's funeral. "I'm sure Joey will have no problem memorizing something longer. After all, he seems to have no trouble with Sir Walter Scott's 'Lochinvar.' All *eight* stanzas."

"Whatever you want," says Joey.

Joey is an easy kid in most ways, muses Hayden. You could give a person like that a job where he has to be on the road and he'll get the work done without constant supervision.

"Anything else?" asks Diana.

"Yes," says Hayden. "I just read a new study saying that oncology patients live longer if they have a dog. I'd like to get a dog. Maybe a border collie or a Labrador."

"Dad, what about Joey's asthma?"

"So we'll get a doghouse."

This time he catches a faint smile on Rosamond's lips. Hayden steers the car under the viaduct and they pass the Little League fields where boys and girls in brightly colored mesh shirts and white stretch pants dot the neatly mowed baseball diamonds. With the windows rolled down it's impossible to ignore the loud whoops coming up from the set of bleachers nearest the roadway.

In the rearview mirror Hayden sees Joey trying to catch a glimpse of the game that is providing all the excitement. "Can you see anything Joe-Joe? Is it a double? A homer?" But the light flickers green and Hayden must turn the car in the opposite direction.

Upon hearing her son's name Diana instinctively swivels her head to check on Joey in the backseat. Who will be Joey's best friend when Hayden is gone? she wonders. For the first time, Diana considers that she may have made a parenting mistake with regard to baseball. It was so difficult being the single mother of a growing boy. After a moment's pause she asks her son, "Honey, do they give you one of those uniforms or do we have to buy it?"

Joey suddenly bobs up between the two seats like a hungry seal about to be fed a fish. "They fund-raise. Why? Can I really play baseball?" he asks incredulously. It's become such a lost cause that he's even abandoned his regular Saturday morning pleading sessions. He can't believe what he's hearing! Thank God that Rosie and his grandfather are witnesses to this miracle. "You heard what she said, right, Grandpa?"

"From her lips to my ears," confirms Hayden.

"Well, you'd better wear one of those hardhats," insists Diana.

"It's a *helmet*, Mom. You wear it to bat," he shoots back, a result of reflex annoyance and sheer disbelief.

"I don't care what they call it, you'd just better wear it, the *whole* time. I've got enough gray hair on my head as things are right now, and don't want it to turn white overnight. All I need is a child with brain damage or amnesia. Or worse, a son in a coma."

chapter thirty-two

They drive through Bay Ridge and over the Verrazano Narrows Bridge, giving Joey an opportunity to point out to Rosamond one of the peregrine falcons that nest in and around the graceful suspension bridge. The water below them is alive with choppy white waves and sailboats making good progress as a result of the steady breeze.

Then it's across Staten Island toward the Goethals Bridge and the turnpike. The industrial parks of northern New Jersey are gradually replaced by double carriageways with jug handle turns, auto dealerships, strip malls, and finally leafy green suburbs with bags of fresh-mown grass stacked at the curb.

A hush falls over the car as they turn into Chicory Circle and pass one starter-mansion after the next, all hermetically sealed in white aluminum siding, made starker by the surrounding bright green chemically treated lawns. Rosamond assumes that the sudden silence is out of respect for the deceased, unaware of Hayden and Diana's collective dread regarding family visits.

"All the houses are so *white*," says Joey.

"That's not the only thing that's all white," says Hayden.

"Dad," objects Diana, "not now."

By this time Joey is the only one smiling as he strains to peer down the street and make sure that his aunt and uncle's basketball hoop is still intact. This was leftover from the previous tenants but, Diana presumes, Ted had decided it gave the house a nice family atmosphere and left it up. She also notices that the maroon shutters and garage door have recently been painted and stand out against the immaculate ivory siding. The surrounding grass and hedges are practically emerald-green and so perfectly manicured they could serve as a backdrop for a movie.

The navy blue Lincoln Continental and shiny red Ford Mustang convertible glow in the driveway as if it's a showroom, thinks Diana, especially when compared to the beat-up station wagon that pulls in behind them like a mongrel dog. In the days back when they'd been getting along better Linda had confided to Diana that she desperately wanted a Lexus but her politically minded husband insisted that they buy American. At least this was true when it came to the items that potential voters could see. Ted had no problem accepting imported Cuban cigars for himself and designer French perfume for his wife from businessmen in need of favors.

Diana sits biting her lip and holding tight to the dashboard even after the car has come to a complete stop in the driveway and been parked for several minutes.

Hayden doesn't move either, already having visions of being trapped by a decade-long homily from his congenitally campaigning congressman of a son-in-law. Ten minutes with Ted is like listening to every public service announcement ever aired on television without so much as a commercial. The sight of a neighbor washing his car and using a white bucket for the soapy water triggers a flashback to his last visit, when Hayden was forced to collect silt from the nearby Raritan River downstream from the manufacturing plant where Ted's political opponent was a part owner, so that it could be tested for chemical pollutants.

After Rosamond opens Diana's door her friend still doesn't get out. Rosamond glances around the yard to see if there's an attack dog lurking in the bushes.

Diana, however, is preoccupied with mentally reviewing a self-help book she'd recently read on how to have a better relationship with your sister. "Don't rise to the bait," she repeats the book's mantras to herself while anxiously clasping and unclasping her hands. "Just smile and take it in stride." "It's *her*, not you." But Diana can't banish the feeling that even as children Linda hadn't taken nearly as much pride in her own perfection as she had pleasure in the failings of others. Linda's constant stream of well-meaning but condescending-sounding advice has always been a source of tension between the two sisters.

Though Linda is two years younger than Diana, she's a matronly looking thirty-three. And though there had at one time been talk of fertility drugs and adoption, she has apparently resigned herself to being childless, and instead concentrating all her efforts on making a perfect home and being a good political wife. It's Diana's secret belief that Linda has purposely gained a few pounds and fixed her hair in a manner suited to an older woman so as to appear the perfect match for her husband, Ted, who is thirteen years her senior, soft in the middle, and bald except for a gray fringe that flips up at the bottom if not subjected to regular pruning.

Finally they all go up the front walk together. Linda opens the door wearing an expensive yellow linen suit with a fitted jacket that accentuates her plump hips. Her dyed-to-match helmet hair is perfectly coiffed and set, and a canary diamond weighs down her left hand and catches the light whenever she moves.

Diana immediately feels self-conscious, having dashed out of the house in her sneakers, jeans, and T-shirt, her hair pulled back in a ponytail. The cool greeting Linda offers Rosamond in comparison to the Oscar-winning hugs she presses upon Hayden and Diana serve to make clear to them her displeasure that they've brought a non–family member to such a solemn occasion.

Tears run down Linda's face as Diana and Hayden say how sorry they are, and Ted is uncharacteristically somber as he ushers them inside. His blue button-down oxford cloth shirt, navy blue blazer, and tan chinos are as new and tidy and perfectly coordinated as the interior of the house. Hayden's first thought whenever he sees Ted is that those big white Chiclet front teeth must be dentures. But then who would get dentures that looked like *that*?

Tea is served in the formally appointed living room on Linda's best china and starched linen napkins. Diana wonders if this is because she thinks the occasion of a visit by her Brooklyn sister is so special or, more likely, because she uses it to remind Diana that her older sister doesn't have any china of her own. Diana's elopement at twenty-one had not exactly attracted gifts in the same way as Linda's four-hundred-guest wedding at the country club. However, down deep, Diana believes that the real reason Linda feels the need to show off her finery is because whenever they're out together people mistake Diana for the younger sister. Or worse. One time Linda was wearing a hideous babushka, caftan dress, and sunglasses, and the waitress mistakenly thought that she was Diana's mother.

When Linda brings out the teacups she says pointedly to Rosamond, "Do you plan on being part of our *family* discussion?"

Diana opens her mouth to say something she'll regret, but Rosamond tactfully excuses herself by saying that she'll keep Joey company out in the front yard. Soon the regular thud of the basketball hitting up against the backboard and Joey and Rosamond's playful shouts can be heard through the open window.

For a long time Ted, Linda, Hayden, and Diana pass around photos of Dominick and talk about what a fine boy he was and contemplate aloud the million to one chance of such a freak accident ever occurring. Diana finds it odd that there are no photos of Dominick after elementary school and wonders just how close he and his father actually were. She knew that Ted and his first wife had split up only a few months after their son was born, and that Dominick had always lived with his mother, but she assumed that they'd continued to see each other, at least once in a while. On the other hand, Diana vaguely recalls Linda talking about an argument when Dominick formed a band, peroxided his hair, and pierced his cheek. Or was it his lip? Either way, when the recollections of Dominick's elementary school career eventually run out of steam, the details of transferring the burial plot are settled once and for all.

After that business is finished they sit in silence until Ted begins explaining how the census has just determined that for the first time New Jersey has a higher median household income than Connecticut. This is followed by a detailed list of the ramifications that this "startling fact" is expected to have on the political landscape in the tri-state area.

Hayden twitches through the long-winded exposition and drains his scotch glass. Dear Lord, he silently performs a mock prayer, If you're really up there, please don't let Ted become president. This is my one and only dying wish.

Diana follows Linda into the kitchen carrying the empty cookie plate and napkins. The large, airy room is perfectly organized with bright copper pots lined up according to size above the island in the middle. A tall, neatly ordered spice rack stands next to all sorts of modern and undoubtedly expensive gadgetry.

"You would just *adore* this new Cuisinart," says Linda, fully aware that her sister can't even afford a new set of wooden spoons.

Diana ignores her kitchen commentary and gets straight to the point. "You shouldn't have given Dad two glasses of whiskey," she chides her sister.

"Honestly, Di, what difference does it make? Let Dad enjoy himself while he still—"

"Linda! They're working on something right now, maybe even a cure. Just look at the progress that's been made with AIDS. And you could help me by encouraging him to try this experimental treatment instead of attempting to kill him with booze. How will you feel at the funeral knowing that you were an enabler?" Diana's breath comes in short gasps and she appears ready to sob or explode.

Placing her hands on her older sister's shoulders Linda says, "Calm down. It's just that you know Dad—he's going to do whatever he wants to do. Which is something we need to talk about," she adds in a sinister hush, as if hatching a conspiracy.

"What do you mean?" asks Diana. "If it's suicide you're thinking about, he's already—"

"What I mean is *financial suicide*," says Linda and she nods toward the kitchen window, through which they can observe Rosamond and Joey playing some sort of a game in which they move farther from the basket after every successful shot. "What if *that woman* tricks him into marrying her so that she can inherit his money? I mean, she shows up out of nowhere right before he's supposed to die . . . don't you find that a *little bit odd?*" Her eyes narrow as if she's a TV detective about to unmask the murderer.

"Linda! For one thing, Rosamond is a very nice person. You'd find that out if you'd stop being so rude to her. And second, she's a nun! She took vows of poverty and celibacy." Diana carefully avoids mentioning that Rosamond appears to have resigned from the convent.

Linda purposefully towels the crystal cookie platter so that every potential water spot is thoroughly eradicated. "How do we know she's *really* a nun? I mean, who's to say she doesn't get reports from a friend at a medical lab and go around town with this sister act. You can pick up a nun's habit at any costume shop. Honestly, dying men must love that—a sexy virgin who can grant forgiveness for all their sins."

Diana's mouth opens in amazement at the contemptibility of her sister's imaginings. "You can't be serious. Linda . . . she's dying! You should hear the way she used to cough when she first arrived. Look at how thin she is."

Linda glances out the window just as Rosamond sinks a basket from the grass next to the driveway and she and Joey cheer and high-five each other. "She looks pretty healthy to me."

But Diana has become too emotional to argue with Linda, between dealing with Hayden's illness and the unfortunate circumstances of their visit. "It's getting dark. I'm going to call Joey inside."

"He's fine. There's nothing to worry about out here. It's not like Brooklyn."

That's another of Linda's favorite jabs, that Diana isn't raising her son in a well-to-do neighborhood. By now Diana's livid and ready to stick Linda's head in the new Cuisinart as a way of testing just how well it really works. "Have you forgotten that Joey has *asthma!*" Diana shouts and storms out of the kitchen.

Linda reenters the living room as Ted hits upon the idea of employing the coasters in order to demonstrate to Hayden how a person gets appointed to the president's cabinet. Only Hayden is restlessly wandering around the room, pretending to study the lithographs of ships that line the far wall. When he does catch a glimpse of Ted yammering away, all he can concentrate on is the way his son-in-law looks like a horse raising a thick upper lip as if about to bite down on an apple.

"You know, Dad, you're welcome to come and live with Ted and me," Linda says as she refills her father's glass with expensive Chivas Regal. "I mean, if it's too much of a strain being with Diana."

It's all Hayden can do not to laugh at the very notion. Move in with Linda and Ted? Talk about dying a thousand deaths. He coughs and then clears his throat. "Yes, well, it's awfully kind o' you, but Diana needs me to watch Joseph while she's at work." My God, did he just say *Joseph?* Something about the vaulted ceilings, dark stone fireplace, and Ted's blue blazer with the bright gold buttons makes him feel that a high degree of formality is in order.

Diana walks into the room leading Joey by the hand and with Rosamond following a few steps behind. "I think we'd better be heading on home," Diana announces, her voice still quavering from being so upset. "I have to work in the morning."

"Of course, your new job!" says Linda and gives her big phony smile. "It must be so exciting."

But Diana is certain her meaning is more along the lines of Diana rarely holding a job for more than a year, and that she shouldn't be working in the first place with Joey off from school for the summer and not away at an expensive camp.

They all exchange stiff hugs and kisses, except for Rosamond and Linda, who coolly shake hands. Rosamond musters her inner resources to hide how hurt she is. But then she chastises herself for thinking of her own feelings at such a difficult time for the family. She resolves to pray to Our Lady of Perpetual Help for Linda's sorrow to be lifted and to be freed from all her sufferings, whatever they might be.

As Diana backs the car out of the perfectly edged driveway Hayden lets out a sigh of relief and says, "Hurry up so I can get home and have a drink."

"You just had three drinks and if you dare pour another one when we get home I'll turn around and bring you back here for good," threatens Diana.

"You drive a hard bargain woman, but I'd much rather drown in your prune juice than have to hear how Ted is solely responsible for Newark airport winning the best safety rating of any transportation center in the Northeast."

chapter thirty-three

By the first week of August the summer heat lies in a thick blanket across the ground. The air no longer cools during the night and the pitch in the driveway adds a sticky residue to anything left on it for more than a moment, including a person's foot.

On Sunday morning, Hayden, Rosamond, and Joey pile into the station wagon and travel down Atlantic Avenue toward the intersection of Utica and Pacific, in the neighborhood known as Bedford-Stuyvesant. Flags from Honduras, Haiti, and Jamaica announce the types of cuisine at the various restaurants. Islamic and Catholic schools stand directly across the street from each other. Hayden finds a parking spot on Pacific Avenue and the three make their way to the Grace Tabernacle Christian Center Church of God in Christ.

Inside the hot sanctuary sits a predominantly black congregation, with a few tan and white regulars, and several rows of Evian-clutching tourists in the back pews. The chance that a parishioner is wearing a neatly pressed suit or a fancy dress and a matching woven hat with cloth flowers and netted veil increases with proximity to the altar. The women in the front pews clutch well-worn Bibles and plastic lace fans that click like metronomes as they stir the heavy air. Both Bibles and fans double as disciplinary devices for the swarm of little children in their Sunday best who squirm and giggle and run pell-mell between the rows of wooden benches.

Rosamond is amazed at the contrast between this busy and lively place of worship and the hushed atmosphere of the convent chapel, where noise by humans is viewed as a disruption. Whereas here the confusion of people bustling about seems to contribute to an ambience that soothes and reassures.

"If anything is going to make me a believer it's gospel music," Hayden whispers to Rosamond as the service begins. "Wait 'til you hear this."

The soaring but rhythmic hymns reach deep into the souls of the congregation and many close their eyes and wave a hand or a purse-sized Bible above their head or rock back and forth as if in rapture of the Lord. All three clap their hands to the uplifting choruses and harmonies of "Oh Happy Day."

An African American woman wearing a brightly flowered dress adorned with two strands of large white pearls and a corsage of orange carnations and baby's breath shuffles to the front of the choir. The only incongruity to her outfit, which would be more than appropriate for a wedding, is the pair of fuzzy pink bedroom slippers on her feet.

There's an air of expectation and everyone sits up a little straighter. For a few moments she simply stands before them, swaying and nodding down at the floor as if in a trance. At last she is upright and looking out at the crowd with large brown luminous eyes and a knowing smile, the way a cleanup batter sizes up the pitcher and the playing field. And the congregation seems to collectively inhale as if anticipating that she's deep in concentration, preparing to hit one out of the ballpark. The woman produces a few preemptive murmurings as the choir continues to clap and hum and build up the backbeat, as if they're the launching pad that's going to assist in sending this rocket heavenward.

She takes a deep breath using her entire body, and it appears that something monumental is about to happen, but she suddenly pulls back, and returns to swaying. The tourists glance around to see what could have caused the false start. The regulars, on the other hand, know that the atmosphere must be perfect for the spirit to come, and that such hesitations can occur another four or five times. But these only serve to increase the impact when it finally arrives, and after the next round of preparation, the moment is right. The woman seizes upon such a lungful of oxygen that she has to lean forward to catch it all and when she comes upright it's only to bend so far back that she's pointed way above their heads. When her mouth opens a stunning solo takes to the air that can make dreams come to life with its powerful message of praise, sacrifice, and hope. The final "Jesus" momentarily stops the pulse of every person in the sanctuary as the last s hovers in the air long past any remembrance of the middle s. The note goes straight up past the altar and directly to the gates of heaven. As the vocalist comes in for a landing the worshipers bow their heads in thanks for being blessed by experiencing such a moving encounter with the truly divine and otherwise inscrutable.

Following the service Hayden manages to shake hands with half the congregation and gets invited to a revival meeting along with the annual pancake 'n' prayer breakfast. Then the trio clamber back into the sweltering car and head to the waterfront village of Red Hook, with its cobblestone streets and old-fashioned clam shacks. The neighborhood is cut off from the rest of South Brooklyn by the Gowanus Expressway, out on a peninsula that even the subways don't reach. Hayden explains how during World War II it was a bustling center of shipbuilding, shipping, and warehousing.

Now the streets are quiet except for summer Sundays when a converted barge acts as a stage for vaudeville acts, jugglers, comedians, and sleight-of-hand artists. While Joey and Rosamond compete with each other to figure out how the magic tricks are accomplished Hayden becomes bored and wanders across the street to argue with some nicely dressed Jehovah's Witnesses handing out copies of their spiritual newsletter *Awake!*

On the way home they pull up in front of a ramshackle shop on Court Street in Carroll Gardens to pick up fresh mozzarella, as per Diana's orders, so that she can make lasagna the next day. The local scene is reminiscent of the movie *Goodfellas*, where a good cannoli takes priority over most everything else. As they pass the bakery favored by both the Colombo and Gambino families, Joey begs Hayden, "Can we please get napoleons?"

They pause in front of the bakery where the windows are filled with cookies and chocolate éclairs and the luscious smell of fresh baked bread drifts out onto the street.

"What are napoleons?" asks Rosamond.

"Pastry with custard cream." Hayden points to the flaky pieces of cake topped with a delicate coating of brown-and-white icing. "Best baked goods in the world! I sure wouldn't mind a chocolate éclair." And though it's only forty-five minutes until dinner, they rush into the bakery.

Hayden orders Joey's napoleon and the chocolate éclair for himself. After torturous indecision Rosamond finally settles on zabaglione, a foamy custard flavored with Grand Marnier poured over fresh raspberries.

While enjoying the forbidden treats they stroll through the old section of Carroll Gardens where the row houses are set back from the street behind lush gardens containing painted Madonnas, Saint Francis birdbaths, and plaster sheep. Old folks relax in folding chairs on the lawns and children romp in plastic bathing pools. There's no traffic to break the serenity and it's possible to hear the birds scuffling in the trees above while the crickets tune up for their nightly concert. The narrow sidewalks are canopied by foliage and beyond the treetops the evening star flickers like a lamp just lit. It's a perfect summer evening.

Even Joey realizes that the moment is special, as if the unstoppable river of time has temporarily been brought to a standstill. He suddenly looks up at them and somehow articulates exactly what Hayden and Rosamond are both thinking. "I wish this—this right now—could be forever." He stretches his lanky young arms out wide in an attempt to describe the indescribable.

"Just enjoy the moment, Joe-Joe," says Hayden, contentment in his voice, though he takes his grandson's hand as if to say that he, too, wishes the soft summer twilight would never turn to darkness. "It's a gift. That's why they call it The Present."

Joey reaches over and takes Rosamond's hand so that he's strolling down the dead-end street safe between the two of them. Rosamond is surprised, not by his gesture, because they'd often held hands, but because she'd envisioned heaven so many times while praying. It was always a mansion in the sky bathed in golden light with an endless number of rooms where God and the angels lived among all the souls granted salvation.

Only now she has another version of paradise to contemplate, entirely different from the previous image. Heaven is a tranquil street in Brooklyn where one can eat fresh raspberry custard and walk hand in hand with a sweet young boy. And on the other side is the ever-confident Hayden, who possesses the miraculous ability to cure the sad and make them happy again. Rosamond is convinced that nothing bad could ever happen with Hayden around.

chapter thirty-four

In the morning Father Hank is expected to arrive at any moment to continue his work restoring Hayden's faith. "And remind me just who is supposed to be converting whom here?" Hayden asks Rosamond.

"May the best man win." She grins.

"And what do I get if I win?" Hayden demands to know in his best deal-maker's voice.

"Eternal damnation," Rosamond tells him with mock sweetness. Though she doesn't accompany the remark with her usual good-natured smile.

"C'mon, I'll bet you two dollars he throws in the collar."

Rosamond automatically gasps at the idea of wagering. Look at what happened to poor Job when Satan made a bet with God over his ability to remain steadfast in the face of tremendous suffering.

But Diana isn't swayed by Hayden's bravado or Rosamond's apprehension. She calmly sits at the kitchen table in her nightgown reading the newspaper and catching up on all the latest disasters. Her dark beauty is even more outstanding at moments like this, when she's without any makeup, her raven hair is pulled back from her face, and she's concentrating on something, completely unaware of her appearance.

Diana takes a sip of coffee and wipes her mouth with her arm like a sailor at the end of a bar. "You're on!" she says, surprising them both. "Twenty bucks for converting Hank."

Before Hayden can attempt to raise the wager, knowing that even though his daughter is in debt, she's employed and therefore still considerably more flush than someone just out of a convent, the phone rings. Diana picks up the receiver and they can all hear Linda's high-pitched voice squawking on the other end.

"A lawyer?" Diana says with surprise and waves Hayden and Rosamond away as if to indicate that she'll deal with her meddling sister alone. But they stand in stunned silence and so she takes the phone along with her coffee mug and goes upstairs.

Hayden is very much aware of how upset Rosamond has been since their visit to Linda's. Most of the time the two converse so easily that it feels as if they share each other's dreams. But when it comes to Linda, she won't be reassured.

Hayden attempts to convince Rosamond once more. "There's no reason to let her bother you."

"I don't understand why she doesn't like me," says Rosamond, thoroughly perplexed. At the convent there were occasionally petty jealousies and even differences of opinion, but the objective was to quickly eliminate such nonsense because it interfered with the overarching commitment to contemplation, prayer, and of course God.

"She's always been insecure," says Hayden.

"Linda acts as if I'm trying to . . . to *be* with you, or something," she tells him, her voice filling with dismay.

Hayden is startled to hear Rosamond bring up the eight-hundred-pound gorilla in the room. Maybe this is his chance to revisit the relationship issue—specifically that he wishes she *would* try to "be" with him, especially since he thinks about making love to her almost all the time. "Now, now, she's just concerned about my health. Don't be put out by her sourpuss behavior. It's just that . . . never mind."

"What? If I said or did something to offend her, then please tell me."

"No, no." Hayden sighs, which is unusual for him. "Diana has always had people remarkin' on how attractive she is, even as a baby. While Linda was the straight-A student and perfectly behaved. We—Mary and I—we always told the girls that it doesn't matter how you look so long as you're a good person. And it doesn't matter how smart you are as long as you try your best. And not ten minutes later some well-meaning friend or relative would say to the girls, 'So you're the smart one and you're the pretty one!' And soon they were marked, or scarred, for life—Diana thinking she's stupid and Linda convinced that she's ugly."

"But Diana isn't stupid, and Linda isn't unattractive."

"Of course not. But I don't claim to understand you women." With Diana upstairs he takes advantage of the opportunity to make another pot of coffee.

For a moment Rosamond feels guilty. As a nun she's supposed to have sympathy for those who are unkind to others. She's been taught that people behave in such ways in an effort to find the love that is missing in their lives, and oftentimes the faith that has been lost. For that reason alone it's her duty to show compassion and pray for Linda to find whatever it is she seeks.

However, Rosamond quickly decides that she's no longer a practicing nun and therefore she doesn't have to like Linda and she's not about to. No one has ever been so mean to her. The worst thing anyone had done to Rosamond at the convent was report that she'd pressed wildflowers in a hymnal during her first year and so she had to beg soup for her supper.

Rosamond exhales as if to agree with Hayden that the situation truly is hopeless. She takes her polishing cloth out of the drawer and heads off to work on the picture frames in the living room. Polishing silver always helped her to relax while she contemplated difficult matters.

chapter thirty-five

When Hank's car finally pulls up Hayden is out on the front stoop enjoying the exuberant morning sunshine and trying to come up with a fix for the Linda problem. Hank apologizes for being delayed. One of the altar boys had forgotten about an egg salad sandwich that he'd left behind a pile of hymnals in the vestry and Hank had been charged with tracking down and eliminating the noxious odor.

Hayden laughs over the story and then asks, "Are you sure it was an accident?"

"An accident of youth," Hank offers generously.

The two men sip coffee ice cream floats concocted by Joey and eventually pick up their conversation from the previous week. For Hayden has discovered an additional incentive to succeed in bringing Hank around to his way of thinking about God, other than to satisfy his salesman's ego.

Hayden genuinely likes Hank. And he would feel a lot better about leaving Diana with a guy like him around the house. Not to mention that Joey will probably grow up to become an expert on infectious diseases if there isn't some rational being on the premises to offset his mother's highly developed hypochondria. Hank had played sports in high school and rebuilt car engines, and except for those little stumbling blocks of celibacy and the priesthood, seemed like a pretty good catch.

"You know, Hank, some of the Apostles were married," says Hayden.

"Yes, well, they've changed the rules a bit since then."

Hayden tries another approach. "So tell me why women can't be priests? Now that doesn't seem very fair, does it?"

"Because they don't share a physical likeness with Jesus."

"If that's the requirement then why don't all priests wear beards? And why aren't they all Jews?" Hayden slaps his hand on his thigh so hard that he almost knocks over his mug.

Hank scrunches his forehead, looking more like a college student contemplating a calculus exam for which he hasn't studied than a seminarian trying to come up with answers to The Big Questions. Finally he says, "Let me tell you a story."

Hayden closes his eyes so he can pretend to listen, since he assumes it's going to be one of the parables his mother was always recounting, emphasizing Jesus' love for us.

"There were about a dozen pigeons living in the bell tower at Saint Agnes," Hank begins and points in the general direction of the church. "Every time we went to ring the bells they desecrated our robes. Father Ryan and I tried everything to get rid of them—clanging garbage cans together, playing loud music, even shooting off rounds from a BB gun."

Hayden has never before heard the Parable of the Pigeons and he opens his eyes with interest. "So what happened?"

"Father Ryan baptized and confirmed them and they never came back."

"Ha, ha!" laughs Hayden and slaps his knee. "That's a new one for me. You'll have to tell that joke to Joey."

The screen door opens and both men turn expecting to see Joey. It's Diana on her way to catch the subway. As she steps between the two men Hank is once again distracted by her shapely figure, accentuated by a dove gray pantsuit and accessorized with chunky silver jewelry. Out of the tips of her black high-heeled sandals peek shiny red toenails. Matching red lipstick glows against her pale Scottish skin and sleek black hair pools around her shoulders. Diana and Hank greet each other cordially as she sweeps by like an unexpected wind on an otherwise calm day, the scent of jasmine trailing in the air behind her and floating heavenward like a prayer.

"It's a bonny day, isn't it Diana?" says Hayden in an effort to slow her down for a minute.

She gazes critically at the hot sun and cloudless sky. "It's the kind of weather where people catch flu by going in and out of air-conditioning."

Hayden only smiles and looks down at the second hand on his watch. One of his favorite games is to make a positive statement about anything that comes to mind and then time how fast his daughter can translate the remark into a health risk.

Hank's eyes follow Diana's steps down the front walk until Hayden mischievously remarks, "Take a picture, it'll last longer."

When she turns and lifts her arm to wave good-bye her breasts majestically swell just below the neckline of her silk camisole.

Hank finds himself in the awkward position of being caught by Hayden as he stares wide-eyed at the man's daughter. He feels the need to confess, or rather explain. "She's just so . . . so sophisticated."

But Hayden's thinking of that other s word—sexy. The men, they all went crazy for her, and after things fell apart he practically had to call in the National Guard—the raging phone calls, the drunken scenes in the driveway. Good God, he often wondered what she did to them. Cast spells? Even her high school boyfriend had to be put on suicide watch after Diana left him for a student art teacher. Diana is what the boys on the street corner call "hot." And this brings Hayden to another question he's been saving for Hank.

"If heat rises, then shouldn't heaven be hotter than hell?"

Hank is relieved to change the subject. "Hell as a pit in the center of the Earth is a more recent idea from Dante's *The Divine Comedy* rather than anything truly biblical," replies Hank. "The Book of Revelation describes hell as a lake that burns with fire and brimstone where the wicked will be eternally punished."

"Sounds like the Gowanus Canal during the 1980s," jokes Hayden. "So Father Hank, tell me how you got into priesting. Is it the family business?"

"Hardly. My dad was a dockworker in the Brooklyn shipyard. There are five of us boys, and my mother had the typical upwardly mobile Catholic plan—a doctor, a lawyer, a politician, a black sheep, and of course a priest."

"I see. So you became a priest to please your dear mother?"

"Oh, no. She just always hoped that one of us would become a priest. But no one did. I majored in architecture."

"You're losing me here, Hank."

"She passed away when I was a junior in college. Though at the time I was more the candidate for black sheep than a bachelor's degree."

Hayden recalls being a boy about Joey's age and sitting at his own father's deathbed. As the soon-to-be "man" of the family, he was instructed to sell the land and move them to the city so his mother could have a few years of rest, Hayden could get an education, and his little sister could eventually find a husband. Only his father hadn't known about the debts incurred during his long illness, and had likewise underestimated the value of the moribund farm.

"Ah, so it was a deathbed pledge."

"Not exactly. A month after she was buried I visited her grave at Parkside—"

"I go there all the time," interjects Hayden. "Lovely cemet'ry."

"Yes, it is," Hank agrees. "Anyway, I . . . I had an experience. I received the call."

"Cell phone?" asks a roguish Hayden.

"No, I mean to the priesthood."

"Lightning struck or you heard a voice?"

"I was kneeling by Mother's grave and about twenty feet away was a little garden with a lilac bush in the center. In front of it was a lovely Madonna."

"Yes, yes, I know the exact spot, wonderfully restful."

"And when I looked up from praying, the Madonna . . . the Madonna . . . she was weeping."

Hayden sets down his drink and put his head in his hands. "Oh my, my, my . . ."

"What's wrong?" Hank asks defensively. "You think I'm crazy. Or that I'm making it up? Like people who insist they saw Jesus in a potato chip?"

"Oh no," replies Hayden slowly, "I can say without a doubt that you're not fabricatin'."

Hank isn't sure whether to be puzzled or angry.

"I think we'd better take a ride over to the cemetery," says Hayden. "Just the two of us." He goes inside to get the keys and asks Rosamond to keep an eye on Joey.

Joey jumps at the chance to spend time alone with Rosamond. He loves playing Go Fish and Old Maid with her. Especially if he gets cranky over losing and she tickles him, or else brushes his hair from his eyes when he's trying to peer at her hand through his overgrown bangs, which he refuses to let Diana trim until school starts.

Joey's well aware that he loves Rosamond differently from the way he loves his mother. Why couldn't he and Rosamond have grown up at the same time? And instead of going into the convent she would have married him and they would have lived in the woods and trained bears for the circus and she would have never caught cancer in the first place.

At the large stone archway that is the front entrance to the cemetery Hayden has a few words with the attendant while Hank waits in the car. They drive past the iron gate and park as close as possible to the rock garden and surrounding gravesites, and then walk the remainder of the way.

"Okay, go kneel in front o' your mother's grave," instructs Hayden. Meanwhile, he walks to a tiny shed behind a small mausoleum about ten feet from the garden.

Just when Hank is about to rise in order to look for Hayden, he hears the Scottish voice vibrantly shout, "Thar she blows!" The garden and surrounding statues are immediately covered in a torrent of sprinkler mist. After a few moments Hayden manages to adjust the spray so that the jet is hidden by statues and just barely rises above the Madonna's head causing tearlike drops to trickle down her face.

Hayden walks over and joins Hank, who is now aghast. "A sprinkler!" he finally says.

"On a timer."

Then Hank falls back down to his knees in front of the grave and cups his head in his hands. "Oh no, what am I going to do?"

Hayden squats down next to him and jokes, "I suppose you could sue God. Though he wouldn't be able to get counsel since there probably aren't any lawyers in heaven."

Hank looks grimly at Hayden.

Hayden tries again. "I hear there's a big demand for architects right now."

Hank checks to see if Hayden is still joking but it's obvious he's not.

"And Diana may be in the market for a new boyfriend, if I were willing to give my approval and put in the good word, o' course."

chapter thirty-six

The following Sunday evening Rosamond and Diana are vacuuming and putting trays of fancy hors d'oeuvres on the coffee table in preparation for a meeting of the book club. Meanwhile Hayden readies himself for a Greyfriars Gang session, which has been shifted to Alisdair's, due to the female invasion. He stands in front of the refrigerator with the door open drinking directly out of the milk carton, coating his stomach before a night of alcoholic revelry.

"*Dad*, will you please use a glass!"

"What for? I'm finishing it." He shakes the now-empty carton as proof and wipes the milk mustache from his face with the back of his wrist.

"It doesn't matter. You should still use a glass. There could be germs on the carton."

Hayden changes the subject in order to work on his latest sales scheme: love insurance. "I thought you might like to know that young Father Hank is gettin' out o' the Gospel business and going back to makin' buildings, where he belongs."

Diana quickly looks up to see if he's pulling her leg, as he is wont to do. "I don't believe you."

"But I'm serious as cancer." Hayden chortles.

Diana scowls unappreciatively at his gallows humor.

" 'Tis true," Rosamond confirms as she gathers up the toothpicks and napkins, then chuckles at the realization that anyone who spends enough time around Hayden eventually starts saying *'tis* instead of *it is*. "Round one goes to Hayden."

"And you owe me twenty dollars on our wager!" says Hayden. "I knew I'd start to turn a profit on you kids if I waited long enough."

Unwilling to give Hayden the satisfaction of knowing that she might be interested in a man who meets with his approval, Diana warns him, "Don't go and get into any trouble tonight. And you're *not* taking the car." Thank goodness she'd thought to hide his keys earlier in the day. Taking Joey home from a ball game after a beer is one thing, but getting behind the wheel following a meeting of the Greyfriars Gang is just asking for an accident.

This is a familiar routine and Hayden has hidden a spare set of keys in the back of the liquor cabinet. Only he decides it's not worth aggravating Diana since the subway is just as convenient.

Joey enters the room carrying his box of baseball cards. "I want to go with Grandpa."

Diana takes a deep breath in preparation for the long version of her lecture on why no such thing will happen in her lifetime, but Hayden merrily preempts her. "Ha! Good luck!" he says. "I possess naked baby pictures of her and I can barely get through security."

"Joseph, I need you here to serve the punch and put the sliced fruit and sherbet into it," Diana firmly tells her son. "It's so warm out that if we do it now everything will spoil. And we'll all get botulism."

Joey grudgingly agrees only because he has his own idea for excitement. When Hayden saw how sweet Diana's punch was going to be, he gave his grandson a pint of vodka to spike it. Joey imagines that some of the more attractive women will get drunk and start to feel the heat, since Hayden is too cheap to have air-conditioning, and hopefully remove their blouses. And then, if all goes well, he'll be able to see *real live* breasts, maybe even some for his Top Ten list.

Hayden departs singing "Comin' Thro' the Rye" in full voice: *"If a bod-y meet a bod-y, Co-min' thro' the rye, If a bod-y kiss a bod-y, Need a bod-y cry? Every lassie has her laddie, None they say ha'e I; Yet all the lads smile to me, When com-in' thro' the rye."*

Rosamond is certain that he winks at her as he walks out the door on the words *need a body cry*. Why does she feel so terribly guilty at the prospect of being intimate with Hayden? She isn't a nun anymore. Well, she hasn't officially resigned, but what does it matter since in her heart she is no longer a nun. In her twenty years Rosamond had known two sisters who had quietly disappeared, no explanation, no good-bye. The paperwork from the archbishop relieving her of her vows might take months to come through. With her cancer there was no point in even filing it.

The doorbell rings and returns Rosamond's attention to the many tasks at hand. The members of the book group begin to arrive, full of gossip and good cheer. As Joey passes out large glasses of punch they cluck over how adorable he is and pat his shoulder while remarking on what a "good little helper" he is to oversee the punchbowl for them. Joey takes full advantage of this perceived cuteness and smiles and continually offers to refill their glasses, all the while silently guessing what size bra cup each woman wears. He's encouraged by the way they sit with their legs slightly apart and fan their faces with their paperbacks in an effort to combat the heat. A few even kick off their sandals and pumps in an effort to get more comfortable. Joey determines that this is a good omen, and that the rest of their outfits can't be far behind.

In honor of their newest member the book group has chosen *A Nun's Glory*. But the story of a feisty nun who works at a homeless shelter in South Central Los Angeles only serves to make Rosamond realize that all she's done over the past month is think about herself. Suddenly she feels horribly guilty. What business does she have wearing a knee-length pink skirt with a white lace blouse, laughing and sipping punch with a group of secular women who wear gold jewelry, nail polish, and makeup? Perhaps this is why ever since leaving the convent she's been having a recurring nightmare of angry-looking men in red jumpsuits dive-bombing her while she sleeps. If she's lucky the terrifying images produce a coughing fit that yanks her to consciousness. Otherwise she awakens standing next to the bed, having leapt up to avoid their nonstop attacks.

Completely unaware of Rosamond's internal conflict, Joey is quite certain about his frame of mind at this moment: severe disappointment. When a cool evening breeze begins wafting through the town house the women are no longer perspiring. Diana even dispatches him to get a wrap for Selma, who is in a sleeveless dress, and then orders him off to bed. His life is so unfair. Whenever anything good is about to happen—an R-rated movie, a grown-up fight, naked people—he's always marched off to bed.

After the discussion about the book has concluded, Selma turns to Rosamond and asks, "If it's not being too personal, do you mind my asking why you left the convent?"

Diana quickly appears in the archway, as if this is the million-dollar question she's been dying to ask Rosamond ever since the night of her arrival, or whenever the right moment arose. But until now, it never has.

"I began to break the rules." Rosamond looks tentatively from one woman to the next. "I . . . I said I was going to the doctor when I was . . . I was actually going to the . . . the circus."

Three more women who'd come in from smoking in the backyard gather in the small corridor between the rooms, staring at Rosamond as if they're trying desperately hard to understand.

"It's . . . it's like a marriage," Rosamond struggles to explain. "If you break the rules—your vows—it's the same as being unfaithful to your spouse." And the women, almost all with diamond rings of varying sizes on their fingers, nod their heads empathetically.

No one asks anything more and so the conversation naturally turns to whether their beloved French actor is making any new movies. And would they rather be trapped on a deserted island with him or their favorite Latino heartthrob.

After the book party, Rosamond and Diana straighten up the downstairs and chat about the evening. Finally Diana asks the specific question that's been on her mind since Rosamond arrived. "So then, you didn't really leave the convent because you have cancer and suddenly decided to see the world before dying?"

After a long moment Rosamond softly says, "No."

Diana waits for a moment hoping there might be a "but" to follow. Only there isn't. "So, are you going to tell him?" she gently asks.

"I don't know." Rosamond sighs. "What difference would it make?"

"Being in love with someone makes a big difference."

"But what if . . . what if he doesn't . . ."

"He went to a department store with you. With Dad, if that's not total devotion then I don't know what is. And maybe you can convince him to look into this experimental treatment the specialist mentioned." Diana finally lays out the reason for her own interest in the situation.

But enough has been said for one night and the two women silently hug each other before going upstairs to bed. Birth and death and love now seem to be sewn from the same fabric, and there isn't the urgency to untangle such complex matters once and for all, assigning every emotion to its proper place, the way they'd approached life in their twenties, as if it were a puzzle to be permanently solved. Black and white have turned to gray and every sunrise inevitably brings with it a shift in circumstances, subtle, yet as predictable as the tides and immovable as the mountains. Believing that one can plan tomorrow is a game for the young, and for those as yet untouched by love.

By eleven o'clock Hayden still hasn't come home. But this isn't unusual when he's out with the Greyfriars, and so Diana makes sure the front door is unlocked since she's taken his keys. However, she doesn't notice the bulky shadow waiting outside in the bushes next to the front stoop. Diana leaves a light on in the living room and goes up to bed.

chapter thirty-seven

At half past midnight Hayden stumbles down the tree-lined street gaily singing, his bright baritone voice strong but slurred: *"You take the high road and I'll take the low, and I'll get to Scotland afore ye, but me and my true love will never meet again on the bonnie bonnie banks of Loch Lomond."*

When he opens the front door Hayden thinks for a moment that he really did overdo it and his eyes are suddenly playing tricks on him. Because what he thinks he sees is Diana's boyfriend Anthony hefting the new large-screen television off its stand.

"What in bloody hell do you think yer doin'?" shouts Hayden.

"Nothing, Mr. MacBride. Now-now, there's no reason to get upset."

"Suffering duck! Yer robbin' me blind and you expect me to burst out in fairy lights?"

Awakened by Hayden's bellows, Rosamond and Diana come running down in their nightgowns. Joey follows in his pajamas, rubbing sleep from his eyes with his fists.

"Tony!" Diana switches on the nearest lamp. "What on *earth*—"

"I just figured the insurance would pay. You're covered for everything, and you know, I'd give you guys half, fifty-fifty, even steven."

"Have you lost your *mind?*" asks an incredulous Diana.

From off the wall Hayden yanks an eighteenth-century musket that was used by his great-great-great-grandfather to defend Scotland against the British in the Battle of Culloden. Rosamond stands at the bottom of the staircase with one hand on Joey's shoulder and the other engaged in vigorously crossing herself.

" 'Tis a sad thing but I'm goin' to ha' to send ye where the woodbine twineth, you good for nothin' blackbeetle." Hayden's brogue is thick and his cheeks are ruddy from whiskey. He leans over and whispers something to Joey, who immediately scampers off to the kitchen. Then he raises the gun. "You'd better say more than yer prayers now."

A panic-stricken Tony raises his arms high above his head. "There's no reason to . . . to get all sore, Mr. MacBride. It was only a business proposition. But we can forget all about it . . ."

Diana whispers, "Somebody had better call the police." But Rosamond just stands on the landing in shock. So Diana dashes back upstairs to use the phone.

"Intruder, turn 'round and face the wall!" Hayden pokes Tony in the back with the sharp point of the musket. Without missing a beat Tony turns to the fireplace still pleading, "Mr. MacBride, let's talk about this, because I think you've been drinking and homicide is a serious—"

"Shut yer verminous trap! When I want the monkey to dance I'll grind the organ." Hayden again prods him in the back with the musket. "I'll be long dead by the time my case comes to trial. It makes no difference to me."

Joey returns from the kitchen with two frying pans and silently holds them up for Hayden's inspection. "I'm goin' to have to shoot ye." Hayden counts to three and then nods to Joey, who, on three, bangs the pans back to back as hard as he can. Tony slumps down on the carpet in a faint.

Diana's scream can be heard up in the bedroom. She races down the stairs and leans over Tony's body. "You shot him!"

"O' course not." Hayden chortles as if this is the best joke he's played in years. "I was just teachin' him not to tangle with the Greyfriars Gang. Now dump a pitcher o' cold water o'er him and tell the layabout that if I e'er catch him in this house again I *will* shoot him and then carry his noggin' around on a stick just like Macduff totin' Macbeth."

Diana places her hand on Tony's heart to confirm that indeed he's still alive, and as she does so a tear glides down her cheek. Only it's not for Tony but herself, in the realization that through becoming so familiar with betrayal, she's more saddened than stunned by it. Maybe Hayden is right about her inability to find a decent boyfriend, that it's time to give up on men entirely and concentrate on being both mother and father to her fast-growing son.

chapter thirty-eight

The following morning, Hayden, Rosamond, and Joey are up early and out in their rented motorboat fishing along the southern coast of Long Island by sunrise. It had rained during the night and the sky is gradually turning from gray to blue as if recovering from an illness. Using fresh minnows for bait they try for striped bass and flounder, and Joey secretly hopes for a baby shark. At least Rosamond and Joey are planning to catch fish.

Hayden gleefully retells the story of discovering the "hooligan" in his living room, careful not to leave out the look on the poor devil's face when it was announced he'd be dining on lead. Hayden turns to Joey and says, "Yer mother nags about my drinkin', but there's no rehab for stupidity now, is there, lad?"

Rosamond doesn't see the humor in a man becoming so wayward in his faith that he resorts to robbery, but somehow Hayden's hilarious reenactment of the incident overwhelms her sense of spiritual duty. She silently promises to say a prayer for intercession on behalf of the troubled Anthony. And Rosamond is heartened that Hayden had displayed his own form of forgiveness by not filing charges with the police, and thereby offering Tony another chance. (Though she's blissfully unaware of the promise Hayden privately extracted from the guilty party to paint the town house for free.)

The green water sparkles in the fresh morning sunlight and seagulls fish from overhead, occasionally swooping down and then rising high above with a wriggling silver snapper clutched in their beaks. Hayden leans back with the sunshine coppering his face and savors the rhythmic slap of the sea against the side of the boat.

"Fishing is a boon to the soul. I don't know why I ne'er did it afore . . .

there was a lovely stream near the farm . . . I suppose I was always busy wi' the chores."

Rosamond laughs as she recasts her line. "Hayden, you don't fish. You drink beer and whiskey and tell stories and sing songs."

"For your information, Sister Know-It-All," he loftily preaches to Rosamond, "drinking and telling tales is the most important part of fishing—that's why the fish come." His mischievous eyes flicker between green and hazel, and when caught by the light from a certain angle appear to be almost golden.

To prove his point Hayden begins singing in his cheerful rich brogue: *"Where ha'e ye been a' the day, Bon-nie lad-die, Highland lad-die? Saw ye him that's far a-way, Bon-nie lad-die, Highland lad-die? On his head a bon-net blue, Bon-nie lad-die, High-land lad-die, Tartan plaid and Highland trew, Bon-nie lad-die, High-land lad-die!"*

As if the gods are on Hayden's side Joey feels a tremendous tugging on his line and reels in a medium-sized flounder. He stutters with excitement, "It . . . it's huge! Look Grandpa! I . . . I caught a fish all by myself!"

Hayden lifts his beer to Rosamond and gives her an I-told-you-so smile. "There's the fishes! After some more refreshment I'll set to conjurin' up the loaves." He laughs uproariously at his own joke and proceeds to sing "Annie Laurie."

Rosamond nods her head as if he's either completely mad or has somehow conned the Lord. At this point neither outcome would surprise her in the least.

After stopping to fill the boat with gas they moor at Hickory Island in Jamaica Bay for a picnic lunch. Hayden explains how the thirty or so islands surrounding Brooklyn and Queens were once a vital part of the urban economy, supporting such diverse enterprises as shipbuilding, military training, summer resorts, and mental health institutions. But now, most are abandoned and off-limits to the public.

While Joey wades near the shore and digs for clams, Hayden and Rosamond lie next to each other on the blanket and enjoy the perfect mix of warm sunshine and salty air. There can be no doubt for either that love had snuck in while they were both preoccupied with other things. But what kind of love is it?

Hayden has almost resigned himself to the fact that it's platonic, a wonderful friendship with a woman in an earthly purgatory, trapped between the worlds of flesh and spirit.

Rosamond believes that their regard for each other may simply defy definition. Perhaps it is ineffable, as many believe God to be, unconfined by logic or reason, His mercy boundless and unfathomable. Or maybe she, as a mere mortal, just isn't capable of comprehending such obscurity.

Hayden gazes skyward and points at one of the thick fluffy clouds. He's always finding liquor bottles in cloud formations and was particularly thrilled the other morning when Joey pointed out a scallop-shaped Remy Martin. At least he savored the moment until Diana beaned them both with her handbag.

"That one looks just like a bottle o' Glenfiddich, do'an' you think?" says Hayden, pointing toward the horizon.

"Will you stop it!" Rosamond chides him but then laughs heartily. "Sometimes even I agree that you're a bad influence on your grandson. Besides, there's no alcohol in heaven."

"No pubs? Then I think a few priests will be changin' their tickets."

Rosamond stops smiling and turns serious. "Hayden, I have a confession to make."

He rises to his elbows, secretly hoping that the hour is finally upon them, the moment Hayden has been playing out over and over in his mind, when Rosamond gives him some sign that her divorce from God has finally come through and she's available. And that she might even welcome a date from a dying geezer such as himself. While he feels his appetite waning by the day, and has half the energy he possessed only six months ago, Hayden is often puzzled by the fact that Rosamond's hacking cough has all but disappeared and her cheeks are positively rosy. Has Rosamond's cancer slowed or has she dived into Diana's makeup jars in a significant way?

"A confession, eh? And what are your sins, my child?"

"I . . . um . . . I had a talk with your neighbor yesterday," Rosamond begins.

"Old Mrs. Trummel? The one who's always calling the Mounties whenever we play the bagpipes? I hope you gave her a good dressing down."

"No, the other neighbor."

"Bobbie Anne?" Hayden feels a surge of protectiveness rising within. Yes, he's in love with Rosie, but no one is going to give Bobbie Anne a hard time as long as there's a single breath left in his body.

"I just . . . I just suggested that maybe she could go back to school. There's a Jesuit University not far from here, in Jefferson Heights, that offers scholarships and financial aid to women in her situation."

"I'll have you know that the Church and the whorehouse arrived in this country at about the same time and I do'an' know that one has a superior claim to the other." Hayden adopts a combative tone and his cheeks turn ruddy as they do when he becomes annoyed. "And what did she say to all your friendly advice?"

"She told me to mind my own business and *how*." Rosamond sounds contrite on two counts—for interfering, and for angering Hayden. Aside from the burglary episode with Tony and occasional comments about Joey's father she's never seen his temper flare so suddenly.

Joey comes running over with big handfuls of shells and rocks worn smooth by the sea and plops down on the blanket to sort his plunder like a modern-day pirate. It seems as if he'd grown an inch that very week. There's no doubt in Hayden's mind that this is Joey's last summer of building sandcastles and collecting seashells. Next year he'll most certainly be listening to music and bikini watching.

"She said that she'd been raised Catholic, married in the Church, had her daughters christened, and given time and money to the Church all her life," Rosamond continues in a quiet voice. "And then when she needed financial assistance they had nothing to offer but a bunch of hot dishes from the Ladies' Bereavement Battalion and grief counseling by an assistant priest."

"That girl calls a spade a spade!" Hayden announces, obviously pleased.

"I'll say. Then she proceeded to tell me that she guessed I'd probably never worked a day in my life or had to worry about paying taxes! Oh Hayden, it was terrible. All of a sudden I . . . I didn't know what to say."

"Oh, do'an' worry about it," Hayden reassures her. "I'm sure she knows you were just tryin' to help in your own way."

"Well, it's just that . . . that she was right. I mean, about my never having had to pay room and board. I don't even pay *you* rent."

"Yes, I've been meaning to talk to you about that," Hayden jests.

Joey chimes in, "Are you talking about Bobbie Anne? Andrew told me that he's saving up his money to go on a date with her, that she'll date anyone for two hundred dollars."

"Well do'an' you be paying no mind to Andrew Drummond!" says Hayden. "He's got a bad case of the teenagitis."

"I feel bad for Bobbie Anne's daughters," Joey says while building a sandcastle, using the shells he'd collected as exterior wall reinforcement. "I wouldn't want people saying things like that about my mom."

Joey's remark shocks Hayden into finally considering that Bobbie Anne's line of work may not be as reasonable as he'd once insisted, that perhaps he hadn't taken into account all the variables. He turns to Rosamond with a serious face and says, "Hmmm," as if to indicate he's going to rethink the matter.

"So Joey, do you still want to be a lion tamer when you grow up?" asks Rosamond, realizing that it's time to change the subject.

"I want to be a catcher for the Mets!" says Joey, thrilled by her interest. "I'm going to signal all the pitches." Joey could easily imagine himself traveling around the country as a baseball hero, going on talk shows, waving at large-breasted women wearing halter tops jumping up and down in the stands.

"Maybe you can be an inventor during the off-season," suggests Hayden. "Tell Rosie about some of the great Scottish inventions."

Joey recites from memory, "The Scots invented the telephone, bicycle, golf clubs, steam engine, continuous electric light, and the television."

"Oh really?" Rosamond is genuinely impressed. "I thought the Americans—"

"The Americans!" Hayden harrumphs. "We Scots come up with it and then the Yanks make all the money and take all the credit. Just look at penicillin, antiseptic, color photography, and even Dolly the cloned sheep! And tell her the most important invention of all, Joey."

"The thermos flask—so your whiskey doesn't get hot in the sun," Joey answers proudly.

Hayden takes his thermos from its place weighing down the corner of the blanket and raises it above his head as if it's the Heisman Trophy. "*Uisga beatha,*" proclaims Hayden.

"That's Gaelic for whiskey," Joey translates, "and means 'water of life.' "

Again Rosamond nods appreciatively at Joey's display of knowledge, though she's not entirely sure whether she should be amused or concerned by the direction his studies can take him under Hayden's roguish tutelage.

Joey glows from Rosamond's expression of admiration and makes an effort to earn even more. "There were two presidents with Scottish roots— James Monroe and Woodrow Wilson. Same for the astronaut Neil Armstrong and Allan Pinkerton, the founder of the detective agency."

The recitation achieves its intended goal and Rosamond leans over and hugs him. "Just wait until school starts and your teachers find out how smart you are!"

Meanwhile, Hayden is envisioning how Joey will get pummeled by the other boys if the teachers take too much of a shine to him, especially since he's starting middle school and will be in the youngest class. "It's important to be smart Joe-Joe, but remember never to show off." He doesn't add the part about getting plastered for being a brownnoser. "Only respond when the teachers call on you, even if you know the right answer. Do' an' go a wavin' your arm around like a flag on a windy day."

On the way home Hayden sees a sign for a nearby animal shelter and pulls off the highway. Strolling down the rows of kennels he likes the look of a St. Bernard-ish mutt. "Mom's going to kill you," says Joey, who's already fallen in love with a teacup poodle.

"Joe-Joe, how are you ever going to learn to steal second base if you always have one foot on first? Sometimes it's better to beg forgiveness than ask permission."

Rosamond calls them over to see a lively Irish setter named Red, but Joey returns to the apricot poodle. From the sign on its cage door the little puppy has apparently been given up due to a lack of appreciation for the more established family cat. "Joey, that's a dust mop, not a dog." Hayden scowls at the orangish ball of fluff.

"Please, Grandpa, this is the one I want! And next Sunday is my birthday."

"How about a German shepherd or a golden retriever? Maybe we should look around a wee bit more—check the newspaper."

"No, I want a little dog that can come with me when I go places. And one that doesn't shed so Mom will like it."

It's becoming obvious to Hayden that Joey has not only inherited his powers of persuasion but some of his determination as well. He rolls his eyes at Rosamond, who is now playing with the carrot-colored puppy.

"We'll name her Ginger," Joey announces while Hayden pays for the dog and signs the papers.

"Just what I need, one more woman around the house," grumbles Hayden.

"They make very good watchdogs," the desk attendant says helpfully. "When I was in prison I asked a lot of the burglars what the best dog to get was, thinking they'd say a rottweiler or a Doberman, but they all said poodles and Yorkshire terriers."

"Well, a good watchdog is certainly something we can use as long as Joey's mother insists on dating," Hayden agrees.

chapter thirty-nine

It takes two days for a hysterical Diana to calm down and acknowledge that Joey isn't going to die from having a dog. And once she does, she finds it impossible not to dote on the sweet little poodle. However, adjusting to the rest of Hayden's antics is not nearly as easy.

When Diana arrives home from work on Thursday, Hayden reminds her that the Greyfriars Gang is coming over that evening and this time he doesn't want her around for the gathering. "The boys and I are sick and tired o' you chaperonin' us—tryin' to cut off our licker, keep down the telly, and hide the bagpipes."

"*Me?* It's the police who keep coming over to break things up when I'm *not* around!" she scolds. But it's not the police Diana worries about so much as the whiskey Hayden consumes when he's with his buddies, and that it's sending him to an even earlier grave. "I'm staying!" She defiantly slices up an orange and presses it into the juice machine to make sure he understands that's her final word on the matter.

But Hayden's anger boils over and he knocks the juice machine into the sink, much to her surprise. "You're not my wife, dammit!"

"No, I'm not. I'm your daughter!" Diana rescues her precious juicer from the sink and checks to make sure it's not broken.

"The last thing the Brooklyn police care about is some noise coming from my living room," says Hayden. "It's that bloody Mrs. Trummel always complainin' and makin' them come by because one of her girls works as a cop. And I'm sick of her, too! I'm tired of all you women. Tonight I want you and Rosie to go off to a nice dinner and then to one of those female movies where they all run around cryin' and tryin' to find a cure for a baby with a rare disease." From out of his pocket Hayden digs five crisp twenty-dollar bills, a monumental amount of money for him, and stuffs them into her hand. "My treat!" he barks.

Diana defiantly crumples his money and hurls it onto the countertop. "I have no interest in going to a restaurant for dinner when I enjoy cooking and can make a better meal right here."

"You think I do'an' know that you purposely cook us food we like so you can keep an eye on us? That's a little trick you picked up from yer mother."

"Well this is my house now, I have the paperwork to prove it, and to get me out of it *you'll* have to call the police! Meanwhile, for dinner I'm planning braised lamb with rosemary, Cullen skink soup made from smoked haddock, and mashed potato. I'm sure Paddy, Duncan, Alisdair, and Hugh will be more than happy to enjoy it. *You* can go out for pizza if you want!"

Hayden hasn't possessed much of an appetite lately, but braised lamb with rosemary . . . he could already smell it! Mary used to serve mint jelly on the side and make croutons out of fresh bread for the soup. But Hayden refuses to let on that he's interested in the meal. "Your Scottish grandparents are turnin' over in their graves hearin' the disrespect American-raised children have for their parents. I just want you to know that!"

"You, the big atheist, want me to believe that your parents are looking down on us from heaven and then feel guilty about trying to keep you alive."

Rosamond is waiting outside the door and only enters the kitchen when she senses the exclamation points have been exhausted and the argument is winding down. Diana and Hayden regularly engage in rows and Rosamond has observed that having bystanders around only seems to encourage them. It was easier for the defiant Hayden and the equally stubborn Diana to accept defeat without an audience.

"Oh-uh." Hayden grasps for an explanation when he sees Rosamond. He doesn't want her to think he's being unreasonable, especially since Rosamond and Diana appear to get along so well together. "I was just askin' Diana if she'd be so kind as to make some extra supper tonight since I've invited the boys over. We can't get enough of her fine cookin'."

"Yes," agrees Rosamond. "Diana's a marvelous cook. And I'd better help if she's going to make enough for everyone."

"Then I'd better leave you girls to it!"

Diana exchanges knowing looks with Rosamond and begins organizing the ingredients for the meal.

"Dad, run to the Italian bakery with Joey and get some fresh bread for the croutons."

"Righty-o," says Hayden with unexpected enthusiasm. "Always happy to help." He's already thinking about the chocolate éclairs.

Later that evening the men eat in the living room with plates balanced on their laps and watch *Rob Roy* for the millionth time, while a frantic Ginger races about the room scarfing up anything that even briefly strays from plate, fork, or mouth.

In the kitchen Diana teaches Rosamond how to make a Dundee cake with spices and dried fruits and then topped off with almonds. Joey sits at the table polishing his school shoes with WD-40, the way Hayden had showed him, insisting that it's cheaper and better than shoe polish.

"I always wanted a pair of patent leather shoes as a girl," says Rosamond. "But the nuns claimed that the boys would be able to see our underwear in the reflection."

"Is that true?" Joey holds up his shoe to check for his reflection, as if this piece of information might open the door to a whole new hobby.

"Actually, it was probably just one of those old nun's tales, like communion doesn't count if you have gum in your mouth."

"I want to eat dinner with Grandpa and watch the movie," complains Joey. He's pretty sure there's sex in it, because even though Diana doesn't like him to watch violence she doesn't forbid it. Sex is another matter. "Why can't I watch the movie?"

"You can't watch the movie because you're eleven, that's why."

"I'll be twelve in a few days!"

"Well *Rob Roy* is rated R! It's bad enough the way you and your grandfather read those gardener's catalogs." Diana says this in her best "the things I put up with around here" voice.

"Gardener's catalogs?" Rosamond is curious.

Diana smiles as if it's against her better judgment, but she can't help it because at the end of the day Hayden makes her laugh. "Oh, go ahead. Show Rosamond."

Joey digs a glossy color catalog out from under a pile of newspapers near the basement door and randomly opens it to a middle page. Then he clears his throat and begins reading in a throaty voice as if he's narrating luscious pornography, obviously something picked up from Hayden: " 'The Bristol onion demonstrates a healthy erect green stalk on the surface and matures into a variety with excellent smooth skin cover and very uniform well-

shaped bulbs, hard when ripe, with a delicate flavor.' " He is careful to emphasize all the words that lend themselves to a double meaning the way
Hayden does.

At first Rosamond blushes and looks down at the table but Diana's
hearty laughter puts her at ease. Rosamond joins in and soon the two
women are laughing so hard that they need to stop decorating the dessert
and Joey is thoroughly enjoying being the center of attention. He certainly
has Hayden's ability to entertain, thinks Diana. Maybe she should enroll
him in some drama classes offered over at the Y. That would be safe, so long
as they don't allow duels and that sort of nonsense.

When Joey finishes the Bristol onion and the Guatemalan red pepper
Diana says, "Do the strawberry."

Joey turns the page to his mother's favorite. In a good imitation of Hayden's brogue he slowly purrs: " 'The strawberry Eros are a bright, firm fragrant
fruit with a voluptuous conical shape and when ripe deliver a tantalizing
sweetness. They have superior yield and mature quickly with proper care
and are surprisingly disease resistant.' "

By now all three of them are convulsed with giggles. "Here," Joey says
and passes the catalog to Rosamond. "You do one."

"No, no, I couldn't." Rosamond is laughing so hard that tears are streaming
down her cheeks. She takes a sip of tea but only proceeds to choke on it so the
liquid runs out her nose, which makes Diana and Joey hit the table with their
hands and lean back in their chairs. Diana holds her stomach with one hand
as if she's about to become ill from laughing so hard. Rosamond finally com-
poses herself, takes the catalog from him and in a serious voice begins: " 'This
exotic black beauty aubergine is rich dark purple with pear-shaped fruits that
are springy to the touch and taste.' " But her cheeks quickly redden and they
all burst into gales of laughter before she can go any further.

While the women finish drying the dishes Joey takes the Ouija board
from the pantry.

"I haven't seen one of those since I was a kid!" exclaims Rosamond.

Joey and Diana sit across from each another at the kitchen table with
their fingertips resting on the molded plastic roamer with the gold pointer.
They ask questions and then wait for the subway to rumble underneath the
neighborhood and the pointer to head toward "yes" or "no," spell out an answer, or skate over to a number. Diana asks the board if Joey's new teacher
will be nice and the pointer eventually glides to Y for yes. And then Joey
asks, "Will Dad take me camping this summer?"

Diana lifts her fingers from the cream-colored triangle and looks up. "I don't know, Joey. Your dad is pretty busy doing construction work up in Providence so he can pay off some debts."

"But he promised me for my birthday—"

"I'll take you camping, Joey," Rosamond interjects. "I may not be able to cook but—"

"That's not true . . . anymore," says Diana.

"I used to camp in the North Woods with my dad," explains Rosamond. "He taught me how to track bear and deer, and I even know how to shoot with a bow and arrow."

"Really?" Joey's amazed that a woman, especially one who was a nun when he met her, is in possession of such worthy talents. "Can we sleep outside and cook over an open fire just like cowboys?"

"Sure. We'll go up to the Adirondacks and explore some caves and look for Indian arrowheads." Though Rosamond wonders if she'll live long enough and be well enough to undertake such a trip.

After the men have been served their Dundee cake Diana tells Joey it's time for bed and kisses him good night. Joey kisses Rosamond on the cheek and she runs her fingers through his hair as she gently brushes her lips across his forehead. Being kissed by Rosamond almost makes going to bed so early bearable. Joey imagines that her kiss probably feels the same as the feathery touch of an angel from heaven.

"You'd better put on your headphones," Diana says and nods toward the battle cries and beating of a snare drum coming from the next room. "And stop sleeping with Ginger on your pillow and that big baseball mitt underneath your mattress."

"It's a catcher's mitt," Joey specifies.

"I don't care what it is, if you don't take it out you're going to be an asthmatic humpback!"

chapter forty

While the men's voices rise and fall in the next room, contingent upon which side is prevailing in the blood-soaked battles, Rosamond and Diana sit across from each other at the kitchen table. Diana places her fingers on the roaming piece in the middle of the Ouija board and moves it to the center. "Didn't you do this sort of thing when you were growing up?" she asks.

"A girl used to bring one to school for playing at recess. But not having any siblings I didn't own board games. Dad and I used to whittle at night—slingshots and knife handles and that sort of thing. He wasn't very talkative. I think he missed my mother a lot. And then, after he finally remarried, my stepmother had enough conversation for the three of us."

Diana and Rosamond rest their fingertips on the plastic triangle. "Now ask a question, and then we wait for an answer from the spirits, or in this case, the F train."

"All right." And with a twinkle in her eye Rosamond says, "Will Diana go out on another date with Hank?" After a few moments they feel a slight rumble underground and the pointer slides in the direction of the zero.

Diana grimaces and then removes her hands from the triangle and places them over her face. "That's correct, definitely a big zero with a zero chance."

"I thought we were supposed to let the spirits answer," says Rosamond.

"I think they just did. Don't get me wrong, Rosamond, I know Hank is a friend of yours, and he's a very sweet man, but if the spirits had experienced how he kissed *they* wouldn't go out with him again either."

"He kissed you?" Rosamond is surprised. "On the first date?"

Diana laughs at her friend's innocence. "Uh, Rosamund, these days a good-night kiss on the first date is considered pretty conservative. Some of those movies we watch are from the 1950s."

"Oh yes, of course."

"Now it's my turn," Diana says and puts her hands back on the triangle, opposite Rosamond's. "Will Rosamond kiss Dad?"

Rosamond stares down at the Ouija board and attempts to avoid eye contact with Diana. But her cheeks flare with color and she feels her heart thudding in her chest until it's overtaken by a subway train thundering into the nearby station and the silver pointer slides to "maybe."

"You wouldn't mind?" Rosamond asks almost shyly.

The men's voices rise in the next room as Rob Roy MacGregor ambushes the king's soldiers.

"Of course not." Diana smiles at her. "You two should have a good time together. I never thought I'd be able to handle the thought of Dad having feelings for another woman, other than Mom, but . . ."

"But what?"

"You're . . . you're good for him. I mean, you're a terrific person in your own right." Then she leans over as if they're co-conspirators. "And I'll tell you a secret, Dad's a terrific kisser. Mom always said so."

"Oh dear," says Rosamond with alarm.

"What's wrong?"

"I'm . . . I'm just afraid I might be in the same boat as, well, poor old Hank. My first and last kiss was in high school."

"I see," muses Diana. "When I was a teenager Linda and I used to practice kissing, you know, with our pillows. We practiced some other things, too, but there's no need to go into that now."

"Has kissing really changed that much?"

"It's not that it's changed." Diana smiles with encouragement. "It's just that *we* change as we get older. It's hard to explain. Why don't you try? Put your lips together like this." Diana demonstrates from her position across the table. "Now Hank was doing the teenage throat plunge with too much inner lip, tongue, and suction." Diana again demonstrates as if she's looking in a mirror. But Rosamond only seems confused.

"Do you know any poems?" asks Diana.

"Not really. I mean, I used to," says Rosamond. "But now I only know a lot of prayers." Though she doesn't see the connection to kissing. Maybe

Diana means poems about kissing or love, like Shakespeare's sonnets. "Wait a second . . . I remember 'Trees'?"

The word *trees* doesn't immediately call up an image in Diana's mind. She'd always been a fan of the romantics and the French symbolists.

Rosamond recites the first stanza. *"I think that I shall never see a poem lovely as a tree."*

Diana has a flashback to the many Arbor Day celebrations in elementary school, standing around a newly planted tree and reciting the Joyce Kilmer poem. The words rise from the dusty recesses of her mind, back where the Pledge of Allegiance is stored along with the Lord's Prayer and her mother's recipe for sugar cookies—the first thing Diana was allowed to bake on her own. *"Poems are made by fools like me,"* she recites, going directly to the last lines.

And then Rosamond and Diana finish together: *"But only God can make a tree."* They giggle at this shared remembrance and Diana almost forgets why she brought it up in the first place.

"Oh yes," says Diana. "A kiss is like a poem without words. Or maybe you can say the same thing about a prayer."

"A prayer without words?" Rosamond sounds even more puzzled.

"Here, stand up." Diana rises and stands in front of her. "The adult kiss is soft, see . . ." She delicately wets her lips with her tongue and then parts her mouth very slightly. "You don't lock lips and shove your tongue into the other person's mouth like a dentist's drill."

Rosamond faces Diana and copies her. She wets her lips and opens them ever so slightly.

"Then you just close your eyes and put your lips between each other." Diana opens her eyes and exclaims, "Oh, this is impossible. Here." She leans over and kisses Rosamond.

At that moment the black Irishman Paddy Fitzgerald clambers into the kitchen for another beer, slightly tipsy, advantageously using the refrigerator door handle for ballast. "Delicious Dundee cake, Diana," he says while opening the door and then does a double take when he registers the women kissing. But he only shakes his head as if he's had either too much or not enough to drink and walks back out mumbling, "Absolutely delicious. Just like Mary used to make."

"Thanks, Paddy," Diana says to the retreating broad back and confused nodding of the head that Paddy shaved every day to give the overall effect of an even baldness.

"Yes, I see the difference," Rosamond says. "Thank you."

Then they hear Paddy in the living room saying, "The girls are kissing in the kitchen. Do you think that's a bit peculiar?"

Diana and Rosamond look at each other and cover their mouths to stifle giggles.

But Alisdair, Hugh, Duncan, and Hayden are well into their cups and it's the scene of the final duel between MacGregor and the British noble, so they all sloppily hush Paddy and cheer for Rob Roy.

chapter forty-one

Despite drinking and falling into bed well after midnight, Hayden rises early the next morning. Much to the delight of Joey and Bobbie Anne's daughters, he's been putting his sheep farming experience to work by teaching Joey's little poodle to herd ducks. Every morning Hayden supervises Ginger as she moves a quacking mob of mallards from the edge of the pond across the street and into their backyard for some bread crumbs and mash, and then returns them to the park.

A side benefit of these morning maneuvers has been the frightening off of all the rabbits destroying Mrs. Trummel's garden, which in turn has considerably cut down on calls to the police about the boisterous nights of the Greyfriars Gang.

Hayden employs the Gaelic commands that his father used with their border collies, which were specially bred and trained to drive sheep. He explains to the children that the name of the breed of dogs known as collies, the best herders, is actually the Gaelic word for "sheep." And how it was often said that without border collies there'd be no sheep at all in Scotland.

Between shouting what sounds like gibberish and a tiny orange poodle halting traffic as it chases a group of zigzagging and loudly quacking ducks across the street, Hayden appears quite the eccentric, even for Brooklyn. This is especially true on the days he wears his green, blue, and black plaid MacBride clan kilt to lend an air of ceremony to the proceedings, and Alisdair stops by to accompany the drill on his bagpipes. Hayden's parade begins at nine o'clock sharp and by the start of the second week it attracts a regular crowd. Even the ducks honk and leap up with giddy anticipation when they see Hayden approach the pond or hear the first few notes on Alisdair's pipes. They know that at the end of their march a reward will be forthcoming in the form of a homemade breakfast.

The community newspaper runs a story titled "Highland Fling in Prospect Park," in which Hayden is quoted as saying that animals feel better when they work at a job and earn their food by using their minds and bodies. "It's the same with people," he adds, hoping that Diana's ex-boyfriends will read the article.

Ginger the poodle is equally enthusiastic about duck herding and has a natural aptitude for it. Hayden shows the children the webbed feet on the little poodle and explains how they were bred as hunting dogs and being able to swim enabled them to go fetch a grouse out of a pond. The word *poodle*, he tells them, is derived from the German word *Pudelin*, and means to splash about in the water, which the little girls think is very funny.

"I'm surprised no one has made duck herding into a circus act," Joey comments as a particularly large crowd forms to watch the show. "People would pay good money to see this."

"Perhaps you'll become a famous breeder of herding poodles, eventually training some to move large gaggles of toddlers through preschools. Now thar's a business!" says Hayden. "And just wait until I get Rosie to teach them the Stations of the Cross. We're going straight to the Vatican."

"I've decided that I want to be a subway conductor," says Joey. Hayden has recently introduced his grandson to the boyish pleasure of riding in the front car and watching for the signals to change from red to green as they hurtle through the dark twisting underground tunnels.

Upon completing his duck march on this particular day Hayden checks to make sure that Diana has left for work. When he's sure that his daughter is gone, he takes Joey over to Mrs. Trummel's for the self-defense lessons he organized with her daughter who works as a local police officer. Once Joey is set up next door he tells Rosamond that he's off to see an old colleague. When Rosamond offers to accompany Hayden he insists that it's better he go alone since his friend is getting senile and the daughter doesn't think it's a good idea to bring any strangers along as it might upset the man. Hayden is a good liar but not that good. Rosamond can't help but wonder if it's a woman friend whom Hayden is going to visit, since it's rare that he ventures off without her.

Hayden quickly heads over to the cemetery sculpture garden for a pre-arranged meeting with Hank. "Well," he demands, "what in tarnation went awry?"

"*Nothing,*" says Hank. "I mean, Diana doesn't like me."

"Why do you say that? Did you make a pass at her? Not that such a move should cause a problem, from what I gather."

"*No!* I kissed her good night. Just one kiss."

"That's all?"

"Heck, Hayden, it sounds as if you want me to throw her over my shoulder and carry her up to the bedroom."

"Probably not a bad idea. Diana's a very romantic girl from what I understand—probably has a bunch of kids out there that she do'an' even know about."

Hank appears startled until he realizes that Hayden is joking.

They sit on a bench next to the garden and the sprinkler makes a sputtering noise as it starts up and they both laugh, recalling the circumstances of their earlier visit to this spot.

"You must not ha' kissed her right," Hayden eventually says.

"Oh shut up! What do you know about women—stealing virgins out of convents!"

"I'll have you know that nothing untoward has passed between the lady and myself. Besides, I refuse to kiss a woman who can catch more fish than I," Hayden declares with pride. "But to answer your question, I do'an' know anything about women. However, I do know someone who does. Come with me."

chapter forty-two

Diana arrives home from the grocery store to the plaintive strains of Dan Hill's "Sometimes When We Touch" coming from inside the house, quite the contrast to Hayden's Highland reels and spirited Scottish folk songs. She finds Rosamond alone in the dining room intent on polishing all the silverware and a tea set. This is the one domestic chore where Rosamond far outshines Diana. Apparently the convent has a trove of urns and crosses that are in constant need of buffing.

"You don't have to do that," says Diana. But then she notices the tears like pear-shaped diamonds sparkling on her friend's cheeks. "Rosamond, what's wrong? Are you ill?"

Rosamond sets down her rag and dabs her face with a clean paper towel. "No, no, it must be an allergy to the silver polish."

The sound of the front door opening can be heard and Joey enters the dining room, having arrived back from his lessons at Mrs. Trummel's. Though he dutifully reports that he was using the swimming pool at the Y, just as Hayden had instructed him to. One needn't be a mind reader to know that Diana wouldn't approve of lessons in how to fight.

Joey notices that Rosamond is wiping what appear to be tears from her eyes. "Do you want an ice cream float?" His voice fills with concern. "I have some Pop Rocks we could mix in and make it explode." Some days it's just too much to consider that his two best friends in the world are condemned to death for reasons he doesn't entirely understand. How can God allow good people to get cancer?

"Thanks, sweetheart. A glass of water would be nice. To be honest, I don't know what's wrong with me." Rosamond looks up at Diana and Joey and continues with forced cheer, "Just feeling a bit weepy, I guess."

Joey goes to the kitchen and pours Rosamond a glass of water and drops in a few maraschino cherries in an effort to raise her spirits. He reasons that if she's unhappy then she might leave, and that would be a disaster. Hayden would return to his funerals and suicide manuals and Diana would have more time on her hands to monitor Joey's pulse and blood pressure. And worst of all, it'd be the end of their fishing trips and future plans to go camping in the Adirondacks.

Meanwhile, the ever-suspicious Diana glances around the room as if she's looking for clues to a robbery. Her gaze settles on the portable radio in the corner that has been steadily wailing away and is now playing the Phil Collins hit song from the eighties "Against All Odds." Diana marches over and flicks off the radio. "I'll tell you exactly what's wrong. You're in love and you're sitting here by yourself inhaling toxic chemicals and listening to syrupy ballads on Lite FM."

"Lite FM?" Rosamond is apparently confused by the diagnosis.

Joey appears with the cherry-flavored water. His mother sends him back to the kitchen with orders to start unpacking the groceries. Then Diana heaves a great sigh, as if she just can't be responsible for catching up another woman on twenty years of romance. "Rosamond, there are only two situations when a woman should be listening to love songs on Lite FM, and one of them is when you're in a *reciprocated* romantic relationship, not pining."

"And what's the other?" asks Rosamond. Perhaps there was a category for distracted ex-nuns.

"The other," Diana pauses as if it's her ill-fated lot in life to have to be the bearer of bad news, "is after your boyfriend dumps you, or worse, sleeps with your best friend *without* first dumping you. And so you stock up on Mallomars and Rocky Road ice cream, pull the shades, get incredibly drunk, and play a continuous medley of Air Supply's 'All Out of Love,' Foreigner's 'I Want to Know What Love Is,' and right before you vomit or pass out start 'The Rose,' by Bette Midler."

Now that the radio is off Rosamond collects herself and takes a sip of the pink water. "I suppose you're right, ballads do seem to have an unusual effect on a person's soul, especially those bits about 'I can't live, I can't live without you baby.' No wonder the convent only sanctions madrigals from the sixteenth and seventeenth centuries. And even that was without harmony or accompaniment."

But what about love? Rosamond wonders what's been holding her back since admitting to herself that she's in love with Hayden. Perhaps being in love is the pursuit of pleasure for one's own gratification, and therefore the same as self-love, and thus exactly what she's been trained to guard against ever since taking her vows.

"You know, I could talk to Dad," offers Diana. "The two of you are acting like teenagers a month before the prom—you agonizing over whether or not he'll ask, and him worrying that you'll say no. In fact, Dad's so distracted that yesterday he was checking under the hood and almost poured oil where the antifreeze goes. Fortunately Joey stopped him."

"He's just fretting about The Cancer, that's all."

"Rosamond, I'll tell you a little secret. You know that song Dad is always humming?"

"He's always singing one song or another."

Diana softly sings, *"Kiss me each morning . . . if it don't work out, then you can tell me good-bye."*

Rosamond nods to indicate that she indeed recognizes the melody, though she's never before heard the words.

"I haven't heard Dad sing that since before Mom died. He used to do this imitation of a famous sixties crooner Mom adored named Eddie Arnold. Dad could copy his smooth American accent perfectly and it made her laugh like crazy." Diana smiles as she thinks back to her mother's reassuring presence, and briefly notes that she should try to relax and stop worrying all the time, or else she, too, is going to have heart trouble. The first thing her mother had taught her about art was that you couldn't always control every element—light, mood, space, hue—and thus after a certain point had to let go so the work could chart its own course. And when Diana was frantic with despair while in the throes of her first crush, at age six, her mother had said the same thing about love.

"Anyhow," Diana continues. "How about I tell him that I spoke with you and—"

"Oh no." Rosamond's delicate hands flutter up to her face. "I mean, I'd be mortified. I wouldn't know what to do. I'll just pray." She suddenly feels startled and overly warm, similar to when she awakes from the nightmares in which the men in red jumpsuits are attacking her.

"Suit yourself, as my mother used to say." Then Diana realizes this probably isn't the best time to keep raising the subject of Hayden's departed wife. And sure enough, Rosamond visibly blanches. Diana immediately drops the subject. "Why don't you come into the kitchen and I'll show you how to make poached salmon with chive mayonnaise sauce and a nice plum pudding?"

What am I doing trying to act as a matchmaker between my dying father and a dying nun anyway, Diana asks herself. Hayden isn't going to try those treatments, not for anyone. And furthermore, since when have any of my romantic couplings ever met with success?

chapter forty-three

At the same time that Rosamond and Diana are talking together inside the town house, Hayden and Hank are locked in a heated argument at the end of Bobbie Anne's driveway. Both men gesticulate wildly but are careful to keep their voices barely audible so that to anyone passing by it appears as if they're engaged in an intense pantomime that at any moment will call for one to strike the other with an oversized plastic bat.

"I've fixed everything," Hayden reassures his new friend. "She understands you need a tune-up so that you can get back into the courtship game on the level of a seasoned professional."

Hank has a miserable expression on his face. "I don't need any love doctor, and certainly not a . . . a . . ."

"*Do'an'* say it. She's a friend of mine. Just go in and meet her," he urges, his brogue swelling. "You do'an' have to stay if she isn't to your likin'. Maybe you just do'an' fancy women," Hayden goads Hank. "It's nothin' to be ashamed of."

"Oh shut up! I do so fancy women. I'll talk to her but I'm not going to *do* anything with her." He's vowed not to be another victim of all Hayden's pent-up salesmanship that is currently without an outlet. How the business-savvy Mormons had failed to engage Hayden as a missionary would forever remain a mystery.

Hayden pushes a reluctant Hank toward the front walk.

"Isn't there another way?" asks Hank.

"Sure. You can go off and date women for ten years and come back, but Diana will be long off the market by then. I had the electrician in for fifteen minutes last week and he sent her roses and calls practically every night after dinner."

"If only she didn't know that I'd been training to become a priest. If only I'd moved here from somewhere else as a regular guy . . ."

"Well, not even Jesus was a success in his hometown, but a few years later he was their big claim to fame. So just stick with the program here."

Hank approaches the front door as if headed for his own crucifixion.

Bobbie Anne is waiting just inside and greets him sweetly. "Hey y'all. Come on in. Hayden has told me so much about you."

Hank isn't sure if that's good or bad. "Let me be honest with you and say that I think this is the dumbest thing I've ever heard of." He glances back through the screen door and spies a satisfied-looking Hayden standing at the end of the driveway with his arms folded victoriously over his chest. "And as soon as *he* leaves, *I'm* leaving." With a swat of his hand Hank motions for Hayden to get going. But Hayden gives a friendly wave back as if he's saying hello from the deck of a cruise ship.

"I see," says Bobbie Anne diplomatically. "Then why don't you at least have a glass of iced tea." She turns and goes into the dining room without turning to find out if he's following.

Hank does follow. He's mesmerized by the sound of her voice, which has a peculiarly engaging quality. It's deep and a little husky and he can hear the breath vibrating behind it as if every word seems to come right out of her heart.

Bobbie Anne pulls out a chair for him at the dining room table. "I'll tell you what, why don't I give you a quick little quiz and if you pass then we'll just inform Hayden you're an expert on women and there isn't another thing that I could possibly tell you."

But Hank's soft brown eyes widen as visions of what a "love test" might include dance in his imagination. "That'll probably be faster than waiting for him to leave."

"We'll start with the oral part," she continues.

His look of alarm at the word *oral* registers with Bobbie Anne.

"I mean that I'll ask you a few questions," she clarifies.

"Oh, sure." Hank attempts to convey a confidence he's far from feeling. "Fire away."

She pours them both a glass of iced tea and sits down next to him at the table.

"How old are you, then? Mid twenties?"

"Thirty-one, actually," he replies tersely. It aggravates Hank to no end that he still can't buy beer without being asked for ID.

"Question one. A woman can get pregnant the day after her period, the day before, or for a few days somewhere in-between?"

"The day before."

"Wrong. In-between."

He gives her a dismissive look that says, "Yeah, whatever."

"Okay," Bobbie Anne continues, "let's say you want to talk to a woman about seeing her exclusively and having sex without condoms. What medical information should you bring with you?"

"I don't know," he answers irritably. "A breathing strip so I won't snore?"

"Results from an AIDS test," says Bobbie Anne.

"I don't need an AIDS test! I've been celibate for the last five years."

"Of course you need an AIDS test. And besides, it shows that you care. Next question. A woman's breasts are least sensitive during her menstrual cycle because all the blood flows away from that area. True or false?"

"True."

"False." Her red-gold ponytail swings behind her neck like a whip of fire as if to reinforce his blunder.

"That's a trick question!"

Bobbie Anne ignores him. "Last question. If you're kissing a woman and things are heading toward making love and she informs you that she's bleeding, the correct answer is: (A) let me know when you're finished and I'll come back; (B) can you temporarily stop it? or (C) why don't we just get a towel?"

Hank has a look of horror on his face. "Come back later?" he guesses.

"Hank, the female cycle is the life force. I would think that having studied for the priesthood you would have a greater appreciation for that particular miracle."

"These are all trick questions," mutters the aggravated young man. How did he ever let himself get involved in all of this insanity? He should stay in the Church. When you don't have an answer you say that everything happens for a reason and then you pray with the person.

Bobbie Anne is getting ready to admit the situation is hopeless. "Hank, how many openings does a women have down there?"

"Two."

"Three."

He pushes his chair back and abruptly rises. "I don't see why I need to know all this women's stuff."

"Hank, if you have a shiny new truck but you don't know where to put the gas and oil or where the ignition is, how are you going take care of it? Or even drive it for that matter? And furthermore, how do you think *you* got here?" asks Bobbie Anne, now starting to sound somewhat annoyed herself. "The woman's body is the fount of reproduction, don't you see? We're talking about the pope-sanctioned act of procreation. Women often feel extremely sexy when they're ovulating or right before or during their periods."

Every time she utters the word *ovulation* or *period* he flinches as if swallowing battery acid.

"Okay, you're free to go!" She abruptly rises and pushes the two hundred dollars back across the table, picks up their empty glasses, and strolls toward the kitchen.

"No, wait a second. Come back."

She turns in the doorway. "Why? I can't teach you anything."

"Sure, you can. I'm sorry," he apologizes. "I want to know how the engine works, honest I do. It's just that I had sex with a lot of girls in college and it went okay."

"That's because it was sex. And you were a boy and they were girls. Hank, we're talking about *making love* . . . to a *woman*. And if you have Diana in your sights, she's a thirty-five-year-old woman with a capital *W*—"

"Yeah, that's what I need—lessons in . . . women . . . Diana . . ." he trails off pensively.

"I can't help you unless you have some innate ability. So I'll have to evaluate your performance."

He looks uncertain. Does she mean what he thinks she means?

She approaches him and in her sumptuous alto voice says, "Kiss me, Hank."

They kiss for a moment and then Bobbie Anne steps back, pauses, and appears to be carefully critiquing a soufflé that she's just tasted.

"Too much interior lip," she says. "Don't start with the tongue so fast. And when you do, move it slowly and gently, not like a harpoon. You're not fifteen anymore. Now try again. Think of Diana as a fine wine."

"And what am I?" Hank asks playfully, his earlier anger and embarrassment having slightly subsided. "Root beer?"

Bobbie Anne also relaxes now that Hank has let down his guard. "More like a slushie."

Hank laughs and pulls her to him in an appreciative hug. They kiss a while longer and this time when they part Bobbie Anne smiles at him.

"Mmm, very nice." Meanwhile Hank takes a deep breath as if trying to shrug off any arousal he felt from the kiss.

"Now this time, after we've been kissing for a few minutes, I want you to begin caressing me."

He takes a shaky breath and says, "Right, caressing," trying to sound matter-of-fact, as if he's reading a manual.

After they kiss and embrace for a few more minutes Bobbie Anne can feel his hard cock pushing through his jeans against her waist and decides it's a good time to break for an appraisal. "That's fine, Hank. But you need to have a plan when you're caressing."

"What kind of a plan?"

"Did you ever play Battleship or Stratego when you were a kid?"

"Sure, all the time, with my brothers."

"Well, the winner usually had a system of covering the board, right? Those who guessed haphazardly usually lost unless they got lucky. Same thing with making love. Start in one place, like the hips, and then slowly work your way to the breasts and neck."

"Got it. Have a plan. Like putting up a building. No random fondling."

Once again she puts her hands on his waist. "I have to be honest with you, Hank."

"Yes?" He's clearly worried.

"I can tell that you'll be a magnificent lover. But I wonder, do you want to continue? I mean, you paid for it, and I'm more than willing."

"Oh, yes. I mean, thank you. I mean, no . . . no, I don't think I'd better."

"I didn't think so. You're in love with her, aren't you?"

"Yes, I suppose so," he admits shyly.

Bobbie Anne slides her hands off his waist. "That's sweet," she says sincerely. Then she points down the corridor. "The bathroom is down that hall."

An hour later Hayden leaps out from behind the side of the house the moment Hank emerges.

"Darn Hayden, you scared me!" says Hank. "Have you been here the entire time?"

"She's incredible, right?" Hayden winks at him.

"She's very nice," Hank says matter-of-factly. "And knowledgeable."

"Did she . . . you know, did you give her a climax?" Hayden is still curious if Bobbie Anne really experienced an orgasm with him or just faked it to be polite.

"She showed me what I needed to know."

"And what was that, exactly?"

"That's for me to know and Diana to find out."

He gives it one last try. "Bobbie Anne's a very stimulating woman, if you know what I mean." His brogue strengthens.

"*You* made love to her?" Hank looks astonished.

Hayden gives him a smug smile in return. "Let's just say the very thought of it brings a tear to me eye . . ."

chapter Forty-Four

On the way out of the house in the morning, Diana finds Hayden busy at the dining room table, one hand on the phone, the other flipping through the Yellow Pages and scribbling what Diana sees are the names and numbers of doctors onto a notepad.

Hoping against hope that Rosamond has indeed changed Hayden's mind about trying the experimental cancer therapy, Diana attempts to sound nonchalant. "Is that list for Rosamond?"

She's even more pleased when Hayden, annoyed by the distraction adds, " 'Tis for the both of us. What did you think, it's a hit list for your friend Anthony?"

"Oh, Dad!" Diana gives him a big kiss on the forehead before she leaves. "Rosamond's been such a good influence on you."

"Me influence your father?" Rosamond says as she comes through the archway from the kitchen carrying two cups of coffee. "That'll be the day."

Diana is in a hurry to get to work early and doesn't have time to talk. She simply kisses Rosamond on the cheek and says under her breath, "Call me at the office if there's any news."

As she watches Diana leave the house, Rosamond wonders what kind of news Diana is after. Sitting down at the table she takes a sip of hot coffee in an effort to fully wake up and only then gets a look at Hayden's latest research project.

"We have to start seeing doctors today," Hayden announces as he rips his list in half and hands the top portion to Rosamond. "You call and make appointments with these four."

She takes the paper from him and looks skeptical.

"Don't worry, yours are all women," he assures her. "I thought you might feel funny about men, you know . . ."

"Hayden, I don't understand . . . I thought we'd decided to go out naturally—no chemotherapy, ginseng cures, or experimental drugs."

"Exactly! And I just realized that we do'an' have any pills for you. Cyrus only gave me enough for one person."

"What pills?"

"For our suicides, o' course."

Rosamond looks at him with horror. Hayden has often discussed how he refuses to put himself in the hands of life-extending physicians, but she wasn't aware that he is actually planning to kill himself. She drops the list onto the table as if it's poison.

"But Hayden," she stammers, "that's a sin."

"A sin! 'Tis a sin to be charged five thousand dollars a day to be kept alive by machines in a hospital. 'Tis a sin to lose all your dignity and have the family change your diapers and wipe the drool from your chin." Hayden slams the phone book closed and marches into the kitchen.

As Rosamond hears the clink of the whiskey bottle and a glass tumbler being removed from the cabinet she begins to weep. Her tears make round stains on the Yellow Pages and she doesn't know if they're for death, God, man himself, or for a particular man. Her life was so much less confusing when there were rules for everything—how to wake, think, walk, communicate, and even how to eat your soup. There were of course rules on how to die, but suicide was definitely not among them. Only she doesn't know what or whom to believe anymore, or what to decide, not about how to live, and certainly not about how to die.

Hearing her sobs Hayden returns to the dining room but anxiously paces back and forth while searching for words. He was a natural joker and thus at his worst and most impatient when confronted with other people's grief. "Listen Rosie, I know we're at opposite ends of the spectrum on the religion thing, but there just isn't time. I'm not feelin' all that well these days and I'm probably goin' to strike bedrock first. Do you want them to hook you up to a machine for three weeks, or worse, three months? I mean, I respect your beliefs, honest I do, but will you try to have an open mind? You've got to stop worrying about the hereafter and start concentrating on the here and now."

Rosamond wipes away her tears with a napkin. "How do you mean?"

"Well, for starters, can you show me any proof that this God of yours exists?"

"Of course I can, Hayden—there are miracles all around us. Just look at the grass and the trees and all the babies being born . . ." In her fervor to persuade him, she's stopped crying.

"Okay, if I promise to go out and take a good look at the vegetation and whatever else you want then will you come and look at my proof?"

"As long as you're not going to try and take me to the morgue again." She visibly shudders at the memory of that particular educational adventure.

"No, no. I just want to show you that people make up all these gods and fables as a way of explainin' what they do'an' understand. It's a damn business is what it is. And people like the idea of all that hocus-pocus. That way they do'an' have to think for themselves."

"Fine," she agrees. "And I'll prove to you the power of faith."

The two shake hands as if concluding a business deal.

Hayden mysteriously claims that he can't divulge his proof for another two days and so she should go first. Rosamond takes him to the nearby church where Hank had his internship. It's an imposing sandstone edifice with a barrel-vaulted ceiling and copper dome-shaped roof resting on a circular drum that is surrounded by stained-glass windows. There's a Latin cross at the top and twenty-four saints carved onto the outside walls.

Hayden and Rosamond enter through richly decorated double doors and pass ornamental panels depicting popular sacred stories such as the angel appearing to Mary, the birth of Jesus, and the Last Supper. Glass-and-wrought-iron light fixtures are strung from the ceiling with long black chains. On the back wall is a large tapestry depicting Jesus being crucified at Calvary and shaking his head "no" at the offer of an opiate to dull the pain.

Several people kneel in the darkened sanctuary and pray. A few more sit in quiet contemplation and one or two nap, escaping the hot, humid summer air outside. Midway down the side aisles is a mahogany shrine containing burned-down votive candles and vases of wilted flowers. Above them is a mural depicting Saint Teresa of Avila's recurring visions. In the center an angel lifts her habit and thrusts a golden spear toward her heart as Teresa appears to swoon, both powerless and welcoming.

Rosamond's gaze easily rests on the crucifix above the altar, with its suffering, bleeding, life-sized Christ. She contemplates how her illness has taken her so far from Him, rather than so much closer, as suffering should, and how in many ways it's a relief. And yet she misses the daily marathon of striving for perfection, the joy of always reaching but never realizing such a lofty goal.

Meanwhile, Hayden stares up at the elaborate panels of stained-glass windows, fascinated by their ability to filter one ray of pure light from the sun into so many different colors, all splashed across the marble floor as if it were the work of a kaleidoscope. He's not overwhelmed by the religious splendor of it all so much as the architectural majesty, the phenomenal fight human beings appear willing to wage against the unpleasant notion of being temporary. And that they'll go to such incredible lengths to create an afterlife for themselves, complete with expensive monuments and paid clergymen.

There are certainly many reasons Hayden doesn't want to die—the exhilaration of being with his family and friends, especially the uproarious fun he has with the Greyfriars; the chance to see Joey graduate from high school, and hopefully college; Diana settling down with a decent bloke like Hank.

And Hayden is curious about the future of the world as well, what his beloved Brooklyn will be like in fifty years, and if there will be a woman president by then. And if so, he prays that she will have beaten out his son-in-law to win the election. No, he doesn't wish to die. At the same time, he can't accept the idea that a free trip to heaven awaits him and that the Church has the tickets, that there is anything other than eternal nothingness. He's resigned himself to the belief that the best a person can do is to make one's life worth dying for. And of course support the spirits industry in accordance with one's means. On those two counts, he's satisfied that he's done both to the best of his ability.

While Rosamond and Hayden stand in front of the life-sized depiction of the crucifixion she takes his hand, leans over, and whispers to him, " 'For God so loved the world, that he gave his only begotten Son, that whosoever believeth in Him should not perish, but have everlasting life.' John, the Apostle."

Hayden whispers back, " 'I have made a ceaseless effort not to ridicule, not to bewail, not to scorn human actions, but to understand them.' Baruch Spinoza, the *Scientist*."

But Rosamond only turns and starts to walk away.

And she is right, in her own way, thinks Hayden. Because the Church will stand tall longer than all the philosophers. It will stand much longer than the two of them. Hayden looks up at the forlorn Jesus. "Tell me about it," he says to the figure nailed to the cross. "I believe I'm in love with her."

From a few feet away Rosamond hears Hayden's distinctive voice but when she turns she's surprised because it appears that Hayden's talking not to her but to Jesus. And she's encouraged that perhaps he's finally coming 'round to her way of thinking after all.

chapter Forty-Five

For Joey's twelfth birthday a celebratory lunch has been planned. Hayden and Diana try to make the day as festive as possible in an effort to gloss over the fact that Joey doesn't have any friends in the neighborhood and that his father broke his promise about fishing. Diana had tried to round up some boys from their old neighborhood but they were all away at summer camp.

Undaunted, Diana runs blue, white, and orange streamers in honor of the Mets from the chandelier in the dining room and makes Joey's favorite foods: fried chicken, french fries, and chocolate ice cream cake. She presents him with a new computer to replace the one that Tony never brought back, and a gift certificate to buy some games for it. Rosamond puts a big red bow around Ginger's neck and she and Hayden give Joey a brand-new aluminum bat and a baseball autographed by the famous Cincinnati Reds catcher Johnny Bench, one of his idols.

They sing "Happy Birthday" and Joey blows out all the candles. Rosamond adds a verse of "May the Good Lord Bless You" for good measure. Hayden disappears into the kitchen for a moment and when he returns it's with a goblet of white wine in his hand.

"Dad," says Diana, "it's not even one o'clock yet."

Rosamond looks at him as if she agrees with Diana.

"It's only water," Hayden casually lies.

Diana leans over and sniffs at the top of the glass. "It's white wine!"

Hayden pretends to look utterly taken aback. "Good Lord, He's done it again!"

They can't help but laugh at Hayden's dramatic double take.

Diana worries about Joey using such a large knife to cut the ice cream cake. Since it's still partially frozen one slip would be enough to take off his entire hand. However, Hayden is pleased to observe that the lad uses a tall glass of hot water to warm the knife before cutting and manages to put his mother's fears to rest with aplomb.

After lunch Hayden sits on the living room couch fingering his nametag for the yearly convention of the Metro Mutual Insurance group while Joey oils his mitt. Though Hayden is still a member, as a retiree the color of his badge has been switched from gold to green. He feels old and worn, like the faded brown couch on which he sits, the first piece of furniture he and Mary had so excitedly purchased after moving out of her parents' home all those years ago.

"Are you still worrying about the color of your nametag?" asks Diana as she passes through with a basket of clean laundry. "It's just a color, for goodness sake. Green is the color of money and so it's in honor of how successful you've been."

"Green is for grass, as in being put out to pasture."

"And you still won't accept the Lifetime Achievement award?" asks Diana.

"Lifetime Achievement award!" exclaims Hayden. "Ha! They should just call it what it is: the You're the Next to Die award."

"It's an honor."

"I don't need honors. When Edward VII of England offered Andrew Carnegie a title he refused it." Hayden turns to Joey. "Isn't that right, Joey? What did the great Scotsman Andrew Carnegie build throughout the land?"

"Libraries!" says Joey.

Hayden pulls his grandson close and hugs him. "That's right," he says with great pride. "*Free* libraries!"

"Please take me with you to the conference, Grandpa," begs Joey. "I want to go fire walking." Joey's been searching for ways to appear heroic in front of Rosamond, and often fantasizes that he rescues her from some great danger, such as an avalanche where he throws his body over hers, or else fends off an escaped zoo lion that has climbed into her bedroom.

"Over my dead body!" Diana warns the two of them in boldface type from the stairwell.

"I think it's possible to do away with the aerial on the roof if we can just hoist one of your ears up there instead," Hayden retorts loudly enough so his daughter will hear. "Listen Joe-Joe, at this shindig there's going to be alcohol and rock music and insurance agents—all three instruments of the devil. And the fire walking isn't a carnival event, it's part of a motivational program to help improve sales."

"But Mom's going out with that priest guy and she's going to hire a *baby-sitter*. I'm too old for a baby-sitter! Rosie's going, and she's my friend, too!" Did he have to remind his grandfather that they met Rosamond on the same day? And if Joey hadn't suggested going to the game farm instead of Hayden's funerals they may never have seen her again. They can't just leave him behind. It's not fair!

When Rosamond and Hayden are ready to leave for the convention, Diana has also just finished preparing to go out for the evening. She looks captivating in a sleek-fitting red crepe dress with spaghetti straps, a black pearl necklace, and black high-heeled evening sandals. With silver shadow highlighting the lids, Diana's vibrant green-gray eyes shine like moonlight bouncing off a dark sea. And yet there's something tender about the way she checks herself in the mirror, unsure that any man could possibly be interested in her. As much as Hayden never again wants his darling daughter to know heartache, he has to admit that it will also be a crime if she doesn't love and experience love in return.

"Hot date tonight?" Hayden teases her as he tries to imagine what he would think if this woman was not his daughter and he just happened to run into her walking down the street. But the idea is enough to make him consider hiring a bodyguard and so he quickly dismisses it from his mind.

"Oh, just dinner with Hank."

Hayden can easily deduce that she's faking her nonchalance and is actually somewhat nervous. Just like he could always tell which customers were lying about having found a better rate elsewhere and pretending to consider canceling their policies with him. "But I thought he wasn't your type?"

"I'm giving him one more chance," she says as if she's doing Hank a big favor. The truth is that Diana enjoyed Hank's conversation and sense of humor. His awkward fumbling and shyness were rather sweet, too. But the kissing . . . ugh, she doesn't know what to do about that. Maybe they'll have to settle for just being friends, like Rosamond and Hayden appear to have done. Yet she still rises to Hank's defense. "He said that last time we went out he'd taken too many antihistamines and wasn't himself."

"Aye, the Drixoral Defense," says Hayden. "Well I do'an' like him one bit. He's probably after your fortune." Over the years Hayden had noticed that whenever he and Mary indicated that they approved of a particular boy, Diana immediately broke off with him, and so he isn't about to make the same tactical error now.

"Dad, I don't have any fortune. I owe $1,246 to Visa."

"Looks to me like he could be another layabout."

"For your information, Hank's uncle got him a job at an architectural firm in Manhattan. It's just entry-level, but he'll be able to finish school and get experience at the same time. In fact, he's taking me to Gage & Tollner in order to celebrate." The legendary eatery with its gaslight, mahogany tables, and polished nineteenth-century mirrors was a Brooklyn institution and favorite for romantic occasions such as engagements and anniversaries.

Rosamond and Hayden say good-bye to Diana and then go and wait at the end of the street until they see the baby-sitter arrive. Shortly after that Hank's battered Dodge Omni churns up the road and pulls into the driveway. Hayden crosses his fingers as he strains to see through the leafy trees and catch a glimpse of what's transpiring in the driveway.

"Stop spying on them," says Rosamond.

"Last time he honked the horn as if he was expecting Diana to run out the door like she was a waitress at a drive-in. I had a word with him about that."

Rosamond joins Hayden and together they watch as a smartly dressed Hank escorts Diana down the front steps and opens the car door for her. When the Dodge has disappeared from view Hayden waits another few minutes and then doubles back to the town house. While Rosamond waits in the car Hayden goes inside, hands the baby-sitter thirty dollars and in a thick, cheery brogue explains that his meeting was canceled and he's decided to spend some quality time with his grandson, take him to see the new Disney movie and so on and so forth. Hayden is pleased that she's not the least bit suspicious about this sudden change in plans and for a split second regrets retiring. Nothing is quite so exhilarating as the moment a deal is sealed and the money actually changes hands.

Hayden, Rosamond, and Joey drive across the Williamsburg Bridge and into New York City. Joey insists that Rosamond sit in the back so they can compete on his Gameboy. When he first introduced Rosamond to video games she hesitated before gathering the courage to blow up the monsters and space aliens. But she's quickly evolved into a swift and coldhearted killer with lightning reflexes, every annihilation only whetting her appetite for more destruction, and Joey must concentrate hard to win.

When they reach Sixth Avenue Hayden points out the tall chrome-and-glass building where he worked for ten years before moving to the Brooklyn office. He parks the car in a garage over near the West Side Highway since it's cheaper than the prime real estate of Midtown. As they make their way back toward the hotel a wind from the west whips the trash into small twisters that rise in the caverns between the soaring skyscrapers.

Hayden nods toward a homeless man who has reinvented himself as an anger management consultant, sitting on a camp chair with a sign at his feet saying TELL ME OFF FOR $5. A line of five men and one young woman impatiently wait their turn.

"It must have been a lousy day for the stock market," quips Hayden.

As always, Rosamond is fascinated by the more unusual sights and sounds of Manhattan—the performance artist dressed as the Statue of Liberty and the man outfitted in aluminum foil telling people he's collecting money to repair his spaceship. Meanwhile, Joey is particularly enthralled by the rumpled Tell Me Off man. For a few minutes the three stop to enjoy the show.

"Most people pretend he's their boss," explains Hayden. "But a lot of women yell at him as if he's their unfaithful boyfriend, lazy husband, or son who never calls."

When the businessman currently shouting at the Tell Me Off man finishes his tirade with "You can't fire me because I quit!" the remainder of the line along with the ring of assembled spectators gives him a big round of applause. The customer happily places a five-dollar bill in the cup and with a spring in his step melts into the pedestrian traffic.

"It's just the opposite of confession," says an astonished Rosamond. "You say what you really want to instead of telling the priest what you think he'd like to hear."

"I thought confession was the same thing as pleading guilty," says Hayden. "All I know is that whenever there's a big layoff or interest rates go up this guy has a line around the block."

"But he isn't giving them any penance or advice in return," observes Rosamond.

"Maybe they do'an' want advice. Isn't that the definition of suicide— telling God 'You can't fire me because I quit'?"

Rosamond gives him a sharp jab in the side with her elbow at the mention of suicide. She had assumed that subject was off-limits for the time being.

"C'mon, Grandpa, the fire walk!" Joey tugs at his grandfather's sleeve.

Rosamond often tells Joey how smart he is. And now he'll have a chance to prove his bravery, just like the noble knight Lochinvar.

The trio cross Seventh Avenue to the city-block–sized hotel where the yearly convention is held. Cadres of uniformed bellhops dash around the entrances, navigating taxi cabs in various stages of loading and unloading towers of luggage. Businessmen and airline employees are heading into the hotel after a long day of work while tourists gripping maps and theater tickets are coming out of the revolving door dressed for a night on the town.

"Okay," announces Hayden, "I'm ready to make my case!"

Once inside the hotel, Hayden busily works the ballroom and introduces Rosamond and Joey to some of his old cronies. His pals know him well enough not to ask questions about his health, and instead rattle off all the latest industry jokes. A man who had started as Hayden's assistant makes a beeline for him and begins shouting while he's still several feet away. "Hey, Hayden, know why sex is like life insurance? The older you get the more it costs."

"Hey, Micky," retorts Hayden, doing a perfect imitation of Micky's thick New York accent. "Did you hear about the guy on Long Island who I told to take out hurricane insurance? He says to me, 'Now how do you start a hurricane?'"

Hayden's tremendous magnetism attracts people like insects to a bright light. Rosamond and Joey are amazed at how the air around them seems electrified as they become the epicenter of the crowded room. And though it's obvious that many old friends are momentarily taken aback by the visible decline in Hayden's health, no one appears to make an effort to avoid him. When he walks to the bar the throng seems to glide right along with him like iron filings in pursuit of a magnet.

One of Hayden's former colleagues makes polite conversation with Rosamond and Joey until Hayden saunters back with two Cokes for them and a generous serving of scotch for himself. "I hope you didn't sign your name to anything," warns Hayden. "This man's so crooked he'd steal the dimes off a dead man's eyes."

A pleasant-looking woman in her forties with a heart-shaped face and stylishly arranged chestnut-colored hair maneuvers through the crowd until she's close enough to kiss him on the cheek. Hayden introduces the woman as Vivian, a former coworker in the Brooklyn office who had made the transition to Manhattan. "Rosie is just recently retired from the business," says Hayden. "She dealt in afterlife insurance."

Unlike the others Vivian inquires about his health. But he fobs off the question by jauntily replying, "I tried to get life insurance but they'll only give me fire and theft."

Hayden efficiently changes the subject by inviting Vivian to accompany them out to the courtyard for the big fire walk. As they make their way from the crowded ballroom, Vivian takes Hayden's hand in hers, which doesn't go unnoticed by Rosamond.

They haven't gone ten feet before another old buddy passes by, slaps Hayden on the back and announces, "It's crazy Haydy! Playing lots of golf? Off to Saint Andrews for a few rounds?" It's apparent that the man knows about Hayden's love for the country where he was born, but not about his illness.

"For me, you might want to think more along the lines of reincarnation than retirement," Hayden says and laughs heartily as they walk on.

"Grandpa, how come guys keep calling you crazy?" asks Joey. He's aware that his grandfather is lots of fun, all the neighbors say so, and that his mother is always yelling at him for one thing or another, but why do they think Hayden is crazy?

"No one ever tangles with a mad dog, Joey, always remember that," says Hayden. "It's only the tame and timid ones who get kicked around."

Outside in the courtyard a twelve-by-four-foot pit of steaming black and gray coals has been set up, surrounded by two layers of flaming logs. Glimmering stars silhouette the towering silver skyline and the surrounding air reeks of charcoal and lighter fluid. Against the smoky darkness the scene looks dramatically forbidding.

Most of the agents participating in the fire walk are doing so as a capstone to their daylong seminar on positive thinking. The motivational expert stands at the head of the burning pit and issues each participant final words of encouragement before shouting "Go!" Whereupon the individual scampers down the middle of the track as fast as possible while involuntarily hollering every time a foot alights atop the baking coals. Whenever someone reaches the end the crowd of spectators gives a big cheer. After catching their breath the insurance-peddling daredevils seem totally unharmed and thoroughly ecstatic.

"Are you really going to do the fire walk?" Vivian looks at Hayden with admiration as they stand in the burning glow and mop sweat from their brows with blue cocktail napkins that have "Metro Mutual" stamped on them in big gold letters.

"O' course I am. That's why we came!" Hayden sinks down on a nearby bench and begins removing his shoes and socks.

"Can I do the fire walk?" begs Joey, so accustomed to his mother saying no to everything that looks the least bit dangerous.

"Sure," says Hayden. "You can't get hurt as long as you keep moving. It's all a hoax really. That guy makes a fortune running these silly things." He nods toward the man sending everyone out onto the coals.

"Aren't you going?" Hayden asks Vivian.

"Are you kidding?" says Vivian. "There's no amount of liability insurance that would get me to walk over hot coals."

"C'mon. I'll bet you fifty dollars that you won't get burned." Hayden removes his wallet and lays two twenties and a ten on the table. However, Vivian just shakes her head "no" all the more vehemently.

"Are *you* going to do it?" Vivian turns to Rosamond.

"Absolutely." She certainly hadn't been planning on it. But with the flirtatious Vivian now cozying up to Hayden, and knowing how he detests cowards and admires women with "pluck," Rosamond acts as if it's been her plan to go all along. She moves brazenly between the two of them and sits down next to Hayden in order to remove her sandals.

When it's Hayden's turn to brave the blazing pit he disregards the peppy words of encouragement being proffered by the gatekeeper and lunges out across the coals, stopping just long enough in the middle to do a little jig and let out some whoops so that Rosamond can't be sure whether he's being burned alive or thoroughly enjoying himself.

Joey follows Hayden and runs a hard straight line through the smoldering furnace like a fox being chased by a hound so that it's questionable whether his small feet even touch the coals for more than a second.

Finally it's Rosamond's turn. The program leader calmly explains that if she believes in herself she won't get burned. Rosamond hesitates just long enough to cross herself and mouth a short prayer before walking hurriedly onto the steaming coals. She determines that if she makes it safely across she'll never doubt her faith again.

When all three have completed the trial-by-fire Hayden seems pleased with the results of his experiment. "Do you see now? It's all science! If you put your hands in a four-hundred-degree oven do they get burned? No! And if you touch a cake in that oven you do'an' get burned either. But if you touch the *metal*, whoa! Because that's what conducts the heat." He points to the fire walk. "Meanwhile, those coals do'an' conduct as much heat as a cupcake."

But Rosamond only stares at Hayden as if he's being completely ridiculous. "The reason I didn't get burned was because of the strength of my belief, just like the man in charge explained. You should have listened to him instead of running off like a madman."

"Oh, that's just a bunch of malarkey to pump the agents up to sell more insurance," Hayden mutters with his trademark cynicism.

But Rosamond is adamant. " 'With man this is impossible; but with God all things are possible.' The Gospel of Matthew 19:26."

Hayden quickly retorts, " 'The most common of all follies is to believe passionately in the palpably not true. It is the chief occupation of mankind.' The gospel of H. L. Mencken."

Rosamond counters, " 'In God have I put my trust: I will not be afraid what man can do unto me.' Psalms 56:11."

He throws up his hands in exasperation. "Well, if you still believe in God then *why ever* did you leave the convent?"

"I don't wish to discuss it." Rosamond sits down to put on her sandals. Fueled by envy, she wonders if now isn't the moment to take Diana's advice and just admit to Hayden how she feels. Only she cannot find the words or the courage to tell Hayden that the divine has become elusive. Just as she cannot complain to Him that love on earth is proving to be equally fraught and mysterious. And worse, now she'd furthered her slide down the slippery slope of sin by adding envy to the fast-growing list.

"So, Joey," asks Hayden, "what do *you* think of the fire walk? Science or God?"

"I think it's *really* cool," Joey says as he inspects the bottom of his right foot. "But either science or God gave me a blister."

"That's just because you do'an' have any calluses yet. You only get those from living."

chapter forty-seven

The next morning Rosamond hears a loud noise coming from the kitchen that sounds like an explosion, quickly followed by a woman's cry. She rushes downstairs to find Diana apparently covered in blood, along with the walls, counter, and floor. Meanwhile, the ceiling fan continues to fleck bits of red around the room and onto their hair and faces. Just as Rosamond is about to scream she sees the top of the juice machine on the floor, floating in a pool of chopped beets and sliced papaya.

Diana is so startled and mortified by the mess that she sounds as if she's in shock when like an automaton she states, "Beets are supposed to be excellent for detoxifying the liver. And papaya is good for lowering blood sugar."

When Rosamond realizes that her friend is unhurt and that it's bright red juice and not blood everywhere she begins to laugh.

Diana looks around at the spectacular mess, as if a kindergarten class had gone through with spray paint, and also concludes there's nothing to do but laugh. The women use paper towels to start mopping up the mess. However, it soon becomes clear that the walls and ceiling are permanently stained and will have to be repainted.

Once they get most of the juice off the floor Diana goes upstairs to change out of her stained bathrobe and Rosamond continues to wipe down the sink, table, and countertops. Hayden pops his head in for a cup of coffee and lets out a low whistle when he sees the red-splattered walls and ceiling. "Jaysus, it looks as if ye slaughtered sheep in here. Did I miss some sort of a sacrifice?"

Rosamond hands him a mug of coffee. "It's just beets and papaya. Now don't make a big fuss. Diana feels embarrassed enough as it is. Go herd your ducks and by the time you get back breakfast will be ready."

When Diana returns she asks about the insurance convention and Rosamond is careful not to make any mention of Joey having joined them. Rosamond heard Diana come in long after they'd all gone to bed.

"You didn't by any chance use the opportunity to tell Dad that you like him, did you?" asks Diana.

"Shhh!" says Rosamond and looks through the archway to see if anyone is coming. She hastily changes the subject. "Tell me about *your* date."

"What can I say?" Diana raises her arms above her head as if to suggest that there was divine intervention. "Hank is a *completely* different person. If I didn't know better, I'd think he was taking dating lessons." She laughs at the absurdity of this idea.

"Is that so?" says Rosamond. The surprise in her voice makes it clear that Hayden has done a good job of keeping his behind-the-scenes activities from both women. Though Rosamond wishes that Diana wasn't joking and someone truly did offer dating lessons. She'd be the first one to sign up.

"We were standing outside his apartment and when he asked me up, I said, 'I'd go upstairs with you, honest I would, but I'm at the end of my period.' " Diana takes the mixing bowl from Rosamond and demonstrates how to crush the lumps against the side of the metal bowl with the back of the wooden spoon. "You have to break these or the waffles will be lumpy." She hands the bowl back to Rosamond. "And you'll never believe what he said."

Far from worrying about believing what Hank said, Rosamond is so stunned that Diana is talking about going up to a man's apartment on the second date that she drops the wooden spoon into the waffle mix and has to clean it off in the sink.

But Diana doesn't notice her friend's discomfort and excitedly continues, "He ran his fingers up and down the small of my back and it felt soooo good and said, 'Oh, well, if you feel okay then why don't we just get a towel?' "

"You're kidding?" says Rosamond. "So then what did *you* say?"

"I was astonished. I mean, it's what you wish men would say, even if they don't really mean it, but of course they rarely do." Her face beams with pleasure. "So I said, 'Are you sure? I'd understand if you . . . ' but he stopped me, put his hands on my shoulders, looked directly into my eyes and said, 'Diana, your cycle represents the life force within us, one of the greatest miracles of all.' "

"Really?" says Rosamond, with obvious interest in the details. "And then what happened?"

"It was incredible. Next we—"

"I smell my favorite blueberry waffles!" Hayden strides into the kitchen tossing a baseball back and forth with Joey, who is wearing a baseball uniform and has his catcher's mitt on his left hand.

Diana shields her face with the bowl containing freshly cut cantaloupe, plum tomatoes, and crushed macadamia nuts, another recipe from her latest trip to the health food store. "Don't throw that thing in the house. You'll kill somebody."

"Looks like somebody already died," says Hayden. "I've been meaning to paint the kitchen anyway." He gives Diana a big kiss on the cheek to prove he's not angry and then nods toward the dark red splotches on the walls. "Though it would appear you've started without me."

"Cool!" says Joey. "It's like a crime scene."

"These waffles don't look very good." Rosamond appears worried as she oversees the waffle iron.

"The first two are always terrible, don't ask me why," explains Diana. "Just throw them away."

"Now what were you lassies just giggling about in here?" asks Hayden while ignoring Diana's pleas to stop tossing the baseball.

"None of your business," Diana replies and grabs the ball in midair. Then she runs her fingers through Joey's hair to inspect for signs of recent shampooing. "Joey, you're going to get head lice if you don't wash your hair. Now how many times do I have to remind you before it actually happens?"

"Eighteen to twenty," Joey replies matter-of-factly.

Diana twists his hair so that his head is forced to turn and face her. "Don't be a smart aleck."

"Ouch." He manages to slip out from under her. "I'm *not*. I counted. Eighteen to twenty is the average number of times you remind me between hair washings."

Before Diana can continue to argue Hayden rescues his grandson. "Do'an' think I didn't hear what time you came in last night," he teases her. "Honestly, I believe you're a bad influence on the boy."

"We watched *Dracula*," says Joey.

"*Dad*, will you stop showing Joey horror films. He's been sleeping with the light on!"

"Rosie's the one who looks like she didn't catch a wink," observes Hayden, the playfulness now dropping from his voice. As cavalier as Hayden is about disregarding his own illness, he doesn't seem to want to afford Rosamond the same consideration.

"Now that you mention it, you look more exhausted than Dad," Diana concurs. "Don't you feel well?"

"To be honest, I didn't sleep much. I kept having strange dreams and then waking up."

"Those horror movies are bad for your health, I'm convinced of it," Diana says in typical motherly fashion. "I was just reading a book by that natural healing doctor who is always on TV and—"

"I didn't watch the movie," says Rosamond. "I felt so tired that I turned in right after we got home. But I couldn't fall asleep for several hours."

"You should have come down and watched *Dracula*," says Joey. "I vant to suck your blood!" He raises his arms and bares his teeth in imitation of a vampire.

"The Reverend Mother always says that if you can't sleep then lie in bed and count your blessings."

Hayden catches Joey's eye and they have to stifle a laugh. Sometimes Rosamond sounds just like one of the spinster primary school teachers from Hayden's youth.

"Are you in any sort of pain?" Diana demands to know. She removes her yellow dish gloves and places her hand with the built-in thermometer up to Rosamond's forehead.

"I've been feeling all right, better really . . ."

"A person with The Lung Cancer is like a dog," Hayden chimes in.

"Beg your pardon?" asks Diana.

"They tend to linger. People with The Liver Cancer are like alley cats—fine one night and then poof." He snaps his fingers. "Next day as stiff as a board."

"*Dad!*" Diana exclaims sharply and then turns to Rosamond. "Is it being too presumptuous if I suggest you see a doctor? At the very least maybe he can give you something to sleep . . ."

"Sleeping pills?" shouts Hayden. "Why, I have enough Nembutal to knock out an entire—"

"No, thanks. I'm sure it will pass," says Rosamond. "I've had strange dreams before."

"Last week I had nightmares about giant snakes," offers Joey.

"That's because Grandpa let you watch *Anaconda*," says Diana.

"This time it was really just a dream . . . about a beach," continues Rosamond.

"Did you see *Jaws*?" asks Joey. "I had nightmares about man-eating sharks after that one."

Diana's eyes become wide and round until she's competing with her favorite actress, Bette Davis. She turns to Hayden with a look that says, "You
let him watch *Jaws*? I'm going to kill you before any cancer does!"

But Rosamond doesn't notice this visual exchange. "No, Joey. There
weren't any sharks in this dream. Though there's an ocean. I wake up on a
deserted beach—it's very beautiful, with turquoise water and a pale blue sky
and shimmering white sand. And there are signs of others—picnic baskets,
umbrellas, red-and-white-striped towels. Only they've all gone and I'm
alone waiting for them to come back . . ."

"I believe in dreams," Hayden firmly states.

"You don't believe in *anything*," scoffs Diana.

"That's not true," he corrects her while secretly pouring the prune juice
into the sink as soon as she turns around to take the milk out of the refrigerator. "I believe in sin."

Rosamond appears surprised. "You do not!"

"Yup. Only one though, Zephaniah 1:12."

"This is too much," says Rosamond. "You expect me to believe that
you've read the Bible. And on top of that, you believe in just *one* sin."

"Of course I've read the Bible," says Hayden. "You get stuck on Kodiak
Island for three weeks without electricity after selling liability insurance to
a logging company and that's about all there is to do. Unless you happen to
like hunting caribou, which I don't."

"You don't know Jesus from Adam," says Diana.

"Adam Smith happens to be a famous Scottish economist. So he and
Jesus were both in the business of teachin' people how to save," Hayden
shoots back at her. "Anyway, I believe in the sin of complacency—of not
acting upon your convictions. And I believe that dreams are your convictions rising to the surface from your subconscious."

"Then you've fooled me twice," says Rosamond. "I'd never have imagined that you, of all people, had ever opened a Bible. And if I knew that you
had, then I would have assumed your favorite line was in Genesis, where
Abram says to Lot, 'If you go to the left, I'll go to the right; if you go to the
right, I'll go to the left.' "

"Ha ha!" says Hayden. "I was attempting to be *see-rious*. You know, lead
me not into temptation. I can find my own way just fine, thank you."

"Dad, serious?" exclaims Diana. "It must really be getting near the end."

"Aha! You finally did it!" Hayden claps his hands. "You made a joke
about me dyin'! We're goin' to have to ice skate to the museum today since
I'm pretty sure that hell just froze over!" Hayden jumps up and practically

does a jig, but a sharp jab of pain in his gut quickly stops him and he doubles over. Rosamond helps him to sit back down.

After determining that he's all right Diana resumes the argument. "Dad, watch your language! And I *did not* make a joke."

"Did so," from Joey.

"Stop always siding with your grandfather," says Diana.

Hayden pours a cup of coffee and Diana scowls at the deadly liquid.

"I've never believed in astrology or dream analysis," muses Rosamond.

"Me neither," says Diana. "I never dream. I just think of all my favorite movie scenes until I fall asleep." She looks out the window and dramatically recites: " 'My love for you is the only malady I've contracted since the usual childhood diseases . . . and it's incurable.' "

They all turn to look at her as if she's losing her mind from inhaling too much Clorox, and Diana says, *"What?"* But it's obvious that she's embarrassed about having released this information about her sleeping habits. "It's what Clifton Webb said in *The Dark Corner*."

"I've never seen love and disease so inextricably linked in one human being," says Hayden.

"Well, this is definitely a dream and not anything from a movie," says Rosamond. "I've had this same vision in one form or another since I was a teenager. I wonder if it *does* mean something."

Hayden studies her. "You say it's a white sand beach with clear blue water?"

"Sparkling blue water, as if thousands of tiny sapphires are floating on the surface."

"Have you ever been to that beach?" asks Hayden. "Is it tucked away somewhere in your memory bank?"

"No, I don't think so. The coastline in Maine is mostly rocky and rugged. Once I visited my mother's family in Allentown, Pennsylvania, but there wasn't any water nearby. And that's as far south as I've ever been."

"Sounds like the Gulf of Mexico or the Caribbean," Hayden decides. "Was there a golf course? The Bahamas lay claim to some of the world's top-ranked golf courses."

"No golf courses that I could see. But there were seagulls. And on the blankets were some of those brightly colored drinks with wedges of fruit and paper umbrellas in them."

"I'll bet it's the Caribbean," Hayden affirms.

"Oh, Dad," Diana says dismissively. "It could be anywhere. It could be the southern tip of Africa for all we know. It's probably a scene out of a movie."

However, Rosamond is intrigued. "It's funny you should say the Caribbean because I remember red hibiscus surrounding the stone ruins of an old sugar mill."

"Maybe it's the alkahest!" Joey shouts with excitement. "And then you'll live forever!"

"Aha!" Hayden slams his hand down on the Formica-topped kitchen table so that Joey's now-empty plate jumps. An idea shoots through his mind like a meteor, its urgency made apparent by its very brightness.

Rosamond is becoming increasingly caught up in the excitement. "So what does it mean?"

Hayden hops up and paces like a restless zoo animal. "There's only one way to find out."

"What's that?" asks Rosamond.

"We'll go there!" proclaims Hayden. He has the fervent look of a convert about to be baptized.

"To the Caribbean?" Rosamond asks wide-eyed. "Together?"

Diana drops the pot she's scrubbing into the sink and it makes a loud clang.

chapter forty-eight

Of course together," Hayden continues, his voice now raw-edged with restlessness. "We'll go to Saint Croix."

"But Dad . . ." Diana says with alarm.

"But Hayden . . ." Rosamond concurs.

"Can I go, too?" pleads Joey.

"No, you may not!" Diana states firmly. "You begged me to play baseball. And now you're going to *play*!"

"That's not fair!" shouts Joey. Until now Hayden and Rosamond have included him in all their outings. And if The Cancer Monster really is trying to take his grandfather then Joey needs to be nearby to protect him. Though there is something about the idea of Hayden having Rosamond all to himself that also bothers Joey. After all, isn't she more *his* friend—while Hayden rests they play cards for hours or go on long walks in the park to search for fossils, Indian arrowheads, and buried treasure. "I can go, right, Grandpa? Right, Rosie?"

But Hayden's look is the same one that accompanied the news that his grandma Mary was not coming back from the hospital.

"No one is going *anywhere*!" Diana attempts to restore calm.

Only Joey knows that Hayden cannot be stopped. He's as sure of his grandfather's willpower as he is of his own. Hayden *is* going. He's planning to take Rosamond away and leave him behind—unloved, abandoned, practically an orphan. Joey hurls his chair away from the table and runs from the room so they can't see his torrent of tears.

"Oh dear," says Diana and wipes her hands on a dish towel. She's torn between rushing to comfort her son and staying to reason with her father. The only thing that keeps her from running after Joey is that she doesn't know how to explain what he only feels in his heart—that Rosamond is his first love. And that she's Hayden's last. Joey possesses a bargaining chip that Hayden does not, the luxury of time. And given that the heart is one of the few self-regenerating organs, despite how Diana aches with tenderness for her son, she's certain that Joey's will eventually heal.

"What's all the fuss?" Hayden demands to know. "Where does it say that dying folks can't have a holiday, I'd like to know? Monotony is a slow death. And besides, I was busy goin' to funerals until you came along, Miss Let's Do Everything We've Never Done Before."

"Yes, but I meant things like taking the Circle Line and going to the Natural History Museum," insists Rosamond. Yet the words from Romans are flashing in her mind like an "accident ahead" warning sign on the highway. "Count yourselves dead to sin but alive to God in Christ Jesus. Therefore do not let sin reign in your mortal body so that you obey its evil desires."

"Well, I've never played golf on Saint Croix and it's next on my list of things to do afore dying," continues Hayden. "There's an incredible course in the northwest valley designed by Robert Trent Jones. In fact, I'll get you a set of irons and teach you the game, Rosie. And of course there's the rum! Come let me lead you by distilled waters."

Rosamond looks to Diana, who is still staring at Hayden in disbelief. What would her mother do in such a situation? Diana wonders. She might ask Diana if she is trying to stop Hayden for his sake or more for her own.

Finally, and much to Diana's relief, Rosamond says, "I don't think it's such a good idea, Hayden . . ."

"For someone named 'Rosie' you aren't much fun," he proclaims. "I'm a goin' to Saint Croix tomorrow. Are you in or out?"

"I . . . I," Rosamond stutters and turns to Diana for assistance.

"Dad," asserts Diana, as if to bring all this nonsense to an end once and for all, "this is the most ridiculous thing I've ever heard of. Don't think I haven't noticed that you've not been at all well lately. You hardly eat. What if something happens?!" She punctuates her admonition with a walrus-sized sigh of exasperation.

"I'm leavin' tomorrow. I'm tired of lookin' for death all the livelong day. It'll find me sure enough. Dyin' is the cost of livin'. And I want to do something that makes me feel alive."

Rosamond glances reluctantly out to the living room, where she can hear checkers bouncing off walls and board games being overturned as Joey angrily protests being left out. "Let me think about it," she replies in a soft voice, but the expression on her face conveys doubt rather than excitement. Rosamond rises, and as she leaves the room she turns in the archway and tells Hayden, "In the meantime, you'd better go and have a talk with your grandson."

Diana throws up her hands, acknowledging that she's been bested, though it's not without having become conscious of the fact that sick people live at varying distances from the real world. And as much as she'd like to believe that she's able to protect Hayden by keeping watch over him every minute of the day, in truth there isn't anything at all she can do to stave off the inevitable. She turns toward the sink to hide the tears welling in her eyes.

"Then we're off like a prom dress!" exclaims Hayden.

"Dad!" Diana quickly recovers from her momentary lapse. "Joey will hear you." It suddenly becomes clear to Diana that Hayden is totally oblivious to Joey's desperate crush on Rosamond.

"So what? Do you think he's never kissed a girl? Why, Joey's got so many girls trying to kiss him that he has to run like a sheep avoidin' the shears to get away from them all!"

Diana is truly stunned, especially since from the gleam in Hayden's eyes her maternal radar senses that for once he's not just provoking her. Oh good heavens, she hasn't even talked to Joey about picking up germs through kissing, not to mention cold sores and other sexually transmitted diseases. She dashes into the living room to make sure he's all right.

When the doorbell rings, Rosamond assumes it's Hank, whom she'd called the day before to say that she wanted to go to confession. She didn't want to ask Hayden and thereby risk becoming even further conflicted by the ranting of an atheist.

But it's not Hank. Giving Rosamond an icy stare through the screen door is Hayden's daughter Linda, dressed in a dark gray suit that appears more appropriate for a winter funeral than an August morning.

chapter forty-nine

O h, it's *you*." Linda pushes past Rosamond into the living room. "I came to discuss this with Diana but I may as well tell you myself. I've talked to a lawyer and have in my possession a notarized letter from Dad's doctor saying that he refuses treatment and is not of sound mind and body. Therefore he's unable to make decisions and enter into legal agreements." She removes a sheaf of papers from her expensive leather bag and waves them in Rosamond's face. "So there's no way you're going to get your hands on anything that belongs to Dad, not even a pair of his shoes. And so you may as well give up your little nun act."

"How dare you accuse me of trying to defraud Hayden!" Rosamond feels a rage rising within her that she hasn't experienced since her hospital stay.

Linda raises the papers above her shoulder. "If you think you're going to marry my father—"

"Marry Hayden?" Rosamond yells back in disbelief. "I think *you're* the one who's not of sound mind!"

"Hi everyone?" Hank calls from the front porch as he opens the screen door. However, it quickly becomes apparent that the two women are in the midst of a monumental argument.

"I've heard all about *you*." Linda turns her wrath on Hank. "Diana's boyfriend, my foot. The two of you are in cahoots trying to con my father and my poor gullible sister! And I'm not going to allow it."

"What are you talking about?" Hank looks over their heads for Diana.

"Linda!" Diana appears on the staircase. "What are you—" and then she notices the apoplectic look on Rosamond's face and Hank points and yells, "The nerve of this woman, accusing me of—" he stumbles for the next word.

"Accusing you of *what?*" Diana asks Hank and then turns to Linda.

But Rosamond interjects. "She's accusing me of trying to defraud your father!" Her face is bright red and her blue eyes are flashing dark with insult.

Hayden and Joey hear the ruckus from different parts of the house and rush into the living room, where the melee has spilled over from the front hall. Hank is gesticulating, Linda is waving papers and yelling threats, Diana is trying to grab the papers and shouting insults right back, and Rosamond is insisting that she's not a fake nun. Joey's face is still tear-stained and his hair is rumpled from lying with his head underneath the pillow to muffle his sobs.

"Jumpin' Jehoshaphat!" yells Hayden. "What's all the yabberin' about?" But this only causes them to simultaneously shout and pound the air at each other while Rosamond buries her face in her hands as if it's all too much to bear. Hayden grabs his musket off the wall and this gets everyone's attention.

"Oh my God, Dad!" screeches Linda. "You *are* senile. Put that thing down or I'll have you committed this instant! Joey, call the police."

But Joey ignores her. Angered by seeing his mother so upset, he doesn't even think about the words that cascade out. "The only reason I'll call the police is to arrest you for trespassing!"

Between Joey's debut of talking back to grown-ups and Hayden wielding his musket, silence falls over the room. Rosamond is closest to Joey and she automatically pulls him to her on the off chance that Hayden's gun is loaded.

Struggling free from her embrace Joey screams, "Why did you have to come here? Everything was fine until *you* showed up!"

Rosamond's emotions are so frayed that she begins weeping and races up the stairs. The rest of the combatants gasp as they turn to Joey, which gives Hayden an opportunity to snatch the pile of legal papers from Linda's hand.

"Joseph, how *dare* you?" Diana chastises her son. "Go apologize to Rosamond immediately and then go straight to your room!"

Joey looks at her with MacBride defiance and then stomps up the stairs.

After glancing at the heading on the first page of Linda's paperwork Hayden practically snarls, "Power of Attorney!" He puts down the musket and with two hands tears the papers in half and tosses them in the air. "Linda, if I hear one more bit o' nonsense about Rosie bein' a gold digger I'm cuttin' you out of my will *entirely*."

chapter fifty

By early afternoon a calm, if not actual peace, has settled over the town house. It's an unusual quiet in that Hayden can actually hear the grandfather clock ticking in the dining room. Normally Diana would be well into her weekend cleaning routine, which involves the whirring and spinning of at least five different appliances.

Nor is there any of the usual laughter and conversation between Rosamond and Diana coming from the kitchen. In fact, Rosamond still hasn't come down from her room, and it was almost an hour ago that Linda's convertible went squealing out of the driveway.

"Rosie!" Hayden eventually calls up the stairwell. "Linda's gone!" But there's no reply, not so much as a door creaking on its hinges.

Hayden climbs the stairs and gently knocks on the door, but there's still no answer, and so he opens it a crack and peers inside. The bed is made, the afternoon breeze causes the calico curtains to dance above the windowsill, but there's no sign of Rosamond. In a moment of panic Hayden quickly opens the closet and checks for the dresses that Rosamond and Diana picked out the day they'd all gone shopping together in the city. They're all there, hanging neatly in a row.

He reviews the morning's events to determine if perhaps he's angered or offended Rosamond in some way. But his mind draws a blank. Hadn't she practically said yes to their taking a vacation together alone, just the two of them? He knows she's upset over Linda, but that was all nonsense. He'd reassured her about Linda on several occasions. Then there was Joey's stupid comment. That had to be it—Joey! Certainly they'd made up by now.

Hayden hurries across the hall to his grandson's room, expecting to find the two of them engaged in a card game or playing with Joey's Gameboy.

Rosie had developed a real talent for video games under Joey's expert tute-lage and could easily clear fifteen boards of Dr. Mario.

But Joey is sprawled on his bed, underneath a giant poster of the Mets star catcher Mike Piazza, sorting his baseball cards and playing with Ginger, who likes to dive under the covers and try to pull his socks off.

"Have you seen Rosie?" Hayden asks, unable to conceal the anxiety in his voice.

"Nope." He shakes his head and then ignores Hayden in a way that brings back memories of what it's like to have a sullen young adult lying around the house.

Hayden heads downstairs and checks the yards, both the front and back. Then he goes to the basement where Diana is sorting laundry. "Have you seen Rosie?" he asks.

"No, I haven't. I assumed after not having slept well and all the excite-ment this morning that she was having a rest before lunch. I know I could use one myself." Diana shakes her head as if to clear away all the morning's insanity. Between Hayden's usual antics and now this craziness with Linda, Hank is probably thinking that mental illness runs in the family. "Rosa-mond knows not to pay any attention to Linda. And I've spoken to Joey. He's more upset with *you* than anyone else. Dad, could you please try and be sensitive to the fact that Joey has a crush on Rosamond."

But Hayden is too distracted by Rosamond's absence to take note of a silly schoolboy crush. "She's . . . she's not in her room or the yard. And she doesn't drive . . ."

"Did you two have a fight?"

"No, we didn't fight!" says Hayden, further agitated by the very sugges-tion that this is his fault. "You heard her, Rosie said she wanted to go on the trip with me. And she never takes a nap."

Diana senses the worry in Hayden's voice and automatically begins imagining worst-case scenarios. "Okay, calm down. I'm sure she just went out to do something with Hank." Diana raises her hand as if she's just re-membered something important. "That's it! Yesterday they talked about going to church together. When Hank left he probably met Rosamond over at the church. Why don't you call him on his cell phone? The number is on the fridge."

He hurries back upstairs, dials Hank's number, and asks if Rosamond is with him. But no, Hank hasn't seen her since the scene at the townhouse. After that he had to deliver some drawings for a new building in Long Is-land City to a client's home in Syosset.

Hayden explains the situation, including the vacation plans and Joey's disappointment at being left out and Rosamond's concern about his injured feelings. There's a long pause on the other end of the phone and Hayden can hear the sound of Hank's measured breathing in comparison to his own uneven gasps.

"This trip was going to be just the two of you?" asks Hank.

"It wasn't as if I held a gun to her head," Hayden says defensively. "I . . . I thought she'd enjoy a little R and R."

After a few seconds pass Hank asks, "Have you seen her habit anywhere?"

"No . . ." Hayden follows where Hank's train of thought is leading. "The convent!"

"I'll be right over," says Hank.

Not knowing what may lay ahead, Hayden changes out of his shorts and polo shirt and into his good khakis and a button-down-collar shirt. By the time he's putting on his loafers Hank's beat-up Dodge is pulling into the driveway. Hayden is sitting in the passenger seat and closing the door before Hank has put the car into park.

Though the sun is high in the sky the dark gray convent appears ominous, with its brooding Gothic solidity, small recessed windows, and dark crevices. In front of the small wooden message door a dozen burnt-orange monarch butterflies with silken wings dance in the dust-speckled light. Hank places a note in the compartment, closes the door, and then rings the bell. After about ten minutes the note is returned. In perfect cursive writing at the bottom it says, "Not here."

"She must be in there!" exclaims Hayden.

"No," says Hank. "It's part of the nuns' job description not to lie."

Hayden leans against the front of the car for a moment to think. Perhaps Diana is right and Rosamond has become ill from all this stress. They get back into the car and Hayden directs them to the hospital where he first met her.

The man at the information desk says that no one by the name of Rosamond Rogers is registered. Hayden heads to the emergency room to see for himself whether his friend is among the crowd waiting for treatment. She's not there, either.

Still not satisfied, Hayden attempts to slip past the security desk in order to check the oncology ward where she and Cyrus had once been patients.

"Can I help you?" says an older woman at the desk as Hayden rings for the elevator.

A quick study shows a neat bun of gray hair that, based on the faded freckles and pink cheeks, was probably once red, and a volunteer nametag that says: Maureen O'Rourke.

"Father MacBride," Hayden says in his best imitation of an Irish brogue. "Going to give the last rites on seven." He briefly looks down at the linoleum floor. "The Cancer."

"Oh, I'm terribly sorry, Father," says the flustered woman as she reaches for the small silver cross at her neck. "I didn't, I mean—you aren't wearing your collar."

"No, 'twas to have been my day off." Hayden delivers his most irresistible smile and severely rolls his r's. "A good reminder that there's no vacation from doin' the Lord's work, is there, Sister?" With a little nod of his head he acknowledges her sacrifice for volunteering on a weekend.

The color in her cheeks rises and she gives him a shy smile in return, as if simultaneously sharing a moment of devotion and receiving his blessing.

On the seventh floor Hayden casually strolls up and down the corridors, acting as if he's going to visit someone in a particular room, but really trying to get a glimpse of who is occupying each bed. It eventually dawns on Hayden that if Rosamond didn't tell him she was checking into the hospital, then she probably doesn't want him to know about it. Or, likewise, to be found.

Hayden rejoins Hank in front of the main entrance and they drive to a nearby diner to strategize over coffee. Hank's years in the seminary have left him calm in a crisis, a good thing compared to Hayden's anxious foot tapping and table drumming. He takes a break from making noise only long enough to anxiously push his fingers through his wild mop of hair. Hayden pounds his fist on the table to emphasize the answers to Hank's careful questions. Did they have a fight? Had Rosamond been acting strangely lately? Did she mention any old friends or relatives who had recently been in touch? Negative to all. Sure, Joey is going crazy lately, but that's the onset of adolescence and his feelings about his grandfather dying. Hayden can deal with all of that later.

"Maybe you should deal with it now," suggests Hank. "Sometimes alleviating one problem automatically solves another. It's called taking care of business."

"Taking care of business my arse," says Hayden. "Don't go givin' me your religious hogwash sayings at a time like this."

"That's not from the pope," says Hank. "It was Elvis Presley's motto."

But Hayden is too distraught over Rosamond's disappearance to concentrate on any other business than finding her as fast as possible. "What was I ever thinking?" he mutters woefully and sinks his face down into his folded arms. "I can't compete with her old boyfriend."

This is the first thing to come out of Hayden's mouth that sounds to Hank as if it might be an actual clue to Rosamond's whereabouts. "What old boyfriend?" Hank asks. "From before she went into the convent? One of the doctors at the hospital?" Or worse, he thinks to himself, *a priest? Is that* why she left the convent?

"Fer chrissakes!" Hayden lifts up his head and casts his bloodshot eyes up toward the faux Tiffany light fixture, "Him!"

On the way home they stop at the local police station and Hayden attempts to file a missing person's report. However, he runs into a few problems: Rosamond hasn't been gone for twenty-four hours, Hayden's home isn't Rosamond's legal address, and she's not related to him. When the officer suggests checking the bridges, Hayden is at least able to report that she's definitely not suicidal. Otherwise, the policeman is sympathetic, especially when he hears the unlikely story of their respective cancers, and assures Hayden that he'll keep an eye out for an amnesiac woman possibly wearing a nun's habit.

Diana is anxiously waiting for Hayden back at the house. She's gone through directory assistance in Maine in an effort to locate Rosamond's father. But no one seems to have a listing for a George Rogers. Though she's not surprised since Rosamond had said that he was suffering from Alzheimer's disease and being cared for in a nursing home. In fact, she was planning to go and visit him as soon as she'd made her departure from the convent official.

Joey is tearful and beside himself with guilt because he didn't do as he was told and apologize to Rosamond. What if a car hit her? It would be totally his fault. Only yesterday Diana had read him a story out of the newspaper about a woman standing on the sidewalk who was struck by a van when the man behind the wheel had an epileptic seizure. Joey is certain that he's going straight to hell. He advances the suggestion to Diana that perhaps Rosamond ran away to join the circus. She'd once confided to him that she'd like to be a tightrope walker, since you need unwavering faith, and in exchange for that you're allowed to work up close to God. Joey promises God that if Rosamond comes back he'll never say anything mean to anyone ever again.

When Hayden and Hank return they all sit around the kitchen table and try to determine where Rosamond might have gone and discuss any clues she may have dropped as to her possible whereabouts. Hayden takes one of Joey's more sensible suggestions and calls the boathouse at Sheepshead Bay.

"I'll bet you five dollars she's out in the boat," says Joey. A bet was a sure-fire way of cheering Hayden up. And Joey is by now feeling horribly guilty that he's upset Hayden, in addition to causing Rosamond to run away.

But Hayden's in no mood for wagering. And Joey would have lost that bet anyway. Fred reports that he hasn't seen her either. In fact, the water was choppy all weekend and at one point the Coast Guard issued small-craft warnings. Most boaters came in and tied up for good before lunchtime.

Eventually they must concede that Rosamond's left on her own accord and apparently does not wish to be found at the present time.

Dinner is a somber affair with none of the usual antagonizing or argu-ing, even when Hayden, thin as he's become, barely touches his food. The emptiness in the dining room makes Diana realize she hasn't truly appreci-ated how much Rosamond has become part of the family, not to mention her best friend and confidante. Meanwhile, Joey continues to punish him-self for causing her departure. He wants so desperately to apologize and feel her arms around his sagging shoulders and her soft curls against his cheek.

As if reading Joey's mind, Hayden finally addresses his grandson. "Joseph, I know you think it's your fault she left, but it's not. It's mine. My lips to God's ears, I should have left well enough alone."

"It's not *anybody's* fault," Diana says in a maternal effort to rally the troops. In her book, sad spirits inevitably lead to weakened resistances and poor health. "Wherever Rosamond went, I'm sure she's just fine."

After the dishes are put away Hayden sits in the darkened living room reviewing everything he's said and done since the moment he met Rosie. Why did he have to try and make a terrific friendship into something more? Was it his vanity? Was it his old salesman's ego wanting to close a deal just to prove that he still could? And he should have known better than to chal-lenge her faith. Hadn't his dear mother been a believer right up until her death, even after a life filled with so many setbacks and misfortunes? Hay-den should have known better than to fight City Hall. He pours himself a large tumbler of whiskey but it sits on the dresser untouched.

Hayden misses Rosamond so much that it's absolutely unbearable. It's as if she had taken the whole summer with her and left the house empty. He hasn't felt this bad since the day he was rigging up the garage to commit sui-cide after Mary died. When he finally climbs into bed that night Hayden stares into the myriad of black dots that make up the darkness and for the first time actually feels the cold arms of death trying to encircle him. Rosamond was the warmth and light that enabled him to keep at bay his worst fears about leaving this world, even during the moments when he was most in pain. Because the pain isn't what terrifies Hayden when it comes to facing death. It's the loneliness. And he can't imagine feeling any lonelier than he does at this moment, unable to sleep, watching a slow-moving moon pass his window on its way up to the heavens.

Diana awakens the next morning with a start, feeling certain that she knows where Rosamond has gone. It's almost as if the awareness had entered her consciousness through a dream just before waking from a brief and fitful sleep. It had been impossible to rest, her mind constantly imagining the horrors befalling Rosamond out on the streets of Brooklyn, without a credit card or bank account.

Pulling on her robe as she goes, Diana rushes downstairs and out the front door. She jogs barefoot across the dew-damp lawn and hurries up the steps to Bobbie Anne's. The front door is open and through the screen Diana sees the little girls watching cartoons in the living room.

A second later, when Diana glimpses Rosamond, she's momentarily startled that her premonition was so accurate. She experiences the mixed emotions of a parent locating a runaway child—relief that the fugitive is unharmed and fury at all the distress she's caused. Certainly Rosamond is an adult and can pack up whenever she wants. But she's also Diana's friend, and as such has a responsibility not to worry her unnecessarily—or Hayden, Joey, and Hank, for that matter. The more Diana dwells on that sentiment the angrier she becomes. She knocks on the metal frame and calls "Rosamond!" through the screen.

As Rosamond approaches the door she's wearing a smile that quickly vanishes when she sees Diana's stern look and arms akimbo, after the fashion of an irritated high school principal. "We've been worried to death about you! Hayden and Hank checked the hospital and even went to the police!"

Rosamond quickly joins Diana on the front porch so the children can't hear what's being said.

"I thought you were my friend!" Diana continues. Suddenly the stress of

Rosamond's absence and Hayden's illness all bubble over and Diana begins to sob. "I thought you were *our* friend."

It's only at this moment that Rosamond understands the full impact of her behavior. In the convent when you had difficulties it was simply accepted that you would go to confession, sequester yourself, and pray, or if worse came to worst, talk to the mother superior. "I'm sorry." Rosamond places her arms around her friend.

Diana's relief at finding Rosamond alive and in one piece rapidly overcomes her anger and she hugs her friend in return. They sit down on the steps while Rosamond pours out the story of what happened, the events of the previous day flashing in bold relief as if they're occurring all over again.

Rosamond had arrived at Bobbie Anne's house the evening before, after spending the day wandering around Prospect Park and meditating on her situation. It was one thing to leave the convent. Many nuns worked as teachers and nurses and even artists and lawyers. But going on vacation with a man was another thing altogether. And so was causing rancor and chaos in the household of people you'd grown to love.

She'd strolled aimlessly around the circular walks flanking the Soldier's and Sailor's Memorial Arch, gazing at the gardens and staring into the fountain until she was almost hypnotized. Then she watched the carousel with its brightly painted horses spinning round and round, and the carnival-like music making the perfect accompaniment to the joyous shouts of children. A few tears fell as she attempted to reach the center of her sorrow and determine what it really was that she ached for.

While digging in her purse for a tissue Rosamond found the baseball card that Joey had given her the day they'd gone to the game farm, almost eight weeks before, seemingly a lifetime. On that day the rows of tiny numbers on the back hadn't made any sense to her. But since then Hayden and Joey had taught her the meaning of TBS, SBs, RBIs, averages, fielding statistics, and shutouts. With this knowledge she now studied the back of the card for the first time. What became clear was that a baseball player, even a great player, didn't always have a good game, or even a good season, for that matter. Their luck, skill, and grace, whatever one wanted to call it, was intermittent. Perfection was elusive and often short-lived, even for those in the major leagues. And so where did the faith come from? The team, the coach, from within?

Pondering all this, she wandered into the serene and unobtrusive

Quaker Cemetery near the Sixteenth Street entrance to the park, pausing among the headstones as she wondered if, at the end of their time on earth, the people resting here thought they'd made the right choices in life. If they could do it all over again would they change anything, or perhaps everything? She sat on a granite bench and prayed, but grace eluded her. Eventually the sun began to set and the trees cast long dark shadows across the lawn and surrounding hedges.

It was in front of the park that Rosamond spotted Bobbie Anne walking down the street carrying two heavy bags of groceries. She was beautifully dressed in an ivory-colored two-piece suit with threads of silk running through the material, a taupe camisole underneath, matching hose, and high-heeled pumps. A dainty white straw handbag with a gold clasp swung at her side. Rosamond was afraid even to consider where Bobbie Anne had spent the afternoon.

Hurrying to catch up with her, Rosamond took one of the bags before Bobbie Anne could protest. Though Bobbie Anne made it clear from her expression that she wasn't at all pleased to see Rosamond, who wasn't as a rule the bearer of glad tidings, or at the very least willing to engage in a live-and-let-live truce between neighbors.

"I was wondering if I might ask you a question," said Rosamond, accelerating her pace to keep up with Bobbie Anne's long-legged stride.

Bobbie Anne looked at her unwanted helper and sighed. "To be honest, I'd really appreciate it if you'd mind your own business, for a change."

Rosamond's breath quickened more from the sting of the insult than walking hurriedly under the weight of the grocery bag. "That's what I wanted to talk about—I'm sorry. I mean, you're right. How you live your life isn't any of my business."

Bobbie Anne, indifferent to hearing what she already knew, nodded her head ever so slightly, as if acknowledging a crack in the sidewalk.

However, Rosamond was aware that their neighbor had been raised in the Catholic Church, and that no matter how far away you may travel, the experience is never completely erased. And therefore it was doubtful that Bobbie Anne would be able to withhold forgiveness in the face of a sincere request. Those were the rules. Everyone knew it, from God to Jesus to Paul and right on down the line.

Eventually Bobbie Anne peered down at Rosamond as she trotted along beside her, silently awaiting some sort of absolution, as if Bobbie Anne herself were the pope. "Yeah, whatever. Forget about it," she said at last.

When they reached Bobbie Anne's front door Rosamond insisted on carrying the bag into the kitchen. The twins came tumbling down the stairs in their nightgowns and fell into their mother's arms, a cyclone of light brown ponytails, pink cheeks, and Powerpuff Girls insignia. Rosamond knew the little girls from watching them play in the yard and going duck herding with Hayden and Joey, and said hello. They had no idea about any differences between Rosamond and their mother, and were very friendly toward her.

Rosamond continued to wait while Bobbie Anne handed the baby-sitter three crisp twenty-dollar bills that appeared as if they'd just been drawn from a cash machine. What was the origin of the money, Rosamond couldn't help but wonder—a banker, a stockbroker?

After exchanging scheduling notes about the following week, the baby-sitter hugged the girls, said good-bye to everyone, and left.

"Thanks for the help," Bobbie Anne said to Rosamond, indicating that she was welcome to follow the baby-sitter out the door.

Yet Rosamond still wanted to ask her a question, though she was no longer sure exactly what it was. She felt that if she could just stay there for a while it might all be revealed. Rosamond continued to stand in the living room but no words came. Bobbie Anne looked at her expectantly.

"I . . . I can't go home yet," Rosamond finally blurted out.

Now most people would ask "why" after a statement like that. But Bobbie Anne had worries enough without involving herself in other people's problems. Also, she'd been around long enough to know full well all the usual reasons a person can't go home, and that they were all pretty much the same. However, being raised in the South, hospitality was ingrained in her. "You're welcome to join us for dinner."

Bobbie Anne made them hamburgers and after the girls were tucked into their beds she showed Rosamond to the alcove off the kitchen, which had apparently served as the maid's quarters when the town house was originally built back in the 1920s.

"Aren't they going to be worried about you?" asked Bobbie Anne. Had Rosamond been in the convent so long that she didn't understand how if you live with a bunch of people who are not omniscient, unlike her old boyfriend, God, and then suddenly disappear, in most cases they go looking for you?

"I've only created a lot of chaos and unhappiness over there," replied Rosamond. "Joey hates me. Hayden's daughter Linda believes I'm a con artist. And he asked me to go on vacation with him." Rosamond carefully pulled back the bedcovers while Bobbie Anne leaned against the door frame.

Bobbie Anne had never known a crew of neighbors with so many dramas, not even when she was a sorority sister in high school. Ever since the nosy daughter moved in there were men either shouting or serenading every time Bobbie Anne opened the window at night. Furthermore, Bobbie Anne had been under the impression that Hayden and Rosamond had been shacking up all summer, that the moment that old black habit disappeared it was replaced by the old black magic, and all bets with The Big Guy were off. She briefly wondered if Hayden had confessed to their little fling last winter, and that's why Rosamond had given Bobbie Anne such a hard time about plying her trade. But she'd eventually decided no, Hayden was too much of a gentleman to kiss and tell.

"As for Joey, if kids don't hate you at least once a day then you're not raising them right," Bobbie Anne said in her pleasant drawl and softened her countenance with a smile. "And Hayden told me about that loco daughter Linda. She doesn't know if she's washin' or hangin'. Sounds as if someone went and stole her rudder."

Rosamond finally smiled, too. "Do you think I should go?"

"Stay here for the night. It makes men crazy when they don't know where you are—it's a lack of control."

"I meant on the vacation?" Rosamond asked in a voice all trembly, her emotional state disintegrating at the very mention of the trip. "Will it make things better or worse?"

Why were people constantly asking Bobbie Anne these kinds of questions? she wondered. For starters, she was considerably younger than most of them. And except for the house, which was mortgaged to the hilt, she was broke. On top of all that, she didn't even have a college degree.

Bobbie Anne was tempted to tell Rosamond to do whatever she felt was right, or that she should just go and have a good time, especially since she knew from speaking to Hayden that Rosamond also had terminal cancer, though probably not as advanced as his. But of course those were the kinds of answers people came up with for themselves and so they were never found to be very satisfying.

"You've kissed him, right?" asked Bobbie Anne.

"Not really," admitted Rosamond.

"Have you kissed *any* men?"

"I kiss Joey every night before he goes to bed."

"That's a good example," said Bobbie Anne. "Kisses can have different meanings. When you kiss a child it's to tell them you love them in a parental way. A kiss with a friend might mean hello or good-bye. You can kiss a lover and feel unexpected passion or else watch the passion run right out the door. But you have to start somewhere."

Rosamond nodded her head as if this made sense, though it didn't, and she still couldn't tell whether it meant she should kiss Hayden and then decide about the vacation. Or if she should go, but make sure to kiss him only as a friend. Even the word *passion* was confusing. In the Bible and in Latin, passion means "to suffer," specifically the suffering and death of Jesus. And if that was the correct definition then Rosamond had been experiencing more than her fair share of it.

Bobbie Anne realized that Rosamond was still bewildered. "The point is, you can decide what a kiss means. They're like words—they are nothing but the meaning we invest in them. It's the same with sex. It doesn't have to be—you know—as meaningful as you're making it. It *can* be. But you can also decide that it didn't mean anything." Then she added in a softer, world-weary tone, "And if you do it for money you can decide it's just a job."

"I keep thinking about God," Rosamond whispered, as if He might overhear them.

"Well, God is another word that we invest with meaning. My God knows that I've had to do some things I'm not particularly proud of to provide for my family, but I don't think He's going to hold it against me in the end, as long as I try to be a good mother. Because I *love* my children. And at the end of the day, isn't that what it's all about?" Bobbie Anne's smoldering voice charged her words with an authority and even a sense of enchantment that belied her youth, sex, and lack of higher education. She kissed Rosamond good night on the cheek. Exiting the room Bobbie Anne recited the only prayer from her vast childhood repertoire that she still employed: "Saint Anthony, Saint Anthony please look around, something is lost and must be found." Rosamond recognized the Prayer for Lost Objects from when she was a schoolgirl. There wasn't a Catholic anywhere, lapsed or otherwise, who didn't trust in the prayer to Saint Anthony.

As Rosamond finishes telling Diana what happened, Hayden appears on the front porch, his pajamas wrinkled and his face haggard from a sleepless night. Seeing the women sitting together on the neighbor's stoop causes him to rub his eyes in order to make sure they're not playing tricks on him, as they sometimes did after a few whiskeys. It doesn't help that a curtain of emerald leaves sifts the piercing August light until it glitters and trembles on the lawn, turning the tiny yard between the houses into what looks like a river of broken mirrors. And within the bushes that veil the two women silvery cobwebs flash pockets of sun as if little flames are leaping among them.

But Hayden's eyes are fine and he hasn't had a drink since before Rosamond left. He takes the porch steps two at a time and dashes toward them. "Rosie! I thought you were dead as mutton! I checked every room in the hospital!"

The joy in his voice rings out across the lawn and his entire countenance is transformed by the instant return of his former vitality, like a tree awakened by spring. He hastily makes his way over to where the women are talking.

Hayden's outpouring of concern overwhelms Rosamond and her eyes fill with tears. Never before has she been so thrilled to hear that strong and true baritone voice, the brogue rising up in places to serve as its own system of punctuation.

"Why didn't you tell us if something was wrong?" says an anxious Hayden. But he's come to better understand Rosamond's dilemma and stops asking questions about her disappearance. "The vacation was a dumb idea. Won't you just please come home?"

Rosamond wipes the teardrops from her cheeks. "No, the trip is a good idea. I just . . . I needed to talk to God." And God had sent her back to Hayden, who was like a gigantic beam of light, illuminating what no one would have ever guessed was there in the darkness. She now realizes the moment has arrived when her love for Hayden can no longer remain a solitary one, in the manner that her heart had been conditioned to love for so long.

Hayden runs his fingers through his permanently unkempt hair and says, "That's fine. I don't mind that. But you'll tell me if He starts talking back to you, right?"

chapter fifty-two

That evening Hayden and Rosamond drive Joey to Park Slope for his Little League game. Only Joey doesn't plead with Rosamond to sit with him in the back and play video games the way he usually does. All they hear from the backseat is the metronomelike slap of the ball into the mitt.

Joey is doing everything possible to make it clear that he's still angry with Hayden for planning a trip and not including him, and that it's not too late to get another ticket. Joey *always* goes with them. He could help teach Rosamond to golf and even carry her clubs. They could go ocean fishing for bluefin tuna and swordfish like the ones he saw reeled in on TV, and help net each other's catch. Who is she going to fish with if he doesn't go? Who is going to play hearts with her while Hayden rests? And who will supply all the newest video games, the ones he uses his allowance to trade up for at the computer store? Joey is convinced that Rosamond cannot possibly have a good time on this trip without him.

During the baseball game Joey doesn't so much as glance at the two of them, either from the dugout or when he's playing catcher and positioned behind home plate, practically right next to where they're seated. At one point, with the best hitter in the league approaching the plate, Joey walks out to the pitcher and whispers something in his ear, which makes the pitcher smile and scan the bleachers as if he's trying to locate someone in particular. To Hayden and Rosamond's delight, the pitcher quickly and efficiently strikes out the star of the opposing team.

"I wonder what Joey said to the pitcher," Hayden remarks to Rosamond. "Is there a scout in the stands? Though aren't twelve- and thirteen-year-olds a bit young for recruiting?"

"We'll probably never find out from Joey," replies Rosamond. "In case you haven't noticed, he's not talking to us."

"It'll blow over."

"You *did* have a talk with him, didn't you?"

"No, I didn't have a talk wi' him." Hayden's brogue noticeably thickens, the way it does when telemarketers call during dinner. "I'm no good at talkin'."

"You must be joking! Why, you talk such a good game that if you ever take up the Lord's work all the fallen Catholics will be back in their pews by next Sunday, even if it means buying tickets from scalpers." The absurdity of Hayden's statement makes Rosamond laugh so hard that she leans back on the narrow aluminum bench and almost slips through the bleachers.

However, Hayden catches her with an outstretched arm and doesn't remove it even after she's regained her balance. "Better be careful or you're going to be a fallen Catholic."

"That's exactly what I mean!" says Rosamond. "Anyway, I wish you would talk to Joey, because I hate the feeling that he's angry with us."

"Rosie, that kind of talk is girl talk. Diana and her mother would sit around for hours yammering about their feelings." Hayden places his light blue handkerchief over his hair like a scarf, bats his eyelashes, tilts his head to the side, and offers his imitation of women talking to each other. "How did you *feel* when he said that? Was he being honest about his *feelings.* . . ."

Rosamond attempts to stay serious, though it's hard with Hayden continuing to flutter his heavy-lidded eyes under bushy brows, knowing full well that he's getting her permanently off track with laughter. Because if there's one thing Hayden definitely is not, it's feminine. She turns away from him in order to stay focused on the issue at hand. "It's not just about us taking the trip without him. You're his best friend and he's beside himself that you're, you know, not well."

"He's makin' more friends here at baseball. I caught him and the pitcher tryin' to smoke behind our garage the other day."

"Well, I'm warning you, Diana's threatening to send him to a child psychiatrist."

"A *psychiatrist?* My grandson will see a shrink over my dead body. Speaking of which, we *are* dyin', Rosie. I've told Joey that. And I've shown him lots of dead people at funerals. What else do you want me to do? Tell him we're going to paradise and that he'll see us again in heaven? Come on, you know I can't do that."

Rosamond frowns at him, exhales loudly, and turns back to watch the game, even though she isn't seeing anything. If only she'd had the opportunity to speak with her mother just once. What were *her* hopes and dreams? And were any of them fulfilled? What was it that had attracted her mother to her father, a kindly but solemn man who put food on the table but displayed little emotion, at least not after her mother was gone. Rosamond often wonders if she'll meet her mother again in heaven. She likes to think so. There are so many things she'd like to ask her and tell her.

Hayden is also annoyed. Just when they're about to take this vacation they have to start arguing. He decides that women do this on purpose. It was going to be his one big chance to romance her without a twelve-year-old around. What's equally aggravating is the shrug and sigh business she just displayed. Hayden is convinced that Rosamond learned those moves from Diana. In fact, it occurs to him that his daughter is most likely the inspiration for the entire performance, right down to the furrowed brow, pursed lips, and sweet-smelling perfume she has on. If it were up to Hayden, women would be housed like murder suspects and never allowed in the same room together without an officer present. He's convinced the distaff half spends the majority of their time strategizing against men and exchanging potentially damaging information that can later be used for the purposes of male entrapment.

A summer storm moves in quickly from the west and obliterates the orange sunset with dark purple clouds. Umbrellas come out and spectators start running for their cars. Soon thick walls of raindrops bounce three inches above the white bases, rivers of water begin connecting all the ruts on the playing field, and the coaches briefly study the sky before calling the game. Lightning zigzags across the heavens, causing everything to stand out for a moment. Hayden gallantly attempts to cover their heads with his windbreaker but they end up getting drenched.

Even though Joey's team is behind when the game is called, they go out for ice cream to celebrate the fact that he finally got on base, even if his occupancy didn't lead to scoring a run. Hayden drops off Rosamond and Joey so they can get a booth while he searches for a parking space.

Once they're seated it's obvious to Rosamond that Joey's still sulking about not being invited on the trip, because instead of speaking to her, he buries his face behind the menu that he knows by heart.

Joey wonders if she understands that he's upset by the significance of the trip as much as the trip itself. And that he is heartbroken now that Rosamond has finally chosen between the two of them. Furthermore, he's angered and insulted at the way his mother refers to his feelings as a "schoolboy crush."

By now Rosamond has determined that even if Hayden won't have a talk with the boy, she sure as heck will. "You know, Joey, sometimes your grandpa doesn't feel all that well and he makes a big effort to do things so that you and I can have a good time."

Joey is accustomed to his mother barking orders at him, fretting aloud about safety, and listing all the accidents and illnesses that could befall him at any given moment. But he's rarely been exposed to some well-placed guilt. Eventually from underneath a pulled-down baseball cap comes a remorseful, "I know."

Rosamond gently removes the cap so that she can meet his gaze. "This trip we're going on is supposed to be good for his health, so that he can rest a bit."

"You mean without Mom nagging him all the time?"

"Well, I wouldn't say that, exactly. Diana loves your grandpa, the same way she loves you."

Joey frowns. He is also discovering that guilt can be like cough medicine, the bad taste fading quickly after it's been dispensed. Much to Joey's surprise, Rosamond takes his smooth young hand in hers. "Being that your grandpa isn't up to a more rigorous vacation, how about when I get back the two of us will finally go on that camping trip? Just you and me."

"Really?" Joey's face lights up.

"Cross my heart and hope to die." Rosamond crosses herself. Meanwhile, a shadow crosses her face as she remembers that she really is dying. She reaches over and hugs him to assure him of how much she loves him, but the sight of Hayden waving as he makes his way through the crowded restaurant and over to their booth causes him to wriggle out of her embrace, retrieve his hand and hide it under the tabletop.

Hayden sits down next to Rosamond and faces Joey. "Hey Slugger, you're not trying to take away my girl?" He laughs heartily, oblivious to Joey's heartache and Rosamond's efforts to keep the peace between the men in her life. "Now, I'm dyin' to know what you told that pitcher to strike out their best batter!"

"I told him that if you can get Artie's dad to start yelling then he goes to pieces," Joey confesses with a grin.

"That's my boy," says Hayden and reaches across the table to rumple Joey's hair. "You've got a good read on people. Maybe you should be a coach or else one of those Wall Street traders."

chapter fifty-three

Sometime after midnight Hayden is awakened by a commotion out in front of the house. There's a plaintive cry followed by an angry shout and then the sound of gravel hitting the downstairs windows and ticking against the metal gutters. He assumes that Diana has forgotten her key and climbs out of bed to go and let her in. But Diana appears with Hank at the top of the stairs while Hayden is unlocking the front door. It's clear that they've also been sleeping. Hank is wrapped in a bedsheet and Diana is wearing a filmy green nightgown. Thus Hayden deduces what's awaiting him is a visit from Tony-the-Sofa-Tester, or some other disgruntled ex-boyfriend, and braces himself for a confrontation.

"Joey!" An agitated voice can be heard shouting from the front lawn. Next to appear on the landing is a sleepy Joey, with Rosamond trailing behind him in pale yellow pajamas.

"Jayzus, Mary, and Joseph!" bellows Hayden. "Did you throw a baseball through some guy's window?" He looks up toward Joey.

"Joey!" the voice comes again, this time more plaintive than threatening.

"Evan!" concludes Diana.

"Evan?" echoes Hank.

"Dad!" Joey shouts excitedly, eyes now wide open with excitement. He dashes to the screen door and races outside. "Dad! Dad! I knew you'd come!"

Rosamond feels as if she's in the eye of a hurricane. Diana and Hayden rush past her toward Joey while Hank runs by her in the opposite direction to go back upstairs, presumably to put on some pants. By the time they're all assembled on the front lawn Joey is hugging his father, who is now down on bended knee.

Evan, a tall, lanky man with jutting cheekbones and a ponytail that only serves to accentuate his leanness, places his arm possessively around Joey's shoulder.

"I want my son!" he announces to Diana and Hank, who are standing to the left of the front stoop, and Hayden, who is off to the right. Only it appears as if the energy expended in making this proclamation throws him off balance and he has to cling to Joey for support.

"He's high," Diana tells Hank, loud enough so that Hayden can hear her.

"I'll take care of him," Hank assures her. Having thrown on jeans and an unbuttoned blue dress shirt, he pushes up his sleeves as if preparing for a fight. The urge to protect and defend that has welled up inside him trumps any lingering notions he had of entering the priesthood. And having grown up with four brothers he's accustomed to working things out with his fists if need be.

In the intervening moments Rosamond has pulled on her borrowed white silk bathrobe and now appears on the front stoop. Upon seeing her friend Diana yells, "Call the police!" Then Diana attempts to restrain Hank from tackling Evan and shouts at Hayden, "Dad, *help* me. I don't want to lose custody."

But Hayden enters into the fray with his own agenda. "You want your son, do you?" he threatens Evan in an icy tone that contains not a trace of his regular good humor. "Why haven't you paid alimony or child support since nineteen canteen? And where's the money from the cashed-in life insurance policy that was supposed to be for Diana and Joey in case anything happened to you? Did you think I wouldn't find out about that?"

"I want my son!" Evan repeats in an unsteady voice that sounds increasingly desperate. He continues to use Joey as a leaning post.

"Then be a man," Hayden shouts back. "It's better to die on yer feet than live on yer knees!"

Frightened by the faltering uncertainty in his father's voice and uncomfortable with the weight on his slender shoulders, Joey steps to the side. Without the support of his son, Evan sinks down on the lawn so that he's sitting on the heels of his boots.

Joey becomes increasingly alarmed, his gaze frantically darting from grown-up to grown-up as they all start to shout and gesticulate like angry statues that have magically come to life under the cool glow of the moon.

Having gone inside and made the phone call, Rosamond returns to her position on the front stoop. In the midst of the erupting chaos she slowly raises her arms, the billowing fabric of the robe suggesting an enormous white heron stretching its wings. Joey dashes toward the bathrobe and Rosamond wraps her arms around the frightened child. She leads him into the house so they can wait for the police.

From the kitchen they hear a loud series of arguments out front, mostly men's voices. But occasionally there's an isolated diatribe from Diana, sharp with distress and protectiveness.

Soon they hear the wail of sirens. Rosamond places two dishes of vanilla ice cream on the table and sits down next to the shaken boy. Joey silently spoons the ice cream into his mouth. And the tears that occasionally drop onto his bowl aren't born of sadness so much as discovered strength.

Rosamond understands Joey's frustration with waiting—waiting for his father to act like a father, waiting to grow up, waiting to be able to take control of his life. She'd felt much the same way about waiting to become secure in her faith and devotion to God. Only she'd failed and finally surrendered to her disappointment.

Eventually Joey says, "I don't understand. I prayed and prayed for Dad to find a good job and to come back and live with us. But it didn't work."

Rosamond places her hand on his arm. "All prayers are answered. It's just that sometimes the answer is 'not right now.' "

It takes another half hour for the quarreling in the front yard to subside and a complaint to be filed. Diana, Hayden, and Hank return to the house exhausted. Hayden is muttering "useless as a wet Woodbine" and rattling around the cabinet for his scotch. Diana is too unnerved to stop him and effusively coddles and comforts Joey the same way she always does after he's suffered an injury.

But Rosamond can tell by his trembling lips and rigid body that Joey is no longer the idealistic boy who ran out of the house to greet his daddy. Nor will he ever be again. As farmers feel the weather changing deep within their bones, Joey senses that his childhood has come to an end.

chapter Fifty-Four

The morning of the big trip dawns lush with summer and the scent of freshly mown grass. Trees bow under the weight of overripe fruit and swollen seedpods split open and fall to the ground. Hayden and Joey rise early and go to the service station to fill the car with gas and buy windshield-washer fluid. Or rather, Joey confidently attends the automobile, even replacing a fuse and checking the tire pressure, while his grandfather waits in the driver's seat. Though Hayden hates to admit it, he has limited energy these days, and the same small errands and quick chores that used to start his day now drain him.

There's hardly any traffic on the way home and so Hayden lets Joey sit next to him and steer while he operates the gas pedal and brake. This cheers Joey slightly, but once they arrive home and he sees the suitcases on the front porch he falls silent again, and Hayden reconsiders Rosamond's advice. Only he can't think of anything philosophical to say to his grandson—about fatherhood, life, or even death, the subject in which he'd so recently attempted to make himself an expert. What he considers mentioning is that women are somehow at the bottom of the whole thing. They can give a man more self-confidence than a new suit and old money, or else knock him into the gutter with a single disapproving glance.

When the two enter the kitchen to get some breakfast, Hayden is surprised that the coffeemaker, blender, toaster, juicer, and all Diana's favorite morning appliances aren't going at full speed. Though knowing the way his daughter worries, as if it's a job she gets paid to do, he assumes it was a long while before she finally went back to sleep the night before. Joey continues to mope around and carelessly pours cornflakes into a bowl so that they spill over onto the countertop. It breaks Hayden's heart to see his grandson so world-weary.

"Joey, run and get a rubber band from the mailbox," Hayden says with forced enthusiasm.

Joey appears puzzled, but does as he's told. When he returns, Hayden is standing in front of the sink holding a black Magic Marker and motions for Joey to bring the rubber band over to him. "Now watch this."

Hayden colors the tan rubber band until it's black on both sides. Then he pulls the sprayer out of the sink, presses down on the black plastic bar so it's in the "on" position, and then winds the rubber band tightly around the nozzle before replacing it. Just as the hose clicks back into place they hear footsteps on the stairs. Hayden jumps away from the sink and motions for Joey to do the same.

Diana enters the kitchen bleary-eyed and still in her bathrobe, her hair pulled back into a sloppy ponytail. "What a night," she says to Joey and Hayden and dazedly lifts the top on the coffeemaker as if half asleep.

Hayden sneaks a quick peek at Joey, who suddenly realizes what's going to happen next as his mother reaches toward the sink, and is thrilled by the look of anticipation on his grandson's face. As expected, when Diana turns on the faucet a huge blast of water sprays her directly in the face and also soaks her hair and the front of her nightclothes. She lets out a shriek and backs away from the water-spewing sink while frantically rotating her arms like a high-speed windmill.

Hayden closes in on the sink from the side, turns off the faucet, and while Diana's eyes are still closed from the surprise deluge, he quickly removes the rubber band and slips it into his pocket. Standing a few feet behind Diana, Joey is convulsed with laughter from the sight of his normally glamorous and composed mother flailing like a person drowning.

"Oh my God!" a thoroughly soaked Diana shouts as she wipes her eyes and forehead with a dish towel.

Rosamond comes running into the kitchen. "What's wrong *now?*"

"Nothing to worry about," says Hayden. "Just a little plumbing problem. It happens with these old houses."

Meanwhile Joey is covering his face with his hands as he tries to stop laughing but is unable to reduce his gleeful howls. If anything, he's laughing progressively harder and in danger of vomiting.

"It's not funny, Joey!" Hayden chastises him with a sly wink. "In fact, go and get the toolbox and fix the pipes for your mother, just like I've been showing you."

Diana looks concerned. "Shouldn't we should call a plumber?"

"Don't be ridiculous. Joey will have that fixed in a jiffy."

Diana's too exhausted to argue and stumbles upstairs to change. On the landing she passes Hank, who is preparing to drive the vacationers to the airport.

"Will you please make sure you get a number for a doctor down there?" Diana calls to Hayden from the top of the stairs. "You look jaundiced. I wish you'd see a specialist."

"It's just a suntan." Hayden pulls his red golf visor down to thwart any further examination.

Diana returns to the kitchen where Joey is busy impressing Rosamond by "fixing" the sink. She hands Rosamond a pink-and-white-striped Victoria's Secret bag.

"What's this?" Rosamond assumes Diana has packed some sandwiches for the plane ride, since she'd been worrying that they wouldn't be fed properly.

Diana looks through the archway to make sure that Hayden and Hank aren't nearby. "Just put it in your suitcase. Men are like crows. They're attracted to shiny objects."

"Let's go!" Hayden shouts from out in the driveway.

Rosamond tucks the bag Diana has given her into a carry-on case and Joey comes out from under the sink announcing that it was just a loose pipe and is now repaired. Diana tests the faucet and it seems to work perfectly. She pats her son on the shoulder to show that she's truly impressed. Now that Joey's almost as tall as she, it's no longer as easy to reach the top of his head unless he's sitting down.

They all squeeze into the station wagon for the trip to the airport. The expressway is packed with people heading east to enjoy the beaches in the Hamptons, Fire Island, the North Fork, and Montauk. Others are off to summer concerts at Jones Beach and to catch the ferry to Shelter Island. Hank drives and Hayden busies himself keeping everyone amused. "Hey, Joey, what goes *clump clump, bang bang, clump clump?*"

"An Amish drive-by!" Joey shouts before Hayden can even turn to look at him in the backseat.

"Dad!" scolds Diana. "Don't be sacrilegious."

"I think it'd be an excellent idea to sack religion," says Hayden.

Hank stifles a laugh. Rosamond doesn't appear to hear any of what's being said as she stares out the window, nervously fingering the charm bracelet on her wrist as if it's a rosary.

"Why can't the Amish go to jail?" asks Joey.

"Because no one would ever know," Hayden shoots back. "None of their relatives have phones!"

As they say good-bye, Rosamond suppresses the urge to shout that it's all been a terrible mistake. Somehow removing the bags from the car at the airport has a feeling of finality about it, as if they're being shipped off to an internment camp rather than embarking upon a tropical vacation. Having been on an airplane only once, she tries to convince herself that she's experiencing anxiety about flying.

By the time they reach the airline counter Hayden is in full salesman's mode, endearing but insistent, his brogue at an all-time thickness, and a smile that assures anyone who cares to look that laughter resides at his doorstep. "Yes, we're both dyin'," he informs the agent. "She doesn't look like it right now, I know." He nods toward Rosamond. "But trust me, we're goners." He pulls out the X-ray he'd stolen from his file and shows it to the woman as proof. "So if you can give us two seats together, with hers next to the window, I'd be eternally grateful." Hayden emphasizes *eternal* and accompanies it with a friendly wink.

"Your accent sounds familiar," the agent says, by now completely charmed.

"Well, do'an' go saying anythin' but one of my poorer relations is a famous movie actor."

"Oh!" The woman's eyes widen and then she smiles and nods to indicate that his secret is safe with her.

chapter fifty-five

Rosamond is relieved that she and Hayden have two separate rooms, though they're adjacent to each other. Small vases containing fresh flowers placed on the table and next to the sink in the bathroom make the dazzling white towels and linens appear lovely and fresh. A woven straw carpet gives the room a feeling of casual elegance. The walls are decorated with tranquil beach scenes and delicate watercolors of local flora that appear to have been rendered by an artful botanist. A great silver bowl overflowing with brightly colored exotic fruits sits on the table looking like one of the still-life paintings they'd admired at the Metropolitan Museum of Art. Rosamond has never seen such an exquisite place in all her life, and after the initial thrill of it, she thinks of her tiny barren cell back at the convent and then all the world's poor who don't have so much as a clean mat to lie upon.

Hayden, on the other hand, barely notices his surroundings. And the minute they finish unpacking he rushes them off to the world-famous golf course overlooking the clear blue Caribbean Sea. Along the winding palm-lined road stand rows of tin-roofed houses in faded yellow, pink, and ocher, resplendent with vivid blazes of magenta bougainvillea and red hibiscus out front. By the hillside tall cactuses emerge from the brush every few yards, a half dozen or so topped with flamboyant orangish-pink globes, blooms that are said to appear only once every hundred years.

"I wish I'd brought my wimple and veil to protect me from the sun," Rosamond says while Hayden demonstrates how to swing a golf club.

He gallantly hands her his visor. "Try this. It's what nine out o' ten golfers prefer over a wimple and veil." Rosamond hits her ball only a few feet from the hole. Hayden slices and lands his in the nearby sand. "Oh Christ, I'm my own handicap."

"Hayden!" She blanches at the Lord's name taken in vain.

"Beg pardon," he says contritely and loudly exhales. Hayden occasionally winces or takes a deep breath for no apparent reason, in the manner of a person who carries a pain around inside.

"What's the white flag for?" asks Rosamond.

"For you it marks the hole where you're trying to get the ball," he says. "For me it's saying that I should surrender."

By the time they exit the clubhouse Hayden is enjoying the cheerful and outstanding service afforded an affable local mayor, having befriended everyone from the caddies to the golf pro, the manager of the restaurant, and a group of businessmen from Minneapolis. As usual, his high spirits color the day and easily spread to perfect strangers so that they carry this joy away with them and pass it along to others.

After returning to the resort for a nap in their respective rooms, they stroll on the white sand beach as the wind ruffles the nearby water with waves and breathe in the peacefulness. Overhead the gulls soar and dip, their wings flashing silver in the sunlight. The refreshing tranquillity reminds Rosamond of the Liturgy of the Hours, the seven times a day the nuns went to chapel for prayer. Now her sisters would be gathering for Nones, the ninth hour call for more perseverance and strength to continue as one exceeds her prime and must keep going. By acknowledging this midafternoon hour of Christ's death, one was supposedly able to touch finitude.

While carefully making their way around the blankets and lounge chairs of sprawled pink flesh, the two eventually walk close to a couple lying together and kissing. Rosamond watches unabashedly for a moment. The man notices her and smiles. She smiles back before looking away. The warm sea air and flood of clean sunshine have lent a certain happiness to her face, brushing out the fine wrinkles around her eyes, which are the color of forget-me-nots against the pale blue sky. A few freckles have appeared across her nose and cheeks and shoulders, as if she's been splattered with gold paint. And her shorn hair has grown into a tousled array of pale blond curls that flutter against her cheekbones in the gentle ocean breeze.

Rosamond is overwhelmed by the natural beauty surrounding her. "It is just like a dream!"

"Yes, if you ever do run into God, please tell him that I'm a huge fan of His work."

"Oh, Hayden!" Rosamond stretches her arms out toward the sea and sky. "So, is this the alkahest?"

Hayden laughs. "Good heavens no. When I was a boy that's what Dad said when he nipped out to the barn after dinner for his whiskey. Me mum was a Presbyterian and wouldn't allow it in the house. So when I used to meet up with the Idleonians for a round o' drink I'd joke with Mary that we were going to search for the alkahest. And then I started sayin' it to Joey when we'd go for ice cream too close to suppertime. Only one day he looked it up and thought I was seeking a cure for The Cancer. Of course I've told him there isn't one, that I'm just tryin' to die with as little mess as possible, but he keeps reading books about wizards and finding alchemists on the Internet and is convinced there's a magical remedy out there someplace. You know how kids are. He believes the alkahest stops cancer the way kryptonite stops Superman."

"I see," says Rosamond. "Sounds as if he's revived an old religion."

"Well, I hope it's a tax-free one," says Hayden. After a recent visit to the accountant he'd been appalled by how much estate tax Diana and Linda were going to have to pay when they inherited his savings—money that he'd already paid taxes on.

As they stroll back toward their rooms a black cat leaps onto their path from out of a nearby jacaranda tree and then disappears into the dense shrubbery. Rosamond is startled by the sudden streak of movement, jumps aside, and then pauses to catch her breath. But Hayden just chuckles. "Now I bet you're going to tell me that a black cat means bad luck."

"Of course not. That's just superstition." She relaxes and smiles. "It startled me, that's all."

"Isn't it funny the way we refer to other people's beliefs as superstition but our own we call religion," he says slyly.

"Oh, Hayden, next you'll be trying to find a voodoo priestess to argue with."

Between the doors to their two rooms is a bush of fragrant white oleander with swirling green leaves, gorgeous to look at, but as the bellhop was careful to warn them, poisonous to eat. Rosamond goes inside and closes the door so that she can change for evening.

The open-air restaurant overlooks the sea and when Rosamond stares out at the wide expanse of sky it brings to mind the blue of the Madonna's robes. As the sun falls to the horizon on one side of them a pale outline of a moon can be seen emerging on the other, as if waiting in the wings. Rosamond is reminded of the words of Saint John of the Cross in his *Spiritual Canticle*, "The union between the soul and God is like starlight united with the light of the sun."

The table is beautifully laid with elegant china, crystal water glasses, and a single flower, the reddest of roses, in the center of a smooth pink linen cloth. In the background can be heard the low popping of corks and gentle clinking of glasses.

When a tuxedoed waiter arrives with their dinners he lifts up the sterling silver covers as if performing a magic trick. The food is prettily garnished with tiny pink and red petals shaped to form a starburst.

"It's so exquisite that I almost feel as if we should say grace," says Rosamond.

"One grace coming up," says Hayden, much to her surprise. Rosamond assumed that she'd be the one giving thanks while Hayden impatiently drummed his fingers and tapped his feet.

Instead, he folds his hands, bows his head, and solemnly begins, "Some hae meat, and cannot eat, And some would eat that want it; But we hae meat, and we can eat—And sae the Lord be thankit."

Rosamond says "amen" and then looks up approvingly and yet slightly puzzled.

" 'The Selkirk Grace,' " explains Hayden as he cuts into his filet of sole. "Robbie Burns, o' course."

"Of course," she says. Hayden never ceases to surprise and amuse her.

Over dessert he produces another surprise, only this one is not nearly as amusing. Hayden quietly yet passionately unveils his plan to overdose. "I do'an' want a death vigil—the darkened room, whispered voices, bringing everyone else's life to a standstill, Ted droning about privatizing social security, seeing my reflection in his teeth, no, no. And then these patients who fiddle around with the morphine, they're so weak or doped up that they can't commit suicide even if they have a half a mind left to. . . ."

But Rosamond can't bear to listen to such talk. Out on the dance floor several couples hold each other close and sway to a Calypso band playing "Jamaica Farewell." The metal drums plink out the melody while an ocean breeze causes the hanging plastic lanterns to flicker and sway. Wild purple orchids cling to the nearby trees and a gentle breeze carries their pleasant aroma out toward the sea.

"Hayden, what's it like?" Rosamond asks dreamily and gazes out to where the horizon is stained orange by the last rays of the sun.

"Same as falling asleep, only faster, like when they put you out before an operation."

"No, not that," she says softly. "I meant making love."

Hayden is momentarily startled. He carefully wipes his mouth with the starched linen napkin. "Oh, you've never, no, well, I guess, of course not. Yes, well, it's like, it's like . . . come on . . ." he rises from the table, "I'll show you—"

Rosamond accidentally knocks over the water glass in front of her. Her chest tightens as she envisions a repeat of the scene in the backyard with the ice cream soda.

"No, no," Hayden says and places their napkins over the expanding pool as he softly chuckles. "I didn't mean that." He takes her hand and leads her to the dance floor where the soothing Caribbean music drifts through the balmy air and a handsome man with lustrous coffee-colored skin and swinging dreadlocks croons: *"I'm sad to say I'm going away, had to leave a little girl in Kingston town."*

"I only meant that makin' love is like dancing," Hayden whispers as they come together and float across the floor in the orange glow of tiki torches against a purple-black sky. "Holding each other, moving together to the music, whispering in each other's ear, feeling your heart beat against mine, it's an elaborate ritual that's at once both improvised and rehearsed. Like dancing."

"Yes," says Rosamond uncertainly as they sway to the *plink plink* of the drums under the large and indifferent stare of a pale yellow August moon, like a sun grown old. The sky above is strung with thousands of tiny lights, and she fights an overwhelming urge to break her orbit and fling herself out among the stars.

"Rosie," Hayden asks after a few moments, "how come whenever I pull you close you pull away?"

She giggles bashfully. "Sister Annunciata at the Academy of the Sacred Heart said that when dancing with a boy one must always leave sufficient room for the Holy Spirit."

"Well, if angels can comfortably dance on the head of a pin then I'm sure the Holy Spirit doesn't need a bloody wind tunnel." Hayden gently pulls her to him and this time she doesn't withdraw.

In fact, Rosamond tightens her grip on Hayden's shoulder as she feels released from the small but comfortable world of her life so far and suddenly catapulted into a universe that lacks the reassurance of limits. Love had arisen unexpectedly, like hundreds of flowers simultaneously blooming on a cherry tree one day in springtime.

They move against and around the rich smooth beat of the music. For

Rosamond, dancing with Hayden feels like coming in with the tide. As the song drifts to a close and they unlock their embrace Rosamond looks apprehensive. "Oh Hayden, what's happening?"

He holds her hand as the next song begins, the carefree "Don't Worry, Be Happy" of Bobby McFerrin. In the distance, summer lightning quivers in the moist air and the spicy, thick scent of marijuana drifts down from the bandstand. When Hayden glances up the moon appears shiny and hopeful, like a drunk's last silver dollar. "In your dreams you were alone. But now we're in love and so you're no longer alone."

"But what about God?" she asks with deep concern.

"What *about* God, Rosamond? He, She, It, wants us to love one another."

"I'll bet you say that to all the nuns." It's impossible to deny that Hayden's sense of humor is infectious. And Rosamond loves being rewarded with that warm magical chortle of his that can almost assure a person that everything is going to be made right in the end.

Indeed, Hayden does burst out laughing. "That is the funniest thing you've ever said to me!" He touches his lips to hers for a second, and then gazes into her intense blue eyes before kissing her again, long and languorously this time, and they hold each other close and continue to dance. Her blond hair glows with starlight and every once in a while he touches the delicate strands to make sure she's real.

Only Rosamond can't help but fret and wonder, is this earth-bound man with his arms around her body, sharing the very breath she draws, her great misfortune or her great redemption?

Slightly after midnight they stroll together, hand in hand, down the path back to Hayden's room. The sea and the sky have turned the same shade of deep blue, as if they dissolved into each other. White lanterns glow from within the trees every few feet and the air is filled with the sweet perfume of flowers and fruit borne on the breeze. The staccato of drums fades into the background, replaced by the slap of banana leaves against the trees and the plaintive chirping of crickets. A curtain of night moths softly beat their velvety brown wings against Hayden's screen door beneath the outside light.

Inside the room the bed has been expertly turned down in his absence and the radio softly plays in the background. Hayden's attempts to find a jazz station with some Miles Davis and John Coltrane have turned up only All Reggae—All the Time. But after awhile the plaintive strains become almost hypnotic, molasses smooth voices against a strongly accentuated offbeat.

Hayden lights candles that cast crisscross shadows of bamboo furniture onto the walls. He pushes back the curtain and opens the sliding glass door so they can see the moonglow atop the ocean and hear the surf crash onto the beach only a few yards away. After locating the key to the mini bar he offers Rosamond a drink. When she declines he pours a scotch for himself, takes a swallow, and walks back to where she's seated on the edge of the bed.

"I . . . I've been waiting for this moment for a long time," Hayden says with a gentle burr in his voice, and then leans over until the space between them melts into darkness and he kisses her slightly parted lips.

From the clock radio Bob Marley chants soulfully in the background. When they come apart Rosamond exhales nervously, glances toward the top of the TV and asks, "Aren't you going to have the rest of your drink? Or maybe you'd just like to knock it over?"

"No, I'm fine now." But it's Hayden's turn to appear puzzled. "Why?"

"Suddenly I'm a little thirsty." She stands and retrieves his unfinished cocktail from across the room with the defiant grace and resolute step of the healthy. Lifting the glass to her lips, Rosamond hastily dispenses with the last half of Hayden's scotch. The radio fills the silence, *"Won't you help to sing these songs of freedom, because all I ever had, redemption songs."*

When Rosamond returns to where Hayden is seated on the edge of the bed she's no longer slightly distressed but overwhelmed by her own inexperience. "Hayden, doesn't it concern you that I've lived my entire adult life as a nun?" Though her uneven voice hints that in reality it's more worrisome to her than to him.

He raises her left hand to his mouth and delicately kisses her third finger, the one where she used to wear the ring sealing her marriage to God. "To be honest, it's . . . it's exciting and terrifying all at the same time. I do'an' think I ever, with a, I mean, Mary had been engaged before, and there were some others, mostly from the nurses college . . . very fast, those nurses, must be the anatomy classes."

"I see." Now that she's approaching the point of no return, Diana's tales of Hank's clumsy inexperience reverberate in Rosamond's head like chapel bells and she suddenly withdraws her hand. Surely she'll disappoint him.

Hayden touches his lips to her other hand. "To tell you the truth, I'm more concerned about bein' a dyin' fifty-five-year-old who's tryin' to make this worthwhile for you. As far as finding a partner goes, you could have made a better choice . . . a healthier choice, I mean. I'm not exactly setting the heather afire anymore."

She squeezes his hand with hers and draws it toward her heart. "When it comes to certain things, I don't believe the choice is ours."

"Huh? Oh, right, the God thing. I get it. Well then, God could have made a better choice for you, other than one of his defective products that's just about to be recalled."

"My father was a fisherman," says Rosamond, "and he used to say that the stars shine brightest when the moon is on the wane."

"Well, my father was a farmer. And he was fond o' saying that the rain is God's way o' cleaning the sheep."

"See! I knew you were from God-fearing people. That was a bunch of boloney about reading the Bible in Alaska."

"Yes, you finally got me. I'm a born-again heathen. After reading the parable of the Lost Sheep and learning that God loves sinners most of all, I have since devoted all of my energies in that direction."

"Stop it. You're making me laugh."

Hayden gently slides one hand to her front and unfastens the top button on her blouse.

"This is very sexy, by the way."

"Thank you. Diana gave it to me for the trip."

"No wonder I'm constantly havin' to shoot at blokes in my livin' room."

"Oh, Hayden!"

Hayden lets his hands flow like two rivers from Rosamond's face down to her neck, across her smooth shoulders and along her sides, without letting so much as a shadow come between his fingertips and her soft skin.

"What shall I do?" she whispers, as if there's a chance they could be overheard.

"You know Diana's spirit board?"

Rosamond giggles. "You mean the Ouija board?"

"It's just like that. The hands move on their own. You do'an' have to think upon it. And there's no need of a subway to make it work."

Rosamond's hands explore his legs, gradually absorbing the texture of his skin and the wiry hair on his calves as it springs to life around her fingertips. Hayden strokes every alcove of the slender womanly form he's been admiring from afar for the past few weeks; the nape of her neck, the inside of her elbow, the soft underside of her ankle bone, and her delicate earlobes, lingering at each sumptuous curve with a kiss. The tremulous candlelight casts their silhouettes onto the walls like windmills along a moonlit Dutch countryside.

And when their lips finally meet again they become lost in an infinite kiss, the kind known only to lovers who have no objective other than love itself, tender as the dawn, yet insistent as a tide. The radio pauses between songs and it seems as if their hearts are ticking in synch with the clock on the bedside table, beating to the music of time. They silently remove the last articles of clothing that remain between them and finally experience the simultaneous thrill of knowing each other as one and thereby defying death.

Outside a summer rain has begun to fall and the air in the room becomes heavy with humidity and secret urgencies as their bodies melt together like two flames. Tenuous moods of firelight and shadow pass between them as the ceiling fan overhead rotates and casts pinwheels on their intertwined forms.

A feeling of deep satisfaction burns within Hayden's flesh, in the way that only happens during those rare moments when what one most longs for is finally realized.

Streams of tears run down Rosamond's cheeks as she tries to concentrate on evening out her breathing in an effort to calm her heart, which is still racing like the desperate beating of birds' wings.

Hayden encircles her with his outstretched arm and runs his fingers through her soft hair, a sinking drowsiness descending upon him. They slip away from each other slightly, into a loose knot. And Rosamond's heartfelt weeping slowly fades as she ponders this ache of tenderness and everything that has happened leading up to it. She savors the feeling of his warm breath against her cheek while her consciousness lazily drifts between dreams and reality.

The cloudburst passes and the steady drip of rain finding its way back to the earth is joined by the dying song of crickets. And Rosamond, floating off to sleep, feels as if she has finally been visited by love, a sudden awakening of the spirit and a stirring of the flesh that makes a difference where previously there was no difference.

chapter fifty-seven

When they return to Brooklyn Rosamond feels relaxed and renewed. The street is quiet and with the end of a long, hot summer, the houses appear slightly faded. Though the MacBride residence sports a fresh coat of paint, inside and out. Anthony and his friends had gone to work while they were away, apparently eager not to run into Hayden. What seems to be a permanent haze has settled over the dry lawns and wilted shrubbery. Diana and Hank immediately notice that Hayden and Rosamond have "gone public" with their affection, smiling at each other and occasionally kissing after short absences.

Rosamond and Hayden also become aware that things with Diana and Hank have progressed while in their absence. Hank has moved a few personal items into the upstairs bathroom and Diana glows with the radiance of new romance, exuding the quiet assurance of a woman who knows that she's loved unconditionally.

Joey has made some friends on his baseball team, despite the fact they've lost all their games so far. Ginger is finally completely housebroken and the dishwasher has mercifully melted the top of Diana's juicing machine. It's only Hayden who appears subdued, as if he expended the last of his vitality on making the trip.

"Did you find the alkahest?" Joey eagerly asks.

"Yes, we most certainly did." Hayden pulls Joey close and whispers into his ear, "But it's the most secret and ancient science and has to do with kissing girls. And so you'll have to find it for yourself."

"Yuck," says Joey and wriggles free. Though while Hayden was away, Joey and Giovanni, the boy his age who'd moved in next door, discovered a hole in the men's locker room at the Y through which they can watch the girls take showers.

On the way into the kitchen Hayden steadies himself against the wall, suggesting that it's an effort just to balance. His face is the color of ashes, as if the light and warmth is slowly draining out starting from the top of his forehead.

"You should stop drinking once and for all," Diana reproves him.

"I prefer the term *self-medicating*," replies Hayden. "Tell them to read from *The Wrath of Grapes* at my funeral."

The Cancer has left him thirsty all the time, so Hayden takes a beer and shuffles toward the front porch. But Diana's attuned ears pick up the sound of the can opening from the dining room and she chases after him with Rosamond in tow.

"Diana's right that you shouldn't drink anymore," says Rosamond.

"Harping all the time will not make you an angel," replies Hayden.

"Dad, do whatever else you like but I'm putting my foot down when it comes to—"

Bobbie Anne's car pulling into the next-door driveway momentarily distracts her. Out of the back pop her two daughters along with the light-brown-skinned boy who'd recently been playing with Joey. Normally the women just exchange tight smiles or forced waves, but today Bobbie Anne saunters across the small patch of grass dividing the two driveways and says a friendly hello in her smoky alto voice. She's dressed in a smart lavender-colored suit with matching spectator pumps.

"Where *were* you?" she asks Hayden.

"Rum country!" he declares and nods toward Rosamond, who is standing next to Diana, waiting for her to continue leading the charge on the alcohol ban.

"That's terrific!" says Bobbie Anne, pretending she hadn't already heard about the proposed trip from Rosamond two weeks earlier. "I was afraid you'd moved back to Edinburgh. You know what they say about Scots always going home to die," she tells him with a laugh.

Rosamond and Diana visibly blanche at the death reference, but Hayden appreciates those brave enough to be frank about his fate, and better yet, have the courage to joke about it, like his beloved Greyfriars Gang.

"Nope, just a little R and R—rest and resurrection," says Hayden.

"Listen, I . . . I just wanted to tell you all that I got a job—a real job," Bobbie Anne announces, although she looks directly at Diana and Rosamond, who couldn't be more surprised if Bobbie Anne declared that she's running for borough president.

"Congratulations!" Hayden is the first to speak. He toasts her with his beer can and takes a big swallow, much to the chagrin of Diana and Rosamond. Then he turns and smiles at them, too, knowing full well that his daughter won't start a row about his drinking in front of their neighbor.

Bobbie Anne checks the yard to make sure that all the children are out of earshot. "I'm working as a sex counselor."

The way Rosamond and Diana glance at each other suggests that they're not sure whether this is better or worse than running a midday brothel out of one's home.

Bobbie Anne immediately senses their doubtfulness. "It really *is* a job." She smiles proudly. "Remember that psychiatrist who used to talk for his entire hour?" She directs this question to Hayden.

"Yeah, sure, the guy who after fifty minutes always said, 'Our time is almost up,' " Hayden says, causing Diana's eyes to widen at how intimately her father seems to know the details of Bobbie Anne's business.

"Right," Bobbie Anne continues. "Now I work in his office and talk with people about their problems. It's totally legit because he has a license and oversees everything, it pays well and has benefits, and I don't have to . . . to, you know . . ."

The women nod vigorously as if they'd rather not have her say it either.

"I mean, it's just like my old job . . ."

When they all appear startled she amends that statement, ". . . in that I can make my own hours, even on Saturdays. For instance, today I'll go in between ten and two. But the clients, I mean the *patients*, they're not even allowed to ask me out on a date, you know, because it's a professional relationship. And the best part is, get this, I'm paid more for talking about sex than actually having it." She throws her head back with laughter. "Can you believe it?"

"There's capitalism for you," Hayden says with approval and toasts her with his beer can.

An attractive woman with mocha-colored skin and long disheveled coppery curls wearing a tank top and shorts appears on Bobbie Anne's front stoop and calls for the children to come in and have their snack.

"Did you hire a live-in baby-sitter?" asks Hayden.

"No, that's Gabriella, my girlfriend. She moved in while you were away, after I was sure that I had the job. I'm just so burned out on men right now. No offense," she says, more to Hayden than the women and then chuckles.

"None taken," says Hayden with a meaningful smile.

"Anyway, her son Giovanni will be in the same grade as Joey." Bobbie Anne points to the dark-haired boy talking to Joey in the narrow space between the two houses. "Gabriella's going to stay with the kids while I work during the day. She has a waitress job on Sundays and evenings, when I'm off, and so I'll watch the kids then. That way we won't have to pay baby-sitters."

They all congratulate Bobbie Anne on her success and by the time she's headed back to her house Hayden is enjoying the last sip of his beer.

chapter fifty-eight

By the end of the third week in August Hayden has finally given up on false displays of energy and accepts the fact that he needs assistance to do everything but raise a glass to his lips. He passes the hours in his bed on the sunporch, accompanied by Rosamond, and occasionally Joey, when his grandson isn't out playing baseball or running around the neighborhood with Giovanni. After dinner Joey sits at Hayden's bedside and recounts the plays from his ball games—though more often than not they are unsuccessful ones. "No matter how hard I try I'm just not very good," Joey shamefully admits.

Hayden knows he should lecture him about practice and teamwork, but he'd raised Joey not to depend on tired advice. "Well, Joe-Joe, the way in which we're all cursed, and we all are in one way or another, is also our blessing—just ask Rosie about her friend Jesus. Anyway, maybe you'll find a career other than as a catcher and it will turn out to be even better."

Joey saves up the jokes he hears from the other boys and Hayden has to admit that his material and presentation is improving by the day. He's mastered the twinkle in the eye that lets you know you're supposed to chuckle even though he's not acknowledging it was a setup. Hayden actually chokes with laughter when Joey saunters in saying, "So these two fleas leave the movie theater and the one says to other, do you want to walk or catch a dog?"

Joey also reports back to Hayden any observations on the state of the American female. If Rosamond or Diana are present then Joey describes in code language any good sets of "twins" that he managed to see during his wanderings, and the two delight in sharing an inside joke.

Hayden constantly struggles with the urge to try and pass on to his grandson all the wisdom he's collected over the years. Even when Joey reads aloud to him from Robert Louis Stevenson's *Dr. Jekyll and Mr. Hyde*, Hayden's urge to philosophize is sparked.

"You see, Joe-Joe, Stevenson is saying that a man can have a hidden nature, and you have to understand what it is if you want to do business with him. Such duality in men is also a good reason to wear a clip-on tie, in case a bloke takes issue with you and attempts the Glasgow Kiss by pulling you up by the necktie and bopping you in the face."

"Mom says that Robert Louis Stevenson wrote *Dr. Jekyll and Mr. Hyde* while taking mind-altering drugs."

"Well, yes. Mr. Stevenson enjoyed the occasional hallucinogenic the way your grandpa enjoys his single malt Glen Grant. However, he was of sound mind when he said to disregard most things taught to you by your parents."

While Joey is off playing with Giovanni, Hayden and Rosamond sit and hold hands like two people grown old together, no longer needing more than a glance to communicate their feelings. Through the glass they watch nature's summer dance play out around them—a mother robin teaches her young to fly, brown and white rabbits scamper past to raid Mrs. Trummel's lettuce patch, and squirrels dart across electrical wires overhead.

Hank usually sits with Hayden for an hour in the evening while Rosamond helps Diana in the kitchen. He shares the plans for a new office building his firm is constructing along the East River and brings old maps of Brooklyn from his company's archives, which Hayden devours with great interest.

With Hayden's blessing Hank has started taking Joey to see the Mets play when they're at home. He's wise not to try too hard in winning the boy's affection, and thus they're building an easy friendship.

"You and Hank make such an attractive couple," Rosamond says to Diana one evening as they watch Joey and Hank play catch in the street out front.

"You're not upset that he left the Church?"

"Oh heavens no. In retrospect I think he was more attracted by ecclesiastical architecture than anything else. And he does still go to Mass with me on Sundays."

"Yes, he's invited me to go, too," says Diana. "I don't know. I suppose it can't hurt. Though I'm not sure if I can believe in a God that, well . . ." she nods toward Hayden's room. "You know . . ."

"Of course. It's not for everyone. And you seem happy, different almost, since we came back."

Diana gives Rosamond a knowing smile. "I remember what you said about confidence. And when I realized how much Hank believes in me, I guess it finally gave me some confidence in myself. Not to mention the strength to let Joey go out and make his own mistakes. Heaven knows, I've made enough for the both of us."

"No more than anyone else," says Rosamond, taking her friend's arm. "I only wish that I'd had the courage to go out and make a few myself earlier on."

When the guys have finished playing catch Joey comes rushing over with his glove still on and asks if Rosamond has had a chance to pick out a campground. While Hayden and Rosamond were away he'd painstakingly researched parks and hiking trails in the Adirondacks. He's been hoping with all his might that she wasn't making up the story about going camping, just the two of them.

However, not only had Rosamond enthusiastically reviewed all of Joey's careful notes, but she'd arranged to borrow a tent from the Palowski family, where they'd enjoyed their Fourth of July feast.

"Don't worry, I've chosen the place," she says. "Only we'll have to wait until your grandfather's feeling a bit better, so he can be left on his own."

Though Rosamond knows in her heart that Hayden is the one who will be going, and that they'll be the ones left on their own.

chapter fifty-nine

On overcast days Hayden watches the lines of silver rain make adjoining rivers on the tall panes of glass while Rosamond reads aloud from *The Crow Road* by the Scottish author Iain Banks. And if a rainbow appears after dark clouds pass he is sure to tell Joey not to believe the Irish with their cockamamy yarns about leprechauns and a pot of gold. "The rainbow is right here in your own backyard, Joe-Joe. You have to go to school, work hard, and don't hit the bottle until after the five o'clock whistle blows."

To Rosamond the streak of pastel colors painted across the sky brings to mind the waters receding after The Flood and Noah's ark surviving the test of God's might, with the first rainbow symbolizing the new covenant between God and everything that lives.

When evening comes a swathe of purple rises up to the horizon and then melts into the sky, leaving in its place a sliver of a moon suspended above the Brooklyn Bridge like the broken edge of a white porcelain disc, and they lie atop the bed holding hands, safe within each other's love, at ease in the mutual knowledge of each other's flesh.

They are calm, resigned in the face of the inevitable, and even cheerful. When Rosamond plays Hayden's favorite Bach cello suites and they have a glass of cabernet with dinner Rosamond is surprised at how both romance and Catholicism rely so heavily on incense, music, candles, and wine.

Diana, on the other hand, is increasingly overcome with anxiety regarding Hayden's decline, and has accelerated the frenzy of her search for remedies, dragging hope along behind her like the fading tail of a comet. From a neighborhood aromatherapist she's purchased tea light candles and incense cones scented with sandalwood and juniper that are purported to have healing properties. She has, however, abandoned her nutrition campaign, instead concentrating on making Hayden's favorite dishes in an attempt to encourage him to take a few bites. Only he's all but lost his appetite, and Diana is struggling not to admit to herself that he's becoming more shadow-like every day.

The Greyfriars Gang now gathers around Hayden's sickbed, with Diana serving up sweet mutton hot pot and dumplings and peeking her head in every so often to make sure they're not plying him with scotch. But she appreciates the presence of Hayden's friends and their stalwart good cheer, the way they boldly continue to argue as if everything is normal, hotly debating whether the English monarchy should be abolished and if the British should leave Northern Ireland once and for all.

Whenever one of the men tells a particularly first-rate God joke Hayden insists that Rosamond come in to hear it. "Do that one again, Hugh," he says and watches her appreciatively as Hugh repeats: "When God created Scotland, He gazed down on it with great satisfaction and called the Archangel Gabriel to have a peek. 'Look at the splendid mountains, beautiful scenery, brave men, fine women, and nice cool weather,' God said to Gabriel. 'Plus I've given them beautiful music and a wonderful drink called whiskey. Try some.' Gabriel takes an appreciative sip and says, 'Excellent, only perhaps you've been *too* kind to them. Won't they be spoiled by all this?' But God only laughs and says, 'Not at all. Just wait 'til you see the neighbors I've given them!' "

Rosamond laughs heartily, which pleases Hayden. And on this particular evening she ventures into male territory by saying, "You know, we had some jokes at the convent . . ."

"Pour another round, Alisdair," says Paddy. "Rosie's going to tell us a joke!"

Rosamond clears her throat and hesitantly begins, "So this nun gets lost on a rainy night and stumbles upon a monastery."

The men are already howling with laughter. But this only confuses her. "What's so funny? I haven't told the joke yet."

"A nun walks into a monastery!" shouts Hugh, doubled over with laughter. "Saints be praised, it's brilliant. Sorry, go on now."

"Yes, yes, go on," Alisdair encourages her, his hazel eyes glowing with merriment.

"Well, it's dinnertime," continues Rosamond, still unsure of herself, but the men are nodding that she should go on. "And they serve the nun the best fish and chips she's ever tasted. So afterward she goes into the kitchen to thank the chefs, Brother Michael and Brother Charles. 'That was the most wonderful dinner I've ever had,' she says. 'But just out of curiosity, who cooked what?' Brother Charles replies, 'Well, I'm the Fish Friar.' And Brother Michael says, 'And I'm the Chip Monk.' "

The men hoot with laughter, less a result of the dreadful punch line than the fact that the proper and reserved former nun is telling jokes of a "guy walks into a bar" variety. And in even larger part because they've been drinking for several hours and at this stage would find Joey's knock-knock jokes to be hilarious.

Hayden takes Rosamond's hand. "Tha's wonderful. I do believe that in a former life you were a stand-up comedi*nun*."

Once again the men roar with merriment and clink their glasses. They offer her a drink but Rosamond leaves the men to their fun and returns to the living room where she's promised to help Diana sort out photographs.

"Sounds as if the boys are in fine fettle," says Diana. "Talk about a curse and a blessing."

"Yes, it would certainly appear that we can't enjoy the benefit of their high spirits without their bottles of spirits," says Rosamond.

Rosamond enjoys looking at the pictures of the MacBride family throughout the years, especially Diana as a little girl with ribbons in her hair and a youthful Hayden waving gaily at the camera, usually with a cocktail glass nearby. Diana sorts the photos by approximate date and hands them to Rosamond to organize in the different albums. As for pictures of Linda, Diana rules that if she's with another family member then they can be placed in the album, but all solo shots go right back into the box. Unless of course it's a particularly bad photo.

An hour after Joey has gone to bed it's so quiet in the back room that Diana and Rosamond decide to check and make sure that the men haven't all passed out.

Diana opens the door a crack and peers into the darkened room. "Dad, is everything all right?"

A resounding "Shhh!" serves to hush her. In the soft glow of the television the men are wiping tears from their eyes, clearing their throats and blowing their noses into handkerchiefs. For a moment Diana fears that Hayden has not only passed out, but also passed away.

Then she follows their glassy eyes to the television, where an athletic Gene Kelly shares the screen with a stunning Cyd Charisse. With a catch in his throat Gene Kelly explains that he must go home and leave his love behind in her enchanted Scottish village of Brigadoon, which appears only once every hundred years.

"*Do you understand at all?*" asks Gene Kelly, playing Tommy Albright in a plaintive I'll-never-forget-you voice to Cyd Charisse's Fiona Campbell. "*You're not sorry I came?*"

"*No,*" replies Fiona in her soft melodious brogue. "*I'll be less lonely now. Real loneliness is not being in love in vain, but not being in love at all.*"

And after a few balletic parting steps Gene is on his way back to New York with shouts of "I Love You" reverberating throughout the encroaching Highland mist.

This touching moment is immediately followed by Paddy, Hugh, Duncan, and Alisdair sniffling and clamoring for another round.

Diana and Rosamond quickly slip out of the room and when the door is closed they burst out laughing from all the times Hayden has made fun of their movies. Diana wipes a tear from her cheek. Rosamond does the same. And then she wipes away another.

"It *is* awfully sweet," says Rosamond.

Diana nods her head in agreement, tears up again, and they both sniffle and hug each other in the hallway.

chapter sixty

Day by day death continues to steal over Hayden's failing body. The future slowly becomes the past as the hours dissolve into one another, and it becomes apparent that there's no way anyone can reach out and extend them. Every night feels like a lifetime and it's as if Rosamond and Hayden have left part of themselves behind, on an island in the bright blue Caribbean Sea.

Rosamond is no longer hopeful that Hayden will make a miraculous recovery. In fact, Diana is more optimistic than Rosamond at this stage. Then again, Rosamond's view of miracles has changed considerably since she fell in love with Hayden. She now realizes that they rest not so much upon seeing visions, hearing voices, or the sudden acquisition of a healing power, but rather on our perception being enhanced, so that for a moment our eyes can see and our ears can hear what has always been around us.

The past two months have been like the long twilight between the Fall and the Redemption. The weight of doubt and loneliness in her heart and soul has dissolved while the faith that had once receded like a tide gone out has gradually restored itself.

On the last Sunday in August they awaken before daybreak, the yard outside still wreathed in the last mist of a dream. A solitary bird chirps in the darkness, secure in its faith that light will soon appear. There's no reason to look at the bedside clock. Time has ceased to exist for the two lovers, as their lives have become woven into a single strand. But this particular sunrise will live forever in Rosamond's memory.

Spokes of yellow-gold light appear on the horizon like the dawn of creation in a children's Bible. Hayden slowly opens his eyes and gazes at Rosamond as if she's a far off melody. "I have something to tell you," he says. For the first time she can sense fragility in the halting rhythm of his breathing.

"I have something to tell you, too," she says.

"Ladies first." Hayden graciously waves his hand in her direction and then closes his eyes, as if it's exhausting just to move. His lids feel grainy, like they're scratching against his pupils.

"The other day, when you thought I was out shopping, I went to one of the doctors where Diana works. I . . . I thought I might be pregnant."

"Great Scott!" Hayden opens his eyes and leans forward. In the midst of so much death the possibility of new life is the farthest thing from his mind. "And . . ."

"No. No, I'm not."

Hayden visibly exhales. Talk about health care complications—a baby . . . he can't even imagine it.

She pauses, not knowing exactly how to go on, then plunges ahead. "But my cancer, I mean, it's not lung cancer. They did another CAT scan. I had pneumonia. It was apparently someone else's biopsy report."

Hayden stares ahead in silence, avoiding her eyes, as if calculating what this actually means. And yet it is something he has been sensing for a while, and perhaps just didn't want to admit to himself because he thought it would lessen his chances with her. Finally he looks at Rosamond, takes her hand in his, and smiles. "See, it's like I always told you. Those bone benders have no idea what they're talkin' about."

"Well, I *do* have a tumor in my left lung. But it isn't cancerous. In fact, it's gone down by half, to a centimeter." Rosamond feels guilty delivering this news, as if she's betraying him, and has been holding off for the right moment, which never seemed to arrive. She finds it incredibly difficult to recall that only two months ago she'd been so distressed upon learning that she was going to die. Because it's as if an eternity has passed since then, and now Rosamond feels totally prepared, if indeed death is what God has planned for her. In fact, in some ways she would prefer it.

"I'm so happy you're not goin', Rosie. I always said you had too much life left in you to be dyin'," says Hayden. "It was probably just the haircut you had when the doctor first saw you that made him think you were a goner."

"Oh stop it! Now what did you have to tell me?"

"Never mind. It wasn't important. The main thing is that you're well." He gently squeezes her palm with his fingers.

"Hayden, please. What were you going to say?"

"It was silly. Just a dyin' man's last wish. I was . . . I was going to ask you to marry me." He has the jagged respiration of an aging athlete who's just finished a difficult marathon. "But now o' course it do'an' make sense, you being well and all . . . and me headin' south for the winter."

"Oh Hayden, that's the sweetest thing anyone has ever said to me." She kisses him on the cheek.

Hayden looks hopeful. Outside the bright August dawn spreads like a flower of fire and the darkness quickly recedes while a vibrant end-of-summer-green fans across the damp earth. Everything sparkles like a garden after a shower.

"I'm sorry . . ." Her voice is as delicate as ice on a spring brook, and there is true sorrow in her gaze.

"No, no, do'an' be sorry. I just thought if we were both goin' to buy the farm, that if we pooled our resources we'd get more land, that's all. But now you're . . . I do'an' want you to be a widow. . . ."

"But that's not the reason, Hayden." She pauses and then takes both his hands in hers and softly says, "It's just that . . . I'm returning to the convent."

He stares out the window for a long while before meeting her resolute gaze. Was being with him so satisfying that she wasn't interested in meeting other men, or more likely, had the experience sent her fleeing the opposite sex forever? "I see. They've held your place, have they? No scheming young replacement from a temp agency performed an *All About Eve* while you were away?"

"I'll be given a leave of absence for health reasons."

"Very good. Like temporary insanity. That's all it was anyway," he says dismissively. "The crazy things we do and say when we think we're dying," he jokingly adds. But it's apparent he's crushed by the belief that their romance was nothing more than a fling on her part.

Rosamond is also distraught. "No, Hayden! It wasn't like that, not for one minute. I was never thrown out of the convent. I left. I mean, I . . . I felt that I was falling in love with you. And I had to see . . . and I was . . . I mean, I am."

"What about Him?" Hayden nods his head toward the ceiling.

"It wasn't that I didn't love Him so much as I didn't know how to love fully, with all my heart."

"But what about the fact that we, uh, you know?" Hayden's not sure if he should feel guilty for having made love to a nun, especially so close to the hour of his death. He suddenly feels rather vague and thinks he hears the voice of his Presbyterian mother saying that near the end is when you should be busy polishing up your copybook, not sullying it.

"Yes, *that*." Rosamond's cheeks flush. "Actually, a substantial number of sisters enter the convent later in life, after being married, or at least after leading normal lives. Many have even raised families. And of course indiscretions occur. Celibacy is a Church principle, not a divine one. Some even believe the vow of chastity is a contradiction, that a life need not be devoid of love in a worldly sense if it is filled by Him who is all graces."

"All right then." He leans back into the pillows and loudly exhales. "I guess I'll just have to wait for you on the other side."

"I know you don't really believe that," she chides him, and yet there's a trace of hope in her sky blue eyes.

"No, but I thought it might score me some points." Hayden's mischievous smile turns up the corners of his mouth ever so slightly. "Not with *Him*, I mean. With *you*."

"You don't have to score any more points with me. I'll never love another man." And it's true. Now that love has finally ventured into her heart, mind, and soul, there can be no higher form of expression for Rosamond than to love her God. She looks at Hayden and a solitary teardrop trembles on her cheek like a diamond coming loose from its setting. The room is silent except for a dry leaf stirring against the door to the backyard.

By the time Joey enters the room with his breakfast cereal the sun has risen above the tree line and the room is filled with pure morning light that causes Rosamond and Hayden to appear pale against the yellow walls and sheets. Hayden nods toward the bagpipes in the corner and says to him, "Bring me my pipes, son." Only his voice sounds too loud, as if in a fever, or else magnified by fear or hope or longing.

Joey brings the heavy set of bagpipes to his grandfather's bedside. Hayden takes the gleaming black pipes in his hands and admires them one last time as one would a beautiful woman. "Here." He hands the bagpipes over to Joey. "You're an official member of the Greyfriars Gang now."

Joey beams with pride and anticipation, not yet realizing that this is the moment signifying his grandfather's departure.

"Listen to me now. Whene'er you blow those pipes I'll hear you."

A shadow suddenly crosses Joey's face. "Grandpa, you're not . . . you're not going to die today, are you?"

Hayden musters all his remaining energy. "O' course not!"

But Joey looks dubious.

"Tell you what, I'll bet you a hundred dollars that I make it to see the Mets in the World Series!"

"You're on!" Joey feels relieved. Hayden is never one to throw money around unless it's a sure thing. Joey attempts to balance the heavy bagpipes in his arms. "But Grandpa, I hardly know how to play these."

"Alisdair is going to finish teaching you. In fact, go call Alisdair right this minute and tell him that I've given ye my pipes."

After Joey's out of earshot Hayden quietly adds, "And that I'll get to Scotland afore him." But Joey is gone and only Rosamond is there to hear him.

Hayden scribbles something on a piece of paper and tucks it into an envelope that he hands to Rosamond. "I want you to give this to Joey as soon as I'm gone."

"Of course." She takes the envelope and sets it on the night table.

"Now hand me the pills, please." His voice has acquired a hoarse, passionate timber.

"What!" says Rosamond, unsteadied by shock. "Why? Why now? Why today?"

"Rosie," he says as he squeezes her hand, "I'm starting to be in a lot of pain." Hayden's face visibly tightens as he says this. "It's no good anymore. Let's face it, I'm ready for a clap in the head with a spade." Only he's not joking. His lips are thin and tense as wire.

Rosamond stares at the pill bottle on the dresser as if it's a loaded handgun while a series of tiny pleats visibly deepen around her eyes and mouth. "You know I can't do that Hayden . . . please don't ask me . . . suicide is against . . ."

"I didn't ask you to *take* them. Just *hand* me the blessed things. Besides, I've always wanted to have the courage to say to a woman: If you won't marry me I'll off myself."

Rosamond hesitates and when Hayden starts to reach for the pills she seizes them. "Oh Hayden, oh God," she says, as if it's impossible to decide between the two. She clutches the plastic container to her heart as if she might scatter the pills out the window like birdseed rather than hand them over.

But after several moments of silence, eyes brimming with tears, she opens the small plastic bottle and slowly offers it to him.

Hayden takes Cyrus's special capsules into his palm, breaks them open, and empties the contents into his waiting glass of scotch on the night table, which shines like liquid gold in the morning sunlight. He raises the glass and expertly swirls it until the powder dissolves.

"Last call!" Hayden announces cavalierly as he raises the glass to his lips, and empties it in a few quick swallows.

"Oh, Hayden, do you really not believe in God?"

"Rosie"—he smiles as he hands her the empty glass—"My God . . . my God took our farm with drought and disease. So no, he's not the one for me anymore. But I believe in the God that's in your head, honest I do."

"Then don't you at least believe in miracles? Like Jesus walking on water during the storm?"

"Maybe he did," Hayden offers a cryptic smile. "On the other hand, maybe the lake was frozen."

But Rosamond's not sure if he's answered yes or no to either of her questions, or else it's the mumbo-jumbo of someone who's just ingested a massive amount of drugs. "Please let me call a priest . . ."

"Do'an' you *dare* let a priest into this house. Hank is priest enough. Now tell me one of those nun jokes."

"Oh, Hayden!" A teardrop quivers on her cheek. "I couldn't possibly, not at a time like this."

"C'mon Rosie, one for the road."

She's flustered and can barely remember the Lord's Prayer, no less a joke. But his charm hasn't diminished and Rosamond finds him impossible to refuse in this bizarre last request. She wracks her brains and finally begins, "A man broke his arm and went to the emergency room of a Catholic hospital."

A tiny smile plays across Hayden's face to indicate that he's enjoying the words as if they're Chivas Regal turned into text.

Rosamond stumbles slightly from the awkwardness of the situation and continues through her tears. "And the nun tells him, I mean, she asks him what type of insurance he has. 'None,' the man replies. So the nun asks, 'Do you have a relative who can help?' And he says he only has a spinster sister who's a nun. 'Well,' the nun says, 'nuns aren't spinsters, because they're married to God!' So the man says, 'Then send the bill to my brother-in-law.' "

Hayden squeezes her hand to indicate that she's turned in a tremendous performance under the circumstances. He tries to lean forward to kiss her but can't muster the energy. She bends down and kisses him one last time, for the past, for the future.

"You'd better call them in," he says. His green eyes are turning the color of leaden winter skies.

Rosamond begins to pray desperately, not for Hayden's soul to pass quickly into heaven but for intercession by an angel. Surely a man who has embraced life with such heroic force isn't meant to be snatched away in his prime like this. They will grow old together and live as love has made them. It must be some sort of test, like Abraham being asked to sacrifice his son Isaac for the sake of mankind. After all, it's an angel who stays Abraham's hand at the last moment, after having successfully tested his fidelity.

Her silent appeal is interrupted by the arrival of Diana and Hank, who appear in the archway as if they've been summoned. Having seen Joey with Hayden's cherished bagpipes Diana sensed what might be happening.

"Now Diana, do'an' forget to return this bed and get back the deposit. The receipt is in that top drawer." Hayden rises slightly and nods toward the dresser.

Diana's laserlike eyes immediately land on the open pill bottle and Rosamond tightly clutching Hayden's hand. "Oh, Dad," she says tearfully.

"You're a bonny lass Diana, just like your mother," he whispers, as if it takes all his remaining energy to speak the words. Hayden sinks back onto the pillows and closes his eyes, the latticework of wrinkles on his forehead turning smooth. Diana sobs into Hank's shoulder and then sits down on the bed and takes Hayden's other hand.

"Should we call Joey?" Diana sobs to Rosamond, so paralyzed by anguish that for once she is unable to gather her wits enough to make a decision.

"No, I think he said good-bye the way he wanted to," Rosamond assures her.

"And what about . . . what about Linda?"

"He phoned her last night," says Rosamond. "When he knew Ted was at Rotary."

A few minutes pass in fretful silence, as if the entire room, including the air, is suddenly made of glass. It's Hayden who finally breaks the stillness, whispering softly, barely moving his lips. Rosamond leans over to hear him. "It sounds as if he's saying that the lights are falling." She automatically glances toward the windows where the sunshine is smashing through the glass panes. "But the shades are wide open."

Diana moves closer. "Dad, do you want me to close the window shades? Is it too bright?"

Hayden's breathing has become measured and shallow and it takes great effort for him to move his mouth. Diana leans very close to listen for his answer.

Again Hayden murmurs the same syllables.

"The pipes are calling," Diana slowly repeats, anguish tightening her throat. The significance of this shatters her remaining composure. "Oh, Hank! Do something!" she clutches at him with her free hand. "I . . . I think he's hearing bagpipes."

chapter sixty-one

What exactly it is that he's supposed to do Hank is not at all sure. He looks to Rosamond but she is off in a distant place with Hayden. He can't give last rites. For one thing, he's not a priest. And for another, Hayden would wake up just long enough to clunk him over the head. Hank quickly flips through his mental prayer Rolodex, clears his throat, bows his head, squeezes Diana's hand and begins:

"They come God's messengers of love,
They come from realms of peace above,
From homes of never fading light,
From blissful mansions ever bright.
They come to watch around us here,
To soothe our sorrow, calm our fear:
O heavenly guides, speed not away,
God willeth you with us to stay."

On the final mention of God Hank tentatively lifts his head. If Hayden is still alive there's no doubt that this is the point he'll start an argument or crack a joke about God e-mailing people directly with His Will for faster turnaround time. But Hayden does not respond. His face has become altogether natural and lost any expression of suffering. He breathes softly for a few minutes and then appears to breathe no more.

Rosamond unconsciously murmurs "amen" when Hank has finished and then places her delicate fingertips on Hayden's pulse. As the life fades from his body without a sound large tears glide down her cheeks. Unable to meet Diana's gaze she slowly moves her head from side to side. And with the final beat of Hayden's heart she is freed forever from the desire to possess another person or the temptation to belong to any other human being.

Rosamond touches his cheek one last time, which is turning cool, like a smooth stone. "He's gone," she says, and something inside her splinters like broken glass, leaving only razor-sharp edges and spiked points in her heart, head, and abdomen.

Then a strange thing happens. All the love and compassion trapped and aching within her body begins to flow outward like water pouring from a shattered vase, and is gradually replaced by a deep sense of calm. For Rosamond becomes aware that she has indeed been visited by an angel, and through an extraordinary voyage of the senses has had her faith restored. At last she feels the ecstasy of the spirit that had so eluded her in the convent and her entire being is flooded with peace. Is it possible to become more holy by becoming more human? Before Hayden her quest had been like a hand trying to grasp itself.

Rosamond rises slowly and Hank takes her place by the side of the bed, next to Diana, whose world has momentarily gone dark, as if the only candle illuminating it has just been blown out. All those long months of holding on and hoping had taken such energy. In imagining this moment Diana had somehow thought that it would be easier to let go than it had been to hang on. But it isn't so. To bid farewell takes even more strength than she believes she possesses.

Rosamond dutifully removes the envelope from the nightstand and goes in search of Joey. The front door is open. He's standing out on the lawn, engrossed in a conversation with Giovanni, who is throwing a plastic ball for Ginger. Off to the side of the front stoop fallen rose petals curl in the grass like bits of paper. Rosamond carefully selects her path to avoid the dark red berries from the overhanging cherry tree that are smeared upon the walk like bloodstains.

However, she's distracted by an unmistakable sound rising from the far end of the street. The Greyfriars Gang comes somberly marching into view wearing full Scottish regalia; kilts swaying in time to their step and caps perched uniformly on their heads. Alisdair is playing the bagpipes, Duncan is on snare drum, Hugh holds his fife to his lips, his son Andrew at his side with a musket slung over one shoulder, and Paddy Fitzgerald carries the blue-and-white flag of Scotland, lowered so that it's almost parallel with the ground.

Neighbors appear on their front stoops one by one, as if there's an unscheduled parade. Some are still in their nightclothes. Mrs. Trummel wipes her hands on her apron before solemnly lowering the billowy American flag that hangs next to her front door, as if to announce that a great man is no longer among them.

A random group of Trinidadians, Irish, Poles, and Pakistanis follow the procession until it ends in front of the MacBride house, where the Greyfriars Gang dutifully concludes their tribute with "Scotland the Brave." Bobbie Anne stands on her porch, hands clutching the children's shoulders and eyes clouded with tears. She bows her head as if the funeral cortege of a world leader is passing before them.

Suddenly the loud and insistent quacking of ducks is heard from the direction of the park. The mallards respond to the familiar sound of Alisdair's bagpipes at this time of the morning. The ducks begin to waddle over the embankment, just a few at first, and then Hayden's entire herd clumsily joins the throng of mourners. Among the mostly brownish-black females a few emerald green heads and necks rise above silver-feathered bodies and catch the morning light.

Rosamond puts her arm around Joey's waist as the crowd continues to gather. "Your grandpa wanted you to open this right after he died," she says and solemnly hands him the white envelope.

"But he *promised* he wasn't going to die today!" Joey struggles to hold back his sobs because he knows that's what his grandfather would have wanted.

Rosamond glances up at the fluffy white clouds floating across a sky as blue as the seas of eternity. The filtered rays of the sun cause her cheeks and forehead to glow with fresh yellow light. She places her hand on Joey's shoulder, wanting to share with him the wisdom of Teresa of Avila, on how God makes space within us and then later fills it. But instead she says, "It always *was* difficult to know when your grandfather was telling the truth."

Still fighting back tears, Joey tears open the envelope. He removes a crisp hundred-dollar bill, two tickets to the final game before the playoffs and a note in Hayden's thick scrawl: *You win the bet! Go Mets!*

It's a milky Saturday afternoon in late August with heat rising in shimmering waves, not unlike the day we buried my grandfather almost twenty years ago. And after which Rosamond kept her promise and took me camping in the Adirondacks, just the two of us. They were the most wonderful three days of my life—tracking animals through the forest, fishing in a cool green mountain stream, and at night gazing up at the stars and together remembering Hayden so hard that he became forever preserved in the misty landscape of our souls. And when the dawn came his presence was felt in the warm sunlight that slowly surrounded us. Thus we became eternally connected to each other, even though it was to be the last time I would ever see her.

Hundreds of small white butterflies with black smudges dart and pirouette among the overgrown honeysuckle that clings to the high granite walls of the convent. I am not permitted to attend the service. So I stand outside the iron gates and my mind wanders back to the many funerals Grandpa had taken me to as a boy, cursing the medical establishment all the while.

I'm surprised by how the past has stayed with me throughout the decades, always just beneath the surface, invisible and heartwarming, threaded to the future, the way the end of summer seamlessly stitches itself into the fall.

Goodness, how my grandfather would be pleased to know that Rosamond had eventually become a mother superior, though perhaps she was the first to use a baseball card as a bookmark in her hymnal. I like to think he'd be amused that I'd grown up to be a surgeon. And that he'd be happy to know that just as Rosamond was blessed with the love of her God, I was equally fortunate to have found the love of a good woman. It's certain he'd be relieved to know that I never watered down my whiskey, and that I would discourage my young son from doing so as well. Of course, the key to teaching my own eight-year-old boy anything worth knowing and truly Hayden-like is not to let his ever-fretful and vigilant grandmother Diana find out about it.

When I left for college, Diana married Hank, who'd been made a partner in his architecture firm. My mother has maintained her extraordinary beauty throughout the years and continues to amaze us with her infinite capacity to worry about our health and safety, calling each morning with warnings about everything from the West Nile virus and dengue fever to black ice on the roads and a potentially contaminated municipal water supply.

Finally the bells in the dilapidated tower begin to toll, signifying the end of the funeral. Raising my bagpipes toward the sun I begin to play "Oh, Love Will Venture In," to announce her arrival on the other side, just in case Grandpa is off herding ducks, or more likely placing bets at the bar. With his kilt round my waist and his beloved Robbie Burns in the air it's certain that I appear a solitary lunatic weeping for lost things, pacing the dusty old gravel driveway where we'd first dropped Rosamond off on that June evening so many years ago. It was the year the Mets finally won the pennant.

LAST CALL

A Reader's Guide

LAURA PEDERSEN

A Conversation with Laura Pedersen

*Julie Sciandra and **Laura Pedersen** have been friends and occasionally colleagues for more than twenty years. They walk each other's dogs and also bowl together. Julie usually wins, but Laura insists that this is because Julie's family owned a bowling alley in Buffalo, and thus she has had an unfair advantage.*

Julie Sciandra: Did you always want to be a writer?

Laura Pedersen: I was a slow starter, basically a turnip in a sleeper the first few years of my life, and I didn't come on strong academically until much later. Just learning to read was a huge accomplishment for me. I would say the prospect of telling stories first arose in seventh grade. An only child and pathologically shy I realized I had to do *something* to facilitate interaction. So I started telling a few jokes and funny stories, and found a positive response that led to friendships. After getting yelled at for talking during class, I was forced to start writing and passing notes.

JS: When did you first receive recognition for your writing?

LP: In middle school I won an essay contest for writing about Teddy Roosevelt. And then I won a prize in the declamation contest for a speech about Carrie Nation. But it wasn't until high school that I really hit it big—I was sentenced to community service for a poem I'd written that contained a hidden message.

JS: How do you set about writing a novel like *Last Call*?

LP: I hear a lot of writers say they start with the seed for an idea, such as a character or one particular event, and they don't know where it's going to lead them. That could never work for me. I don't start a book unless I have the beginning and the end. Only the middle is something I can work out as I go.

JS: Do you write every day?

LP: I definitely write checks every day. But I probably work on what will eventually become a book or short story about four days a week, usually between 10:00 A.M. and 3:00 P.M., with an hour break for lunch and a few other breaks for running errands or playing with the dogs. I have a very short attention span and work best in spurts, then I need to do something else for a while, like go Rollerblading or play basketball with the kids.

JS: How long does it take you to write a book?

LP: That's a real time-motion study, like how long between when a traffic light in Manhattan turns green and the cab driver behind you leans on his horn. But I'd say a book takes me a year, while doing other things. I suppose that if I sat down with a freezerful of burritos and a vat of chocolate, I could write a novel in eight weeks.

JS: Where do your ideas come from?

LP: From daily life. I live "hard" in the sense that I enjoy being on the go and having lots of experiences. For instance, I went to the floor of the stock exchange shortly after I turned eighteen. That environment created the foundation for my first book, *Play Money*. Journalism has taken me to exotic places like Russia, Turkey, and Cuba. If you want to tell a story but you don't have an idea, I think it's best to go out and do something and then write about it. There are a lot of things I'd love to do but haven't had time yet, and so I'll occasionally imagine a character doing them and use that in a novel. But at the end of the day, my stories are always about living, loving, and dying.

JS: Are the characters based on people you've known in real life?

LP: I borrow bits and pieces from different individuals and then create new people, sort of like a medieval dwarf going from house to house in the middle of the night and stealing the essences of the townsfolk. For instance, my friend Peter Heffley's ninety-year-old mother, Mildred, is the patron saint of worriers and pessimists. We actually look forward to her negative pronouncements and often attempt to evoke them just for entertainment. (Hence the catchphrase, "Who put the *dread* in Mildred?") I know if I say, "My, that's a lovely orchid, Mrs. Heffley," she'll retort, "It's just about dead." Or if Pete says he has the Fourth of July party all organized, she undoubtedly replies, "There's a storm heading this way." So for the character of Diana in *Last Call*, who is unlike Mrs. Heffley in every other way, I borrowed the fretfulness along with some of her best lines. And many of my characters are built on a small slice of me that I then exaggerate. For example, in *Beginner's Luck* Hallie plays poker, goes to the racetrack, and trades in the stock market. Gil likes plays by Tennessee Williams, Craig is an only child, Olivia is a vegetarian, and Bernard is optimistic and enjoys humor. Those are all based on my own experiences or personality. Plus, I'm a lazy researcher.

JS: How does being a minister influence your writing?

LP: I'm an ordained interfaith minister (we respect all paths), but I don't have a congregation, and I don't give sermons, except to the teenaged Michael. In the not-for-profit world it helps to accomplish things if you're a minister or a politician. As for organized religion, I'm a lifelong Unitarian Universalist. Most Sundays you'll find me sitting in a pew on the far right over at All Souls in Manhattan, reflecting on the UU Trinity—reduce, reuse, and recycle.

JS: But there's a lot of religion in *Last Call*, especially Catholicism.

LP: I've always had an interest in religion, especially since it's been the cause of so many wars and so much strife. Also, my earliest childhood memory is of my mother yelling, "Jesus Christ, is it *ever* going to stop snowing?"

One of my favorite stories is how in the late 1300s there were two dueling popes, Clement VII and Urban VI, both busily excommunicating each other. Finally, a council was called to decide between them. Pietro Pilarghi, who helped bring about the council, made *himself* pope and told the others to take a hike. Neither did, and so then there were *three* popes.

As for making Rosamond a Catholic, when I was growing up outside of Buffalo in the 1970s, eighty percent of the population was Catholic. As James Joyce famously said about his faith, Catholicism means "Here comes everybody!" Catholics live out loud in a terrific way. So everywhere you turned there was a big church, battalions of habited nuns, outdoor celebrations on feast days, and of course the Friday fish fry. (Word of the Vatican II council that ended in 1965 apparently hadn't yet reached Buffalo. Cowboy comedian Will Rogers once explained that he wanted to be in Buffalo when the world ended because it would happen there five years later.) So my friends were constantly dashing off to Mass, confession, religious instruction, and CYO (Catholic Youth Organization). Having had so much exposure to that particular faith, I thought it would be interesting to set up a sort of fictional showdown between an atheist and a Roman Catholic. Also, if Rosie had been a Theosophist, I don't think the story would work as well because there aren't the lifestyle constraints and concept of an afterlife to work with. And worse, I would have had to do research.

JS: I notice you have a pair of snazzy new red-and-blue bowling shoes. Is there a big game tonight?

LP: Not tonight, but I haven't given up on my idea of bringing about world peace through bowling. It's a sport that allows almost everyone to play, regardless of race, religion, economic background, and body type. You can wear a sombrero, burqa, kilt, saffron robe, or whatever you like.

JS: So what's next? I've seen you scribbling on your jeans, which usually means a new book is in the works.

LP: After *Beginner's Luck* came out people asked, "What happens to Hallie?" It was open-ended, so I've written a sequel called *Heart's Desire*. Hallie has finished her first year away at college and returns to the Stockton household for the summer, which is in a greater state of chaos than usual, if that's possible. Gil and Bernard have broken up, and Ottavio is pressuring Olivia to marry him. Meanwhile, Hallie is contemplating that age-old teenage dilemma: Should she or shouldn't she?

1. Have circumstances driven Diana to become more overprotective and fretful than she might be if life were easier at the moment—if she had more money and a nice husband, and if her father wasn't ill? Have you ever gone through a rough period when you felt like a person on the verge of a breakdown due to events beyond your control—when life temporarily eclipses your true personality, or at least the person you want to be?

2. Is Hayden a good or bad influence on his grandson? Is Hayden helpful in counteracting Diana's coddling of her son, especially now that he's almost a teenager? Or is Hayden the one making Diana anxious in the first place?

3. Does Hayden's appreciation of the freedom and opportunity he's found in the United States, combined with fierce pride for his homeland, bring to mind the mixed attitudes shared by immigrants you know?

4. Does it matter what religion, if any, Joey becomes when he's older? Or have Hayden and Rosamond imparted other valuable lessons?

5. Do you know people who have fallen out over religion, or decided not to marry because of the issue? Would you agree or disagree that there are certain situations where the differences and difficulties just can't be overcome?

6. Has Rosamond truly lost her faith, or, as a woman coming to the end of her childbearing years, is she suffering from a vacuum of human affec-

tion? Is it possible to live a rich and full life and not know physical intimacy?

7. Why does Diana suddenly allow Joey to play baseball after her sister's stepson dies in a freak accident? Shouldn't this event serve to make her more fearful that Joey will be injured?

8. Is Hayden really an atheist or does he have his own spiritual program to live a good and full life—perhaps "Haydenism"? Would you say that you subscribe to all the tenets of a specific faith or that you've assembled your own guidelines?

9. Is it possible that any events in the book were meant to be miracles? Or are they just life's typical accidents and coincidences?

10. If you wanted to find biblical equivalents for the characters in *Last Call*, who might have the most in common with Bobbie Anne?

11. Being a good parent often involves making difficult choices and personal sacrifices. What are some real-life examples of this made by people you know?

12. Rosamond lost her mother when she was young. Hayden lost his father and had a difficult youth because his family lost their farm. Joey's parents are divorced and he no longer sees his father. Do you think such childhood events forever change the way we see and react to the world? When you look back, is there anything you experienced early on, good or bad, that you'd say has had a tremendous impact on later decisions, or the way you've chosen to live your life or raise your family?

13. Diana and her sister, Linda, appear to have had a pleasant childhood, complete with two parents who love and provide for them. Yet the sisters don't get along. Why do family tensions often arise even when there's no apparent reason for it? Are there siblings in your family who aren't close and it's hard to determine when or why it all started?

14. By the end of the story has Rosamond converted Hayden or vice versa? Or are they both able to love in their own way and stay true to opposing belief systems?

15. Is it possible to overcome some religious differences by focusing on the similarities between religions?

16. Why does Rosamond return to the convent at the end of the story?

17. What do you think Rosamond and Hayden would say about I Corinthians 13:13: There are three things that will endure: faith, hope, and love, and the greatest of these is love? Is it true that love can transcend everything, including religion and even death?

Denise Winters

ABOUT THE AUTHOR

Laura Pedersen grew up near Buffalo, New York, and now lives in Manhattan, where she volunteers at the Booker T. Washington Learning Center in East Harlem.

Visit her Web site at LauraPedersenBooks.com.

Please turn the page for

an exciting preview of

Laura Pedersen's next novel,

the sequel to *Beginner's Luck*

HEART'S DESIRE

CHAPTER 1

Someone is cracking open the bedroom door. "Hallie? Are you in there?"

Upon hearing the familiar voice I wake slightly and assume that I'm having weird dreams due to excessive body heat. Lying next to me is my boyfriend, Ray. And on the other side is Vanessa. I push down the blanket.

"Hallie, are you up?" the voice comes again.

Only now I'm definitely hearing and not dreaming Bernard's stage whisper. And also smelling the rich aroma of freshly baked bread. Wakefulness and reality strike simultaneously. "Oh my gosh!" I shout and raise my head. "What time is it? I have an exam at eight!"

The only thing that's not surprising is to find Bernard Stockton in the hallway of my apartment. After all, he's the one who'd saved me when I was sliding down the slippery slope of adolescent rebellion the previous fall by taking me on as a live-in yard person. And now at least one weekend a month he arrives early and cooks us all a big breakfast. Only this isn't Saturday or Sunday. It's Thursday of finals week.

Bernard opens the door the rest of the way and steps inside the room. "It's just after seven," he says. But his voice breaks and I can tell immediately that something is terribly wrong. Not only that, he must have gotten up at four in the morning to make the one-hour drive to Cleveland and then bake bread.

"What's the matter, I mean, I'm coming . . ." In climbing out from my position as pickle in the middle I realize that I'm still in my underwear. "Um, could you wait in the kitchen?"

"Oh, yes, of course. How indelicate of me." His footsteps become faint and then I hear him tackle the mess of dirty pots and pans.

Meanwhile, I stumble through the minefield of packed duffel bags and piles of dirty clothes and finally pull on the first T-shirt and sweatpants that come into view. The whole place smells like old pizza and even older laundry. As I pass the living room the sound of loud snoring comes from behind stacks of books and model cardboard buildings that rise in the middle of the floor to form a miniature skyline. A closer look reveals Debbie and Todd passed out on the couch, surrounded by notebooks and empty pizza boxes.

In the kitchen Bernard has lined up his numerous shopping bags on the floor since there's no available space on the countertops or table. Those are all covered in a collagelike mishmash of art supplies, stained coffee mugs, and pizza crusts. Fortunately, he's accustomed to the mess. With four busy young women sharing three rooms and all the various friends and boyfriends hanging about, housekeeping rarely rises above the minimum required for pest control. Particularly during exam time, when we're all cramming for finals and working like crazy to finish up papers and projects.

I rub the sleep from my eyes. "What's wrong? Is it Olivia?" Though I'd called Bernard's sixty-ish mother the night before to ask her a grammar question for a paper I was writing, or at least attempting to write, and she'd sounded fine.

Bernard stops whipping eggs in the clean metal mixing bowl he brought from home, bows his head, and shuts his eyes as if in pain. "It's Gil."

Never before have I seen him so grave when referring to his longtime companion. And so of course I assume the worst. "What? Is he *dying?*"

When my eyes become accustomed to the light I notice how completely wrecked the normally dapper Bernard looks—bags under his eyes, worry lines furrowing his brow, and something I've never seen on him before, brown socks with black loafers!

Bernard turns away from me and dabs at his eyes. "I promised myself I wouldn't cry." He waits a moment to compose himself, takes a deep breath, looks me straight in the eye, and in a trembly voice blurts out, "Gil left me!"

"You broke up?" I'm truly stunned. I'd have voted my parents more likely to break up than Gil and Bernard, and even the thought of *that* is impossible.

"We didn't break up." Bernard starts sniffing again. "Gil *left* me! *Abandonnement.*" He switches to French for greater effect.

I'm not sure that I see the difference between breaking up and one person leaving, but it doesn't appear to be the right moment to ask. Tears begin to stream down Bernard's cheeks and I've never seen him full out cry like this before, not even when his father died.

As I reach out to put my hand on his arm a hiss comes from the stove and he leaps up to adjust the heat on his beloved Calphalon nonstick crepe pan. Then he starts concentrating on making apple-cinnamon crepes and this seems to calm him slightly, to my great relief. Hopefully Bernard is overreacting and he and Gil just had an argument that will eventually be resolved. Perhaps it was about Bernard's junk taking up the entire garage. In the spring Gil always gets cross when bucketfuls of pollen land on his car because it has to sit out in the driveway.

"What happened?" I ask. "Did you two have a fight?"

"No. I mean, here he is, always insisting that *he's* the normal one. Then all of a sudden he goes berserk and announces that he doesn't want to be part of a committed relationship. Gil hasn't been the same since his older brother Clifton died unexpectedly last month . . . he became more and more distant and then . . . he said . . . it was over . . ."

Bernard begins crying again and uses the dish towel over his shoulder to wipe away his tears. He always brings his own Marshal Field's British icon dish towels when he comes to cook for us.

All of my friends love Bernard. He's like an eccentric uncle who unexpectedly shows up and cooks, helps to decorate, rearranges the furniture, and even organizes theme parties. In fact, one of my professors had even invited him to guest lecture in a pottery class. Having bought and sold ceramics for his shop the past fifteen years, Bernard knows everything about all the different schools and designs, and most of all, exactly how much any lump of painted clay you might have lying around your attic is worth. However, this morning his usual expression of irrepressible lightheartedness is nowhere to be found.

Either the noise from us talking or, more likely, the smell of fresh bread and vanilla-flavored coffee awakens the couple on the couch in the living room and we hear them carefully making their way toward the kitchen. There are design projects in various states of completion all over the apartment, transforming it into an obstacle course.

Bernard quickly pulls himself together and says to me, "I can't have anyone seeing me so upset. Now don't say a word to them about this calamity, all right?"

"Mum's the word," I say. Bernard does indeed have a reputation for inexhaustible zest and witty remarks to protect.

Debbie and Todd appear bleary-eyed in the archway. Todd is bare-chested, wearing only jeans that hang low on his waist, suggesting an absence of underwear, and Debbie has a mint green sheet wrapped around her, Statue of Liberty style. I'd rather we were all exhausted from partying, like at the beginning of the semester, but everyone is beat as a result of hitting the books hard all week.

"Hey," they say sleepily, but in unison.

Debbie is used to Bernard arriving early, though usually on weekends rather than school days. And her boyfriend, Todd, is around often enough to have met Bernard a few times as well. They also know that he's very generous with his cooking. Bernard always claims that he's trying out new recipes and needs tasters, as if we're all doing him a huge favor by eating a five-course breakfast.

"Something smells terrific," says Todd, hungrily eyeing the platter that by now has three crepes smothered in crushed apples on it.

"Come on now, I know that everyone is tired and hungry with all these horrible tests!" With forced cheer Bernard digs into his shopping bags and starts taking out cartons of cream, fruit salad, and powdered sugar.

"Your eyes are all red," Debbie says to Bernard. "Are you okay?"

Bernard looks at me searchingly.

"He was just chopping onions." I quickly supply a plausible explanation.

"It's no use," says Bernard and begins to weep again. "Gil left me and I'm just a wreck!"

Bluffing was never his great strength. At least not like blanching. Bernard crumples into the nearest chair and cradles his face in his hands.

It so happens that Debbie's mother is a rapid-cycling bipolar, and as a result she's excellent at dealing with unexpected mood swings. Debbie calmly pours him a mug of the fresh coffee and pulls a chair up right up next to his. "That's *terrible!*" She places her arm around him. "Tell us *all* about it."

"Oh, no. You have enough to worry about with exams." Bernard takes a breath and begins, "Gil's older brother died a little over a month ago. They weren't on speaking terms because of course the family had disowned him when he came out of the closet . . ."

Just then I notice the clock on the microwave says a quarter to eight. My exam in motion graphics starts in exactly fifteen minutes. Leaping up from the table I say to Bernard, "I'll be back in two hours. Can you stay that long?"

"*Stay?* I *can't* go home!" He waves the end of the dish towel with the Buckingham Palace guard wearing the big black furry hat at me. "I've driven Mother insane the past two weeks with all my keening and wailing.

She says that if I can't let go then I need to see a psychiatrist before she'll let me back in the house. And to make matters worse, she keeps reminding me that Shaw's *Pygmalion* didn't have a happy ending—Hollywood added it when they transformed the play into *My Fair Lady*."

I leave Bernard at the kitchen table while I take a quick shower. By the time I return, my other roommates, Suzy and Robin, have emerged from their cave in the back and he's recounting the story to them, starting at the beginning.

As I'm racing out the door Bernard interrupts himself to ask me, "Uh, Hallie, that was Steve in your bed with you, wasn't it? But I didn't recognize the woman."

"Actually that was Ray, my latest boyfriend of two weeks. And on the other side was Vanessa. She stayed over last night."

"Obviously." He gives me a curious look. "A ménage à trois. Mother would be so proud!"

"Oh my gosh, no! Vanessa is Ray's neighbor. She's planning on going to school here next year. We ran out of beds."

"Of course. I've forgotten how *loose* everything is at college."